ROYAL FAE GUARDIANS

THE COMPLETE SERIES

HEATHER RENEE

ISBN: 979-8686628243

Editing: Jamie from Holmes Edits

Cover: Red Umbrella

CONTENTS

OF SWORDS AND DRAGONS

OF DREAMS AND SORCERY

OF BLOOD AND SACRIFICE

OF SWORDS AND DRAGONS

A PREQUEL STORY

DEDICATION

For all of the warriors in the world. No matter your battle…
Keep fighting. You got this.

CHAPTER 1

I gazed at the morning horizon from the front porch, unsure of what I was going to do with my rare day off. The lavender sky and warm yellow sun called to me, making me want to go out to explore, but that would require too much effort when all I wanted to do was relax.

I'd been on assignment after assignment for the council as of late, and even if it was almost too nice outside, I sighed and decided to stay home. I was determined to have today be a lazy day in which I did absolutely nothing.

Closing my eyes, I leaned back in the cushioned chair, listening to the birds chirp and the rustle of leaves as a soft air blew through. Maybe I could still have my languid day *and* enjoy the nature that was Arvayta.

A loud thud sounded from behind me, and gone was the peace I'd been experiencing. In its place was a guardian ready to attack.

Instead of a threat, all I found was my best friend.

"What the hell, Ryland?" My morning was officially ruined, and he was going to pay the price for it.

"We have an assignment." He leaned against the porch railing, crossing his arms.

I shook my head. "Nope. Today is my day off. The only one in *weeks*. I have plans. One of which you've just interrupted. Come back tomorrow."

He stormed across the porch. "It's a dragon issue in the Otherworld."

Crap.

I sighed. There would be no avoiding this. Dragons didn't come out of their caves in the fire sector often and were too dangerous for their own good, at least from what I'd been taught. I'd never personally met one.

"Meet me at Oliver's as soon as you're ready and we'll fill you in on what the council said." Ryland turned, and I shoved my foot into the back of his leg, making him buckle at the knees.

"That's for wrecking my day," I called out, but he ignored me as he disappeared without another word, and I knew I needed to hurry.

Ryland was one of my two best friends. The other was Oliver. I'd known them since I'd begun guardian training more than four decades ago. Ryland had refined my skills and helped me channel my anger when my parents chose to leave Arvayta and me behind.

I'd had no idea where they went, and I no longer cared. Brooks and Daliah Atwater had taken me in, allowing me to stay in their spare bedroom since Ryland had already claimed the guest house most nights. I'd considered getting my own home by now, but the Atwaters had been forced to Earth when their daughter was born, and I now watched over their house with Ryland.

Once I was dressed in jeans and a tank top, I went to the mirror, my emerald eyes staring back at me as I put my blonde hair in a high ponytail. Lastly, I slipped on my favorite strappy sandals before heading outside. I inhaled the fresh air and let the sun warm my skin, drawing the calm I'd been focusing on before I'd been rudely interrupted. I knew Ryland wanted me to hurry, but sometimes a girl just needed an extra minute.

I double-checked the door was locked, then ported to Oliver's—a useful perk all Arvaytans were capable of.

Even though Oliver wasn't the one who barged in on my quiet time unannounced, I did the same to him and Ryland.

"You idiots still around?" I called out as I threw open the door. "The brains of the operation is here and ready to slay some dragons. Maybe we'll even find a princess for one of your ugly mugs."

I chuckled at my own joke. They loved me whether they *liked* me or not.

Neither of them was *un*appealing, though. While I'd never been attracted to them, I wasn't blind. Ryland rocked the "I don't care" vibe with his perfectly tossed russet hair and soulful brown eyes that stood out against tanned skin. He also had the ability to control the winds, which might not sound exciting, but it could be intense to watch.

Oliver was the complete opposite of Ryland. His blond hair was unruly like the earth and plants he controlled with his elemental abilities. His skin was lighter than even mine, and his eyes were a soft cobalt. But what he lacked in color, he made up for in personality and skill.

Oliver shuddered. "Don't joke about princesses. I could use a few more decades to enjoy my freedom."

I peeked at Ryland and could see the longing in his eyes. Even though he was only a couple years older than my sixty-three years, he was an old soul. It also didn't help he'd already found his princess, but she'd been killed nearly two decades ago. Ryland assumed that meant he had to spend the rest of his life alone, honoring the bond he'd had to Sara, but I didn't believe it. Ryland was too good of a person for a life of solitude.

Typically, Arvaytans found their Meraki soulmate sometime

between twenty and forty years old. I tried not to be spiteful that I hadn't found mine, but I knew there was a reason for everything and trusted the Fates. Plus, who needed a soulmate when I had these two idiots for best friends?

A lie I told myself on a daily basis.

Ryland cleared his throat. "I was in the Otherworld a few days ago and saw the chaos. I'm surprised we weren't asked to step in sooner. Everyone is on edge; hostile, even. There's dark magic fueling the turmoil, so we'll need to be extra careful who we engage with. We can't risk being affected by whatever is happening."

"I haven't sensed anything here. Do we need to worry about anything filtering into Arvayta?" I asked.

Ryland frowned. "Not yet."

Arvayta resided between the Otherworld and Earth. Most of the people who lived here trained to be guardians who help keep dark magic out of Earth. Though on occasions like this, we also stepped in to help maintain the balance of the Otherworld. I didn't mind it most days. I enjoyed a good battle, which was why Oliver and Ryland had accepted me as one of them. They knew it was better to be on my good side than my bad.

"So, what does the council expect us to do about the dragons?" I asked, annoyed they hadn't called us all together to give us the assignment.

"We need to travel through the earth sector to the fire sector. The quickest way to get there without porting, which we won't be allowed to do, is through Meadow Lane, Web Jungle, Mineral Valley, and Inferno Ponds. Several other groups will be handling other situations around the Otherworld, and we'll be on our own for the most part. We just don't have the exact location of the dragons, and it could take days to find them."

Oliver slapped his hand on Ryland's shoulder. "Don't stress. We've gone out on missions with less information and still won."

"But we've never been at such a disadvantage. I don't like being so limited in our abilities," Ryland replied.

"Uh, excuse me? Why can't we port?" I asked.

Ryland sighed. "Queen Navi put a block across all four sectors."

"There's no way she can lift it for certain people? You know, like the ones trying to save her damn world. This isn't good if one of us gets hurt." Normally, the risk of death was minimal, because we could port away before an injury got too bad. Having that option taken away from us made things much more complicated.

"Unfortunately, not. We're going to be on our own out there, from the sounds of it. We follow the map and hope we don't run into trouble before getting to the dragons. We'll need every ounce of our strength to face them," Ryland answered.

I tossed a fire orb in my hand, needing magic to distract me from the irritation of the mission. "When are we supposed to leave?"

Oliver groaned. "At first light tomorrow. No sleeping in for us."

"So, I could have enjoyed my tranquil afternoon on the porch, but you chose to ruin my day off anyway?" I glared at Ryland and he just shrugged.

"How about we go to the training fields and get some sparring and dragon defense practice in? I think Jordan needs to release some pent-up emotions. She seems a little grouchy this morning." Oliver winked, a gleam in his blue eyes.

"You're on. Just remember this was your idea when you're crying on the ground later," I taunted.

"Sparring is a good idea. Then, we can all stay at the Atwaters' instead of meeting up in the morning," Ryland said, ignoring my and Oliver's ribbing.

"Sure thing, *Dad*," I mocked. He was always the responsible one, keeping Oliver and me out of trouble. "I'll see the two of you in an hour. Don't forget your tissues."

Without waiting for a reply, I walked out of the house and ported home. I already had a 'go bag' for situations like this, so I didn't need to pack much. Just a few essentials and I'd be all set. One thing I was always prepared with was clothes. My wardrobe filled my closet and three dressers. The guys liked to tease me about my obsession with shopping, but I didn't care. I'd lived through decades of fashion trends and couldn't help myself.

Even though most things weren't bought in Arvayta—we only traded for necessities with no money ever exchanged—guardians received bonuses after completed missions. Mine were almost always spent on clothes.

When I arrived back at the house, I ventured into the kitchen first to fill up on some food. I'd need the extra calories before sparring since my guys didn't take it easy on me.

I made a turkey sandwich with all the toppings and added a salad on the side. Making myself comfortable on the couch, I ate my lunch with a smile, thinking about all the fun we were about to have in the Otherworld.

While the magical obstacles would prove to be challenging, I wouldn't let it ruin my mood for long. Even though I'd never faced a dragon before, the more I thought about it, the more eager I was to go on this mission.

"DAMN IT, JORDAN!" RYLAND YELLED AT ME, AND I SNICKERED. "Take it easy."

Oliver was pinned beneath my staff, choking from lack of air. I leaned in and whispered in his ear, "Say 'Jordan is the best fighter ever' and I'll let you up."

He shook his head while trying unsuccessfully to buck me off him. "Never."

I dug my heels into his sides, hitting a pressure point. "I can do this all night, Ollie."

Ryland might have yelled at me just moments before, but I heard his low chuckle from across the field. He was enjoying this almost as much as I was.

Oliver's face was turning ten shades of red. I gave it less than a minute before he caved. His feeble attempts to beat me at my ground game had been cute the first few times, but he should have known by now that there was no point in trying to outmaneuver me when we wrestled.

"Fine! You're the best fighter," Oliver coughed out, and I lifted the pressure of the staff.

"You forgot one part," I taunted before pushing back down.

"Seriously, Jordan?"

I held the staff down, watching his eyes bulge before he tapped my leg and I let up once more.

"Jordan is the best fighter *ever*." He glared at me, and I smirked.

"That's a good boy." I patted his chest before jumping up and taking a few steps away. I had no doubt he'd retaliate eventually.

"Was that necessary?" Ryland asked me.

I grinned. "It absolutely was. I have to keep you boys in check and remind you that I'm no damsel in distress."

Ryland laughed so hard, he bent over holding his sides. "I think we can manage that without you beating on us."

I shrugged my shoulders, walking away. We were on the training field just beyond the town, and we'd been training hard for the last few hours. I grabbed my water bottle from the table and gulped down the whole thing.

"You guys ready to call it a day? My beauty rest is just as important as my training."

"Yeah, I'd rather not have my ass kicked again. My ego can only handle so much of it," Oliver whined as he lay down on the ground, utilizing his earth connection to recover from the beating.

"Your ego needs to be put in check more often." I laughed. "So, back to the house and up tomorrow morning at five?" I cringed at my own words. I hated getting up that early. My body protested. A lot.

"If we stayed anywhere else, you'd be late, so that works," Ryland jested.

I rolled my eyes and grabbed my workout bag. "See you losers later. Don't bother me until it's time to leave," I called out as I ported home. A steamy, hot shower was calling my name, and I was determined to finish my evening the way my day had started, because mental health was just as important as physical.

I may not have hands-on experience with a dragon, but I'd heard the stories. Our strengths were going to be put to the test over the next few days. If we weren't one-hundred-percent ready for this, we were about to become dragon snacks.

CHAPTER 2

Before the sun rose, I made my way downstairs, my body driven by the sweet aroma of coffee. The guys were smarter than I gave them credit for sometimes. If they had some sort of food waiting for me, too, they'd really be on my good side.

When I made it to the bottom of the stairs, I was assaulted by the scent of cinnamon rolls. I raced around the corner and snagged one before even muttering a polite good morning to my friends. The gooeyness melted in my mouth, causing me to make inappropriate noises.

"You're welcome." Oliver grinned.

"Have I told you lately that I love you guys?" I asked around my mouthful of the treat, hoping they understood me.

They laughed at my ridiculousness, but they really did know how to make sure I was in a good mood this early in the morning. Decades of friendship had taught them well.

"As soon as you receive your morning dose of caffeine, we'll take off," Ryland said between bites of his own breakfast. "The earlier we start the trek toward the fire sector, the more time we'll have to find somewhere to stay for the night. I doubt we'll wrap this up in one day."

I let out a small sigh. "A girl can dream, though." I attempted to savor my breakfast, but Ryland tapped his foot impatiently at me. I ignored him for as long as I could before he became relentless.

"Okay! I'm done. Let me go grab my bag and sword. At least I packed already. Jerk."

Ryland smirked at me. "I didn't say anything."

I rolled my eyes and jogged back to my bedroom. It was too early to argue with him. I grabbed my bag, attaching my sword sheath to it before swinging it onto my back. Normally, I preferred knives, but dragons were huge, and I wasn't going to get any closer to one than I had to.

This sword was definitely still a favorite, though. It was lean and light, making it easy to handle. The hilt had a detailed carving of the main waterfall that channeled most of the magic to our world, along with flames around the backside to complement my elemental ability.

The Elves had made the sword from special metals that absorbed my power and allowed me to funnel extra magic through it, including my fire. Nothing screamed badass like a flaming sword, and it fit me perfectly.

After adjusting the straps on my pack one last time, I decided to snag a boot dagger before heading back to the kitchen again. "Alright, nerds. Let's get this show on the road," I said.

Oliver shoved another cinnamon roll in his mouth and nodded his head, proving he had no manners.

Hurriedly, I made sure nothing was left on downstairs and the breakfast mess was cleaned up, just in case Brooks or Daliah made an appearance. They'd been known to show up without notice for a quick check-in with the councilmembers. Even though I'd always been told to treat this as my home, I still kept it as neat as I could at all times.

Once we were outside, we ported to the waterfall that would take us to the Otherworld. Porting only worked within the world we were on. We used gateways through the falls to get to the many different parts of the two worlds around us.

"Ladies first." Ryland gestured toward the entrance. I had no qualms about going first and walked through without pause.

The travel between worlds was short but stunning. I floated along the course surrounded by twinkling lights and a dark sky, pretending I was flying among the stars.

A bright light emerged in front of me, confirming I was almost to the Otherworld. I closed my eyes against the glare, and before I knew it, my feet made contact with the ground.

I walked forward, not wanting Ryland and Oliver to come toppling down on me, and surveyed the area, relieved to not see anything out of the ordinary so far. The lands were mostly green in these parts with spots of color popping up here and there. Red, yellow, orange, and purple were the most prominent, weaving their way through the landscape. A breeze ran through, making me shiver and want to curl up with a warm blanket and a cup of coffee.

"What the hell?" Oliver groaned. "Why is it so cold?"

"Don't be such a wuss," Ryland said from right behind him.

"Children, we just got here. I don't want to hear any whining yet," I scolded with a grin.

"Whatever," they both replied in unison, and I laughed. They'd be so lost without me.

"Should we go to the market or head on out?" Oliver asked.

For once, I had no desire to go there and shop. With the lockdown on porting, I doubted anyone had hauled anything good in to sell or trade anyway. We just needed to be on our way and get this dragon business done with as soon as possible. Ryland spoke up before I could, though.

"We brought all the supplies we need, and I doubt there is

anything we can glean from anyone inside that we haven't already learned from the council. Let's just get going."

I snatched the map from Ryland's hand and led the way. There were four sections to the Otherworld that were originally created by the pure fae who lived centuries ago and died in the Dark War, leaving only partial fae beings like the three of us behind. Earth, wind, fire, and water lands made up the Otherworld and we were currently in the earth lands.

In order to reach the fire sector where the dragons should be, we'd need to go through four territories that consisted of very different terrains. While it wasn't the best way to get there, it was the shortest and the fastest, as long as we didn't run into too much trouble.

The first one was Meadow Lane, which wasn't too far ahead. Most of the time, that area was safe, but we couldn't be lax. There was very little that was completely innocent in the Otherworld unless we were within one of the main areas surrounded by guards or shields.

The second was Web Jungle. It consisted of obnoxious trees whose sole purpose seemed to be keeping people from passing through. There was no easy way to the other side except to ram through it in the straightest line possible. Next would be Mineral Valley. Though, the only dangers to us there were ourselves. We needed to be physically fit enough to tolerate the steep terrains and rugged paths.

Lastly, and certainly most dangerous, was Inferno Ponds. It was where the fire sector began. Of all the guardians I'd known to be lost when crossing sections, Inferno Ponds was the one that usually did them in. We needed to be extra vigilant as we traveled further along.

"Where should our stopping point be for the night?" I asked.

"Depends on how long it takes us to get through the first two valleys, but I'd prefer to stay in one of the caves in Mineral Valley," Ryland answered.

"I agree," Oliver chimed in. "We're going to be exhausted after Web Jungle. Even if it's not night when we get to Mineral Valley, we'll need the rest before tackling the rocks leading to the ponds."

I glanced back at the map. "According to the scale, it will take us about an hour to get through Meadow Valley. There are two forks in the path. We need to take the left one first, then the right. After the ninth bend, we're only ten minutes from the jungle."

Instead of giving Ryland back his map, I put it in the side pocket of my pack and picked up speed.

"In a hurry to find yourself a dragon?" Oliver teased.

"We're sitting ducks out here. Of course, I'm in a hurry. If you think for one second that we're safe right now, then you're not as smart as I rarely give you credit for."

Realizing I had a point, they both glanced around as I focused on what was ahead of us. Nothing was out there that we could see, but I had no desire to wait and find out if there was more we couldn't.

"Jordan's right," Ryland agreed.

All of us picked up the pace until we were jogging down the path, keeping an even speed without wasting too much energy.

Within a half-hour, we reached the first fork and took the left I'd seen on the map earlier. So far, so good. We hadn't come across anyone else, but our guards were still up. We didn't speak the entire time, choosing to stay focused on our surroundings.

We came around another bend, and I could see the next split in the road. I threw my arms out and pushed Ryland and Oliver off the path, behind some brush.

"You could have done that a little more gently," Oliver complained while rubbing his knees where he fell.

"There's a Centaur up ahead. He's standing in the middle of our path. I've never dealt with one. Have either of you?" I asked.

Oliver shook his head as he crouched beside me, but Ryland nodded. "Once, but it's been decades. He was a hustler. They usually turn a blind eye if you have something to bribe them with."

"Well, crap. Did you guys bring any valuables? I just brought clothes and food."

Oliver rolled his eyes. "Why is that not surprising?"

Ryland grinned, and I didn't like the way he was eyeing me. Whatever was about to come out of his mouth was going to make me want to throat punch him.

"Actually, you brought one valuable thing. Your sword."

I crossed my arms. "That would be a hard no. It's my favorite sword. You better find something else in your bag."

Ryland shrugged. "I have some gold pieces. We could try that first, but when he starts turning an angry shade of red, I suggest you hand over that sword."

I let out a heavy sigh. "Fine, but you better get me a new one."

"Sure, whatever you say, Jord."

As I stood up, I jabbed Ryland in his stomach with my elbow, garnering a painful grunt from him, and a smile of satisfaction appeared on my lips. "Well, we don't have all day. You guys coming?"

"You'll pay for that one when you least expect," Ryland grumbled, and they both joined me back on the path.

We made it several more yards before we caught the Centaur's attention. He was as large as a Clydesdale horse with muscle upon muscle covering his torso. His horse body was a charcoal grey color, which matched perfectly with the long hair that hung down his back in wild waves. His eyes were a piercing silver that watched every step we made as we moved closer to him.

"What business do you have on this path?" he demanded, voice deep and grumbly.

I glanced at Ryland, gladly letting him take the lead since he'd dealt with one before.

"We're headed to the fire sector, and our business is with the dragons. If you would grant us access to the right fork, then we'll be on our way and you can go about your day."

"Arvaytans aren't that ill-informed," the Centaur chided. "This is my path, and nobody gets by without payment. Show me your offering."

The Centaur was a demanding asshat. If he wasn't eight feet tall and made of muscle, I'd be begging Ryland to let me kick his ass. But I didn't feel like eating dirt. Ryland was right. I'd have to say goodbye to the one-of-a-kind blade.

I swung my pack around and set it on the ground. I loosened the straps holding the sheath, then pulled the sword free. I gently stroked the blade, saying my goodbyes. It had been good to me, and I was going to miss it. *This oaf better appreciate you,* I thought as I handed the weapon to Ryland and mentally cursed the beast standing tall before us.

"This sword was made by the Elves with the finest metals. It will also channel any magical power directed through the blade into an opponent. Is this a worthy offering?"

Damn, Ryland was being so much nicer than I would have been. I didn't have a political bone in my body.

"I want the girl, too."

For the first time in as long as I could remember, I was speechless. I quickly glanced between Ryland and Oliver, waiting for one of them to object, but nobody said a word.

Finally, I shook off the stupor and placed one hand on my hip while snapping at the Centaur with the other. "First, don't talk about me like I'm not standing right here. It's rude. Second, I'm not a possession. You can't just demand to take me. I've already given you my favorite sword. That's more than enough payment. Unless you want us to come back with an army, I suggest you accept the damn weapon and step aside."

The Centaur trailed his gaze up and down my body, sending shivers of revulsion through my spine. He may be sexy on the top half, but I liked my men to have two legs, not four.

Once again, he ignored me, turning toward Ryland and Oliver. "I prefer my females more docile. You said this sword is Elven-made?"

I took a step forward to throttle this jerk for his snide comment, but Ryland threw his arm out, blocking me as I kicked my bag. "Yes, purely Elven-made."

The Centaur eyed the sword more carefully, running his fingers along the sharp edges and then, as if things couldn't get more uncomfortable, the freak *licked* the blade. A sound escaped from my throat, and Ryland gave me the evil eye, one that told me if I said a single word, he'd likely tape my mouth shut.

"This is a worthy offering. Your group may pass this once. If you have to come to my area again, bring a female with less of a mouth or you won't be allowed through."

Oliver's hand found its way over my mouth before I could tell the oversized piece of trash where to shove the sword he just received. He barely managed to yank me away from the Centaur when Ryland came around my other side, holding my pack, rushing us along.

Once we were out of sight from the Centaur, Oliver removed his hand and we slowed down.

"That disgusting, chauvinistic, ass-gobbler! He doesn't deserve the kind of weapon you just willingly handed over."

Oliver laughed, glancing at Ryland. "And that is why I covered her mouth."

"The beast would have eaten us all for breakfast if you hadn't." Ryland shrugged.

I rolled my eyes. They were probably right. Centaurs were fierce opponents, and we would have been in more trouble than we had time to handle if I had started a fight with him, especially if he had friends nearby, but I would have gladly done it anyway. I hated men who thought they were better than women. I'd dealt with enough of them in my life. My mouth had no filter, and some men were too weak to handle it.

I took my stuff from Ryland, trying but failing to hide my fury at giving up my sword, then grabbed my water before we began our trek through Meadow Lanes. The guys did the same. We didn't want to stop for any preventable reason while going through the varying terrains. I refused to be someone they told stories about because we never returned.

Instead, they were going to tell stories about me because I slayed some dragons.

CHAPTER 3

I was starting to freak out. Meadow Lanes was too docile. We were far enough through that I could see the beginning signs of Web Jungle; the trees grew more wild, taller, and denser. There was a wildness about the jungle that wasn't present in these meadows. I preferred the former. Quietness didn't sit well with me.

My shoulders were tense from being on guard for the last half hour or so. Ryland and Oliver thought I was being paranoid, but I felt like something was following us.

"We just passed the ninth bend, so we're only about ten minutes out from the next territory," Oliver repeated my earlier words. "Are we pushing through or stopping?"

"Pushing through," I stated at the same time as Ryland said, "Stopping."

"Why would you want to stop?" I asked. "You seriously don't get the vibe we're being followed? Some psycho *being* is waiting for us to put down our guards. I know it."

Oliver surprised me by nodding his head in agreement, but

Ryland still wasn't buying it. "Why would whatever it is wait? It doesn't make sense."

I rolled my eyes at him. "This is the Otherworld. Nothing makes sense."

"If you're that concerned with it, then we go straight through the jungle, but you'll have to watch our backs since you're without a sword now."

My blood boiled at the thought of that oversized beast who'd taken it. "You just had to remind me, didn't you?"

Ryland laughed. "Figured it'd give you something else to think about for a while."

We continued our journey and, still, nothing remarkable happened. The meadows were just fields filled with varying flowers and grass. Weeping willow trees could be seen from time to time, along with a stream that curved in and out of sight, keeping the area thriving. Still, nothing out of the ordinary ever crossed our path.

The moment we officially left Meadow Lane and entered Web Jungle, it felt like I couldn't breathe anymore. While only a few steps from the meadows, the humidity was high with the trees, and the pressure bore down on us.

"I'm done. Let the dragons come to us. There's no way I'm spending hours getting lost in this bush," I whined.

"Toughen up, buttercup. We're just getting started." Oliver grinned.

"I've heard some tall tales about Inferno Ponds, so think of this as training. It's only going to get worse from here," Ryland added.

"Thanks for the pep talk, guys. I'm so glad I have best friends to kick me while I'm down." The sarcasm was thick.

They both had a good laugh at my expense, but I'd get them back. Eventually. I was a patient person when it came to revenge. For me, the anticipation was as enjoyable as the act itself.

~

HOURS PASSED, AND THE SUN BEGAN TO DESCEND, WHICH MADE ME start to worry. I would never tell the guys, but I wasn't naïve enough to believe we'd be safe much longer if we didn't find shelter. Being out at night in the middle of the Otherworld and not being able to port was asking for trouble.

Though, so far, the only kind we'd found were more than our fair share of spiders and snakes before catching the attention of some rather annoying monkeys.

Oliver led the way, using his earth ability to move most of the vines out of our way, but he could only do so much without fear of exhausting himself, so he and Ryland still used swords to take out the most stubborn foliage that didn't want to get out of our path.

The monkeys continued to follow us, but never came close enough to make me worry too much about them. They observed from the trees as their large forms swung from branch to branch. The animals had rough ebony fur, long arms and legs, and defined muscles on their torsos. I knew without a doubt that they could manhandle us, but it appeared the monkeys just wanted to make sure we had no other business in their territory besides passing through.

"Look," Ryland called out. I had been paying so much attention to the monkeys, I hadn't noticed the light shining from a large boulder in the distance. The setting sun was reflecting off the minerals, giving us hope. I was exhausted and ready for sleep. It was taking us twice as long to get through the vines as it had the meadows.

"Probably another fifteen minutes or so and we should be out of here," Ryland added, and I could hear the smile in his statement. All of us were ready to be free from Web Jungle.

Suddenly, the monkeys began to howl louder and swooped down closer. My pulse spiked, and I closed the distance between the three of us as Ryland furiously hacked at the vines in the way of our freedom.

"We're almost there. Just stay close," Ryland yelled above the monkey calls.

I grabbed on to Oliver's bag to make sure I didn't get too distracted and pulled out my dagger. There were three giant apes coming my way, and I had no idea what they wanted. They were either trying to warn us to move quickly or they didn't want us to leave. Neither option appeared to be a good one.

"Jordan, duck!" Ryland called out as he glanced back.

Without thought, I dropped to the ground, turned, and positioned the dagger blade up over my chest. When my eyes focused after hitting my head on the dirt, there was a monkey in my face. Literally, nose to nose. I wanted to scream, but something in its eyes called to me. It blinked, and the enchantment was broken.

"What the hell is happening?" Oliver yelled over the noise, but I couldn't see him through the wall of monkeys that now surrounded me. Their screams were in full force, causing the ache in my head to grow.

The one in front of me reached a hand out, as if it wanted to help me up. Ryland called out a warning, but I couldn't understand what he was saying. A calm settled over me as I placed my hand in the chimp's palm, seeming to not have much control over my actions. Oliver joined in with the cautions, but the screams from the primates blocked them out.

"A darkness is coming for you," a voice whispered, but the monkey's mouth never moved. "*Run.*"

Holy crap. That was the creepiest thing ever, but I didn't second-guess the warning. I'd known something was after us as soon as we'd entered the Meadows. I quickly nodded to the monkey and jumped to my feet.

"Run!" I repeated the warning to Oliver and Ryland.

The monkeys helped to clear the path while the guys cut down whatever was still in our way, and I was right at their heels, keeping pace. I heard Oliver say we were almost to the exit, but before I could respond, I was yanked back and my mouth immediately covered with something furry, causing my screams to be muffled. My body was pulled further away from my friends, and they had no idea it was even happening.

CHAPTER 4

Whatever had covered my mouth was continuing to wrap around my face until I could no longer see. I managed to breathe, but my sight and hearing were soon cut off. I flailed my arms and legs around, landing a punch to something hairy, yet firm.

Rapidly, vines enveloped my arms and legs. I was completely defenseless, and I was going to die.

I was going to be a statistic.

Damn it. I really wanted to fight some dragons, but now I was probably going to be a monkey snack instead.

"The less you struggle, the sooner we will get there," a deep, baritone voice snapped at me before my hearing was taken away again.

Yay, me. I get to die sooner.

I didn't listen to the warning of my captor and soon felt the vines getting tighter, wishing I had my sword so I could fillet the furball. Harsh? Yes, but I was beginning to panic. I could barely breathe, and when I started to tire and stopped squirming, the vines loosened. Maybe I should have taken the creature's advice to begin with, but that wasn't my style.

Minutes passed before I began to hear monkeys again. Everything constricting me became more comforting until I was able to breathe normally again. Though, I still couldn't see anything until I was dropped unceremoniously to the ground with a thud. *Ouch.*

My eyes blinked several times as my vision cleared up. I turned my head from side to side to find I was in some sort of hut made from vegetation. Bamboo and vines erected into the form of a teepee, and there were no windows that I could find above me, making me wonder how I'd ended up inside.

Someone's throat cleared, bringing my attention to eye level in front of me. Well, it was more like some*thing*. A giant ape stood there, along with monkey minions at his side. The ape appeared very human-like in shape, but definitely not in size and features.

Coarse, brown hair covered most of his body, and he wore only cut-off tan shorts. Piercing, black eyes stared at me until I finished my assessment. His minions were smaller monkeys with long tails. I shivered at the thought that one of those tails was likely wrapped around my face just moments ago. Disgusting.

"What do you want?" I snapped at them. No point in beating around the bush. I was outnumbered. Though I still had a backup knife in my pack, I doubted it would do me any good against the brute who spoke.

"We saved your life. It would do you good to remember that and show some respect. My name is Titus, and you've brought darkness into my home. We should not have spared you, but we heard you're on a mission to stop the dragons. It's imperative that you succeed."

"You saved *my* life?" I screeched. "What about my friends? What happened to them?" If something hurt Ryland and Oliver, all hell was going to break loose around here.

"The darkness was not after them. They made it out of Web Jungle, but they are trying to get back in to come after you."

A self-satisfied grin appeared on my face. My guys would never leave without me.

Titus continued, "We have blocked their attempts so far and will send you back to them soon, but we have business to discuss first."

"What business?" My curiosity piqued. Annoyed as I was at their methods, they confirmed my earlier unease and, if they knew what we were up against, I wanted to know as well.

Titus nodded to one of his minions, who then scampered off. "There is a serpent hell-bent on stopping you. He tried to get to you in the Meadows, but the water there is blessed, and he couldn't pass the stream you followed. Once you came into the jungle, my people kept him at bay for as long as they could, but the closer to the exit you got, the more relentless he became. Instead of risking more of our own, I told them to bring you to me. The serpent is not fast enough to keep up with my kin in the treetops."

"What does this serpent want with me, and why wouldn't it be after my friends, too?"

"It needs a female sacrifice. The males are of no concern to it."

What. The. Actual. Hell?

"Sacrifice? Like they want to offer me up to their gods and get some reward for it? Not happening. I've already been told once today I'm not docile. Their gods probably wouldn't want me anyway."

Titus grinned, making me shiver. "Be that as it may, you've been marked. You and your friends won't make it through Inferno Ponds to the fire sector alive. Too much darkness resides there now, and the serpent will have help. There is a secret entrance to a place called the Forbidden Tunnels in Mineral Valley. It is hard to find, but you must try. If you don't, there isn't much hope for you to succeed on your own."

I've had some really crappy pep talks today. People needed to have more faith in my ninja abilities. "Got it. Darkness, evil serpent, secret entrances, no hope. I think I can handle that. Can I go back to my friends now?"

Titus nodded. "One more thing." One of his minions entered the room through a door that blended right into the wall of bamboo, and he was carrying a sword across both of his monkey hands.

Wait a hot second. Not just any sword. *My* sword. "How? Why? When?" I stuttered out incomplete sentences.

"That doesn't matter. Just don't let it out of your possession again. You will need it if you plan to survive." I nodded, having nothing else to say to Mr. Dark and Gloomy. "The monkeys will take you back to your friends now. I suggest you find good cover to sleep tonight. If you don't find what you seek in Mineral Valley tomorrow, it's not likely you ever will."

Before I could respond, I was once again swept up and the roof of the hut opened up on hinges that had been previously hidden from my view. I waved goodbye to the monkey king and might have even flipped him off when he couldn't see for his depressing information. People really needed to be more positive. Always thinking the worst would only lead to the worst happening.

As the monkeys swung from tree to tree, I had all my senses as we flew through the foliage, and the two monkeys holding me worked together seamlessly.

Each of them had a tail wrapped around one of my biceps and shoulders, using their strong arms to propel us through the jungle. It would have been nice if they had just approached us earlier and done this instead of letting some psycho serpent stalk me for hours, but whatever. Nothing I could do about it any longer. I was just ready to see Ryland and Oliver again.

Just as I had that thought, I heard loud shouts.

"Where is she?" Ryland demanded.

"If you don't give Jordan back, I'm going to rip those annoying tails right from your body!" Oliver added angrily.

The monkeys were taunting my guys while keeping them from entering the jungle again. I didn't know whether to be thankful or to laugh at the situation.

"Easy now, boys," I called out. "I'm right here. No need for threats."

They each mumbled something under their breath, and it was probably good I didn't hear it. The monkeys stopped on the last set of branches and began to swing me. *Oh no.* They were going to toss me out of Web Jungle. Literally.

Ryland and Oliver realized it right after I did. They positioned themselves close together, and I braced for impact. Before I knew it, I was sailing into the sky and landed with a hard thud on top of Oliver. Ryland quickly pulled me up and ran his hands over my face and arms.

"Are you okay? Did they hurt you? Where were you?"

I dusted myself off and helped Oliver get up as well. "I'm fine. They didn't hurt me. They actually saved me." I went over as much as I could remember in the moment as I checked our surroundings. "We need to find somewhere to rest. Now."

"Or we could go hunting." Oliver waggled his brows.

"Not a chance. Jordan's right, we need to regroup and get our strength up again. Especially you, Oliver. You used a lot of magic to get us through that jungle, then even more trying to get us back in. We'll sleep for a few hours and head out at first light."

Glancing up, the normally pale green sky grew darker and I stifled a yawn. "Of course I'm right. Let's go."

Each of them shook their heads as we moved along swiftly through the rough terrain. I was dazzled by all the gems we passed, but Ryland warned me not to touch anything. Apparently, one didn't take from Mineral Valley without disastrous consequences. While I normally enjoyed testing the limits, after being swung through a jungle by monkeys—twice—I had zero desire to find out what consequences Ryland spoke of. At least, not today.

An hour later, I'd managed to keep my hands to myself and our temporary resting place was set up. I picked at my dinner while wondering about the serpent and using one hand to keep hold of my sword. I was never letting it go again.

"Jordan, you and Oliver are first up for sleep. Hurry and finish eating," Ryland said from the edge of the inlet we'd found in a rock mountain.

I took a few more bites between yawns and nodded. Oliver snorted, likely surprised I hadn't argued, but we'd had a hell of a day and I trusted Ryland with my life.

With my pack behind my head, I slid down to lay in the dirt, uncaring that I was going to be filthy when I woke. Oliver did the same, and his arm looped through mine.

"Worried I'm going to go somewhere without you?" I teased.

"Yes, actually." He fluffed his bag once more with his other hand and closed his eyes. "Night, Jordy.

"Night, Ollie." I glanced at the entrance. "Goodnight, Ry."

He grunted and waved, keeping his eyes on the horizon. That serpent didn't have a chance in hell at getting the jump on us, but even still, I kept my sword tucked into my side.

I'd fry up the bastard if it tried anything again.

My eyes finally closed, and I drifted off to sleep, but the nothingness I craved wasn't around for long. Instead, I was swept into a vivid dream that had my heart pulsing.

"Hello, Jordan, Guardian of Arvayta."

I bowed. "Hello, Fate. Thank you for blessing me with your presence."

The Fates didn't visit often, let alone to guardians. Normally, this kind of action was only reserved for the councilmembers and royals.

The golden-hued woman wrapped in a white silk gown sighed. "I wish it was a blessing, Guardian, but I come with news that no one else could get to you."

Crap.

"How can I be of service?" The polite tone was hard to keep with the storm of emotions rising within me—a strange feeling, given I was supposed to be sleeping. It all felt very real.

She glanced around the inlet, and I realized I was standing just beside my own body with Oliver still next to me and Ryland studiously at the entrance, having not a clue of what was happening behind him.

"The dragon you're going to face is named Zendar. He has been spelled with dark magic and uses it to force other clan members to attack anyone who doesn't stand with him. Dragons are turning against their own without having any understanding of their actions."

Double crap.

Fate continued, "If you can stop Zendar, then his influence will be broken, and the mayhem being caused by the others should cease. If you can't locate him and stop his spell from spreading, then the consequences will be irreversible. All control over the dragons could be lost."

I was never one to back down from a challenge, so I stood up straighter, prepared to accept whatever the Fates needed us to do.

"Are we heading in the right direction? The gorilla Titus said we had to find a hidden tunnel and it would take us to where we needed to go." I really hoped that was right, at least.

She nodded. "Look in the northeast sectors of the largest mountain in Mineral Valley. There, you will find what you need to succeed. Be covert and swift. Time is not on our side. Also, remember not everything is as you've been told."

With those final mysterious words, darkness surrounded me again, but I didn't go back to sleep; instead, I woke up feeling more refreshed than I'd been in days. I sat up slowly as not to disturb Oliver, his arm-linking not working how he hoped.

"Ry, I know who we're up against now," I said as he turned around.

He frowned. "You've been laying there for less than ten minutes. How is that?"

"A Fate visited me."

He laughed until he realized I wasn't joining in. "You're serious?"

"Dead."

He pinched the bridge of his nose. "Tell me everything."

CHAPTER 5

After making plans with Ryland, we woke up Oliver and, since I already knew everything they were talking about, I ended up falling back to sleep. It wasn't long enough before someone was repeatedly jabbing me in my side, though.

I took this to mean whoever continued to drive me crazy wanted to lose a limb. I swiftly kicked my feet out, knocking them on their ass, and climbed on top.

"Why are you annoying me to death?" I snapped at Ryland. The smirk on his face said he had expected this reaction out of me, making my takedown a little less satisfying than it should have been.

"Well, I tried softly whispering your name, but that didn't work. Prodding at you until you attacked seemed like the next logical step."

I sneered at him. "Where's my breakfast?"

"Over here," Oliver called out.

I grinned at my current favorite friend. Their status changed by the hour depending on which one was driving me crazier. I really needed to find at least one of them a Meraki, so I'd have a girl on my side.

I snatched the granola bar and dried fruit from Oliver while searching around for the coffee I smelled. Ryland moved up a few spots on my nice list again as he handed me a steaming cup of life force. It wasn't going to be the flavored kind I preferred, but campfire coffee was still good enough for me.

"We need to leave soon. According to everything we pieced together yesterday, I think we're about two hours from the entrance to the Forbidden Tunnels. Well, that's if we find it right away." Ryland sighed. "We could be out there all day and it might be right in front of us. I don't imagine there is going to be a sign above the entrance saying 'enter here'."

Ryland was right. We needed to get out there as quickly as possible and keep moving. I downed my coffee and gobbled up my food before getting up to throw some fresh clothes on. Once I was dressed and had my bag repacked, I met the guys outside of the cave's entrance.

The warm yellow sun was rising in the once again pale-green sky. I took a deep breath and soaked in the nature of the Earth Sector. It was the calmest in all of the Otherworld, and I really hoped we didn't fail, letting the dragons ruin that.

"Let's get this show on the road!" I said with more enthusiasm than I felt on the inside. What I really wanted to do was curl up in my bed at home and sleep until noon.

Moving swiftly and quietly through the terrain, we had our guards up even more now that we knew what we were up against. Between the dragons and serpent, we couldn't be too vigilant. Conversation was kept to a minimum, and our full attention was on our surroundings.

"Look over there." Ryland pointed to the left. "See how that whole side of the mountain shimmers in the sunlight except the bottom right corner? Think that's worth checking out?"

I pulled out the map to see if we were near the area Titus had told us to go to. Scanning it quickly, I located the mountain Ryland pointed to. It was right at the edge of the area we had circled. I turned the map toward the guys, so they could see, too.

"It's not far off our path," Oliver said. "Let's check it out."

Ryland and I nodded our agreement. I folded the map back up, sticking it in the center pocket of my bag. "Alright, last one there has to let me give them a makeover when we get home."

I didn't wait for their response before I took off running. My bag slapped against my back as my feet pounded on the hard ground. I was laughing at the grunts I heard behind me as the guys tried to catch up. I peeked to see if they were gaining on me, but before I could catch a glimpse of them, everything went dark. My feet lost traction, and my ass hit the ground. Hard.

I began sliding down a dark hole, screaming my lungs out. I couldn't see a thing and had no idea where I was headed. The guys were going to lose it, considering I'd disappeared on them the day before as well. I just hoped they kept their wits about them long enough to find me before they got themselves into trouble. They didn't often do well without me. I was the backbone of the group. The responsible one.

As I was potentially falling to my death, those thoughts brought a grin to my face. I was so not the responsible one.

Ouch! I slammed into a hard surface as the tunnel curved, and my shoulders smashed into several more walls before my battered body finally came to a hard stop on rough ground. There was no light down here, so I created a fire orb and shined it around my surroundings.

The walls were filled with rubies of all different sizes. The individual facets reflected back as my light shone across the room. I took stock of myself once I realized I was alone and in no immediate danger. My arms were scraped up, and a trickle of blood ran down the side of my face. I rummaged through my bag and removed some bandages from the first aid kit I always kept handy.

When I was as cleaned up as I was going to get, I stood back up and shined the orb around again, this time looking for an exit and calling for Ryland and Oliver. Though, I couldn't hear them and assumed they couldn't hear me either. Instead of attracting too much unwanted attention, I quieted down while continuing to inspect my surroundings.

I couldn't find anything that would lead me out of the room I'd been dropped in, not even where I'd come in from, but I did spot an out-of-place circle of diamonds along the furthest wall. I strode toward the cluster and, as I got closer, saw the diamonds weren't in a circle but arranged in some sort of symbol.

The outer stones which had first caught my eye were about half an inch in diameter and pointed. Smoother, more intricate ones were laid haphazardly throughout the center. They were absolutely mesmerizing. I ran my hand gently over them. The steel-colored wall was cool to the touch, while the diamonds emanated a slight amount of heat.

Crap! I shoved my thumb in my mouth to staunch the blood. I must have cut it on one of the bigger diamonds. I glanced back up at the wall, and my mouth dropped open. *What in the actual hell?*

The few droplets of blood I had spilled on the wall began swirling through the stones. As my blood reached a stone, it would turn a crimson color and illuminate. I stared in fascination as this continued with each diamond. Once they were all shining brightly, I heard a groaning sound from the walls. Taking a step back, I watched as the wall separated and a hallway appeared.

I dissolved my fireball, then glanced back one more time. I was worried if I went through this opening, I might never see my guys again, but considering they hadn't followed after me yet, I had to decide which was worse: staying put or exploring.

Choosing the latter because I knew that was what Ryland would have done, I stepped through the entrance. There were sconces on the wall already holding a steady flame and leading the way down a stone path. To where? I had no idea, but it had to be better than being stuck in the ruby room for the rest of my life. Maybe this is what the Fate meant about us finding what we need to succeed, but it made no sense why I kept getting separated from Oliver and Ryland.

I continued walking, then picked up speed as carvings appeared on the walls. I recognized the etchings from the classes I'd attended during Guardian training in Arvayta. There was a thick, winding line that ran through the middle, representing the Serpentine River. On the top half were flying dragons, some breathing fire, while the rest soared the sky. Below the river line was an ancient language. Symbols ran along the bottom, telling a story that would likely give me nightmares.

This was *not* good. Considering I was pretty sure I was still in Mineral Valley, I didn't even know how it was possible. But if these drawings were what I thought, I'd found myself in a dragon's lair, and my chances of making it out alone were slim.

CHAPTER 6

Rumbles could be heard from up ahead. I slowed my pace and glanced around for another exit. All I saw were more gemstones and piles of gold. This dragon certainly liked its flair. *Crap!* I needed to get out of here quickly, before the dragon realized I'd invaded its space.

I turned to go back the way I came. Locked in the first room was starting to sound better than being snack food to the beast I could hear moving around not very far from me.

I made it three steps before being summoned. "Come here, child. You don't need to fear me." The dragon's voice was sweet and almost angelic. I would not let my guard down, but now I was curious. *Was the crazy beast luring me in for an easy kill, or could she really be friendly?* I shrugged my shoulders at that thought. Only one way to find out.

I unstrapped my sword from my bag and unsheathed it, surprised to find it undamaged from my trip down the tunnels. Though, there were a few tears in my bag, making my outside pockets useless.

I balanced the sword in my hands, pushing my flames

through the metal. If I was going down, I'd at least do so like a badass, fighting a dragon. I tentatively stepped around the corner and sucked in a breath at the sight of the dragon sitting in the cavern, not at all ready to attack.

To top it off, the beast was gorgeous. Deep teal scales shimmered around her. Each one appeared to have a different variation of aqua blue, no two alike. Her eyes were a piercing silver color with ebony slits in the middle. She was average size for a dragon, seeming to be around ten feet in height and twice the length. Definitely not the biggest I had heard about, but I imagined she could hold her own in a fight.

Her wings were folded against her body, and I craved to see them extended. Her image matched her voice perfectly until she grinned at me. Well, I think she grinned. I was seeing teeth and hoping it was done in a friendly gesture.

"Come in and have a seat." She nodded her head toward a rock that was shaped like a bench. Her mouth didn't move as she spoke, but her voice somehow still projected. "My name is Yelah. Sorry to have brought you here under such circumstances, but when I felt you near, I didn't want to chance you getting away."

I shook my head in confusion. This dragon was off her rocker and needed to do a bit more explaining. "Felt me near? Care to elaborate on that tidbit for me?" If this really was what the Fate had been trying to say would help us succeed, she'd done a horrible job preparing me.

"Your sword. It calls to me. It contains magic dragons can no longer access. More importantly, it is the only thing that will stop Zendar from destroying our kind."

This dragon mentioned the same one the Fate did, and I had my confirmation. Knowing I was no longer in danger, I pulled my magic back so that the sword was no longer a threat and examined it closer. "This sword right here? Are you sure? This was a gift from the Elves. All they told me was that it could channel my power, nothing about being able to slay dragons in particular."

Yelah let out a snort, which caused me to squeal. Dragon snorts could be dangerous, and she was a little too close for my liking. "Of course, they wouldn't. Elves only do things when they feel like it, but they knew exactly what they gave you when they did. That sword is the last object in all the worlds which can take down Zendar. He will come for you if he realizes the weapon is near, and he won't hesitate to kill you if we don't stop him. So, I'd recommend not using it like you just were until absolutely necessary."

Holy crap! *Thanks for the heads-up, Fates,* I thought sarcastically. It sounded like I was on a suicide mission now. "What about my friends? Why did you leave them behind, and can we find them now? They're a little overprotective and are probably throwing a fit in their search to find me."

Yelah nodded. "You trust these men? You were running from them. I thought I might have been helping when I took only you."

I smacked my hand against my forehead. "We're also competitive." I shrugged. "We were racing, and I was winning. They're my best friends and will have my back during any fight. I wouldn't want to do this without them."

"Very well. I'll summon them. Probably best to do it now, anyway, before they destroy any more of the minerals above. They're causing quite a bit of havoc up there."

Yelah closed her eyes and began humming softly. If she wasn't standing before me in her glorious dragon form, I would have believed her to be a Siren. The melody she used was alluring.

Before I knew it, a circular hole opened in the ceiling. I stood up as Ryland dropped to the ground, followed by Oliver, who landed halfway on top of him. It was quite the sight. "About damn time you two showed up," I teased.

They both scrambled to their feet and gave me hugs, barely

allowing me to breathe until they realized we weren't alone. As soon as they saw Yelah, I was thrown behind them while wind from Ryland began circling the cave, ready for attack.

"Calm down, boys. She's friendly," I said, pushing forward. Nobody put Jordan in the back.

Ryland twisted his head toward me. "Only *you* would fall down a hole and make friends with a dragon."

"I'm talented, what can I say? Speaking of, how did you do that?" I asked Yelah.

"Dragon magic." She grinned at me again with rows of razor-sharp teeth on display. Someone really needed to let her know how frightening that was. Though, I would *not* be that someone.

"Alright, then. Let's leave it at that. What do we do now?" I asked.

"How about you tell us who this is?" Oliver asked, warily.

"Don't be such a wuss. This is Yelah. We're in her lair. My sword called to her, so she brought me here to ask for our help. I know why the Fates asked us to help with the Dragon problem. Apparently, this sword is made from the only metals which can kill the beast causing all the mayhem in the Otherworld."

Ryland shook his head. "Again, I say, only you."

I grinned at him. I was glad it was my sword. I loved a good fight, and this one seemed even more promising now that we had a dragon on our side.

"I need to call on a couple members of my clan," Yelah said. "If you want your friends to come with us, then they need their own dragons. We will be flying over most of the Fire Sector, unless you care to venture through it."

Ryland and Oliver grinned widely at each other and spoke at the same time. "We'll take a dragon."

I sat back down and let Yelah do her thing while finally taking the time to check out her home. Her lair was huge and cavernous. The ceiling was easily fifty feet high, and the cave was even wider than it was tall. More intriguing etchings of ancient symbols were carved into the walls, accented by rubies and diamonds.

Fire sconces continued to light up the area, not only brightening the room, but keeping it warm as well. There were several dozen animal pelts in the corner, laid out where I assumed Yelah relaxed or even slept, and nearby was a small waterfall that trickled down into a basin.

With as big as the room was, I hoped it would be enough to hold three dragons, but just in case, I made a mental note to be as far off to the side as possible when they arrived to avoid being an accidental casualty.

Ryland and Oliver followed me back to the rock bench, sitting so that I was in the middle. "You really scared us, Jordy," Oliver whispered.

"We were blowing holes in the ground with orbs but couldn't get anything to penetrate further than four or five feet down, and our elemental abilities were useless," Ryland added. "Try not to do that again."

I gave them each a hug. "I knew you guys loved me. Yelah thought I was running from you or she would have summoned all of us. Guess the race wasn't the best idea." I grinned. "I so would have won, though."

"Of course, you would have," Oliver said condescendingly. "So, you trust this dragon?"

I shrugged. "I'm pretty sure she's what the Fate was speaking of. This dragon can help us succeed, and she's not at all like the dragons we've been told about in the past. If she was, we'd be dead already. Plus, she's pretty damn powerful if she can just call us to her like that."

"As long as we don't get separated again, I'm good with it." Ryland shuddered. "Twice within twenty-four hours is not what I call fun. Also, I wouldn't want to be the one to tell Brooks or Daliah that we lost their pseudo-daughter. They'd likely fire me as their protector and get me kicked out of Arvayta or demoted. I quite like my life as it is and helping them, so don't die or get kidnapped again, please."

I patted Ryland's knee. "I'm glad your life and job are your biggest concerns. I'll be sure to keep that in mind later."

He let out a belly laugh, and it was good to hear. Oliver and I joined in, and the tension was released from all of us. As long as we managed to stick together, we'd make it out of this okay.

Before I could voice any other opinions on the matter, the walls began to quake. The charcoal-colored rock opened up at the ceiling, allowing two mammoth-sized dragons to swoop in. I grabbed Ryland's and Oliver's arms, dragging them to the furthest corner in search of a safe haven. These beasts were massive, and their tails appeared to have a mind of their own.

The first one to land was golden in color and had bronze, soulful eyes. Its tail was forked and barbed. Scars ran along its sides, telling of the years it had battled. The second dragon was slightly shorter than the first, but its width certainly made up for that. Its scales were smoky gray and silver intermingled together. Its tail was forked like the other dragon, but not barbed.

"Welcome, Ladon and Drake. These are our new friends." Yelah used her snout to gesture toward us cowering in the corner, very unguardian like. "Jordan, Ryland, and Oliver will be helping us with Zendar. Jordan will be flying with me and each of you will be responsible for one of the other guardians. We will prepare and rest tonight, then leave at first light tomorrow."

The silver one, I think he was Drake, eyed us carefully. "How do you know we can trust them?" he asked suspiciously.

"Jordan, will you unsheathe your sword again, please?" Yelah asked, and I complied without pause. "Can you not sense the magic within her weapon? This is what we have been waiting for to defeat Zendar. They will be the key to our success."

I hadn't noticed the excitement from Yelah earlier, but she was radiating with hope now. As nervous as I had been about going against dragons, I was happy to help if it meant keeping these ones safe. Nobody deserved to live in fear. Zendar needed to be stopped, and I would happily deliver his punishment.

Drake nodded, while Ladon remained silent. I wasn't sure what to think of our newest editions, but I was confident Ryland and Oliver could hold their own when the time came. I glanced at my guys, grinning at the expressions on both their faces. I was pretty sure none of us had been in the presence of even a single dragon before, let alone three.

"So, what now?" I asked. "Do we get a tour of this place and a warm bed to sleep in?"

Oliver elbowed me in the side. "What?" I asked. "You can't tell me you don't want to see the inside of a dragon's lair. When are we going to have another opportunity like this?"

"Hopefully never," Oliver groaned. He and Ryland didn't know how to fully embrace life sometimes. I, on the other hand, lived each day as if it was my last. It had been a promise I'd made to myself after my parents leaving me nearly broke me.

"I'd be happy to give you a tour, Jordan. It's the least I can do considering you didn't run for the hills when you saw me for the first time." She grinned again, and I couldn't take it any longer.

"Yelah, you are a magnificent creature, absolutely stunning. But please, for the greater good, don't smile. Your teeth freak me out and remind me I *should* have run from you."

Ryland and Oliver stiffened, while the three dragons before us snorted in what I assumed was their form of laughter. Small puffs of smoke came out of their nostrils, and their eyes squeezed closed.

"I'll keep that in mind. Your honesty is something to be admired, young one."

I elbowed the guys and glared at them. "At least someone appreciates it."

"Drake and Ladon, you're welcome to your usual rooms here, or you can join us in the morning. Which is better?" Yelah asked her dragon friends.

Since he hadn't spoken yet, it surprised me when Ladon answered first. "We'll stay here, just in case. With the sword present, we all need to be ready at a moment's notice." The tenor of his voice was deep and rough, making me wonder if his vocal cords had been damaged in a fight at one point, but I saw no scars around his neck to confirm.

"I agree. Be ready at first light, then."

The massive beasts pounded their way toward the enormous doorway leading to the tunnels opposite of where I had first arrived. Once they were out of sight, Yelah turned back to the three of us. "Who's ready for a tour?"

I grinned widely and nodded my head, while Ryland tried to stifle a groan. I was going to make these guys live more dangerously if it was the last thing I did.

"Right this way." Yelah swung her body around, her tail missing us by mere inches.

Oliver and Ryland flinched, glaring at me. "She's leading us to our deaths," Ryland complained.

I promptly ignored him and skipped after my new favorite friend. My guys had just been demoted.

CHAPTER 7

Morning came way too soon after the previous day's exhaustion. Once the adrenaline wore off that night, thoughts about the day filtered through. A giant snake wanted me dead, I'd been kidnapped by monkeys, then again by a dragon. Thankfully, only one of three meant me harm.

The beds Yelah had provided us were made from animal pelts, but on a much smaller scale than the ones I had seen when I first arrived in the lair. The bed was warm and comfortable, ensuring I slept like the dead once I was able to quiet my thoughts.

Ryland and Oliver shared the bed with me, both having been too afraid to have us separated in the slightest. Big babies. I didn't mind, though. We used to have sleepovers like this when we were younger, and I had forgotten how fun they could be.

"You still snore when you sleep," Ryland complained as we got up for the day.

"You still annoy me on a daily basis, so I guess we're even." I stuck my tongue out at him and went to the makeshift bathroom. There was a hole in a rock seat that was supposed to be the toilet and a small water feature opposite the toilet where I could wash up a little. I laughed at myself as I hovered over the rock and attempted to pee without actually touching the cold stone, but nearly fell in instead.

I finished washing up and changed into my clothes. Once I was back in the room, I unhooked my sword from my bag and strapped it to my back. Anything we didn't absolutely need would be left here. There was no sense in having anything extra to hold us back. I snagged my knife at the last minute and shoved it into my boot. One could never have too many sharp objects.

"Who's ready to go slay some dragons?" I grinned wickedly at my best friends.

"Some days, I really worry about your sanity," Oliver said seriously, causing my grin to expand even more.

"Let's go find Yelah and see if the others are ready," Ryland suggested.

The guys finished strapping their own weapons to themselves, and we headed down the hallway. The closer we got to the dragons, the more tension rolled off my friends. I tried my usual joking, but nothing was lightening their sour moods. Getting annoyed by my lack of success, I stopped trying, in case they succeeded in bringing me down with them.

"Good morning, young one," Yelah spoke as we came around the corner.

"Good morning, large dragon." My grin returned. "Glad to see someone else is cheerful. Normally I'm the grump in the mornings, but tweedle-dee and tweedle-dum over there decided to take that role today."

Yelah tossed her head from side to side but said nothing else. Ladon and Drake were already in the cavernous room, observing us.

We were offered breakfast, which included an assortment of fruits and greens. I was curious about how they appeared and asked as much.

"Dragon magic." The same answer she had used yesterday. I pondered what else her *dragon magic* could do. There was so much unknown with these beasts. Their clans didn't socialize with other species in the Otherworld, so they were often labeled a danger. Something I believed until just yesterday.

People were afraid of the unknown, but in this case, I knew the people had been wrong, or at least partially. Maybe if the dragons hadn't been feared for so long, we wouldn't be in the situation we were currently in.

After we were fed, Yelah opened up the ceiling to her lair once more and glanced at me with a twinkle in her eyes. "Ready to hop on?"

"Hell yes!" I fist-pumped the air and ran for her tail. Before I made it two steps, my body was yanked back.

"Are you sure about this?" Ryland whispered. The look of worry in his creased face had mine softening.

"Yes, I'm very sure. Trust me, okay?"

Ryland nodded and let go. I resumed my sprint toward Yelah and climbed up her tail. Her scales were coarse and sharp, so I had to be careful. Once I was settled, my legs found a comfortable spot at the base of the dragon's neck, and I held on to the small horns that crept toward the top of her head.

The horns were ebony, standing out against her glossy teal scales that weren't as warm as I expected, given she breathed fire.

I peeked over at Ryland and Oliver. They were each mounting their designated dragon, but with much less enthusiasm than I had. Ryland went with Drake and Oliver with Ladon.

Once everyone was situated, Yelah led the way as she flapped her powerful wings up and down. They were smooth but thick like leather, and the edges were covered in scales that matched the rest of her body with sharp barbs I'd missed before on each corner of the wings. Her pace remained steady until we cleared the ceiling, and then we soared.

I was flying with a dragon. Holy crap. Best. Day. Ever.

Wind blew across my face, and I closed my eyes briefly, sighing at the bliss rolling through me. Even though there was a good chance we could all die against the dragon we were supposed to fight, I pushed that aside and soaked in the moment.

When I reopened my eyes, I took in the sights. We were several hundred feet above Mineral Valley. I watched in amazement as the final pieces of rock came back together that led to Yelah's lair. Dragon magic was pure and astonishing. I could see Web Jungle behind us. It looked quiet and peaceful, but I knew otherwise. I would never be venturing through there again, if I could help it.

Inferno Ponds was soon upon us, and we were officially in the Fire Sector. Heat from the eternal flames grazed us, so I pulled my legs up a little higher to be safe. I had no desire to find out how far of a reach those flames had.

"How are you doing back there?" Yelah called to me.

"Better than I thought I would be." I laughed. "You've got some steady wings, my friend."

Yelah snorted, then went back to focusing on flying. Ryland and Oliver were next to me, finally looking more relaxed. The creases from Ryland's forehead seemed to have smoothed out for the time being.

The man was going to age quicker than all of us if he didn't learn how to live a little. I knew he'd had his heart broken and I couldn't understand how that felt, but it wouldn't stop me from trying to make sure he lived the rest of his life as best he could.

Oliver, on the other hand, switched from Team Jordan to Team Ryland and back again almost as often as the sky went from day to night. He evened out our trio nicely, though I'd never tell him that. My guys didn't need me to inflate their egos any more by telling them how awesome they were.

Drake and Ryland soared a little closer, so we were within yelling distance. "How you doing, old man?" I called.

Ryland gave me the middle finger and whispered something

to Drake. Before I knew it, they took off like a bat out of hell, which made me giggle-snort, considering he was riding a dragon over Inferno Ponds.

"Yelah. Do. Not. Let. Them. Win!" I punctuated each word, making sure my point was made.

"You got it." I could hear the grin in the timbre of her voice, thankful I couldn't see all her pointy teeth this time.

I held on tighter and pressed my legs more firmly into her scales. Out here in the sun, they appeared more aqua than teal as the light reflected off of them. The faster she went, the cooler the scales became against my skin. So cold, in fact, that I began to shiver.

"Why is it so cold?" I asked.

"Oops. Dragon magic."

"No way. That's not working anymore. Spill it, dragon." I was giving the back of her massive head the 'don't mess with me' look, but it was wasted. She didn't glance my way, which made me pout in return.

"Our bodies change with the elements and with how much magic we use or what we're using it for. Like right now, we're having fun and I'm using dragon magic to accelerate my speed. Since I'm in no danger, my body is cooling. If I was in danger, my body would heat up significantly. The elements also affect the coloring of my scales. You likely noticed I appeared more teal to you in my home, yet now my scales are light blue. The sun changes them, but if I was lower to the terrain, then my surroundings could influence the color, as well, allowing me to camouflage."

"That is badass, Yelah. I have to admit, I'm slightly jealous. Now, back to the task at hand. Oliver is gaining on us, and Ryland is still ahead. Let's make these boys eat dust and show them who's boss!"

Yelah roared and, not-so-surprisingly, her speed kicked up another few notches. I laughed and grinned the entire time, completely forgetting we were potentially flying to our deaths. Those thoughts could shove it until the threats were nearer.

Once we passed Ryland and the outer limits of Inferno Ponds, Yelah began our descent to the ground. According to what we'd been told the night before, we were going to follow the Serpentine River on foot for a while and see if we could pick up anything new while on the ground.

Shockingly enough, with as massive as the dragons were, their landings were graceful and smooth. Yelah lowered herself to the ground, so I could slide off her easier.

Ryland and Oliver were right behind us and dismounted just as quickly, giving their dragon escorts manly pats on the side. "We never had a chance, but it was fun to try anyway," Oliver joked.

"That it was." Ladon nodded his colossal head.

I smiled as I realized that my guys seemed to have bonded a little with our new friends. I was worried their hesitation would make this whole situation harder than it needed to be. We already had an evil, psycho Dragon to contend with, and possibly a killer snake if he'd managed to follow us somehow. I didn't want to add anything else to the agenda.

"We didn't get to cover the entire plan last night," I said once everyone was together. "I know we're on foot for a while, but what next?"

"The canopy of trees is really thick through this part of the river. Zendar and others working with him could be anywhere between here and the seventh bend of the river. Until our view isn't restricted, we need to be on the ground," Yelah answered.

"What happens when we get to the seventh bend?" Ryland asked before I could.

Ladon answered this time, grinning even creepier than Yelah. "Then, we fight."

"I like your attitude. I'm all for a good fight, but please leave the grinning for people you want to scare." I shuddered once more as each of the three dragons snorted out in amusement. "Am I the only one who quakes at the sight of all those killer teeth?"

"Yes, I think you are," Ryland teased.

"Well then, let's get moving," I said after giving Ryland a quick glare and deciding to change the subject. "I'm ready to be back in the sky."

"Addicting, isn't it?" Drake asked, his heavy feet stomping just a few paces away from me.

I nodded enthusiastically before catching up to Ryland and Oliver, who had already moved several yards ahead of me. "You guys feeling better about our new friends now?"

"Yeah," Oliver answered first. "The flight time gave me a chance to drill Ladon. They're good dragons, and I'm glad we're here to help them."

Ryland nodded in agreement. "We'll take care of Zendar and make sure the good dragons don't take the blame for this idiot and his minions."

I loved my guys. They really were the best.

After the first twenty minutes or so, Yelah froze, halting the rest of us without a word. I strained to hear whatever she might have, but I got nothing. I looked to Ryland and Oliver, but they each shrugged their shoulders. I inched closer to Yelah, but she was intently focused on whatever was up ahead.

I waited not so patiently for her to acknowledge me and tell us what was going on. I was seconds from tapping my foot and clearing my throat when she lowered her head to me. "There are two dragons up ahead. They're young, maybe a century old. I can't quite make out their conversation, but I can sense Zendar's magic on them."

"So, what do we do? Go in breathing fire and swinging swords?" I asked, eager to finally be doing something other than traveling.

"No, we don't know they're a danger. Zendar has forced a lot of good dragons to do things they normally wouldn't. Let's get closer and see what we can learn first."

I let out a disappointed sigh, and Ryland patted me on the back. "Always so thirsty for bloodshed."

"Only when we're stopping evil beings from wreaking havoc on the goodness of the worlds." I smirked. "I dream of these opportunities."

"Only you, my friend."

"That's why you love me."

Ladon shushed us and brought our attention back to the matter at hand. I mouthed *sorry,* realizing if Yelah had heard the dragons, there was a chance they could hear us.

Each corner we came around, I expected to come upon the dragons, but it was another ten or so minutes before Yelah stopped us again. How she had heard anything from that far away amazed me, but I wasn't going to ask, already knowing her answer would be the same as each time before.

Dragon magic.

"Come on, dude. Why are we even here? You know what he's doing is wrong," a young male voice said. Dragon years were way different than any other supernatural I knew. Even though Yelah thought they were around a century old, technically, they were still teenagers mentally.

"Don't be such a wuss. If you want to survive, you need to shut your mouth and do as you're told."

"Is it so wrong that I don't want to hurt people just because someone else tells me to?" This time, the tone of his voice was sad and hopeless.

"Yes, it is." The hardness of the second dragon's voice gave me shivers. I was ready to slice this ass-gobbler's head off. I reached for my sword, but rough scales rubbed against my arm. Drake shook his head at me and, once again, disappointment crashed into me.

When am I going to get to draw blood?

Yelah let out a melody so hypnotic, my eyes began to droop. My knees grew weak and I leaned against Oliver, who didn't seem any better off than me. Ladon noticed and immediately blew in our faces with an icy blast.

"What the hell was that for?" I screeched.

Ladon shrugged. "Only way to keep you out of the trance."

Damn dragon magic.

"Neo! Wake up!" the young dragon shrieked.

Yelah, Drake, and Ladon moved through the trees and appeared before the young forest-green dragon still awake. I heard his intake of breath before the begging began. He thought we were here to kill him.

"Calm down, little one. What is your name?" Drake asked.

"Kort. What did you do to my brother?" he snapped, moving his eyes between us and the russet-colored dragon at his feet.

"He's in a deep sleep, but he'll be just fine, I promise," Yelah said softly. "We heard your conversation, and we mean you no harm as long as you agree to stay here with your brother."

Kort swung his head around, finally noticing us. "Why are you here?" he asked, suspiciously.

"We're here to stop Zendar," Ladon stated. "From the conversation we overheard, it didn't sound like you would have a problem with that."

"What will become of Neo?"

Yelah stepped closer. "The sleep will only last for two moon cycles. If he wakes and sees reason, then you'll likely never see us again."

I was certain I could actually see the lump move slowly down Kort's long neck as he took in this information. "There are more of us, and Zendar has his claws in deep on many of them. How do you plan to stop him?"

"That's none of your concern, little one. Watch over your brother and take care. Don't make us come back here." Yelah narrowed her gaze at the young dragon, seemingly large and in charge. She was my kind of people. Or dragon. Whatever.

Kort nodded eagerly, lowering his gaze respectfully. Our three dragons seemed satisfied with this, and we continued down the path.

Well, that was anti-climactic.

"After the next bend, we'll take to the skies again," Yelah said. "Kort was untrained, with no handle on his magic. His thoughts projected loudly to me, and Zendar only has those he deems insignificant on the outskirts. The ones we need to worry about are with him at the seventh bend."

"Should I even ask how you *heard* his thoughts?" She was full of wonder. I loved it.

The three dragons shared a look as if they were communicating telepathically, which wouldn't surprise me one bit.

"I think it's time you learned a little more about me," Yelah said excitedly.

"Well, spit it out, woman."

"I'm supposed to be the queen of our dragon clan."

CHAPTER 8

Once the shock wore off, I asked, "What does 'supposed to be' mean? And why are you helping us fight? Aren't you supposed to be locked away somewhere being protected?"

Yelah sighed and shook her head. "We are a monarch-led clan. There was a prophecy that a young male dragon would be born who would cause corruption within our ranks. The clan thought we locked away the dragon from the prophecy two centuries ago, but we took Zendar's dad. He was a teen when this happened, and he grew to resent us and became very powerful. By the time we realized our mistake, it was too late.

"A few months ago, when Zendar reached his full power, he killed my mother, who was Queen at the time. In our quest to stop him, my crowning has been overlooked. Queens in our clan do not stand on the sidelines during times of war. We fight alongside our people."

Holy dragon babies! I did not see that coming. "Where is Zendar's dad now?"

Yelah lowered her head in sorrow. "He poisoned himself and

died a week before we realized our mistake. I believe that is what set Zendar off. He killed my mother right afterward."

"Is this why you can do things I've never heard of other dragons doing before?" Ryland asked.

"Yes. Certain abilities are passed down from queen to queen. Each new matriarch receives their own special gift as well as all the gifts given before them."

"What is your special gift?" Oliver asked eagerly.

Yelah grinned. I cringed. Damn dragon didn't listen very well. "Land manipulation. It's how I was able to summon all of you to me."

Ryland let out a low whistle. "That's impressive."

We made it to the next bend, and it was time to fly again. I was equal parts excited and nervous. I enjoyed flying and was anxious to stop Zendar, but after what we just learned, my guard was up even more, along with my nerves going a little haywire. This fight was personal for Zendar, which meant he was going to be reckless. This could go either way for us.

Each of the dragons lowered their bodies, and the three of us quickly took our positions. Yelah flapped her enormous wings first, leading the way toward the seventh bend of the river. Her body was stealthy, and the ride was smooth. Before I knew it, we were landing once more.

"Why are we landing?" I asked.

"I need to summon more members of my clan. They have been waiting for my call since you arrived in Mineral Valley. They will help us keep Zendar's guards away from us while we move in."

I wanted to ask more questions but decided not to. Yelah needed to do her thing, and I wasn't going to be the one to stop her.

Her voice sang another hypnotic melody. Right as I was starting to feel lightheaded from it, Ryland and Oliver appeared next to me.

"What's she doing?" Ryland asked.

"Calling for reinforcements."

We waited for several minutes before Yelah finally turned back to us. "Everyone is in position now."

"Wouldn't Zendar's dragons have heard you if your own dragons were able to?" Oliver asked.

"Only the people linked directly to me can hear my call, and I only have the most loyal of dragons still tied to me, I promise you that. Dragon magic works in mysterious ways, a lot of which I cannot explain to someone who does not belong to our clan."

Yelah had proven herself more than capable time and time again. I wasn't going to question her and was glad when neither Ryland nor Oliver did.

"So, we ready to do this?" I said with a smirk on my face.

Everyone else nodded their heads, and we mounted our dragon friends again. I was getting cozy until I felt Yelah tense beneath me. I leaned forward and followed the direction of her stare. I couldn't see anything, so I peeked at Oliver and Ryland. They both seemed as confused as me, but Drake and Ladon were looking in the same direction as Yelah.

"More dragons out there?" I asked.

Yelah rumbled deep in her chest. "No, a pest. Don't worry. I'll take care of him."

A full-on pout appeared on my face. *Way to rain on my parade, Queen Yelah.* I wanted in on the action at some point.

"You'll get plenty of opportunity to let off some steam once we're at the seventh bend, I promise."

Well, that helped to cheer me up. Some.

Finally, I heard branches breaking and leaves on the ground crunching. I squinted and pulled myself further up Yelah's back to get closer until I saw the head of a serpent. *Crap*. I knew the bastard was going to show up again. This thing was massive and moving quicker than I assumed its size would allow.

Ebony scales covered its body, with small spikes running

down the backside. Its beady yellow eyes met mine, and its mouth opened, revealing some nasty-looking fangs that dripped thick, golden saliva. Chills ran across my body, and I was about to make Yelah really annoyed with me.

When the serpent was within striking distance, Yelah and Ladon both roared and shot fire out of their mouths. Heat carried with the wind toward me, and I scooted back to avoid getting burned. The serpent didn't seem bothered by the fire and struck through the flames, but Drake flicked his tail, slamming the serpent back on the ground.

With everyone else distracted, I launched off Yelah's back and landed on the ground twenty or so feet below. The flames from one of the dragons had blinded the serpent, but his other senses didn't seem dulled as he moved for me.

"Jordan!" Ryland yelled, but I ignored him as I focused on the monster coming at me.

His forked tongue hissed, smelling the air. He might be able to know where I am, but the annoyance still couldn't see.

I swung my sword out and chopped the front of his tongue off. The snake screeched, and its body jerked toward me. I didn't move fast enough, and its tail slammed into my ribs as I fell to the ground.

Yelah was moving toward us, and I knew I only had mere seconds to finish the serpent before she did it for me. Ignoring the ache in my side, I got back up and brought my own fire to the party.

My sword flamed up, and I felt wind on my neck. Ryland might be pissed at me for interfering, but he had my back anyway. I launched myself forward, letting the wind do most of the work as I arced the sword and came down on the snake's head, my blade going through the middle.

Yelah was caught up then and stomped on the back half of the serpent, breaking its spine and keeping it from hitting me again. When it stopped flinching and the head was almost all ash and bone from my flames, I withdrew my sword and walked toward Yelah.

She was glaring at me, but I didn't cower. "That was my problem, and I needed to take care of it."

"You knew he was following you?"

I nodded. "Titus, the ape who kidnapped me and told me to find your tunnels also let me know about the serpent."

"What?" Oliver and Ryland grumbled at the same time.

"Did I forget to tell you guys there was a giant snake following us? My bad." I grinned.

"Seriously, Jordan?" Ryland rolled his eyes. "Can we get out of here now?"

Yelah blew smoke from her snout. "I won't say I'm thrilled with your choice, but I understand your reasons and respect them."

"So, we're good to finish dragon hunting?" I asked as we walked away from the dead serpent.

"I believe we are," Yelah replied.

CHAPTER 9

As soon as the three of us were settled, the dragons took flight. We were once again on our way to find Zendar with hopefully no more distractions. Within ten minutes, I could finally see the area we were headed. It was tucked next to the river with dense trees surrounding the opposite side.

Off in the distance, there were fountains of lava and smoke plumes all across the dry land. I'd only been to the Fire Sector once before and had no desire to ever return. Except for the spots of forest next to the river that ran through, the rest of the land seemed post-apocalyptic.

There was little to no vantage point from up here. I thought I saw massive boulders in the clearing, but as we got closer, I realized they were moving and not boulders at all. They were dragons, and not ones we wanted to have lunch with. *Fan-freaking-tastic.*

We started to descend, and my adrenaline began pumping. I patted my back and boot, feeling for my weapons and making sure they were secure. Everything was in place.

I glanced toward Ryland and Oliver; they flanked each side of me and Yelah with Drake and Ladon. Ryland's face was creased in concentration, his bronze hair tousled from the wind, and he looked as much the warrior as I knew him to be. Oliver's cobalt eyes met mine, and the grin I expected appeared on his youthful face. He was as eager for this fight as I was.

As soon as we landed, I jumped off Yelah and drew my sword. Ryland and Oliver did the same as they moved closer to me.

"Drake and Ladon will stay behind us, watching our backs. Other members from my clan are coming from the opposite direction. We were the distraction for their discreet arrival. I want the three of you at my side. Do not venture off. Do not engage any of the dragons except Zendar. We will only get one chance at this, and we cannot fail." Yelah leveled her silver eyes at each of us.

I felt the power of her words weigh down on me, making me want to kneel before her. She was a powerful queen, and I had a feeling we'd only seen a fraction of her power. We nodded in agreement and followed Yelah as Drake and Ladon disappeared behind us.

I heard grunts and shouts from nearby, causing my body to tense. I didn't like being told I couldn't fight yet, but I trusted Yelah. I would listen. For now.

My magic stirred inside me and I let it flow freely from my core, through my arms, and out to my sword. Flames formed above the hilt, traveling up the blade, but staying small as I controlled the element.

Oliver and Ryland each had their own swords in one hand and deep, ruby-red orbs in the other.

Yelah halted, her wing swinging out, and I almost cut right through her with my magic-filled sword. Damn, that was close. "Why'd we stop?" I asked in a low whisper.

Yelah didn't answer, but I continued to scan our surroundings, waiting for whatever she was concerned with. After several minutes, my patience was running thin. Ryland sensed my restlessness and placed his hand on my shoulder, calming me some.

"Okay, it's clear," Yelah said, finally breaking the silence.

"What was that about?" I asked, with more attitude than she deserved from me, which made me cringe internally. Sometimes I couldn't stop my mouth.

"One of Zendar's dragons was up ahead. Drake and Ladon took care of him for us, so we can continue on."

My head whipped around, trying to sense them. I hadn't even heard a twig snap. For such massive beasts, they were sure as hell stealthy.

"Not that I don't trust your instincts, but why are you trying to prevent us from doing anything useful yet?" I asked, and Oliver stifled a laugh. I shot him a glare as I waited for Yelah's answer.

"We don't need to waste our energy when it isn't necessary. Battling Zendar will take everything you have and then some. Please try to trust me. I know the damage he is capable of firsthand."

Way to be a jerk, I chided myself. Of course, Yelah would know. She lost her mother the last time she faced Zendar. I needed to shut up and do as I was asked for once.

Yelah began moving again, and we followed without saying anything else. Ryland glared at me, basically saying with one look what I had already been thinking. I raised my hands up and shrugged. Nothing I could do about my lack of a filter after the fact.

After several more stops and waiting on other dragons to handle whatever was in our path, we finally made it to an enclosed area at the edge of a dying forest. Oliver cringed.

"What's wrong?" I whispered.

"I can't use the earth here to help us. It's too weak, and I can't ask it to make that sacrifice. The pain of everything is too much and I'll be distracted."

I patted his chest. "Your earth elements don't make you strong, Oliver. What's in there does. We got this."

He seemed taken aback by my sudden kindness, but merely smiled and pulled me along without saying anything else. I hated that he didn't feel whole going into this fight, but with all three of us together, I knew we would be okay. I had to believe it, because there were no other options in my mind.

We approached the perimeter of what I assumed was where Zendar was hiding. Large rocks were stacked together, creating a makeshift fence. We crept around it in time to see Drake and Ladon taking out a dragon twice their size that stood in front of the entrance to whatever lay behind the rock wall. The fight between the three of them appeared to be touch and go. I stepped forward a couple times, but Ryland and Oliver slapped hands on each of my arms before I could do anything.

Drake was bleeding from three large gashes to his neck, and Ladon had burn marks on his golden tail, along with a chunk of scales missing from his back-left leg. I hoped their part in this was almost over, because I didn't see how they could last much longer.

Finally, they caught the dragon by surprise and blood spurted across the gate as Drake raked his front claws down the dragon's neck.

Once the guard was unmoving, we continued forward and I kept my eyes away from the dead beast. Even though it was his life or ours, the humanity in me didn't enjoy seeing gutted dragons.

Yelah stopped at the gate, appearing to have one of those mental conversations with Drake and Ladon again. They nodded and drug the body of the guard dragon out of our way. I tried to not stare at the fallen dragon, but in the end, I couldn't help myself. I nearly gagged at the sight of internal body parts hanging out of the gaping hole Drake had caused and regretted my very poor decision.

"Once we enter this gate, there is no going back until we've defeated Zendar," Yelah said solemnly. "We go in together, and we leave together. Do you understand?"

Ryland, Oliver, and I nodded. That was how we went into every battle when it was just the three of us. No reason why we couldn't add Yelah in as a 'no Dragon Queen left behind' rule.

We crept through the gate. Well, the three of us crept. Yelah stomped. I liked her style better. I left the guys in the dust and kept pace with the dragon. She glanced down at me, nodding her approval of my place at her side.

While we walked, I sent more magic through to my sword until the flames began to lick at my fingers. As soon as I did, a loud roar erupted from somewhere up ahead and heavy steps sounded, heading right toward us and causing vibrations in the ground as they got closer.

We were about to come face to face with Zendar.

I bounced on my toes, rotating my sword between hands as we—or at least, I—waited eagerly to see the beast who'd been causing havoc on the innocents of the Otherworld.

Trees two or three feet in diameter snapped in half like they were mere twigs as Zendar plowed through his little fortress, ready to face whoever dared to enter his domain.

His gaze landed on Yelah first, then on me. He let out a chuckle so horrid, I couldn't be sure if he was crying or laughing. It was quite pathetic, considering how much he had been talked up.

His beady charcoal eyes did one more cursory glance at each of us before he came to a complete halt. His scales were midnight blue and scarred. His black claws were sharp, digging into the dirt beneath him. Lastly, his tail caught my attention. It appeared to have been mangled in battle at some point. Half of the end was missing, while the other was littered with more white scars.

"Yelah, I'm disappointed in you," Zendar reproached. "You dare to face me, and the only backup you bring are *Guardians*."

His tone gave way to his disgust, making me eager to shove my sword straight through his heart.

"I've learned a lot in my time away, and I don't need backup. Your reign of terror is ending today," Yelah answered with all the confidence I hoped she truly felt.

I was almost annoyed that she didn't tell him how awesome we were, and we most definitely weren't *backup*. We were the main event.

"Then, what are you waiting for?" Zendar spat.

"Absolutely nothing." Yelah charged, and my mouth gaped. *This was so not part of the plan.*

Zendar rose onto his hind legs, and when Yelah came close enough, he slammed down, swinging his tail out and smacking her in the face. I cringed at the pain she had to be experiencing, but the fierce dragon queen persevered and kept moving forward as if nothing happened.

Yelah lifted her front leg and swiped out at Zendar, but he evaded easily and quickly. I glanced at Ryland and Oliver, wondering what the hell we were supposed to do. Yelah hadn't quite explained our role in this scenario, other than my sword needed to be the one to kill Zendar. Was I supposed to wait for her to tire him out, then go in for the kill, or join in whenever I felt like it? I wasn't one for sitting on the sidelines, so I already had my answer.

"You boys ready?" I asked as Yelah and Zendar continued to exchange blow after blow, rotating between tail swings, claw gouging, and fire blasts. I wasn't so fond of the fire. It had a heat unlike my own that was laced with something dark.

"We've got your back," Ryland said with a fierce look of determination, but before we could move in to assist Yelah, Drake and Ladon came tumbling through the gates with three dragons pushing in on them. Drake's right front leg was dangling at an awkward angle, and he was attempting to fight without putting pressure on it. Ladon had multiple streams of blood running down his back from several gashes, losing more fluid than I imagined his body should.

I looked back at Yelah. She was still handling Zendar on her own with only minor abrasions. We had to help Drake and Ladon first.

"The three of us need to tag team the third dragon," I said. "Once we have it mostly handled, then one of us needs to break off and help Drake or Ladon. Whoever looks worse off at the time."

They gave curt nods, and we sprinted to help our new friends. A look of relief appeared in Drake's eyes as he saw us coming to their aid.

I leapt first at the second dragon who was tag-teaming Drake with another. He hadn't seen us coming, his focus primarily on hurting our friends. I raised my sword, flames increasing by the second, and swiped at the scales where Drake or Ladon had already done damage.

I pushed my magic through the sword as it connected with the dragon, and the smell of burnt skin filtered through the air. A fierce howl escaped from the beast, and I quickly retreated. As I regained momentum, Ryland and Oliver ran in as well. Ryland slid under the dragon, slicing from one end of its belly to the other, using his wind elements to push him further along. Oliver charged for its neck, swiftly slicing, then turning back around to throw an orb at it. I was glad he knew he didn't need the earth elements to still be a badass.

I was coming back in, focused on the injury Oliver had made. My aim was set to make the wound a deadly one with my sword, but I made the mistake of only concentrating on my target and not on my surroundings.

"Jordan, look out!" Ryland yelled, but it was too late.

One of the other dragons whipped its tail out and gut-checked me. My breath was knocked out of me as I soared through the air, and my head smacked hard against a nearby tree when I landed.

I quickly realized that, at some point during my flight time, my grip on the sword had loosened and it was nowhere to be seen. *Crap.*

Oliver cradled my head and lifted me. My vision was blurry, but nothing hurt more than what I could handle in the moment with adrenaline urging me on.

"You okay?" he asked.

"I'll be fine as long as I get payback." I continued to let him help me up and searched for my sword. I couldn't see it anywhere and was beginning to panic. This was so not good. I'd have to find it after we eliminated one of the three dragons. Otherwise, our usefulness here was about to end.

I pulled my dagger from my boot and called my magic until it made an angry, red, flaming orb. I was pissed, and this was going to hurt that ugly-ass dragon.

I crept up behind the one who had hit me as Ryland and Oliver went back to the beast we had started with. Ladon saw me coming in and kept the dragon's attention off me.

I crawled beneath the brute and found several deep cuts from Ladon's claws already there, but none of them had slowed this dragon down. I slid further toward where I assumed its heart was and steadied my aim. I had one chance at this. Otherwise, I was likely going to get squished by the massive beast.

The dragon kept moving its feet as it continued to battle with Ladon, but I managed to stay unnoticed. Once I felt confident and the dragon stilled momentarily, I thrust my dagger up and continued to push with all my strength until even my hand was fully emerged in dragon guts. Once I was satisfied with the depth, I pulled my blade out and shoved my other hand holding the orb right where my dagger had been.

Once the orb was in place, I retreated quickly. The dragon froze, and Ladon backed up as well. Within seconds, the chest cavity of the creature blew out, causing minced dragon meat to fly everywhere. I'd had my revenge, but the job wasn't even close to over.

Ladon moved on to help Drake, while Ryland and Oliver were just finishing up with the third dragon.

I retraced the path I had been thrown earlier in search of my sword but came up empty once again. I glanced back at Yelah and Zendar and my breath caught. Zendar was throwing her around like a ragdoll. *Crap, I need to find this sword!*

Oliver and Ryland joined me in my search, while Drake and Ladon made sure all three dragon guards were unconscious or dead.

"Got it," Oliver called out.

I turned and saw him pulling it from the bushes about fifty yards from where I had landed. I must have been hit harder than I thought. I thanked the Fates for the adrenaline pumping through my veins right then or I'd probably be crying like a baby.

Oliver ran over to us with sword in hand. He bent over at the waist, offering the sword like a gentleman.

I laughed and smacked his shoulder. "Thank you, Sir Oliver. Now, let's go kill one last dragon."

They both grinned at me and nodded. Drake and Ladon joined us then, looking much worse than I originally thought.

"You two need to stand down," I said, knowing my words would have no effect, but wanting to try anyway.

"Good luck with that, Guardian," Drake said. "Our job is to protect the queen, and we will do it until our dying breath."

I nodded, understanding their commitment. I just hoped that last dying breath wasn't going to be anytime soon.

Drake and Ladon charged off toward Yelah without another word. Drake wobbled while he ran, keeping weight off his injured leg, but still managing to keep up with Ladon. Adrenaline and commitment made a body do things most would never think possible.

The three of us held back until we figured out how Drake and

Ladon were going to play this out. Zendar had Yelah backed into a corner at the base of an oversized boulder. By the time he raised his front leg to deliver another blow, Ladon charged in and knocked Zendar to the ground.

"Why aren't you imbeciles dead yet?" Zendar roared. He opened his mouth, emitting a solid stream of fire at Ladon, catching him completely by surprise with Zendar's quick recovery. The blaze smacked Ladon between the eyes, causing me to let out an audible gasp. The golden dragon went down like a sack of bricks, and Yelah roared in pain while Drake stepped in to get Ladon out of the way. The three of us charged once we recovered from the initial shock of what had happened.

Ladon's head had been incinerated. There was no way he could survive that, even with all the magic in the world. Without looking at Ladon's upper half, the three of us helped Drake push his dragon friend out of the way. He didn't deserve to be trampled on in our attempt to defeat Zendar.

Once he was under the trees, Drake lowered his head to Ladon's chest. "He may not have survived this, but he went out the only way any true warrior wishes. Protecting their queen. This is an honorable death for him. First, his life will be avenged, then celebrated."

Drake's voice was devoid of all emotion, but his eyes were filled with sorrow. I reached my hand out to his front leg. "Let's get the avenging part finished, so we can get to the celebrating."

Drake gave Ladon one more glance, then we all charged toward Yelah and Zendar again. We had to finish the job without any other casualties, because if anything happened to one of my guys, I wouldn't survive that heartbreak.

CHAPTER 10

Yelah had the advantage this time when we turned back toward her. Zendar had empowered her by taking out Ladon, making Yelah an even more formidable opponent.

Drake took the lead, and I was happy to let him have it. His leg already seemed to be healing, but I could tell it pained him to walk on it. Regardless, I was pleased to see the trails of blood dry up.

I sat back, trying to figure out Yelah and Drake's game plan. Zendar was now outnumbered, but he was still keeping his own. They flanked him, taking turns breathing fire at each other or swiping for low cuts. I couldn't figure out where the guys and I were supposed to fit in, so I decided to just make it happen. No more waiting. This was ending now.

"You guys remember that one time in practice when you threw me on the roof?"

"Yeah...," Ryland said, uncertain of where I was going with this.

"Let's do that again, but this time, I need you to throw me on top of a dragon who wants to eat us for dinner."

Both their faces paled, and they shook their heads. Oliver spoke up first. "No way. Yelah said she'd tell you when to go in. Just wait for her."

"Look at them. They're too evenly matched. We have to do something to push the odds in our favor. Unless you have another way, then sending me flying for the dragon seems like the only viable option. Obviously, I can't sneak up on him with a flaming sword."

They both groaned, and I knew I had them. They couldn't deny this was the best idea we were going to come up with.

"Fine, but if you turn into dragon food, I request the right to carve 'I told you so' into your headstone," Oliver said, and I grinned.

"I would welcome it."

We got into formation, and I sheathed my sword for the flight to prevent accidentally impaling myself on landing. That would be no good for anyone.

"On the count of three," Ryland said.

I nodded as I stepped onto their palms and steadied myself. I knew exactly where I wanted to land; I just had to hope my guys still had good aim. They loved me enough to want to keep me alive, so that should be motivation enough to do it right the first time. I hoped.

On three, I went soaring. I got the attention of Yelah, and her eyes widened as I grinned at her and waved. Then, my attention was brought back to the evil dragon I was currently being propelled toward, and I braced myself for impact.

Thankfully, he was as wide as a semi-truck, and I landed with a thud in the middle of his back on my hands and knees. Zendar flicked his head back and roared. I sat up and swiftly unsheathed my sword, smirking at the side eye he was tossing my way.

"Good day to die?" I asked as flames once again walked up my blade.

"I don't know. Why don't you ask Ladon?" he countered, and I cringed. This oversized psycho needed to die immediately.

Before I could finish powering up my sword, Zendar bucked wildly and shot blazing flames at me. I flattened to my stomach on his back, attempting to make myself as small as possible, but before I could pull my legs in, his fire grazed my ankles and feet. I wanted to scream out, because it burned like a mother, but I kept the hurt locked in, using it to push me forward. I army-crawled toward the base of his neck, where Yelah had already done some damage.

I heard shouts from in front of Zendar. Ryland and Oliver were making a ruckus and throwing orbs in an attempt to get Zendar's attention off me. Wind blew past me, likely from Ryland.

I picked up the pace. By the time I reached where I wanted, my sword was completely charged and ready for action. I couldn't stand on my feet, because they'd been burned by the flames, even worse than I thought. Breathing through the agony was harder with every pant I took, but I wouldn't let myself dwell on the dark thoughts for long.

Instead, I grasped on to thoughts that consisted only of killing Zendar and pushed myself up on my knees again, falling over several times as the beast continued to evade the blows he was being dealt by my friends and the dragon queen.

Wind arched around my back, but instead of knocking me over, the pressure came from both sides, holding me up. I sent a silent thanks to Ryland as I focused back on the task before me. I hoped like hell Yelah was right and this sword really was special enough to kill the beast beneath me. If not, I was going to start saying my final goodbyes, because there was no way I was making it out of here if Zendar didn't die.

"*Now!*" Yelah roared.

I sank the long blade as deep as it would go at the base of Zendar's neck and held on tight. The hilt heated in my grip, and Zendar began to flail like a bucking bronco. Even though I could feel blisters forming from the heat, my hold tightened. The fear of getting trampled was stronger than that of getting more burns I was hopeful could be healed.

Zendar continued to roar and twist beneath me while Oliver, Ryland, and Yelah delivered hit after hit. Just as I began to think Yelah was wrong and all my sword had done was piss this dude off, Zendar stilled.

"Jordan, jump off!" Ryland screamed at me, but I couldn't move.

My hands were glued to the sword. I pulled with all my might, uncaring if I lost all the skin on my palms, but they wouldn't budge. Zendar's body began to shake uncontrollably, and my eyes widened. What the hell was happening, and why couldn't I let go?

Soon, I realized my body was being siphoned of magic. The sword was continuing to pull from my well of power in the process of destroying Zendar. I cried out in pain when it became too much, no longer able to hold in the anguish of all my injuries. I could hear Ryland and Oliver frantically yelling for me, but there was nothing I could do except hope I survived.

My body slumped against the sword, and I gave up trying to fight the pain. Instead, I let it consume me until my energy was zapped.

Then, suddenly, everything stilled.

Zendar stopped shaking. My hold was released from the sword. Our surroundings were eerily quiet. But before I could do anything or celebrate, my world exploded. Literally.

I was once again flying through the air, surrounded in blood, scales, and guts. *Disgusting*. I had nothing left in me to brace for impact. I didn't even have time to think of any smart-ass last words. The speed in which I was traveling didn't fare well for me at all.

I closed my eyes, picturing those I loved most and remembering Drake's earlier words. I was going out like a warrior, and it brought a smile to my face just as I slammed into something…soft?

What the hell?

I opened my eyes and screamed a few obscenities when I realized I was floating in the sky, stuck and unable to move.

Yelah and the others approached as I was slowly lowered to the ground. My feet winced as I touched down, and I bit back a few other choice words before falling to my knees.

Ryland and Oliver ran to me as soon as I reached the ground. They each hugged me gently, and I knew I appeared just as horrid as I felt.

"What can we do for you?" Ryland asked, and I appreciated him not asking if I was okay. Obviously, I was far from it, so I might have smacked him if he had.

"I can't walk. Bastard singed my feet. Now, treat me like the princess you always call me and carry me."

"There's our girl." Oliver smirked. "She's going to be alright."

Yelah nudged me with her oversized snout, and I reached up to place my hand on her head. Her eyes said everything I needed to know. I nodded my understanding, not needing words to feel her appreciation of our help here.

"How did I stop from shattering my entire body against one of those trees?" I asked, wondering if Ryland had done some quick thinking or if it was more dragon magic.

Yelah spoke first. "I used a shield. Normally, they're used for catching trespassers. It's meant to keep someone trapped until the creator of the shield releases them. I hadn't been sure it would work, but I'm thankful it did."

So, I was alive due to pure luck. I had a few things to say about that, but before I could, Ryland carried me over to Drake, who stood next to Ladon's lifeless body. My concerns for how I was saved weren't more important than the respect Ladon deserved from us. We had a moment of silence for him until Yelah spoke several minutes later.

"There is much to do, and Jordan needs to see a healer. Drake, will you stay here with Ladon until I can bring others back to help with the fallen?" Drake nodded. "Ryland and Oliver, you'll need to hold Jordan on my back, so I can take you to the nearest healer."

I saw the uncertainty in Ryland's face before he spoke. "Do you mind taking us to a gateway instead? We have a very capable healer in Arvayta, and we'd really like to get back home."

"Very well, but I hope one day you'll come back to visit. After your assistance today, I certainly owe you a debt."

Ryland agreed to our return, and they got me situated on Yelah. I was glad he had spoken up. I was ready for my bed and, when my feet healed, a day at the spa. I could feel dragon bits in places they most certainly didn't belong.

There wasn't a lot of space for Yelah's wings to fully expand, so once we were comfortable on her back, she moved for the gate. As soon as she made it through, she stopped short, and I lifted my head in an attempt to see what caused her to pause.

"There are dragons. Everywhere," Ryland whispered.

Seriously? Could this day get any worse?

"Wait. They're bowing. One by one, they're all kneeling for their queen. It's okay," Oliver added.

Oh, thank the fates. I couldn't handle another evil dragon today. I settled into my best friends and closed my eyes. I was done thinking or doing for the time being. I needed sleep, stat.

With the knowledge that my guys were watching my back, I drifted off, more thankful than ever before to be headed to Arvayta.

CHAPTER 11

Two weeks later, I was no longer a fan of our healer. Lorelle might be powerful, but she had horrible bedside manner. "Now, move your toes," she demanded.

Okay, maybe I was a little to blame for her curtness. I might have called her every insulting name I could think of while I went through hell during the healing process.

My feet had nearly been melted off, and I hadn't been able to properly use my hands for nearly a week. If I hadn't had on my tough-as-nails boots when Zendar burned me, Lorelle was certain I'd have lost them both. I cringed at that thought every time it crossed my mind, which was often.

Finally, I wiggled my toes for her. This was my last visit. After several magical reconstruction surgeries performed by the wench herself, my feet and ankles were finally working together again. The only positive thing about all this was that Ryland and Oliver had been my slaves and I hadn't had to get out of bed unless I wanted to, which wasn't often.

"So, she's all healed?" Oliver asked anxiously.

Lorelle nodded. "She'll have some residual numbness, but

that will go away in time. Other than that, I don't need to see her anytime soon. Unless she decides to tangle with dragons again."

I rolled my eyes. I'd like to see *her* go against the scaled beasts and come out unscathed.

"Thank the Fates." Oliver turned to me. "I'm out of here. Don't ask me for *anything* for a solid month."

"Quit being a baby. I wasn't that bad." He glared at me. "Okay, maybe I was, but I totally saved the day. I deserved the special treatment."

"Whatever you say, *Princess*."

Before I could respond, Oliver disappeared from the room. I glanced over at Lorelle as I slid off the medical table. "Thank you for all your work. I wouldn't have trusted anyone else."

"You're lucky I didn't give you a sixth toe." Lorelle appeared serious, and I stared at her with my mouth hanging open until she smirked. "You actually handled that better than most men. I'm used to being yelled at when I'm breaking bones and moving things back where they belong. Your name-calling was merely entertainment to this old lady."

I leaned in and hugged her hard. "I'll try not to find myself in here again, and I'll make sure to mention to the men they need to toughen up."

Lorelle laughed, long and hard. "Let me know how they take that."

I nodded. "I'll see you around. Thanks, again."

For the first time in much too long, I walked out of the room on my own. As easy as it would be to port home, I wanted to test my feet and make sure they really were all healed up.

Lorelle lived about a mile from home, which was just the right amount of distance to test my newly restored toes without over-doing it.

I pushed up until I balanced on the balls of my feet and stretched out my ankles. Things were still tight, but there was no pain for once. After a few stretches, I began my walk. I made it to the heart of Arvayta where most of the businesses were, but I went around the long way. I knew people would want to stop and talk, and I wasn't up for that just yet.

I'd had nightmares almost every night, reliving the fight with the dragons. It was too close of a call for even me to just play the battle off as no big deal like I normally did. Yelah had asked us to come back, but I wasn't sure when I'd mentally be ready for that.

Before I knew it, I was walking up the yard to the house. I kicked off my shoes, and the grass felt amazing beneath my feet. I lay down in the lawn and stretched some more. Nothing was painful, but it was certainly sore. I was going to have my work cut out for me trying to get back in shape from two weeks off.

When I was done with my stretches, I headed up to my room. I landed on my bed with a huff and decided a nap after my walk was a good idea. As I rolled onto my side, fluffing my pillow, there was a letter on my nightstand.

Don't touch it. Just go to sleep, I told myself, but curiosity got the better of me.

With a deep sigh, I reached over to grab the paper before sitting up. My name was scrolled across the front of folded parchment that was too crisp to be from anyone other than the council. Gingerly, I unfolded the single page.

Ms. Baker,

The Atwaters have been attacked with the focus being toward their daughter. A dark witch, who has already been dealt with, attempted to drown Kaliah and was near success before Daliah found her at the falls. She and Brooks are worried about Kaliah's continued safety on Earth and have requested a protector for her.

Their magic was revealed during the encounter, and we had to remove some of her memory. The action is not something we want to happen again due to the lasting effects it could have. This is the second attack on their family since they left Arvayta, and we need your help to make sure there isn't a third one.

You will be sent to live near them with pseudo-guardian parents and, using a glamour, will appear the same age as Kaliah, growing as she does. You will become her closest friend and, without her knowledge, her protector. Your presence is expected by the week's end. Prepare what you need and expect to be gone until Kaliah's nineteenth birthday.

If you wish to decline this summoning, please see us immediately as there isn't a moment to waste when it comes to the young princess's safety.

With respect,

The Council

I had zero words. How? Why? And, *princess?* Most days, it was easy to forget we used to have a monarchy rule, but with the council's use of "princess", I assumed it meant Kaliah was going to be more than just the daughter of people I cared deeply for. She was going to be important to our world.

I needed Ryland and Oliver. I was going to be gone for *eight* years. Even though we aged way slower than any human once we acquired our full magical powers, I had no desire to be gone from my best friends and my life here for that long.

I'd do it, but it didn't mean I had to be happy about it. Hopefully, Brooks and Daliah had raised a kid I could actually get along with.

After checking the guest house, I ported to Oliver's house, hoping Ryland would be there, too. As I walked in the door, sensing them both, I'd never been more thankful to see my best friends.

"What's wrong?" Ryland asked as he took in the expression on my face.

I explained to them what the letter had said and what I was supposed to do. They both remained quiet until I was done, which made me nervous. I needed them to be upset about this.

"The situation certainly isn't ideal, but Brooks and Daliah have done a lot for us," Ryland said. "I knew they were having some issues, but I didn't realize it had gotten this severe. I'd go in your place if I could, but I'm not the one who received the letter. Look on the bright side, you can go shopping whenever you want on Earth."

A smile appeared on my face, and I hugged Ryland first, then Oliver. "I'm going to miss you guys."

"It's going to be boring without you, but we'll come visit when we can," Oliver said, making me feel better.

Ready or not, I was headed to Earth.

Kaliah better be ready for her world to be turned upside down. I wasn't going to go easy on her. Even if she wasn't allowed to know magic existed until it was time for her to come home to Arvayta, I'd do what I could to prepare her for this world.

By the time I was done with her, she'd be the most badass princess Arvayta had ever seen.

OF DREAMS AND SORCERY

BOOK ONE

DEDICATION

To my daughter Haley…
May you always follow your dreams and believe in yourself as much as I believe in you!

CHAPTER 1

Watching a talking owl fly through a lavender-colored sky while he mumbled about how stubborn I was under his breath was the highlight of my evening. Mostly because it was still hard to believe what I was seeing was real, but also because it was a distraction from the anxiety that flowed through me.

It was my last night visiting with Stryx in the secret realm the owl had magically dragged my conscience to nearly every night for the last year.

He swooped down and landed on my outstretched hand. "Let's take a walk."

"Uh, oh. You have your serious voice on. What's wrong?" I asked, knowing the humor I had toward my unique situation drove him nuts, but that was what he got for keeping so many secrets.

His beady eyes narrowed at me, and his white silky feathers bristled. "Don't be smart with me when you're just upset this is the last night of your true human existence. It's your own fault if you feel like you failed to make the most out of your time left on Earth. It's not like I didn't give you enough warning."

I scoffed. "My fault? First, stay out of my head. Second, how about you overworked me with your never-ending to-do lists?" Not only was Stryx able to speak out loud, but my feathered friend could also read my thoughts. Annoying, but true.

Though, our banter was endless, and I loved it. It was what kept me from losing my composure as I acknowledged there were things that I couldn't know yet but needed to be prepared for anyway. I wasn't big on surprises, so it had been a hard pill to swallow, but I'd managed it over time.

"I'd like to show you something if you're done being difficult," Stryx hooted, then flew from my hand back toward the clear skies.

"Oh, really? Are you going to break some more rules, my little friend? I thought I wasn't allowed to be anywhere but these hills." Inside the realm Stryx brought me to each night was a replica of another world I would soon be visiting called Arvayta. The problem was that I wasn't supposed to know anything about the place until my magic was released, so Stryx never let me leave the grassy knolls to see the world my family was from.

His wise eyes, black with flecks of silver, peered down at me. They were never judging but usually encouraging me to be better and stronger than I was the day before. "Just follow me."

Even though he was a talking animal, I finally accepted that I wasn't hallucinating after a few weeks of knowing him and took a leap of crazy faith to trust the creature who had since become one of the most important people in my life.

Yes, I knew he wasn't an actual person, but other than having feathers and no hands, he pretty much acted like one. Sarcasm and all.

His beak snapped at me, bringing my attention back to him when I hadn't immediately followed, and I began to walk as he spoke, flying only a few feet above me. "With your birthday tomorrow, you're going to know a lot of this anyway, so I don't count it as rule breaking, per se. Just a bit of information to ease you into what comes next."

My hand stroked his wing as I realized there was an important question I'd yet to ask, mostly because I was afraid of the answer, but I needed to know before there wasn't time to find out. "Will you still be around after tonight?"

"Things will be different, but yes, I will meet you in Arvayta after you've settled in with your parents and Jordan. They'll all be going with you, so it's not like you'll be alone."

That wasn't the answer I was hoping for, but it was better than never seeing him again. As I pressed my sweaty palms against my shirt, I calmed my beating heart, reminding myself that everything would be okay. Whatever came next, I'd figure out a way to get through all of the craziness.

"So, what is this information you have?" I asked, trying to get back on track since my mind was a hot mess at the thought of my impending nineteenth birthday.

"Well, you know how I've mentioned your family originated from the fae, but after centuries, the magic of the originals was changed into something else, something less fae and more hybrid which resulted in most of the Arvaytan population that's alive today?"

My head nodded, unsure of what he was getting at.

"Well, there's something I need to prepare you for since you're not exactly like the others who live in Arvayta."

He was lucky he was flying just out of reach from me, because I really wanted to yank him closer and shake him. "What do you mean?"

"You have more fae in you than any Arvaytan born since before your parents. Your grandmother Taliah on your mother's side and your grandfather Cello on your father's side came from a long history of royals. Their fae side was much stronger, because blood lines had remained purer than most due to their standing as royalty."

"Are these people still alive? Will I be meeting them and need to remember to curtsy or something?" I asked when he failed to get to the point.

"Unfortunately, no. They're not still alive, but what is important to know is that they diluted the fae line when they found love with those descended not directly from their kind. And it would have kept diluting the powers in each generation if your parents hadn't met each other."

"Stryx, I don't understand genealogy. You need to be more direct before I lose my mind over here." I hated having conversations that didn't get right to the point.

When I stopped walking, he swooped around to face me and snapped his beak at me like he so often did when I frustrated him. "What I'm saying is that your grandparents on both sides had enough fae magic in them to carry on their powers for many generations to come, so long as the fae line remained predominant between future unions, but they'd each taken bonds with those not of pure blood. That made your parents half-fae, still powerful in their own right, but nothing completely out of the ordinary. When you were born, you became the first being conceived from two royal families in hundreds of years."

My eyes pinched closed as an irritation settled over me. I still felt confused, probably more overwhelmed actually, but I was beginning to wrap my mind around it all.

Stryx landed on a rock near me and continued, "Most Otherworld beings are only a one-third or less fae. When your parents found love with each other, nobody knew what would happen when they decided to have a child until it was too late."

"Too late for what?"

"You carry a significant amount of magic within you that was thought to be lost long ago. When your parents realized this, they had that power suppressed and brought you to Earth in hopes of keeping you hidden for as long as possible. But, sometime tomorrow night, your magic will be set free and there will be no hiding what you truly are."

Part of me knew I shouldn't ask, knew that I didn't really want to know, but it didn't stop the words from tumbling out of my mouth. "What am I?"

"That's something I can't answer for you yet. I wish I could, but there are bigger things at play and I just need you to trust me. What I can tell you is that you're the first royal who has a chance of restoring the balance lost in the Dark War many centuries ago and stopping the prophecy that was given when you were conceived."

A deep laugh escaped me, and once it started, I couldn't stop it. If I understood what he was saying correctly, I was the reason for the doom and gloom he spoke of, yet I was also their only hope of stopping it.

"Kaliah, this is not a laughing matter. I'm only telling you this because your transition will not be easy. You will go through more pain than your human body can handle, and you will die before being reborn into your new fae form."

That's when the laughing stopped, but my hands still shook, and I was finding it hard to breathe normally. Stryx was more serious than I'd ever seen him, and he'd just told me I was going to die. What in the actual hell was happening? Out of all the crazy things he'd said in the time I'd known him, that was by far the worst.

"Is there a way to stop it?" I asked, doing my best not to scream out my frustrations.

It had taken me months to cope with the fact that I was going to be something other than human on my nineteenth birthday. Now, I was suddenly supposed to be okay with dying as well? Fat chance of that happening.

"Just breathe. I promise it will be alright. It's what I have been training you for since your last birthday. I won't lie and tell you that it's not going to be agonizing, but you can handle it. You're stronger than you know, and I hope one day you will see yourself the way I do."

Heat rushed to my cheeks at his compliment as I began to calm down. Stryx didn't often praise me, no matter how many obstacles I conquered that he set before me during training. So, when he did have something positive to say, I actually believed him, even if it was hard.

Stryx spread his wings out and shook his feathers before taking off back into the sky. "Come on. There is still something I want to show you, and it might help ease your nerves. Not everything about coming to Arvayta will be bad."

Deciding things couldn't get much worse than being told I was going to die the next day, I continued walking and followed the angelic creature as he soared in the air just above me.

We moved in tranquil silence as I took in Arvayta the way it was in my conscience for the final night. Above us, the sky was a pale lavender color and cloudless with a beaming yellow sun, which Stryx said was the usual daytime atmosphere. Plants thrived all around me in various sizes and colors; pastel, neon, and every palate in between could be found in the foliage on the outskirts of town. The main area was blocked off by trees more superior and wider in size than any I'd seen before.

About ten minutes passed before Stryx landed on a boulder, and I heard the rushing water before I saw it. Goosebumps pricked at my skin as anticipation raced through me at what I was about to see.

When I rounded the corner, my neck craned up to find the most massive waterfall I'd ever laid eyes on. The width of it had to be over one-hundred feet, and the height? No close guesses on that, but probably nearing one-thousand feet.

A purple hue radiated from the fog that rolled off the water, and a pulsing sensation began deep within me as my body involuntarily moved toward the pool before me that was more like a pond, half a football field in size. Something within it called to me, and there was nothing I wanted more than to submerge myself in the swirling waters until all my worries faded away.

Stryx clicked his beak at me again. "Don't touch that water unless you want to start the transition earlier than planned, which I don't advise, given Jordan isn't exactly equipped to handle it on her own."

Jordan was not only my best friend, but she was also my roommate and probably wouldn't enjoy waking up to what I assumed would be my screams.

"You mean she isn't equipped to handle my imminent death?" I retorted with a roll of my eyes as I forcibly took a few steps away from the waterfall.

"Precisely."

I had no idea what I was getting myself into, but it was time to go back to reality and find out.

I had a date with death and probably shouldn't be late for it.

CHAPTER 2

Pain rocketed through my body as an elbow dropped onto my gut and a body pressed on top of me, giving me a wake up I definitely could have done without. Though, my attacker didn't keep the advantage for long once awareness seeped in.

Flipping her over, I ended up on top and grinned. "Not today, Satan."

"Happy birthday, Chuck," Jordan said with a sideways grin on her oval face. She was my best friend and had been calling me some version of Chuck Norris ever since I started taking Brazilian Jiu Jitsu classes last year and kicking her ass like the Texas Ranger.

In return, I often called her Satan due to the smirk she constantly wore as she pushed any boundaries set before her. Along with the secrets she kept that she thought I knew nothing about, but in reality, I knew just enough.

"Thanks for the warm awakening," I grumbled as I rolled off her and toward my bathroom.

We lived in a two-bedroom, two-bath house on the outskirts

of Portland, Oregon. While our house was simple, my life was anything but. Then again, neither was Jordan's. Instead of going to college, I was training my butt off for this day. My nineteenth birthday.

The craziest part was all the secrets we were keeping from each other. She thought I didn't already know what was in store for me today—and I had to keep up the charade that I was clueless.

It was my last day as a human. The day I would become something more than I ever thought possible. Something I didn't believe even existed until the snarky owl started demanding all the things from me on my previous birthday.

From my view in the mirror, I could see she was nervous about something. I knew it probably had to do with whatever she and my parents planned to tell me when we met up later that day, but I didn't feel bad enough to consider letting her off the hook.

"So, I know this is a big day for you. Last birthday of your teens and all, and I don't want to be a Debby downer, but I wanted to mention something before we go see your parents this afternoon," she said sheepishly, pushing her blonde hair behind her ear.

"Oh, yeah? What's that?" I asked calmly while staring in the mirror at the mess I called hair. My russet locks were wavy, but not quite curly, making it hard to ever know what to do with them.

Jordan's emerald eyes met my icy-blue ones in the reflection. "I was just thinking about how mad you were at me last year after your birthday, and you wouldn't really tell me why. I'm pretty sure you're over it now, but if I upset you again, please don't shut me out. I'd rather you kung fu my ass into the depths of hell than be given the silent treatment again."

Ahh, she was smart. She knew I would be pissed when I found out what I really was today and that she'd known the entire time, but luckily for her, she already suffered those consequences without ever knowing it.

After Stryx had come to visit me the first time and told me I wasn't exactly human, I also learned Jordan was from the same world my parents came from and knew about all of us. Yet, she'd never told me.

To say I'd been pissed was an understatement, but Stryx talked me out of completely writing her out of my life, and I finally forgave her without ever telling her why I'd been angry in the first place.

"You've been my closest friend for eight years, Jordan. I hope that's not going to change anytime soon," I said with a forced smile, because even though Stryx had assured me that Jordan was a true friend, I still had niggling doubts that once she knew I was aware of the truth, and we went to Arvayta, she wouldn't feel obligated to stick around any longer than required.

She waltzed into the bathroom, and her much taller frame hip-checked me as she moved to sit on the counter while I brushed my teeth.

"So, do you want to go to brunch this morning before we head to Bridal Veil?" she asked.

Bridal Veil was a small town outside of Portland where my parents lived. Even though the house was miles from any real store, they'd kept the home for its view.

The story had always been that it was inherited from long-lost relatives before I was born, along with a lifetime supply of money that they'd invested properly. While we weren't swimming in cash, we'd lived a comfortable life that I assumed had more to do with being inhuman than it did with an inheritance.

The modest house I'd called home for my entire childhood sat atop a mountain facing Multnomah Falls, a monstrous waterfall that was over six-hundred feet in height and absolutely stunning to visit. When I was younger, I remembered going there on many occasions and hiking to the top after hours when nobody else was around. There was always a sense of peace that would settle over me when I did, and I never understood why until the night before.

When Stryx had shown me the falls in Arvayta, the same sense of tranquility became rooted deep into my soul. Once I recognized the feeling, I knew I was home. Even if I hadn't been raised in the unknown world, my inner being recognized it for everything that it was.

Jordan kicked me from her spot on the counter as I finished rinsing my toothbrush. "So, brunch?"

"Oh, yeah. That would be great. We can swing by Carver Café on our way to Mom and Dad's," I replied, my mouth was already watering. Not only was the café in the middle of nowhere, far away from the craziness of downtown Portland, but they served the best biscuits and gravy I'd ever had.

"Are you still half asleep or what?" she teased while hopping off the counter.

"Pretty sure I'm wide awake." I rolled my eyes.

"Then what did I just say?" She smirked, and I gulped.

"Uhhhh, you asked about brunch."

She patted my shoulder. "Nope, but maybe I'll tell you again later."

Damn it. The stupid biscuits and gravy thoughts, on top of my looming death, had me distracted. That was definitely still rolling around in my mind, but I was trying to make the best of it. Stryx had promised that while it would hurt, the pain would be dulled as soon as I arrived in Arvayta.

Apparently, I couldn't begin the transition in the magical world as the passageway would reject me if I hadn't at least begun the process of having my powers released.

My head still had a hard time wrapping itself around that one.

I was going to be something other than human in less than twelve hours. If I was just learning about all of this on my birthday, I was pretty sure I would have run away from everyone and changed my name. Likely, my appearance as well.

But, given I'd had the opportunity to take it all in slowly, a part of me was excited for the new adventure, especially if my parents and Jordan were still going to be in my life. As long as the darkness Stryx had warned me of on several occasions—the reason I'd worked my ass off for the last year—didn't completely screw with things, I kept hope that my life would work out for the better.

Jordan left my room, so I could finish getting ready. It was late April, and temperatures were sporadic. While they usually were during all seasons in Oregon, it was almost a guarantee to need an umbrella and shorts on the same day this particular time of year.

Finally, I decided on my favorite ripped jeans, sandals, and my *Avengers* tee. We weren't going anywhere fancy, and I preferred comfort over fashion any day of the week, regardless of what my roommate thought.

"You're wearing *that* today?" she huffed when I came out of my bedroom.

Peeking at my phone, I feigned shock. "Well, look at the date. I'm pretty sure it says April 29th. You know what day that is? My birthday. So, yes, I will wear whatever I want, and there's not a single thing you can do about it."

Her head shook. "One day, you're going to come to me for fashion advice and it's going to be the greatest day ever." She stomped toward the front door in her perfect-fit skinny jeans, strappy heels, and sequined tank top.

The day I did that, hell would have frozen over.

"You still love me anyway," I called down the empty hallway, then grabbed my purse before following her outside.

First part of my last human day down. Just a few more events to go.

THE DRIVE OUT TO MY PARENTS' HOUSE WAS AS STUNNING AS USUAL for the time of year. It was late spring, and the warmer weather was just starting to make its appearance, causing the trees to change from deep forest green to a more vibrant version filled with bright colors from all the budding flowers.

Thirty minutes after stopping for brunch, we passed by Multnomah Falls and made a right turn up the dirt road leading to the wooden home I'd grown up in. The house was two stories with floor-to-ceiling windows and log siding that made it appear more like a weekend getaway than a full-time home.

Jordan parked the car in her usual spot beneath the side overhang, and before we could even open our doors, my mom was waiting just outside my window. Her hand waved excitedly, and her blue eyes a few shades darker than my own shone brightly in the afternoon sun.

"Happy birthday!" she exclaimed when I opened my door.

"Thanks, Mom." My arms opened to her, and her shorter frame stepped into my embrace.

"How was the drive?" she asked when we pulled apart.

"Same as always. Too much traffic until we passed Troutdale, but it wasn't all bad. Before we hit I-84, we stopped for brunch at Carver's, so it made the drive a little more bearable with food in us," I answered.

Mom's eyes sparkled as she licked her lips. "Did you get the biscuits and gravy?"

A grin appeared on my face as I opened the back door of the car. "I did, and I might have even ordered an extra side of them to bring with me."

There wasn't much about my mom that wasn't exactly like me when it came to taste, so I knew she'd be over the moon with the treat. The biggest difference between the two of us was my temper. That, I got from my father, who was barreling his way toward us from the front porch.

After I handed Mom the food, she and Jordan talked about the weather of all things, while I made my way to meet my dad in the middle. He was a gruff man, but more like a teddy bear whenever he was around people he actually liked.

"Hey, sweet girl. Happy birthday," he whispered in my ear as he picked me up off the ground.

"Thanks, Dad," I replied after he set me back down and I could breathe a little easier.

My dad had blue eyes the same shade as my mom's, but his skin was naturally tanned while my mom's was fair. Mine was the perfect mix of both. The same thing happened with our hair. Mom was a natural brunette who never greyed, and Dad was a blondie, so I ended up with dark brown strands that had natural highlights thrown in.

As the four of us moved inside the house, I took several deep inhales of the outdoors: pine, sugar, and water. I knew it seemed weird to smell water, but ever since I met Stryx and my training began, my senses had been heightened, including the ability to smell any type of moisture in the air.

I didn't focus too long on the outside scents, as they were quickly overpowered by the aroma coming from the kitchen. "Are you making sweet meatballs?" I asked my mom.

"Of course, I am. It's your birthday, and I didn't need to ask to know what you'd want for dinner."

Her homemade meatballs were my death-row meal, that final meal I would ask for if the occasion ever arose.

Ha! When I really thought about it, I *was* getting my final meal. Part of me wondered if that was a twisted joke on my mom's part, because she always glared at me when I called her meatballs my death-row choice. Probably not, though. She was too sweet for a devious plan like that. Jordan may have subconsciously suggested it, though, and it wouldn't surprise me in the least.

"Why don't you girls have a seat in the living room while your father and I go get some snacks?" Mom suggested.

"Sure thing, Daliah," Jordan answered before tugging me along.

Dad's shoulders tensed as Mom drug him from the room.

"Do you think they're fighting? What if they're not happy together anymore?" I feigned panic when we both noticed the obvious tension.

Pretending things seemed worse to Jordan was just payback for the hell I went through after learning I wasn't who I thought I was, from a freaking owl of all things.

Jordan choked on the water she'd just drank, then spit it all over her lap. "Excuse me? Why on earth would you think that?"

"They seem really stressed. Actually, all of you do. Do you know something? Is this some sort of last family meal before you all break the big news to me?" My voice rose, and I coughed to cover my laughter as Jordan became increasingly nervous.

"Kali, what the hell is coming over you? Your parents are the two happiest married people I've ever met. They're life goals. Maybe they're just anxious about your gift. Yeah, that has to be it."

My brow raised. "My gift, huh? Do you know anything about that?"

She muttered a few curse words under her breath. "Daliah, Brooks! Are you two almost done in there?" She paused. "What's that? You need help? *Gladly*."

Jordan raced from the room before I could say anything else, and a smirk tugged at my lips. Maybe I was taking it too far, but all of the build-up from the last year was coming to the surface. This was it. There were going to be no more secrets, or so I hoped, and I wanted to move on to my new life without animosity.

Giving them grief was the only way I knew how to move past everything.

Just a few minutes later, I could hear raised voices. They were attempting to be quiet and therefore still muffled, but I didn't mind. I knew their secrets. I was merely interested in how and when they were going to reveal them.

Finally, the three of them came back into the room. "Where are the snacks?" I asked with a grin.

Mom blinked a few times. "Oh, we thought maybe we'd do presents instead, since you had a late breakfast. What do you think?"

Presents. Right.

"Sure, but you guys really didn't need to get me anything. I'm not a kid anymore." I was barely even human.

"Well, no matter how old you are, you'll always be our baby girl, so let's get started." Mom pulled a small box from behind her back, then handed it to me before taking a seat next to Dad on the loveseat.

Leaning back, I settled further into the recliner while Jordan perched on the arm of it, seeming more eager than me to see what was inside the package.

My fingertips slid under the carefully folded silver wrapping paper and tugged on the tape. Moving slowly, I unfolded both sides of the box before working on the middle.

"Seriously?" Jordan huffed. "The paper isn't made out of money. Rip it to shreds, Walker."

Deciding I'd tortured them long enough, I finally tore through the backside of the wrapping to reveal a black velvet jewelry box. My eyes met my mother's. Neither of us had ever been big on flashy things. The only jewelry I'd ever seen her wear were her wedding ring and the necklace currently hiding beneath her beige shirt.

The gift threw me off even more, because I thought I was the only one with secrets for this birthday. Turned out my parents were still capable of surprising me.

"Go on. Open it up," Mom encouraged while Jordan was practically panting above me.

My fingers opened the box, and it snapped open to reveal a thick silver chain with an unusually bright amethyst pendant wrapped in thin white-gold wire hanging from it. My breath caught as my eyes traced over the stone. It reminded me of the foggy lavender hue that radiated from the waterfall Stryx had shown me the night before.

"This is stunning, Mom. Thank you so much," I said while I pulled it from the box.

"The necklace last belonged to your grandmother Taliah. It's been passed down for generations, and we thought you were ready for it," she replied.

My throat tightened as guilt for giving them such a hard time poked at me. It was a thoughtful gift, and this was probably just as hard on them as it was supposed to be for me if Stryx hadn't intervened.

Jordan held her hand out, and I gave her the necklace before bunching my hair together and pulling it out of the way. When the cool metal of the chain hit my skin, I let out a small hiss, but once the stone settled just above my chest, a warming sensation took over.

My parents watched me cautiously, but when Jordan took a seat on the chair next to me, they seemed to relax as well.

"Now, here's one from the both of us," Dad said, handing me an unwrapped wooden box.

Intricate filigree and feathers were carved into the dark oak. My fingers traced over the aged wood before I flicked a golden latch open. As I lifted the lid, Jordan leaned in closer again, and since I was still feeling feisty, I turned the other way so she couldn't see.

Once the box was open, I took a moment to appreciate what lay before me and ignored the edgy silence around me.

This was my life journal. A book that would tell of my birth, my death, and my rebirth, followed by every major event after that until my practically immortal life was over. Stryx had spoken of it before, but he hadn't prepared me for the connection I'd feel to the book as soon as I touched it.

My fingers slid over the cover as a magic pulsed from it so heavily that I swore I was in Arvayta, but the moment was broken when Mom spoke.

"Kaliah Grace, do you know what that is?"

Deciding to end the façade, I nodded, and chaos descended all around me.

CHAPTER 3

All three of them spoke in louder-than-necessary volumes, so I ignored their outbursts until they calmed down and only one of them talked.

"Sweet girl, how do you know what that is?" Dad asked more evenly from his spot on the couch in the living room.

Stryx hadn't said I couldn't tell them about him once I was ready for the transition, just that I couldn't do it any day before. If it had been important to keep him a secret entirely, then I assumed he would have reminded me to keep him out of the conversation.

Since he hadn't, I was going with the old adage that it was better to ask for forgiveness than permission.

"Well, about a year ago, I had a visitor in my dreams, except it wasn't really a dream. My subconscious was transported to another world, and I learned everything I know from an owl."

Nobody moved, and I wondered if I really was crazy. Crap. Maybe I should have played dumb and pretended I had no idea what the book was. Maybe I had just been imagining their nerves and nothing I thought was impossibly real was true.

"Did this owl have a name?" Mom asked.

"Umm, maybe?" I wasn't giving more info until they showed some sort of emotion. I needed to know with absolute certainty that I hadn't imagined the entire last year of my life.

Mom's hands pressed against her thighs as she composed herself. "Kaliah, it's very important you tell us everything you know. Not everything about your birth was as normal as we would have liked. So, whatever information you have, we need to know about it, too. It could mean the difference between life and death."

Okay, so they didn't think I was nuts. I'd just scared them half to death. Super.

Word vomit descended as I told them everything I knew. From meeting Stryx, the small part of Arvayta I'd explored, the history I'd learned, to the training I'd been challenged to complete. When I was done, a weight lifted from my chest and I felt like my true self for the first time in much too long.

I hated keeping secrets from them, regardless of how many they had kept from me. We'd all been trying to follow the same rules, and being able to let it all out was more cleansing than I realized it would be.

Jordan laughed as her body relaxed. "Of course. Only you, Kali."

"What does that mean?" I glanced between her and my parents.

"Well, Stryx is from a remote part of the Otherworld, one that is strictly for bonded animals. They're more human-like, as you've obviously learned, and are there to help guide their bonded ones through whatever troubles may be coming their way. The only thing is, they haven't been around since the Dark War, and it's cause for concern that Stryx is back now," Mom said.

My eyes pinched together as confusion ran through me, because Stryx made it seem like my parents were well aware of whatever issues we might be facing. They had even admitted my birth wasn't normal, so Stryx appearing shouldn't be such a big surprise, in my opinion.

"What did you mean when you said my birth wasn't normal? Why was I raised here instead of Arvayta? Stryx wouldn't tell me much about anything that would have an impact on my immediate future other than my need for training."

Mom and Dad shared a look, but they weren't the ones to answer me.

Jordan leaned in closer to me. "Well, for one, you were prophesied to go all *Carrie* on Arvayta if you were born in the usual ritual as the rest of us." The smirk on her face told me she was enjoying this little shock factor much more than a best friend should, but that was also why I called her my *Satan* best friend. Her mind didn't work like everyone else's.

"Jordan, that's enough," Dad reprimanded, and she slinked back into her seat. "What she means to say is we were told that if you weren't born away from Arvayta that things could be very bad for our worlds. Though, a lot has changed since we learned of this, and we had hopes certain outcomes had been prevented by choices we'd made, beginning with what happened after the war that ended the hierarchy of our world."

Ugh. That reminded me. My parents were supposed to be royalty, which meant I was as well. My body shuddered at the thought. I wasn't one who enjoyed being in the spotlight. That was more Jordan's calling, and I was happy to let her have that role whenever possible.

"As you seem to already know, your ancestors were lost to the Dark War, along with all of the pure Fae we are descended from. Thankfully, those mixed with Arvaytan and fae blood did not perish, or else Arvayta would have completely crumbled," Dad continued.

"What was the Dark War? Stryx just told me many of our

people died and that was when the council was created in place of an actual King and Queen." My hands continued to fidget with the book I'd been given but had yet to open.

"Long story short, your grandfather was led to believe one thing by someone close to him and made several wrong decisions which cost him his life, among too many others. He'd made dealings with a dark fae who posed as a sorceress in need of help. When he agreed to help her, he chose to share his natural power with her. When he did so willingly, she drained him before moving on to as many fae as she could until a group was formed to stop her," Mom answered.

"How was she stopped?" Man, I really wished Stryx would have told me all of this, but I guess I should have asked more questions as well.

"The council we now have killed her, but in order to do so, they had to use a spell that syphoned power from all fae—the good and the bad—killing them in the process. The sorceress who tricked your grandfather grew more powerful by the hour, and the council made the choice to kill off one pure race that consisted of hundreds of people in order to protect thousands of others. It was the only way to save Arvayta," Mom said with tears brimming in her eyes.

That was not at all the answer I expected, and it had my nerves on edge.

So, my grandfather had screwed up, gotten a horde of people killed, including himself, and then put me in danger somehow. Though, the million-dollar question still hadn't been answered.

"All of this happened centuries ago. What does it have to do with me now?"

Jordan opened her mouth to probably spit out another crude response—my bestie had zero filters—but my dad stopped her. "Did Stryx tell you about the Fates?"

Groaning, I thought of all the ways I was going to kill that feathered little monster for making me think he had properly prepared me for this moment. "Nope, not a word."

"They are the purest of fae descendants and have the ability to see the future. They live in the In-Between, a place only those who have died pass through on their way to the afterlife. They're not living; though, nor are they dead. They just exist, watching over the worlds with the hope of keeping a balance of good and evil.

"Sometimes, when they deem absolutely necessary for the survival of our kind, they will intervene. When this happens, the council who now leads Arvayta is given a glimpse of possible futures based on certain choices. Your birth was part of two prophecies given," Mom answered.

I really shouldn't have opened my mouth. I should have just run away and pretended like none of this existed, because the more I learned, the less I wanted to know.

Even still, I didn't stop myself from asking. "And those two things were what?"

Dad grabbed Mom's hand and took over for her. "To put it simply, we could allow you to be born into the Arvaytan waters, as is usual for all newborns, but then we would watch you be lured into a life of darkness by an ancestor of the dark fae. The other option was to hide you away for as long as possible and have a small hope of ending the Dark War so many thought was already finished."

There had better be a whole library on this Dark War, because I *needed* to know more about it, along with this dark fae that Stryx had failed to mention. Though, if I was smart, I'd stay as far as possible from everything mentioned, but I didn't think I had a choice in the matter any longer.

Either way, I was screwed, but thankfully, I was made of strong stuff. As overwhelming as the situation was, I wouldn't back away from a challenge. If I was going to go down, I'd do so fighting with everything I had.

Jordan's face tightened as she spoke seriously, surprising more than just me. "Just as you are the strongest light fae descendant since the Dark Wars, there is also a dark fae descendant, one who is hell-bent on making sure his family has the retribution he believes they deserve. In the prophecy, he comes for you, and one of two things happen. You go with him and turn on your people, causing a ripple effect of great proportions, or we once again go to war, and who knows what will transpire."

On the plus side, we knew who we were up against. I wasn't sure my human training would actually do any good against a dark fae who'd likely been plotting my death for years, but it didn't change my stance on things. I was ready to find out what came next.

"So, what's the plan now? I have my final meal, I die, and then you guys take me to Arvayta to be born again and we find this crazy dark fae?" I asked.

Mom glared at my crassness. "You've been hanging out with Jordan too long."

Jordan grinned. "What your mom means to say is yes, that's pretty much how it will go. You were born at 7:46pm, so we have until then to make the best of your last human hours. So, how about we head out to the falls before dinner and chat some more?"

The book I'd been given that began this whole conversation still sat in my lap, and I held it up. "What about this?"

"That you can worry about when we're settled in Arvayta. Jordan is right. Go explore, but don't be too long. Your mom has been working on dinner all day," Dad answered.

Deciding I didn't want to argue with him, I placed the book back in the box and set it on the table before taking Jordan's outstretched hand. With one last glance at my parents, I smiled at them then left the house. My mom appeared as if she was about to completely lose her cool, and my dad seemed proud of me.

Suddenly, the fate of a world was sitting on my shoulders. I wasn't entirely sure I was ready for it, but I was prepared to fake it for as long as it took to figure things out and preferably not die more than once in the process.

CHAPTER 4

When we arrived at the waterfall, Jordan cut through a path we'd never taken before, and when I tried to question her, she shushed me. Secretly, I sort of enjoyed that I didn't know *everything*. The elation radiating from my best friend at being able to finally share this with me was too good to have ruined entirely. I'd have to give Stryx my thanks for being the pain he loved to be.

"So, where exactly are we going?" I asked as I pushed the umpteenth branch out of my face.

"To the portal," she answered nonchalantly.

Air caught in my throat at her words. Even though I already knew there were portals out in the world from what Stryx had said, I didn't expect them to be somewhere that just anyone could stumble upon.

Of course, normal hikers didn't go off the beaten path and trudge through thick foliage, either.

When Jordan stopped, I ran right into her back, because my head had been down watching for more stray branches. I grasped her arm before she fell. "Sorry."

She glared at me. "These sandals are *not* meant to get wet. You're lucky I didn't fall."

"Then maybe you shouldn't have worn them hiking like a city girl," I retorted.

Jordan ignored my jab and moved over. "Look." Her finger pointed to a small waterfall that was hidden underneath Multnomah Falls. It was maybe eight feet tall and just a few feet wide, but it shimmered like diamonds with the setting sun shining down on it.

A rock path was set in the shallow stream where water swirled, and little white daisies grew all around us. My foot lifted to step onto the first stone, but I quickly realized my own flip-flops weren't meant for this kind of activity either and pulled back.

"So, this is how we get to Arvayta?" I asked when I finished my perusal.

"Yep. You won't remember your first trip, so I thought I'd show you ahead of time. Does anything feel different to you yet?"

My head shook. "Nope. I'm still very human and still alive."

She grimaced. "The dying part isn't normal. I didn't realize you'd have to do that. Most of us grow up in Arvayta, so our magic slowly emerges as we grow. Apparently, yours is going to burst out like a jack-in-the-box."

"Ugh. Thanks for the visual." Glancing down at my watch, I saw it was just before five. "We should probably head back. I want my final meal. No way am I missing out on the meatballs I smelled simmering earlier." My mouth was again salivating at the mere thought of them.

She laughed at me but didn't argue as she led the way home. It was only about a twenty-five-minute walk back once we were on the normal path, but I wished it was longer. As good as dinner sounded, I wasn't in a hurry to experience everything that was supposed to come after.

In about two hours, I was going to die and say goodbye to my human life before entering a whole new world I didn't know nearly enough about.

I was trying to remain positive, but as time ticked by, I really just needed to let out a deep scream and take a nap.

AFTER DINNER HAD BEEN CONSUMED, MY DAD POURED ME A GLASS OF whiskey, surprising the hell out of me. "Here, I know you're not of legal age yet and it's going to taste awful, but maybe it will calm you down, because you're starting to freak me out with all of your fidgeting."

Neither of my parents had ever given me alcohol before, but that didn't mean I was a complete stranger to it considering I'd been to a handful of college parties. Though, on the rare occasion I had tried to drink, I'd always gagged on the taste. Still, I didn't decline the glass he offered, and sipped on the smooth liquid that burned its way down my throat.

Mom couldn't sit still, either, and once my nerves weren't so frayed, I realized why Dad had given me the alcohol. Standing up, I shoved the remainder of my glass in her hand. "Drink this. For the sake of not only you, but the rest of us."

Unlike me, she threw down the rest of the contents in one gulp, and I couldn't stop the laughter that burst from me. My mom had always been so reserved and proper, but watching her down booze like it was water showed me another side of her I wished she'd let out more often.

"Okay, so is everyone calm now?" Jordan teased.

"Not even close, but it's almost time, so it won't matter soon," Mom answered, glancing at the wall clock for the millionth time.

Sure enough. It was 7:39pm and I only had seven minutes left before my official birthday arrived. We all headed to the guest room, and I laid down on the bed. Dad had thought it was best if

I was already comfortable "before things began," which was the polite way to say "before I died."

My hands were beginning to tingle, and my head spun, but that could have been the effects of the whiskey, so I tried not to let it stress me out.

Jordan pulled out her phone, but my mom quickly yanked it from her hand. "Not happening."

"It was worth a try. You know she'd want to see it later," Jordan replied.

As I opened my mouth to respond, my body seized up and no words were able to come out. Though, there were plenty of groans that caught the attention of everyone in the room. The necklace my mom had given me began to burn as everything around me started to glow.

My mind was telling my hand to rip the necklace from my chest when it felt like it was seeping into my skin, but nothing moved.

Mom let out a strangled cry, but I couldn't see her any longer. It felt as if the sun was right above me and I was going to be fried to a crisp from the bright and hot lights. Closing my eyes, I focused on the training I'd gone through with Stryx. While the heat didn't disappear, the light did dim.

When I opened my eyes again, a full-body paralysis was in effect and there was no way I could move at all as the faces of the three most important people in my life stood over me. The only things I thought about as sudden darkness crept in were that I hoped like hell it wasn't the last time I would see any of them and I wished I would have told them goodbye, just in case.

Stabbing pain brought me back to consciousness who knew how much later. I was still unable to move any parts of my body, though I could sense *everything* that was happening to me.

Hands roamed over my body from more than one person as voices talked over each other. Some I recognized, some I didn't.

"Are you sure this is normal?" Dad asked someone.

"Brooks, if you question my methods one more time, I'm going to banish you from Arvayta," a woman snapped.

"She's going to be okay. Lorelle knows what's at stake if Kaliah doesn't wake," a rough male voice said, most likely to my dad, or maybe to both of my parents.

Not being able to see anything was really beginning to piss me off as claustrophobia set in from having no control of my body.

Something sharp stabbed through my chest as my body arched on its own, then I heard the splash of water as I settled back down. Apparently, I was going to be waking up in a body of water of some sort with more than one stranger around me. Super. Just how I wanted to come back from the dead.

"She's coming around. I can sense her consciousness returning already. Now, her body just needs to wake up. I'll come by the house later to check on her, but you all have it from here," the woman said in a much softer tone than the last time she spoke.

"Thank you, Lorelle. We appreciate you meeting us here," Mom said, but I heard no response.

Finally, feeling began to return to my legs and then my arms. Within another few minutes of tense but awkward silence, I finally opened my eyes.

Above me, my mom and dad stood on one side with Jordan on the other and an extremely attractive male next to her. I tried not to stare at the stranger, but my attention was stuck on his eyes, which were an alarmingly similar shade to mine, probably even an exact match, depending on my mood.

Of course, the first guy I'd meet would likely be a relative and having thoughts of how hot he was running around inside my head was far from appropriate, but what could I do? I'd just died and come back to life. I had little control over anything at that moment.

Thankfully, my mom distracted me. "Kaliah, can you talk?"

"Yeah, but more importantly, can I get out of this water?" I asked in return.

I was still submerged in a pool and fully clothed. Wearing jeans probably wasn't the best idea, but nobody had told me I'd be swimming in them later.

"As long as nothing feels off, then yes, you can get out of the falls, but its magic is what brought you back, so if you're not fully transformed, then we should stay in here a bit longer," Dad answered, but Mom shushed him.

"Lorelle said she was fine. If things weren't complete, she wouldn't have left Kali's side."

"Daliah is right. As long as Kaliah is feeling up to it, then we should take her back to the house. It's better for her to be there than out here until she's ready," the guy I didn't know said.

"Kali. Please, call me Kali." Odd as it was, it drove me crazy when people called me Kaliah. Except for Stryx. I'd tried to break him of it, but I usually let it slide for my fluffy owl. When anyone else used my full name, it seemed too proper and reminded me of my mom. Not that being like my mom was bad, but I wasn't ready to be so formal just yet.

"Well, Kali. My name is Ryland. It's nice to meet you finally." He reached a hand to me that I gladly took and was promptly yanked out of the water as if I weighed nothing. The guy was not only good-looking, but strong, too.

Damn it. I needed to quit thinking that. He could be my cousin, for all I knew.

Jordan wrapped an arm around me, then pulled me from Ryland as we walked out of the water together. When I glanced back, I realized we were at the waterfall Stryx had shown me my last night with him. It was even more stunning than it had been in my sleep.

"So, how do you feel, Chuck?" Jordan asked as everyone followed us out.

Twisting my neck, then stretching my arms, I decided I felt pretty damn good for dying. My body was humming with energy, and I had the sudden desire to run a marathon. "All things considered, I feel great. So, what do we do now?"

"*We* don't do anything. You get to go back to the house with your parents, while Ryland and I go attend to some business. But don't worry, I'll be by to check on you really soon. You're not getting rid of me now, I promise." Jordan hugged me tight, and over her shoulder, I made eye contact with Ryland.

He seemed really confused and more than a little stressed by the pinched look in his familiar icy-blue eyes, but I didn't get a chance to dissect it more, because Jordan bounded away from me. I watched as she punched Ryland in the ribs before throwing an arm around him and walking in the opposite direction.

When it was just me and my parents, they seemed worried as well, but when I asked them about it, they shrugged me off.

"Nothing to stress about, sweet girl. Let's go get settled in the house, and then we'll give you a tour of the town if you're up for it," Dad said, and I didn't argue.

I'd been dying to see the town ever since I decided to accept Stryx's word as truth. I just hadn't realized all I'd have to go through to make that happen. Now, all I had to worry about was some crazy dark fae with a vendetta against me just because of who my ancestors were.

Nothing to stress about at all, I thought with an overwhelming amount of sarcasm.

CHAPTER 5

Surprisingly, my parents' home in Arvayta was extremely similar to the one in Bridal Veil, except instead of wood siding, it was stone, appearing more like a mini castle than a weekend cabin.

The lower floor was identical to the other house when I first walked in, but as my parents and I entered into the kitchen, it opened up into a more spacious entertaining area with a huge covered porch and a beautiful fountain in the center just past the French doors.

A deep-rooted sense of serenity ran through me. Considering I'd been dead not too long ago, I felt better than ever. Well, maybe a little tired, but I was trying to ignore that feeling and just soak in as much of this new world as possible.

"What do you think?" Mom asked.

"It's gorgeous, and now that I'm seeing more of Arvayta, it makes me sad I didn't get to grow up here. Don't get me wrong, Oregon was great, but this is something else entirely."

She grinned. "It really is, and I hope you can be happy here. Things will take some getting used to, but as long as we can eliminate the threat of this dark fae, then it should feel like home in no time."

Sigh. The dark fae. For a split second, I had forgotten about him.

"What do we do about that? Just wait for him to show up?" I asked.

"No, we'll be assembling a group of guardians to go searching for him. Once we have his location, a more elite team will be sent to lock him up and end this nightmare before it even begins. We've been trying for years since we learned of his plans, but Alaryk is rather elusive, unfortunately. I'd have much preferred him dead long ago," Dad answered with a grimace.

My parents had always maintained lighthearted personalities, and to see my dad so hell-bent on ending someone's life so casually was sort of freaking me out, even more so than the talking owl.

"It's going to be okay, Dad." I looped my arm through his and leaned on his shoulder, trying not to let my worries increase his own.

"Damn right, it will be. Nobody threatens my daughter and gets away with it. You'll also need to resume training. You have the hand-to-hand part down, but now we need to teach you how to control your magic and bend it to your will. I had a plan for that, but I'm not sure that's going to work out anymore."

Glancing between him and Mom, I saw more concern etched into their faces. "Why? What was the previous plan?"

"Let's not worry about that now," Mom said. "I bet you're famished. How about some lunch? Time changed some with the travel, so it's now the thirtieth and one in the afternoon."

Food didn't exactly sound good, but I knew I'd have to get my body and mind acclimated to the new time adjustments, so I figured I could at least snack. It would also appease my frayed mom, so it was a win-win.

"You ladies enjoy lunch. I forgot I need to go check on something." Dad kissed my forehead and then did the same to Mom before walking out the back door.

My hand reached for the necklace she had given me, and I let out a strangled cry. "It's gone."

She raced to my side. "What's gone, sweetheart?"

"Your gift, the necklace. Did you take it off of me?" I was going to feel awful if I'd lost my mom's gift so soon after receiving it. I should have waited to wear it until after we arrived in Arvayta.

She grasped my shoulders. "Calm down, Kaliah. The necklace wasn't meant to survive. I gave it to you so that it could ease your transition. It is, or was, a conduit of magic. When your powers began to seep out, the necklace filtered as much of them as it could before exploding. I knew what would happen when I gave the gift to you, and it was worth it."

"But it was your mother's." Guilt still assaulted me no matter what she said.

"And she would have made the same choice as I had. Now don't worry about it." She went back around the counter to the food she was sorting and let the subject go, but I worried there was something more wrong than what had already been said.

As I watched her closely, the worry lines around her eyes grew deeper. "Mom, spill it."

She plastered on a fake smile. "Spill what, dear?"

"Don't play coy with me. I know there is more. Dad wouldn't have left so soon if there wasn't. Plus, Jordan took off with that other guy. By the way, is he related? His eyes were eerily similar to mine. How many relatives do we have here?"

I'd always believed we had none, but maybe that was a lie to keep me from asking questions as a child. I wouldn't have minded having an aunt, uncle, or even some cousins. Hopefully, the Ryland guy was not one of them, though. I really didn't want to have to remind myself *not* to ogle him at family functions.

"Arvayta is very different from Earth. We have problems to

worry about here that are much greater than normal human ones. Your father and I used to be part of the council, but we stepped down when we found out we had to leave for your safety. I'm sure your father is just going to check in with them."

My brow raised. Her answer was plausible, so I let it pass for the time being and inquired more about my other questions. "What about Ryland? Who is he?"

She focused really hard on cutting the fruit in front of her and didn't answer for a minute. "He's one of the top guardians of Arvayta. He used to be assigned to us when we had to travel for missions, and he'd stay close if there were threats near."

"So, not a cousin?" I needed confirmation so I wouldn't feel guilty anymore.

"Your father and I were only children and, as you know, your grandparents passed away in the Dark War. So, no, Ryland is definitely not a cousin." She grinned. "Why?"

I shrugged. "Just curious. So, where do I stay?" I changed the subject. I had zero desire to talk about guys at the moment. It had already been a long enough day.

"Well, we have a guest house. I figured you and Jordan could stay there. It's smaller than your old one but should work for now."

I may not have had a job before, but I just remembered, I was leaving behind a lot of belongings. "Speaking of houses. What about all of mine and Jordan's things?"

"That house is paid for. Your stuff can sit there for as long as it needs. Once you have your own place here, we can collect your things and the old house will likely be turned into a workplace for other guardians if needed."

Interesting. I always thought I was taking advantage of the parental system by letting them pay my way when I wasn't in school. Good to know I'd just been utilizing resources.

"So, am I good to go get a nap in before Dad gets back? If so, don't let me rest for too long. I'd prefer to be able to sleep tonight." I'd only done major travel once before and remembered the jet lag like a bad dream. Assuming this adjustment was going to be similar, I wanted to do my best to avoid it if possible.

"Of course. Let me just clean up here and I'll take you over there."

Glancing out the back door my dad had used, I saw the house that I assumed was where I'd be staying. "As long as it's that place over there, I think I can manage."

She nodded. "Alright, well, I'll check on you shortly then."

Grinning, I waved goodbye and headed out the door. That was the best part about my parents. They weren't overbearing and understood the importance of space. While crossing the wood deck, I dipped my fingers into the cool water of the fountain and a tingle ran up my arm. There was definitely something in the water, and I hoped it was good that my body reacted the way it had. I really didn't want to die again so soon.

Moving across the yard, I took in the small guest house. It was a mini version of the main house with the same rock siding, but only a single story and with much smaller windows. It sat higher up on the hill, though, so I assumed the view would be just as impressive.

The door opened up into a small living room that included two couches, a TV on the wall, and a coffee table in the middle with an assortment of board games tucked underneath it. Immediately to the left was a small kitchen with barely any counter space. Major cooking would definitely be taking place in the main house.

Off to the right was a short hallway and three doors. Opening the first one, I entered a bedroom with a double bed, dresser, and small closet. A smirk lifted on my face. Jordan was going to hate this place. The closet wouldn't even fit her shoes.

I found the second bedroom to be the exact same, and the bathroom was nothing to write home about until I caught my reflection in the mirror. Moving into the small space, I held on to the counter as I peered closer. Cheese and rice, my ears were pointy. Okay, not like those of an elf, but there was a noticeable change.

Running my fingers through my hair, I realized it was silky and wavy in all the ways I had always wished. After spending however long in the water, it should have been a tangled mess. Even my skin had a slight glow to it, but thankfully, my eyes were still the same.

Deciding I'd dealt with enough for the first part of the day, I headed back to the first room and plopped down on the bed, not even bothering to remove my shoes before I passed out.

When a weight dipped onto the bed and I realized it was pitch black in the room, I was momentarily pissed my parents had let me sleep all afternoon and evening. That was until the body next to me was pulling the comforter back and I couldn't see a damn thing.

Moving over, I assumed Jordan was getting into bed with me, but when there was a grunt followed by a hand around my throat, I quickly realized that was *not* the case.

Using the skills that I'd worked almost a year to hone, I grabbed the wrist of my attacker and twisted before flipping him onto his back. "What the hell are you doing in here?" I snapped while pinning his arms above his head.

I only knew it was a guy, because he wasn't wearing a shirt and a muscled chest was barely visible as my eyes adjusted in the tiny bit of moonlight that peeked through the closed curtains.

"I was about to ask you the same thing."

I recognized Ryland's voice from earlier in the day, and I was once again thankful he wasn't a relative considering I was straddling him, but that didn't last long. He ripped his arms from my grasp and, with little effort, grabbed my waist to toss me back on the other side of the mattress before rolling off the bed.

"Are you staying here?" he asked as he turned on the bedroom light.

"Of course, I am. It's my parents' house."

He glared as I moved from the bed to stand level with him. "No, this is their *guest* house. A house *I* normally stay in when they're home. Why don't you stay in the main house?"

"Because they offered it to me. Not that it's really any of your business," I retorted. He smelled of alcohol, and gone was the kindness he'd shown me earlier. A scowl marred his face, and I was not awake enough to deal with his diva attitude. "So, run along to your own house," I added when he continued to glower.

Besides the similar eye color, Ryland had tanned skin and russet hair that fell over his forehead in that natural messy way I'd always found appealing. His broad shoulders and muscled abs were also on full display, and I let my gaze wander until he cleared his throat.

"Enjoying the view?" He smirked, which was better than his previous surly attitude, but still not something I wanted to deal with after being rudely woken.

"Nope. Just sizing up the competition," I quipped. Thank the fates I'd always been quick on my feet with retorts. I did *not* need this guy knowing I thought he was hot. Something told me he was already well aware of how good-looking he was.

"So, considering you're supposed to be my parent's guard of sorts, why don't you stay in the house with them? You don't want to be caught slacking on your job all the way out here," I said, then wondered if Jordan had come back at the same time as him, but I wasn't leaving until the sleeping situation sorted out. Sure, there'd been an attraction, but I wasn't giving up my space for anyone.

Before he could respond, the door slammed open in the living room. "Ryland, don't—crap." Jordan was a couple minutes too late.

Ryland threw his shirt back on as Jordan waltzed into the room. "Sorry, Kali. I made it here as quick as I could when your mom said you were sleeping."

"Why didn't anyone wake me up earlier?" I asked, pretending Ryland wasn't still staring daggers at me.

"She tried. So did your dad. You wouldn't budge. Come on over to the house and we'll grab some food while we chat. It's just after nine, so I'm sure you're starving now."

It was only nine? Then, why was Ryland already exhausted and ready for bed? Was he secretly some old man who needed his beauty sleep? That thought made me grin, which seemed to further irritate him.

"What about him? He thinks he's sleeping here." My head nodded toward Ryland and he wasn't at all happy with me.

"Listen here, *Princess*. I don't care what you—"

Jordan cut him off. "What he means to say is that he understands this is *your* family home and he'll be gone before we're back. Right, Ryland?"

He mumbled his reply and stormed out of the room into the bathroom.

Jordan pulled on my hand, and I gladly followed. When we were outside, I asked, "What's his problem? He was nice for like two seconds earlier."

"Don't mind him. He's just going through some stuff and might be a little inebriated."

"So much for him being a top guardian," I scoffed.

Jordan grasped my elbow. "He's had a rough day. He deserved an evening of reprieve. Just try to cut him some slack and things should work themselves out soon enough. Ryland is one of my best friends from here. I promise he's not all that bad."

Deciding she was right—even if I didn't know the whole story —I let it go and continued on to the main house with her. Hopefully, whatever attraction I had to Ryland would pass because he clearly didn't feel anything for me based off his attitude. I was counting on his surly disposition to make sure any blossoming feelings disappeared.

When we entered the house, my mom was already setting out more food in the kitchen, because she was awesome like that, and my dad was sitting on the couch reading a book, which I immediately took interest in. We both had a love of reading, but I hadn't been keeping up nearly as much as I liked.

"Glad to see you're alive," Dad joked when we walked in.

"Yeah, I guess jet lag exists even with portals," I replied with a shrug.

"You'll get used to it after a few times."

Dad went back to his book, and I headed toward the kitchen to check out the spread my mom had laid out. There were several platters of baked goods and light snacks, making me realize I was famished.

"What's wrong?" I asked after taking a seat at the counter and noticing the frown on her face.

She glanced up and smiled. "Just a lot of adjusting today. Don't worry about me."

I wasn't sure I believed her, but I was already on information overload and didn't push. After all, we were in a world where my magic was supposedly putting into motion the plans for some fae who wanted to destroy me. There was a slight chance I was overanalyzing things, because everyone had a perfectly good reason to be acting stressed.

CHAPTER 6

While at the kitchen counter, I focused on sampling the sweets first before putting some protein on my plate. Once I was stocked up with food, I decided to fill the silence with some lighter topics and turned to Jordan.

I brushed my hair back and pointed to my ears. "Why do they look pointy and yours don't?"

She snickered. "Well, you're more fae than me, more than anyone else in Arvayta actually. So, you get perks the rest of us don't."

"You call *this* a perk?" I glowered at her while gesturing again to my ears.

"Yep. Just be thankful you don't have wings like the original fae did. Then, you'd really stand out in a crowd."

Ugh, she was not helping. Time for a different topic.

"So, Stryx says we live for a long time, like centuries. How old are you, really?" I asked.

She grimaced. "I am not old, so don't ever say that again. I'm seventy-one years *young*."

"Got it, Satan. What about you and Dad?" I asked Mom when she finally took a seat.

"We're just over three hundred years young." She winked at Jordan. "You kind of stop keeping track after a while." She shrugged while my jaw pretty much hit the floor.

Cheese and rice, my parents were seriously old, but they didn't look a day over forty. Deciding not to overthink that little fact, I focused on the positive: at least I had good genes.

"So, where do I find Stryx? I'd like to go see him tomorrow," I said, but Jordan and Mom shared a look I didn't like. "What? I realize I've been here for like five minutes, but I've also known about this place for a year. You can take off the kid gloves and tell me whatever it is that has everyone acting so weird."

I hadn't meant to snap, but what I was asking didn't seem like something that should have secrets behind it. It was frustrating to continue being so understanding when it seemed like they were still not telling me everything.

"Honey, we're not trying to keep anything from you because we don't think you can handle it. It's more of a shock to all of us. Nothing about your situation is normal by any means, and while we knew this ahead of time, it doesn't make it any easier," Mom answered. I knew she was right. Though, once the floodgates opened, I had a hard time stopping the words.

"I get it, but not telling me things and preparing me for whatever is coming doesn't help me, either," I responded.

Mom sighed, seeing my point. "So, we don't know where Stryx is. None of us have ever met him. We've only ever heard about him and his kind." She seemed concerned with this tidbit, but I wasn't.

"Well, wherever he is, I'm sure he'll show up soon. He promised he'd be here. What do you know about him?"

All I really knew about Stryx was that he was a talking animal, crazy old, and didn't really like people. Oh, and he was like an encyclopedia of information when it came to all things within Arvayta and the Otherworld, which held the rest of the beings I believed at one point to be fictional.

"He's from a place in the far reaches of the Otherworld called Dásos where other animals like him live. They used to interact more with the fae, given the original leaders created them, but as the pure fae began to die, the bonds broke and were never reformed, because direct heirs started to be diluted of their fae lineage. Until you, that is," Mom said as she slid a plate of food in front of me.

"So, they abandoned the other fae descendants just because they weren't *fae* enough?" The anger at that knowledge was evident in my voice. I thought I knew Stryx well enough, but that wasn't okay. "Did they even help in the Dark War?"

Dad stood and joined us. "They did, and a lot of them perished because of their selflessness. You see, the creatures from Dásos are powerful beings, but they are nothing without their other halves, meaning if they have no equal to balance their magic with, then they cannot control it. Stryx and his people did not abandon us because they didn't care, but because they simply weren't capable without risking their own lives."

Well, I felt like a jerk for my previous comments.

"I don't understand why someone has to be predominantly fae to have a bond with the animals. From the sounds of it, the people around here are pretty powerful," I said.

"Unfortunately, magic is still an unknown, even after centuries of living with it. For every being, it is different, but maybe one day things will change and we can once again come together." Dad grinned, then leaned over me to steal some of the potatoes on my plate.

Mom took a seat next to Jordan. "Speaking of power, you put off quite the show when you were in transition, but I haven't felt much coming from you since we arrived. Stryx did an excellent job of teaching you how to control your magic ahead of time. As much as I wished to have been the one to tell you of our world first, this is actually working out better than I predicted."

"Uhhh, I have no idea what you're talking about. Stryx didn't teach me anything about my own magic. He only told me to expect pain during my transition, and he hadn't been kidding about that."

Once again, my parents shared a look, but before I could say anything about it, Dad reached out to me and took my hand. "There is definitely heavy power within her. Let's just be thankful she's able to control it and figure the rest out together before we make any assumptions. Maybe the necklace did more for her than we thought."

Searching within myself, I tried to sense whatever my dad had, but I got nothing. Now that it was brought to my attention, I realized the only time I'd experienced anything resembling the feeling of magic was when I touched the water in the fountain.

Maybe I needed Stryx close by for my power to come out in full force. If so, that nocturnal pain in my ass better show his face soon or he was going to be missing a few feathers when I got done with him. He'd shown me this world and promised he'd be here. I'd have a bit of a problem if he broke that.

Jordan nudged me and brought me back to the conversation. "What do you want to do now? I'm sure you're not tired after the eight-hour nap."

"I'm actually still kind of sleepy. Plus, it's dark out, so I'm sure there isn't much to do. Will I get to see the main parts of town tomorrow, or am I going to need to stay hidden because of the dark fae stuff?" I asked and really hoped the latter wasn't the case.

Dad nodded. "We can do whatever you're comfortable with tomorrow. We won't be keeping you from anyone, and we have a few days before your scheduled training begins, so don't feel rushed to do anything if you're still tired. You'll need all your strength once magic practice starts."

Ha. It was unlikely I'd be too tired for anything if it meant venturing out. On the way to the house earlier, I'd gotten a small glimpse of the village-style area, but it wasn't nearly enough to sate my curiosity. Though, his comment at the end did give me pause. Hopefully, I wasn't about to have my ass beat over and over again by some deranged trainer.

"The council will want to meet you when you're up for it as well," Mom added.

"Who is the council exactly? I mean, I know they took over once the hierarchy ended after the Dark Wars, but what do they do?" I asked.

"You mean besides telling people what to do? Not much," Jordan grumbled, but Mom glared at her. "What? It hasn't been the same since you and Brooks stepped down. Once I really thought about it, I was actually somewhat relieved when I got assigned to come assist you guys on Earth after I came back from fighting with the dragons."

Screw learning about the council. That sounded way more interesting. "So, dragons are real, too? Please, tell me they're friendly nowadays."

"When we go to the Otherworld, I'll see if I can track down Yelah. She's the dragon queen, and I should check in anyway. They were having some issues, but myself, Ryland, and another one of our friends went to help and took care of it. Bastards almost burned my feet off, but I showed them in the end."

My body shuddered as I considered asking more questions, but even though I'd slept for way too many hours, I was still fairly tired.

"Do you think Ryland is gone?" I asked Jordan.

"Yeah, he's stubborn, but he's not an idiot. You won't find him in your bed just so soon after that little interaction." She smirked.

"Uh, do I need to know more about this?" Dad asked.

My head shook. "Definitely not. I took care of it. I'll be back over in the morning and we can head to town."

Both my parents stood as I slid off my chair and rolled my eyes while Jordan scarfed down the rest of her food like she may not eat again for the next week.

After our goodnights were said, Jordan and I headed out to the guest house together. I was on edge until I double-checked the rooms to confirm Ryland was truly gone. I didn't understand what about him triggered such strong emotions in me but hoped it would pass.

It wasn't like I'd never had a boyfriend or been attracted to a guy before. I should have been able to handle things better. For the time being, I was blaming it on my body adjusting to the new world. Some things were bound to be out of sorts.

Jordan was on the couch with her feet up and the TV on already. "Want to dumb down your brain with late night television?"

"We have cable here?" For some reason, that was even more surprising than dragons.

"Yep, and cell phones and so much more. Just you wait. Magic makes almost anything possible. I've been looking forward to this day since the week after I arrived on Earth and realized you weren't going to be the worst thing to ever happen to me."

Ah, my best friend had absolutely no filter. "Are you saying you didn't actually want the job to come be my babysitter?" I teased even though, if I was being honest, it hurt a little to feel like I had been forced upon her.

"I'd just gotten back from the fight with dragons, so no, I wasn't really looking forward to regressing back to a much younger version of myself and having to go to school again. *But,* once I was there with you, I saw that things really weren't so bad. You weren't the princess I pictured you to be and decided our world would be better off with you growing up under my influence as opposed to anyone else's."

"Selfless as always, Satan." I laughed.

"You know it, Chuck."

Settling on the couch with her, I put the past behind us and accepted that everything happened for a reason. Jordan wasn't going anywhere even though her assignment was done. Holding on to doubts would only make moving forward in this world all that much harder. There was a deep-rooted feeling within me that I had bigger battles to worry about in my immediate future.

CHAPTER 7

Later the next morning, I got ready in the main house with Jordan. The little bit of our stuff that had been snuck over ahead of time was there, and after sleeping like crap the night before, I was too worn out to bring anything out to the guest house.

Stryx hadn't visited me while I slept. It had been the first time in a year, since I didn't count the night before with the time change, and I didn't like the uneasiness that turned within me. My heart was missing him, and I hadn't realized how much he'd grown on me until I didn't have him around.

Jordan nudged me. "Come on. We have to meet with the council first, and then I get to show you around town while spilling all the secrets I've been *dying* to for years."

My smile didn't reach its full potential, but I did my best to embrace her joy. "And I can't wait to hear everything."

After throwing my hair into a ponytail, I took one last look in the mirror and as my eyes caught my attention, they reminded me of Ryland. That was going to be annoying. He was an enigma I wasn't sure I had time to solve. Normally, I loved puzzles, but with the threat of the dark fae, I just hoped whatever had my emotions responding so strongly to him died down.

"Alright, let's go," I said, looping my arm through hers.

We ventured back downstairs to meet my parents who were grinning like children on Christmas morning. Their excitement of being able to share their home with me was palpable, and I almost felt bad about feeling so disconnected when I woke up.

"You girls ready?" Dad asked, dressed in a white collared shirt and tan dress pants.

Looking over, I realized my mom was also fancier than normal in a navy-blue dress that fit loosely enough to be comfortable, but the small gems embedded into it made it appear more than casual.

Glancing down at myself in jeans and a plain t-shirt made me feel severely underdressed. "Uh, should we change?" I asked.

Mom shook her head. "Not at all. The two of us are staying with the council for a meeting that requires us to be more formal, while both of you are fine to stroll through town just as you are."

Deciding to take their word for it, I followed them out the door, then quickly realized there was no car out front and no town in sight from the house.

"How do we get around?" I asked Mom as they kept walking down the drive.

"Well, normally we just port to where we need to be, but since it's your first time exploring, we thought you might appreciate the walk this morning. It's only about fifteen minutes to town. The trees block most of everything, making it seem a lot further."

My face pinched. "What is porting?"

"It's teleporting, essentially, but we can only do it within the world we're in. Otherwise, we have to take portals through the waterfalls like we did to bring you here." Jordan laughed at my gaping face when she finished. "It's not a big deal. I'll teach you today."

Right, because moving from one place to another within the blink of an eye was *no big deal.*

We continued down the path toward town, and I was thankful my parents had wanted to walk. As interesting as porting sounded, nothing could beat the magnificence surrounding me. The area around us was a hybrid of an exotic jungle and the forests back in Oregon. The trees reminded me of the thick woods I was used to, but the vibrant splashes of color from the unique flowers and plants made me think of a jungle.

Animals peeked out and stared but skittered away almost as fast whenever I spotted them. Though, the most intriguing part was just the peacefulness I felt as we silently strolled along. Taking in a deep breath, I could smell the crisp, clean air and hear nothing but the crunch of rock beneath our feet and the rustling of animals.

My skin tingled like it had when I'd touched the water from the fountain, so I closed my eyes and focused on the feeling, trying to draw on it. Supposedly, I had all of this magic within me, but I wouldn't have been surprised if they were all wrong, because even as I actively searched for it, there was nothing coming to me except a light prickling sensation along my body.

"Here it is," Dad said, and my head snapped up.

Sure enough, as we rounded the next bend in the path, a town came into view. Though, it was nothing like any town I'd ever seen. This was a village straight out of a storybook, including a castle-looking structure on the back side of all the smaller buildings.

The dirt path continued to twist downward, and I stopped paying attention to anything else around me, choosing to only stare ahead as my feet picked up pace. With the higher vantage point, I took in the rows of buildings, most of which seemed to be small homes with chimneys popping out of the roofs.

Past the houses were larger structures I assumed to be shops of some sort and couldn't wait to see inside them all. Then, directly in the middle of everything was the largest stone fountain I'd ever seen. From a distance, it appeared to be made from rocks at the bottom, but as I took in the five layers above the base, they shimmered with something more like sapphires.

Jordan snapped her fingers in my face. "Wipe the drool. You don't want to look like a newb as soon as we get around the others. I need them to think I trained you better than that."

My head shook. "So, I need to act right just so you look good?"

"Precisely."

"You're insane," I replied.

"And you're the princess around here, so you don't only want to look good for me. Just remember that." The smirk on her face made mine pale.

For just a little while, I had forgotten all about my royal ancestors. "We're not still considered royalty around here, are we?" I asked Mom and Dad.

"Well, nobody calls us King and Queen," Dad answered sheepishly.

"Don't stress about it, dear. You're not expected to be anyone other than yourself," Mom added.

I groaned, realizing that while they didn't sit on a throne, they still had the power and respect of royalty. That was probably the real reason they were dressed up. I should have known something more was going on.

Deciding to take my mom's advice, I went back to checking out the village, or more accurately, the castle behind the village. The front had four thick pillars holding up a large overhang that covered a set of stairs.

The exterior appeared crazy old, like the structures I'd seen when spending hours dreaming of visiting Rome. Except here, while the coloring was the same tannish brown, the building had no cracks in it.

I thought we'd have to pass through the town area first, but my parents detoured to a side road before we passed the first building, stating we didn't have time to be stopped twenty times before meeting with the council.

Ah, the council. I wasn't sure what to think about them yet. As long as they weren't power-hungry politician types, then maybe it wouldn't be so bad.

Taking the stone steps up, we arrived at ornate wooden double doors that had to be at least twice as tall as me. When we entered, people were moving freely through the grand entrance, but they immediately stopped when they saw my parents to offer a slight bow before moving on.

No longer considered royalty, my ass.

My parents didn't miss a beat. They addressed everyone by name who took a moment to greet them and introduced me before politely excusing us. The way they spoke and held themselves had me feeling like I had no idea who my parents really were. I suddenly felt very nervous about whatever came next.

Jordan must have sensed the shift in my emotions, because she looped her arm through mine and tilted my chin up with her other hand. "You're going to be okay. Just act like you own the place and don't let anyone make you feel like anything other than the strong woman I know you to be."

"Thank you." I smiled at her, because I really had needed to hear that.

We went up one more set of stairs before entering into a room with three men and two women standing around in blue robes.

"Brooks, Daliah," an older man with thick white hair and hazel eyes greeted us. "And this must be Kaliah. It's so nice to finally meet you after all these years." He reached a hand to me, and I ineptly gave him mine as I stepped away from Jordan.

"Uh, hi." I had no idea why I was being so awkward.

"Kali, this is Mathias. He took over for me as the leader for the council," Mom said, and I choked on air.

"*You* were the leader?"

She grinned. "Before the kingdom was disbanded, we were a monarchy, so it had seemed fitting at the time when the council was first formed to keep some traditions in place."

That was some of the best information I'd yet to hear, and I really wanted to give my mom a high five but doubted it would be appropriate at the moment. Instead, I greeted Mathias again, this time without the use of "uh" and was promptly introduced to the other four.

Next was Selene, followed by Rosella, Gracin, and Theo. Once introductions were done, the four of us took seats across the table from the five of them.

"So, we wanted you to meet Kali today, but we'd rather not get into anything heavy with her as we promised her a couple of days rest before we threw her into training, both physical and knowledge-based. Though, if there is anything pressing, she should be aware before we send her and Jordan on their way…" Dad said, leaving the sentence open for someone to finish.

"Unfortunately, we don't have any news on Alaryk, the dark fae, but if Kali has any questions for us, then we're happy to answer," Selene said. Her green eyes flicked to mine, but I couldn't stop staring at the intricate braids in her ebony hair.

"Nope, no questions. Well, actually, maybe one. How long and how often is this training I'm supposed to do? I've spent the last year being told what to do by a feathered tyrant, and I'd like to be mentally prepared for what's coming."

She nodded and smiled, dimples appearing on her umber skin. "Understandable. We'd heard Stryx decided to prepare you some. While that's not conventional, it isn't entirely bad given your unique situation. For future training, you'll begin magic training with Ryland, Jordan, and Oliver serving as your guides. They're some of our finest guardians, and considering your closeness to Jordan, we thought it would be best if she was present as well."

Ugh, Ryland. I was really hoping to avoid him for as long as possible after our interaction the night before, but apparently, that was only going to last for the two or three days I had off.

Selene continued, "As for how long your training will last, well, that's up to you. Whenever you feel confident in utilizing your abilities, then we can move on to more specialized aspects, depending on what you're most interested in doing. As the daughter to Daliah and Brooks, you'll be able to choose whatever you want."

Sigh. Of course, I would be able to.

"Thank you for the information. We'll let the rest of you get to whatever business it is you need to discuss," I said, then stood at the same time as Jordan.

The council members stood as well, followed by my parents. As soon as I hugged them and left the room with Jordan, a sense of dread settled into me.

"You could have prepared me a little better for this, you know? Little hints here and there wouldn't have hurt anything," I grumbled.

She laughed. "But this is so much more fun considering how you tortured me on your birthday with all the crap you kept spewing."

Grinding my jaw, I really regretted finding so much joy from her discomfort, because this payback was *not* what I had in mind.

CHAPTER 8

We exited what Jordan had called the town hall and headed for the main streets we had skipped by earlier.

"Everyone is staring," I groaned when we passed by the first store.

"Nah, they're simply using their peripherals to peek and then turning to whisper about you to the nearest person. Totally different."

I really needed to rethink my friend choices.

Our stroll down the main street wasn't even enjoyable since I was so distracted by all the prying eyes. I mostly kept my head down and wished my hair wasn't in a ponytail so I could hide behind it. When we got near the end and I completely missed everything Jordan had said, I was irritated I hadn't taken a single moment to admire the fountain I'd seen earlier from the distance.

"How about we head to the training field? You told Selene you wanted to mentally prepare for what came next, so this might help," Jordan offered.

"Will there be less people there?" I asked.

"Sort of. More like less people who give a crap about who you are. Guardians tend to not gawk as much as regular Arvaytans."

"What exactly does it mean to be a guardian?"

"Well, think of them like the military you're used to on Earth. Guardians are battle-trained, and the council assigns them duties as needed. Guardians help not only in Arvayta, but also in the Otherworld and Earth as requested, too."

Interesting but not so surprising, given what I already knew. At least it wasn't something that came with a shock factor like almost everything else I'd been told.

We turned left and headed down a hill to a field with a running track, some sand areas, large rock boulders, and a metal building behind all of that.

"So, what will this training consist of?" I asked.

"Hard to say until your magic starts to show what it's capable of on an instinctual level. It could be a number of things depending on how basic we need to go. Since Stryx wasn't able to do anything with your magic ahead of time, it might be back to kindergarten for you."

Well, that didn't sound like fun. Plus, I didn't have high hopes I was going to be an exemplary student, considering I couldn't sense an ounce of anything extraordinary within me.

A guy with shaggy blond hair, fair skin, and a wide smile jogged up to us and wrapped Jordan up in a massive hug. "You're on my bad side for not coming to see me last night."

She grimaced. "Well, I had a bit of a situation I had to take care of with Ryland." Her eyes widened as she realized she'd said something she hadn't meant to.

The newcomer's grey eyes glanced at me, then offered his hand and a grin. "I'm Oliver. You must be Kaliah."

"Please, call me Kali. It's nice to meet you." I smiled in return.

His gaze moved back to Jordan. "These fields weren't near as exciting without you here to put us in our place. It's been rather boring, actually, but I hear that's about to change."

"Yeah, a vengeful dark fae will do that. Have you heard anything about Alaryk? The council was pretty tight-lipped about it when we were in there earlier," Jordan said.

"Nope, not a word. Though, I can sense a shift in things. Might be harder for you since you've been on Earth for so long, but the magic within our waters isn't as strong as it was even a week ago."

My mouth opened to say something, but I closed it right away, because I really had no idea what I was talking about.

"What?" Jordan nudged me.

"It's nothing."

"Your opinion means more than the rest of ours. You're seeing all of this with fresh eyes, so seriously, just say whatever is on your mind," Oliver encouraged with a heavy dose of sincerity. I decided I liked his disposition much better than Ryland's.

"Well, the only time I've been able to feel any sensations of magic since I arrived was when I touched the water. Even in the shower, I felt it."

Jordan laughed. "TMI, Chuck. We don't need to know what you do in your alone time."

Oliver shook his head at her. "You haven't changed one bit, have you?"

"Nope." She grinned proudly. "But what I meant to say was that is normal for you, Kali. Being as though you're the direct heir of the last Arelia, water will likely call to you more than the rest of us. At least, I'm pretty sure. Guess we'll find out."

Oliver shoved Jordan. "Dude, you could have told us she was an Arelia. There hasn't been one of those in I don't know how many years."

"Well, I didn't say she is one. Nobody has confirmed it, but I have my suspicions, given her ancestors. Apparently, Stryx has been paying Kali visits at night for the last year."

He turned to me and wrapped both of his hands around my shoulders. "You have no idea how happy I am that you're here. I need this excitement in my life. Anyway, you two have fun, and I'll be eagerly awaiting the start of your training, Kali."

Before I could even say a word, he was running off in the opposite direction we had been heading and I glanced at Jordan.

"Uh, what's an Arelia?" It was the first time I'd heard the word, and if she thought I had anything to do with whatever it was, I hoped she'd explain right away.

"It's like a fae on steroids. Your power is heightened, you can do crazy things most others can't. I'm sure there's more, but I've never met one, and it's not something they cover in class growing up. If you are one, I'm sure we'll figure it out once Stryx comes back."

Used to disappointment when it came to getting more information, I sighed. "So, there's a lot I still don't know, isn't there?"

She nodded. "But there's a lot all of us still don't know, so try not to worry about it. We're going to figure it out together. Oliver, Ryland, and I won't let anything happen to you."

"Right, I believe two out of three are correct, but not so sure about Ryland. He was nice around my parents, but the look of despise he sent my way in the guest house told a different story."

She grabbed my hand and made us stop walking. "Listen, Kali. There are some things that aren't my place to explain to you, but I need you to trust me when I say Ryland is good people and someone that I consider a dear friend. He's also one of the best guardians we have at our disposal, but he's going through a few things right now. When he's ready, I can guarantee you'll be the first to know about it, or maybe even before then, depending on how things go."

That was intriguing yet ominous. I wanted to interrupt her and ask more questions, but while Jordan normally had no filter, if she said it wasn't her place to tell, then I knew she wouldn't. She was loyal to a fault.

"Even though you've already been physically training, you'll still need to maintain. Chuck Norris didn't become a badass and stay that way by being lazy, you know. So, each morning we'll run five miles before we begin any of our training sessions to help keep endurance up."

"Is there an outdoor or indoor pool around here?" I asked, because I'd love to do some laps in the water instead of on the track.

"Not in the sense of ones you'd see on Earth, but there are plenty of clean bodies of water you can use, and considering where I think your magic is coming from, it's probably a good idea to rotate between running and swimming."

As we passed the track, we came upon a group of fifteen or so guardians practicing hand-to-hand combat. They moved with a precision and grace that I knew was far beyond anything I was capable of, but I hoped to be there one day soon.

Jordan waved to a few, but we kept walking and entered the training building. The door clicked shut behind me, and when my eyes finally adjusted to the darker room, I took in the different parts of the room and the groups utilizing the resources.

There were two guys beating the crap out of each other with bamboo sticks, followed by another handful of people doing archery, but instead of arrowheads piercing into the target, there were orbs of magic—or so I assumed—flying through the air and blowing up the targets. Pure craziness, yet I couldn't wait to try it.

Next, a young woman was on her own and creating a swirling vortex of magic that had me so entranced that I almost ran into two guys wrestling on my right. Once I got my wits about me again, I continued my perusal and found a guy all the way in the back. He had no shirt on and was beating the crap out of a punching bag, but of course, it wasn't an ordinary one.

No, this one was translucent, yet every time his foot or fist made contact with it, there was a bright light that ricocheted off of it. When the flashes became too much for my eyes in the dim room, I glanced down at his back and noticed tribal-style tattoo work along his shoulder blades that continued down the backside of both rib cages.

Then, my gaze traveled further and took in his tapered waist and the fine curves of his lower half before asking Jordan who *he* was.

"You don't recognize him?" she asked, and I shook my head. "Look a little harder. Tell me if you *sense* anything familiar about him."

The way she said it had me on edge, and as I stared harder, trying to avoid the bright flashes of light, I was able to get a good glimpse of his hair and immediately knew it was Ryland I had been ogling.

"Why does he seem to be everywhere?" I complained, and more importantly, why did my chest tighten at seeing him again?

"Or maybe you just keep searching him out without realizing it. I mean, he is all the way in the back corner. For most people, he would have been easy to overlook."

"Shut up, Satan." My eyes tore away from Ryland and searched out the exit. "I've seen enough to satisfy my curiosity. Let's head back to town and do some window shopping until I figure out how to get money around here."

She followed me to the door and kept talking. "We don't actually have true currency around here, more like IOUs. Everyone does their part to contribute, and not many have more than anyone else. Except for the council members, because they pretty much work day and night."

My eyes widened. "So, you're telling me I can walk into any store we passed and get whatever I want?"

"Not exactly. You take what you *need*, not what you *want*. There's a difference." Her tone was almost chastising.

"What if I want a snack or something frivolous? Do those types of things not exist around here?" I was so confused. How could there be no currency? It just didn't make any sense how that system wouldn't be abused. It would never work on Earth. Humans were greedy beings.

"Don't overthink it. I promise, you'll settle in just fine before you know it. How about we start with the bookstore?"

"There's a bookstore here?" My heart was already pounding. There was nothing I loved more than snuggling up on the couch with a good romance or history novel. Romance because I didn't get out much, and history because there was no such thing as too much knowledge.

She laughed. "I pointed it out to you earlier, but you were too busy having a panic attack to notice. Come on. We'll sneak right in, and nobody will even make fun of you when you smell the books."

I snorted. "Nobody but you."

My best friend loved to poke fun at my nerdy side—really it only consisted of an obsession with superheroes and books—but I didn't care. I was proud of who I was and never once in my life tried to impress anyone, which made me realize how ridiculous I'd been by being so freaked out about the stares and whispers from the others on the street.

The people in Arvayta didn't know me, so I couldn't blame them for being curious. The only way to make things any better was to show them the real me, and I was going to get on that just as soon as I finished with the bookstore.

CHAPTER 9

We spent a couple of hours in the bookstore, followed by another hour window shopping as I made mental notes of which stores I wanted to visit again when I wasn't so tired. The high I felt in the bookstore was fading fast until we passed by the fountain.

"Any history to this?" I asked Jordan when I stopped to sit on the edge of the stone before dipping my fingers into the water. Once again, the tingles ran through me, and I shuddered at the overwhelming feeling of emotion.

"It's said to have been a gift to the guardians from Queen Taliah, your grandmother. How come?"

Hmm, I wondered if the stronger feelings were because of who had given the fountain to the people or simply another effect of being connected to the water as Jordan had thought earlier.

"It's stunning is all."

She raised a brow. "Then why is most of your arm submerged in the water like you need it more than your next breath?"

Oops. Standing back up, I shook my hand out. "Just a warm day. No reason to overthink anything,"

She mumbled something as she tugged me along, but I missed it, too busy smiling at the people instead of shying away from them to ask what she'd said. Not being so worried about what others thought of me was a whole lot easier than stressing about it.

When we got to the edge of town, Jordan turned to me with a challenging smirk on her face. "Want to port?"

"Uh, walking hasn't killed me yet." Then I realized I didn't need to be afraid of anything. I'd seen plenty of people disappearing and reappearing while we'd been out. "Actually, why not? Let's do it."

"Really?" Jordan was beaming with excitement. "For the first time, I won't even make you do any of the work. All you have to do is close your eyes and not throw up on me."

If queasiness was part of the process, maybe I needed to rethink saying yes so soon. I was pretty sure my body wasn't yet adjusted to the new world, and I didn't want to embarrass myself by getting sick with something that seemed so easy for everyone else.

Pinching the bridge of my nose, I exhaled and closed my eyes as I considered telling her never mind. Though, before I could voice my thoughts, Jordan latched on to my arm and my subsequent shout was cut off right before I stumbled onto my parent's front yard.

"Are you freaking kidding me? You truly are Satan," I grumbled as I rolled over, taking my time to stand back up since my equilibrium was seriously thrown off balance. On the plus side, I was only dizzy and had no desire to throw up.

"You know it was fun, and I didn't have time for you to overanalyze it. Some things we're just going to have to rip the band-aid off with." She shrugged, then left me on the ground and headed into the main house.

I went to the guest house since I still had bags in my hand from the books I'd purchased, or borrowed. I had no idea, really.

The whole idea of a barter system was a lot harder to wrap my head around than Jordan made it seem.

Dropping them off quickly, I double-checked my hair wasn't a wreck from the porting that still had me feeling queasy, then headed to my parents'. When I walked in through the back door, my insides warred with each other at the sight of Ryland sitting at the dinner table with my parents and Jordan. I was equal parts eager and nervous, because our interactions had been so off-kilter so far.

"There she is." Mom gleamed, but she seemed to be the only one smiling.

"What's going on?" I asked as I took a seat next to Dad, furthest from Ryland.

Nobody answered me at first, and the tension in the room was palpable when Dad finally spoke. "Ryland brings news from the Otherworld. He was there for an errand this afternoon and met with some of our liaisons."

"So, what did they say?" I asked, because he wasn't getting to the point on his own fast enough for my liking.

Ryland cleared his throat but wouldn't meet my eyes. Instead, he focused on Jordan as he explained. "Alaryk, the dark fae with the vendetta against you has made a public appearance and his first threat. He said if the Atwater heir isn't either dead or turned over to him by month's end, then he would start punishing the other races until someone brought you to him."

A hiss escaped my lips as hatred for someone I'd never even met flowed freely through me. This fae was hitting right where it counted most for me: harming innocent people.

"So, when do I go meet him?" I asked, because to me there really was no other choice. I wouldn't be able to handle the death of others on my conscience, so we either needed to set a meeting with the psycho or find a way to kill him first.

"That's not happening, Kaliah. You're not ready," Dad snapped.

"And whose fault is that? Certainly not mine." As soon as the words left my mouth, I regretted them, but the thought of other people dying on my behalf was making me extra snarky.

"Kali, I know this sucks, but your parents are doing their best, given the situation," Jordan said, trying to calm the tension.

"I understand that, but they're not the ones who have to live with being the cause of however many murders. I'm not trying to be a martyr by any means, but I do have a heart. My life isn't worth more than anyone else's."

They all shared a look that said I wasn't going to win the argument, so before I said something else out of anger, I decided I needed a moment alone. Without excusing myself, I headed upstairs and decided to let them keep talking, because I knew it didn't really matter what I said. I was going to be outnumbered and overruled.

Though, I also trusted that Jordan would have my back now that she knew how I felt. She would be my voice if needed, so I didn't worry about it too much. Instead, I went to the upper balcony I'd found when I was done getting ready earlier that day. Opening the door, I sucked in a deep breath of crisp air and closed my eyes.

Stryx, where are you?

I missed my fluffy little friend. He'd know what to do with the information being given, yet he was nowhere to be found. He'd promised he would be here, and I was finding it harder to believe he was going to follow through as more time passed.

I'll be there soon. Quit acting like a baby.

My eyes snapped open, and my head swiveled in every direction. "Stryx? Where are you?"

I'm in Dásos, but I'll be in Arvayta soon. Just be patient and quit yelling. It's giving me a headache.

Are you in my head? I whisper-yelled in my own mind, because this was the craziest thing I'd experienced thus far. As I paid more attention to the situation, a prodding sensation pressed down on my head each time he spoke.

He sighed, like speaking with me was the last thing he wanted to be doing. *Yes, Kaliah. I'll explain more just as soon as I can. Give me a little bit longer to sort some things out. I promise, it will be worth it.*

The pressure released from my head and I knew he'd left. How he even got in my head in the first place was beyond me. Though it was creepy, it was also convenient. Hearing from him did give me some peace.

Moving to the edge of the balcony, I glanced around the property until I felt like my heart rate had calmed enough to go back and finish the conversation with the others.

Stryx was exaggerating by saying I'd been acting like a child. Sure, I could have worded things better, and I did feel bad about blaming my parents for my lack of being prepared for this world. They had been given difficult options, and since I'd never been a mom, I couldn't say I would have made different choices. Regardless, my feelings weren't going to change, and I needed to make sure not to roll over and do as I was told just because I was new to the place.

Arvayta was a complicated world, and I was worried it was going to take me years to figure out. We didn't have the luxury of me taking my sweet time with it. I knew my parents had promised some down time before I was thrust into training, but it was no longer an option we could afford.

Deciding it was time we made a plan that included me being involved, I headed back downstairs, but as the voices drifted up to me, I slowed my pace and listened in.

"You guys can't keep this from her. It's not fair to take advantage of her ignorance. Plus, you know who's going to pay the biggest price for it? Me. She'll kick my ass for not telling her, and I don't call her Chuck Norris for no reason. I know she really can," Jordan said, and my heart warmed a little. She really did love me.

And because I was super curious as to what secrets they were still keeping, I stopped moving down the stairs and waited for someone to respond.

"We know, Jordan, but it's not only up to us," Mom said. "Ryland has to decide as well."

Nothing but silence followed, and my curiosity was piqued at what Ryland might have to do with this big secret.

"Well, Ryland. What are you going to do?" Jordan pushed.

"Not a damn thing. We don't have time for this right now. We can deal with it after we hunt down Alaryk. You of all people should understand that a mission will always come before anything else," Ryland answered.

"Ah, I see. You're afraid. That's okay, because you're right. I do understand, but at least I had tried. There's a huge difference here, though, and you know it. James wasn't my Meraki. Yes, I loved him, but I wasn't bound to him. He wasn't *my* soulmate. We both knew the risks and took them anyway.

"You, on the other hand, are denying your soul the very thing it wants most in this world and causing me to omit extremely important information from my best friend. Now, man up and deal with it or you're more liable to cost us this mission than you are to save the day."

"I remember a time when I was your best friend, too," he grumbled.

"You still are, or I wouldn't be saying anything at all right now and keeping your secrets," Jordan responded and then my parents changed the subject, but I didn't comprehend anything after that.

Jordan had said the words "Meraki" and "soulmate", and she was talking about me. Correction, me *and* Ryland. What in the world did Meraki mean, and why would she think Ryland was my soulmate? If I had some connection to him, wouldn't I have known it?

Sure, I thought he was hot when I first met him, but that didn't mean anything. There was no possible way my attraction was more than that, and I was going to prove it.

After taking a deep breath, I decided I wasn't going to say anything. It was a secret I'd let them think they were keeping for the time being, because if Ryland was actually right—if there was something between us that *somehow* I wasn't aware of—then it didn't need to be discussed until my life and the lives of others weren't in danger.

Strolling into the room, I put on my best poker face and took my seat again. "Sorry about that. I just needed some air."

Mom reached for me. "It's quite alright, dear. Do you feel better now?"

"Yep. Better than ever before. So, I was thinking upstairs, I don't want to wait. I think I should begin my training as soon as possible. How do we make that happen?"

Ryland pushed away from the table. "*We* don't make anything happen. I'm in charge of your schedule, and I'm busy tomorrow. It will begin as previously scheduled."

Okay, being quiet about what I'd overheard was not going to happen if he insisted on acting like a jerk. Even though I knew stooping to his level didn't make me any better than him, I didn't give a crap in the moment.

"Listen, Ryland. I don't care who you are to my parents, to Arvayta, or even to me with whatever this *Meraki* thing is. I realize I don't know everything I should, but I'm willing to learn, and if you don't want to be the person tasked to help me, then go away instead of making things harder."

His eyes widened for a split second before he glared at Jordan. "This is your fault."

Snapping my fingers, I brought his attention back to me. "No, this is *your* fault for acting like you're better than me."

My eyes held his as emotions within me warred. Ryland infuriated me like nobody had before, and that was saying something considering my best friend was Jordan.

"Fine. I'll be here tomorrow morning at five. Be ready or I'll get you ready myself." Then, he stormed off and I couldn't help but smirk.

His irritation only fueled me to be better than he thought I could be. Ryland was going to learn really fast that just because I didn't know everything about Arvayta, it didn't mean I wasn't capable of being a badass guardian who could protect herself from a psychotic fae.

Or so I hoped.

CHAPTER 10

Jordan apologized a million and one times after the brief argument with Ryland, but I didn't really want to talk about it. Instead, I went back to the guest house and headed straight for the stack of books I'd grabbed earlier in the day.

After picking through my horde, I focused on the ones that I thought would give me the most information about whatever Meraki meant. Once I had books in hand, I got comfy on the couch and prepared to read for as long as it took to make sense of the conversation I'd just had.

Of course, I could have asked my mom or Jordan to explain it, but I didn't want the guarded version of anything. I needed facts, and considering they hadn't wanted to tell me in the first place, I wasn't sure they'd be truthful about what I needed to know.

This surprised me, because Jordan was normally brutally honest, but apparently, that ended with all things Arvayta. I missed Stryx even more and went as far as yelling at him in my head like a crazy person, but I hadn't received any words back since our initial conversation.

After staying up for most of the night, I learned a lot of things I wasn't happy with but tried my best to accept. First, Meraki was another word for soulmate, a predestined match by the Fates that watched over our worlds. And second, there was nothing I could do to change who my Meraki was.

I either accepted him or I would never have a soulmate, meaning I had two options: be a lonely spinster for the rest of my extremely long life or deal with him and hope for the best. Unfortunately, those options were only viable pending what Ryland truly thought about the whole situation.

From what I'd observed so far, he wasn't happy about it, nor did he seem willing to attempt to make anything work, so maybe it was option one for me, regardless. In a way, that devastated me.

As an avid reader, romance was my jam. I loved *love*. Dreaming of having my own happily-ever-after happened on more occasions than I cared to admit, but maybe my knight in shining armor was merely a lonely man dressed in tinfoil and not everything the stories made him out to be.

By the time I'd groggily gotten up, the sun hadn't even risen, but I had a renewed determination within me. It didn't matter what Ryland thought about me, or if he was utterly depressed to have been saddled with a Meraki. We had things to do, and feelings aside, I would make sure they got done.

Jordan wasn't up yet when I snuck out of the house at four, but I left a note for her and one on the door for cranky pants in case he actually showed. After learning as much as I could in the books that I'd devoured just a few hours before, I'd decided I could teach myself a few things, beginning with porting.

Closing my eyes, I pictured the training field Jordan had shown me the prior day and tried to summon the magic within me. Flutters erupted in my stomach, but when my eyes opened, I was still shivering in front of the guest house.

The next time I tried, I kept my eyes open and saw when my

arms began to disappear, but when I got excited, they solidified once more. I didn't have time to waste and knew there were other things I could work on, so I began jogging to the fields.

When I reached town, I was completely warmed up and feeling better about my stamina than ever before. Picking up speed, I reached the fountain and dipped both hands into the cool water. There was a momentary boost of power within me, and I decided it was now or never to try porting again.

Keeping my concentration on point, I conjured an image of the field. Within seconds, I was standing on the grassy knoll.

"Yes!" I shouted, then immediately covered my mouth in case anyone else was psycho enough to be out there before five in the morning.

I glanced around and didn't see anyone, so I continued toward the track. Even though I'd run most of the way to the field, I still wanted to do a couple of laps before trying to draw out my magic. My hope was that I could show Ryland I was perfectly capable of becoming an Arvaytan Guardian and wasn't some helpless fae princess.

Before I could make it halfway around the track, Ryland appeared at my side. "Pull your shoulders back, so you're standing tall, and breathe through your mouth instead of your nose." He was running next to me as if he'd been there the entire time.

Instead of responding, I followed his instructions, and surprisingly found my chest feeling lighter at the small adjustments. Maybe Ryland was more of a morning person and training with him wouldn't be so bad.

"Now, head into the building. It's time to show you what happens when you don't wait for your trainer to begin."

Or maybe he was still a jerk.

With a sigh, I did as he said, because at the end of the day, I knew my parents wouldn't have let him be assigned to the group of people responsible for getting me up to speed if he wasn't among the best. Just because I didn't like him, didn't mean I wouldn't listen to him.

Well, most of the time.

"When will Jordan and Oliver be here? Or will I be learning from each of you at different times?" I asked, hoping we could find some sort of common ground and not grate on each other's nerves the entire time.

"Jordan will be here when she feels like and Oliver should be around shortly. I dumped a bucket of cold water on him before I left the house, so I know he's awake." He didn't even crack a smile, which gave me less hope he had any sense of humor.

It was disappointing, mostly because I still found myself attracted to him; even the tick in his square jaw caught my attention. Though, it was likely only because of the Meraki bond. I just needed to do my best to ignore it until we had a chance to talk about our predicament like adults, which didn't seem like it would be anytime soon.

For the next hour, I worked my ass off trying to access my magic until I couldn't stand anymore and asked for a break, which was denied.

"You can rest as soon as you're able to show me your magic," Ryland retorted after my complaints.

"I'm doing everything exactly how you demanded. Maybe you just have no idea what *you're* doing, and I need a different trainer."

"Listen, Princess, I know exactly what I'm doing, and I'm trying my best to believe the Fates weren't wrong about all this, which is the only reason I'm still standing here. So, get it together and show me you're more than a pampered heir to a throne that no longer exists."

My teeth ground together at how badly I wanted to take his words and shove them so far down his throat he was crapping them out for a month. Instead, I took his challenge and decided to show him the only way I knew how to connect with my magic.

Walking away from him, I headed for the drinking fountain at the wall.

"Don't walk away when we're in the middle of training. Giving up isn't an option," he yelled, but I ignored him as I took a long pull of cold liquid.

Thankfully, my assumption was right that the water would be drawn directly from the falls, because I could feel the effects as soon as I drank it. The same as when I had taken a shower the night before and when I touched the fountain in order to port to the training field.

Something *was* broken within me, but I wouldn't let it beat me. I'd take whatever broken pieces I could and use them to build something great, because that was what strong women did, and I refused to be weak.

When I had inhaled as much water as I could without fear of throwing it up, I turned back to Ryland. His normally tanned face was beet red while his hands fisted at his sides.

Grinning, I thoroughly enjoyed pushing his buttons and I was going to see just how far he'd let me before he retaliated. Recalling the books that I'd read the night before, I drew on the power I'd gathered from drinking the water and called it toward my hand. As I felt the magic build, I tucked my hands behind my back and waited to see if Ryland would do anything about my insubordination.

Just when he was about to open his mouth, I shook my head. "I'd choose those words very carefully."

"Why? What could *you* possibly do to me?" He glared, and I decided it was time to show him.

While pulling my hand forward, I focused on Ryland's face as it transformed from confused, to shocked, ending with fury as the magic I'd balled into an orb within my hand slammed into his shoulder.

I'd read that fae magic was all about intention and didn't need spells like witch magic, just power and thoughts. So, when I began creating the orb, I thought about how I wanted it to sting but must have put a little too much weight into that particular word.

"What the hell did you do to me?" Ryland began pounding his fist against his shoulder, then ripped his shirt off.

When I stepped closer, I realized there were tiny red dots all over where my orb had hit. Apparently, magic was very literal, and it appeared as if Ryland had been stung by a hundred bees. Regret filtered through me, but I wasn't sure how to fix what I'd done.

The door flew open before Ryland could retaliate and in came Oliver, followed by my feathered friend. I ran toward the middle of the gym and lifted my arm for Stryx to land on. When he did, I pulled him close before growling in his ear.

"Took you long enough to show."

He snapped his beak at me. "Not now. Let's go see what you did to Ryland, so I can make you fix it."

My face twisted. "Before you see what I did, just know it wasn't what I was going for. You have no idea what's been happening."

His wing came up and pressed against my head. "Actually, I have a pretty good idea. Your thoughts are still very loud."

Ugh. I wondered if I was ever going to get used to having him in my head all day, every day.

"No, you're not, but you'll get over it when I turn you into a magic fighting machine," he said, replying to my unspoken thoughts. "Now, take me to Ryland."

Bossy freaking owl.

Oliver was laughing so hard, I decided it was good for us to go back anyway. It definitely had nothing to do with the beady owl eyes glaring at me until I began moving. When we got closer, I could hear the labored breathing of Ryland between the hiccups coming from Oliver and actually got a little worried I'd done some serious damage.

"That was a low blow hitting me with bee stings. Did Jordan tell you I was mildly allergic?" he tried to snap at me, but his mouth was already starting to swell, and the words were hardly understandable.

Before I could answer, Stryx landed on my shoulder and butted in. "You're going to fix this, Kaliah. Your magic, your responsibility."

"Well, I'd love to say I could right this very moment, but I need to get another drink before I attempt it."

His head swiveled. "Not with me here. Search within you and you'll find your power is just a bit stronger with me around."

My brow pinched as I turned to face him. "Another thing you failed to tell me?"

"Possibly. Now focus before Ryland goes into anaphylactic shock."

Shaking my head, I closed my eyes and did as Stryx asked, focusing on healing magic instead of harmful. When the well of power flowed through me stronger than ever before, I knew my little owl had quite a bit of explaining to do.

I walked closer to Ryland and pressed my palm into his shoulder, but immediately yanked it back when my hand was burned.

"You have to push through the pain. These are the consequences of using magic against someone you care about."

I snorted. I did *not* care about Ryland, but that was an argument for later.

Pressing my hand back against his shoulder, I realized Ryland's eyes were rolling around instead of staying focused, which explained his lack of smartass replies, but also urged me along.

Maybe books weren't going to be the best way to learn more about how to be a better me…

Once the stinging dulled, I removed my hand and Oliver helped Ryland lay on the floor while he recovered. "I'd maybe recommend calling it a day and coming back tomorrow. You don't want to be here when he comes to," Oliver grimaced.

"Yeah, alright. I'm pretty sure Stryx has some explaining to do anyway. At least tell him I'm sorry. I really didn't mean to hurt him."

He nodded. "I know. Don't worry, he'll get over it."

Turning away, I stayed silent with Stryx still on my shoulder. We made it all the way to the door with one foot already outside when I heard Ryland's roar. "Where is *she*?"

"Keep going, Kaliah. You can deal with him tomorrow," Stryx said as I let the door close behind me and ported home.

Porting came so naturally, I hadn't even realized I'd done it until we were standing at the guest house door.

"Talk. Now," I demanded, because I was over being confused and it was going to end immediately.

CHAPTER 11

Stryx didn't say a word until we were inside, and he made me confirm that Jordan wasn't there, either. Why that mattered, I had no idea, but I didn't really care as long as he started to spill whatever it was that he knew.

Even though it had only been three days since I arrived in Arvayta, I felt like I'd been a part of this place for the last year through my dreams. Waiting any longer to figure out what role I played in all that was happening was not an option.

Stryx stood on the arm of the couch, his wise eyes staring at me for much longer than necessary before he spoke. "So, you know Alaryk is the dark fae who feels he deserves retribution for his family that died because of the decision your grandfather made which ended up killing all of the pure fae."

"Yep. Got all that down. Tell me something I don't already know," I replied.

His feathers bristled, but he continued. "When the Fates predicted what would come of you and your magic, they not only said what might go wrong, but they also talked about what could go right. There is a reason I spent an entire year preparing you as best I could, Kaliah, and it's time you know why."

Thank the freaking Fates.

"As you know, we're bonded, but it's not just because your blood comes from mostly fae. When the bonded animals were created for the fae, it was only the purest and strongest who received the gift of a bond. You've already been told that the Fates only step in when the scales of good and bad tip too far in the wrong direction. Well, they are worried Alaryk is stronger than any of us are prepared for on our own."

"What do you mean? Stronger how?" I asked.

"I'm not sure. The Fates have to be careful with what they disclose. I don't have much information other than the bonded animals will be coming back, and even Arvaytans with minimal fae blood in them could be assigned one. The Fates are giving us a huge advantage here."

"So, we know Alaryk is stronger than the rest of us, but the Fates' solution to that is to gift the guardians with bonded animals. What else?" While all of that sounded good, it still didn't tell me how we moved forward or how we were supposed to defeat the dark fae.

"Well, for one, you have to be the one to kill Alaryk."

My face paled. There was no possibility of me being able to *murder* someone. There had to be another way.

"Just breathe before you pass out," Stryx huffed, clearly irritated with my more human side.

"I can't do that," I said when my heart slowed.

"You can and you will, Kaliah. I need you to focus on what it means if you don't. Good people will die if Alaryk continues to live. His dark magic will seep into you, and what you think so horrid at the moment will become a common act, because if Alaryk doesn't die, he will make you just like him."

"So, you're saying that if I don't commit murder, then I'll become a murderer?" Great options. Super freaking great.

"I know it's not ideal, but yes, those are your choices."

"Not ideal. Right." I snorted. "Why me? Why not someone who has been doing this for a few decades like Ryland?" If he was good enough to be my trainer, then he should be good enough to off the dark fae.

"Ryland will have his role in assisting you, but he cannot wield the weapon required to do the job."

"What's his role then?" I asked.

"Well, as you've already found out, Ryland is your Meraki. He is almost as important to you as I am. The stronger your bond grows, the stronger you will become. He will train you and he will assist in making you the best fae you're capable of becoming."

Laughter burst from deep within me. This whole situation was a hot mess. Sure, the bond with Stryx was easy. We'd been building up to that for months, but if the fate of the worlds depended on me and Ryland accepting the predestined bull crap that had been forced upon us, well, good luck. That was all I could say.

"We don't need luck, Kaliah. I understand that you and Ryland haven't gotten off to the best of starts, but it will get better," Stryx said, once again reading my thoughts.

"How come I don't hear anything you think?" I asked, trying to change the subject.

"Because you haven't accessed your full magic yet. Once you're capable of doing so, there is a way to block them. If you're good, I just may teach you how to do so." The little fluffy monster winked at me and I snarled back.

"What now? I play nice with Ryland and hope he doesn't want to pummel me after I almost accidentally killed him?"

"Was it really an accident, though?"

My jaw dropped. "Of course it was. I only meant for it to sting, as in pain level, not actually sting him like a bee."

"Regardless, you need to apologize and mean it, so everyone

can move forward. The two of you need to find a way to get along or you'll doom us all."

My eyes glared at him. "You're a jerk, you know that?"

"No, I'm not. I'm the only one who will be brutally honest with you. I won't sugarcoat anything, especially when it comes to the lives of others. I know you feel like I've given you an impossible task, but I've been watching over you your whole life, and I know you can do this, Kaliah."

That was the creepiest, yet nicest thing anyone had ever said to me. I was going to do my best to believe it, but the thought of killing anyone, even someone evil, was still off-putting to me. I wasn't sure how I was going to conquer that particular task, but I'd deal with it when the time came.

For the time being, I'd focus on training like Stryx was saying and hope the rest would just come to me when I needed it. Assuming it would be a him-or-me situation, maybe it wouldn't be as hard as I was thinking to end his life if it meant saving myself and thousands of others.

"Tomorrow, I'll be back, and we'll try to split your training up more, so not all of it involves so much one-on-one with Ryland. I'll be helping, and Jordan is capable on her own as well. You're obviously not mentally prepared to deal with him yet, but you will be soon. For the rest of the day, I want you to work with Jordan on porting and bringing your magic out. I'll be staying in Arvayta, so it should keep your magic flowing enough for those simple tasks."

"What happens if you need to leave? I'm just helpless again? Why am I unable to do even the simplest things without making contact with the water or having you near?" I rapid-fired the questions at him, because I didn't have a chance in hell of surviving if I had to depend on someone else being around every time I needed to use magic to protect myself.

"I placed a block on your magic. It would have torn your human body to shreds if I didn't. The water gives even the youngest of Arvaytans the ability to use simple magic. As soon as you've gotten a better hold on the power, I'll release the block, but until then, the training wheels stay on."

Frustrated, I glared at him, but he didn't seem the least bit fazed. I wasn't a child, but I was certainly being treated like one.

Jordan burst into the house, breaking the tension. "Girl, what did you do to Ryland? He broke Oliver's nose and gave him two black eyes by the time they were done training."

Sigh. Poor Oliver. I'd definitely have to apologize to him. "I didn't *mean* to do anything. I'll say sorry to them both when I see them again."

Then, Jordan noticed Stryx in the room and her eyes widened. "Oh, I didn't mean to interrupt. Should I come back?"

"Not necessary. I was just leaving, actually. Jordan, will you take Kaliah out to practice porting and basic orb skills?" Stryx asked.

"Uh, yeah. I can definitely do that." Jordan was starstruck, and I was doing my best not to laugh.

The door was still open from when Jordan had come home, so Stryx nodded to me, then took off. Once he was gone, I let the laughter out. "What is up with you?"

"Do you not understand *who* he is?" she gaped.

"Uh, he's an owl who is old, smart, and powerful," I replied with a shrug.

Her eyes rolled. "He's also kind of famous in our world. He was there in the Dark War. He was the bonded animal to Queen Taliah. Most importantly, he's not just *any* bonded animal, he's the leader of them all."

Huh, Stryx was keeping more secrets than I thought, but I also understood. He probably knew I would have been more closed-off to him if I had known all of that. Instead, he'd come to me as a friend with a smartass attitude who didn't take no for an answer. He was exactly what I needed when I needed it.

"Well, I don't think he wants to be treated special, so feel free to be your psycho self when you're around him like you are with me. He's in my head twenty-four-seven, so he already knows you."

She grinned. "True. Let's go do as he suggested. Have you been able to port on your own yet?"

I nodded. "Twice."

"Good, head outside and we'll make it a third."

"Why do we have to go outside?" I asked.

"Because you can't port in or out of any building. That and not leaving worlds are the only two restrictions to the perk," Jordan answered.

That wasn't actually a bad thing. At least nobody could just appear in my bedroom if they wanted.

We went outside and Jordan disappeared right after telling me she'd meet me by the fountain. Not worried at all, I pictured the area and disappeared. Though it definitely took more effort than it had when Stryx was with me, it wasn't nearly as difficult as when I'd tried to do so that morning.

When I arrived, Jordan was watching some kids play in the street with some scooter-bicycle hybrids. One of the boys was on the smaller side and kept my attention as he wobbled a lot more than the others. The poor kid, who was maybe five or six, could barely even see over the handlebars.

My skin began to tingle, and I lost sight of the boy for a few seconds while my attention was diverted. At a quick glance, I saw Ryland walking down the side of the street, also paying close attention to the kids with a soft smile on his face.

Suddenly, there was a crash followed by the sound of crying. My eyes frantically searched for the boy I'd been watching, but by the time I found him, Ryland was already standing over him and untangling his small body from the boxes he'd crashed into.

"See, he's not so bad," Jordan whispered from next to me, but I ignored her as I continued to watch.

Ryland wiped the boy's tears and whispered something to

him that had the child grinning from ear to ear. Ryland then helped him back onto the scooter-bicycle before showing him what I assumed were a few tips on how to maneuver through the cobbled streets.

When the boy pushed away, Ryland stood, and his gaze landed on me. Even though he had caught me staring, I didn't look away. I couldn't even if I tried. He held me captive, and I seemed to be doing the same thing to him.

Maybe there was a bit of hope for us after all. Even if I didn't find my happily-ever-after with Ryland, if we could join forces long enough to save my life and that of others, then it would have to be enough. Or so I kept telling myself.

CHAPTER 12

Surprise came over me when I realized Ryland wasn't going to make attempts at payback for almost killing him once he saw me. It shocked the hell out of me, considering how angry he'd been when I'd left him in the training center. Instead, he did something much worse.

Once our eye contact had been broken, he'd turned away and kept walking, completely ignoring me. I wasn't sure what to think about it or how I felt about his actions. Sure, he had infuriated me before, but we were supposed to be partners.

After speaking with Stryx, I'd mistakenly let my heart consider the idea of having a real soulmate, but had I already ruined the chance? Jordan knew more, and she needed to tell me something, so that I would know how to proceed. I needed to quickly nip whatever budding feelings I was experiencing if it was an utter waste of time.

Maybe he already had a girlfriend and I was basically ruining his life. I'd heard Jordan mention something about an old boyfriend she had to let go, so maybe something similar was happening with Ryland.

Before I could begin questioning her in the middle of town, Jordan zapped us to the back side of the training center. "Are you okay?" she asked.

"Yeah, why?"

"Well, your face went through a horde of emotions back there, and I wasn't sure whether you were going to start crying or yelling when Ryland walked in the other direction."

I laughed. "So, before I could make a scene, you ported us here instead?"

"Yep. So, spill it." She nudged my shoulder before walking toward a medicine ball and tossing it at me.

With a grunt, I caught it and responded, "Actually, I think it's you who needs to spill it. Why was Ryland so nice to me when I first arrived, then he became so angry?"

She grimaced and readied herself to catch the ball. "He doesn't hate you. He's confused by you."

Throwing the ball as hard as I could, I took my frustrations out with my force. "I know he's one of your best friends, and I hate putting you in the middle, but I need to understand. You have to give me something."

Jordan dropped the ball and sat on it. "I don't need you throwing heavy items at me when we have this conversation. Come over here and have a seat."

Thank the Fates, she was actually going to give me something good. Sitting on the ground, I leaned back and rested on my hands while I waited for her to continue.

"Ryland is a bit older than me, so when I started training, he was already established as a guardian, but he took me under his wing when he saw what a fighter I was. Oliver and I began training at the same time, and the three of us have been pretty much inseparable since we became a team. As I got to know Ryland, I also got to know his Meraki."

My mouth opened and closed, but no words came out. Had I been stupid to think that each person only had one soulmate?

Was I expected to *share* him if we found a way to work things out? No freaking way.

Jordan held her hand up. "I know what you're thinking, and we're all just as shocked as you are. It's why I left with him when you woke up in the water instead of staying with you like I planned. I knew he'd have no idea, and he'd need someone to break the news."

"How did you know so fast?" I asked, because I had no freaking clue until I'd overheard them talking.

"His eyes. Before he saw you, his eyes were a light brown color, and now they're identical to yours. It's a Meraki trait. Being as though we come from a monarchy, the male counterpart always changes to match his female mate. But that's not as important as what you want to know and what you need to understand."

My breath held as I waited for what she said next, which was not at all what I expected.

"Ryland was bonded with another woman named Sara. They'd met during guardian training and were together for nearly twenty years before she died on a mission in one of the darker sections of the Otherworld. It took nearly a decade before Oliver and I got our friend back, but Ryland finally came around and accepted he would be alone for the rest of his life.

"He threw himself into work, became an even better guardian, and received a promotion as direct guard to your parents. It wasn't until they knew you were coming that he ever once left their side. When they left for Earth and he wasn't able to go with, Ryland lost his purpose, but Oliver and I kept him busy with other things like fighting dragons."

"And then you left him as well to protect me. I bet he wasn't happy about that one," I said.

"Not one bit. He had wanted to go himself and thought there was no reason for you to need a girl best friend, but now we understand, he couldn't meet you until you were here," Jordan replied.

Cheese and rice. I understood why he was being a jerk, but at the same time, I had no clue how Ryland was feeling. Sure, I'd dated back on Earth. I'd been with a guy for a couple years in high school, but he'd gone off to college in the Midwest and we'd called things off. I never thought of the guy as my soulmate, so it was completely different.

"You can't tell him, Kali. I mean it. I've been put in an impossible situation with the two of you, because I love you both, but I also can't sit by and watch both of you ruin what could be the greatest opportunity in your life. While finding your Meraki isn't super rare, it doesn't happen for everyone, and it should be cherished, never neglected. By doing so, it could be broken and never happen again."

The longing in her voice was evident, and I hated that she'd been without hers for so long.

"Thank you for telling me. I promise I won't say anything to Ryland, and I will try to be more understanding of his actions. I imagine he's pretty pissed at the Fates for doing this to us, and I can't really say I blame him."

The day had been full of revelations, and I was feeling a whole lot better about my place within Arvayta. I had a plan forming in my head that I hoped Stryx agreed with or could use alongside whatever he was cooking up.

I wasn't ready to die, and I sure the hell didn't want to go dark like the Fates predicted, so now that I knew more about myself and what to expect from those around me, I felt ready to continue training.

"Enough with the heavy, and no more physical exercises. I want to learn how to control my magic. Stryx said we needed to work on orbs. Tell me more about them," I suggested.

Jordan grinned before standing and reaching a hand out to me. "I'm more than happy to do so. But only for you, Chuck."

I had a very strong feeling I'd live to regret this moment, but it didn't stop me from placing my hand in hers and following her further out into the fields.

Jordan stood about twenty feet away from me, and we were facing each other. "Okay, I want you to create an orb. I know you read a bunch of the books or at least flipped through them, so I'm assuming you know how to do that much already."

Blushing, I nodded. "I used one on Ryland earlier. It sort of backfired, and Oliver paid the price for it."

"Ah, that makes much more sense, and I really wish I could have been there to see it, but a girl needs her beauty sleep. Oh, well. I'm sure there will be many more opportunities to see you do something completely wrong that causes someone else pain while bringing me sheer joy."

I scowled at her, but she ignored me while creating her own ball of magic. It was perfectly symmetrical and a pale orange color. As she started tossing it between her hands, I focused on my inner well of power and sought out my own orb.

Just like when I was porting previously, gathering the magic and bringing it forward wasn't easy or natural, but it was doable. Pulling it toward my hand, I watched in fascination as a lavender orb shimmered into appearance within my palm.

Jordan cheered for me. "Good job. Now, what were you thinking about when you created it?"

"Nothing except for making it appear. This whole intention thing freaks me out, especially since I almost killed Ryland earlier. I wanted the orb to sting a little and it ended up acting just like a bee sting instead."

"Seriously pissed I wasn't there. Anyway, I know it seems hard, but you'll get the hang of it. I won't let you fail." As soon as the words left her mouth, I knew they were true.

Jordan was the best friend I could have ever asked for, and I trusted her to get me through whatever obstacles lay ahead.

We spent the next two hours creating magical orbs with different intentions and I learned that purple was my magical color as orange was Jordan's, which made sense since she had an affinity for fire like I did for water.

Anything I created would always have a tint of purple to it, but the darker it was, the more powerful it would be. When I was finally able to make an orb that was nearing a midnight-black color, Jordan finally called our session a success.

"Let's go get some gelato and head home," she suggested.

"Dessert before dinner? I will never say no to that, especially when I skipped lunch." We'd been so busy that I hadn't even realized it was nearing four in the afternoon, but it had been a good day. A day that made me feel a hell of a lot better about being thrown into this insane world. I had thought I was prepared for it, but not even close.

When we arrived back at the house, Ryland was just leaving, and I froze in place as soon as I appeared in the yard.

Jordan nudged me, then whispered, "You have to act the same. He can't know I told you."

That was going to be harder than I realized, because I immediately felt sympathy for him instead of irritation.

He nodded to Jordan. "Did you finish her training for the day?"

"Yep. She's proficient in orb creation now. What time are we beginning tomorrow?" she asked.

"Good. Let's see if she can keep from almost killing anyone again. Let's start tomorrow around seven. There's no reason to be there before sunrise."

I knew that last bit was a stab at me and tried not to let it piss me off, but I failed. "Can the two of you stop speaking as if I'm not standing right here?" I snapped.

Ryland glanced me over, then turned back to Jordan. "Don't be late."

Trying to be the bigger person, I held my tongue as he disappeared. I really wanted the animosity between us to go away. Hopefully tomorrow would be a better day.

CHAPTER 13

The following day was utter hell. Jordan was no longer my best friend. Stryx was going to be de-feathered then cooked for dinner, and Ryland... He was going to be gutted just before I tossed him over a cliff. The only person I didn't personally want to kill was Oliver, but it was still early, so anything was possible.

"Kali, quit being afraid of the magic. You're only hindering yourself and making me late for lunch," Jordan complained.

Yeah, easy for her to say. She hadn't been knocked on her ass like I had more times than I cared to admit and laughed at when I blew up one of the boulders instead of just chipping it with the least amount of power.

Apparently, before I could move on, I had to learn control of the storm raging within me, but when Stryx lifted the block even a quarter of the way, I screwed up every time. I'd had all this confidence going into the morning. I was going to do better and prove I was capable of handling things, but that strength was slowly ripped away as I continued to fail at what was asked of me.

On top of not being able to control the endless well inside me, everything hurt. The magic burned my insides and made it hard to breathe when I tried to wield any sort of control over it. Part of me wondered if I wasn't already dark and these were the consequences of it. Maybe no matter what we did or how they tried to prepare me, the ending for me wasn't going to be all sunshine and roses.

Stryx flew into the back of my head and smacked me with his wing before landing on the table beside me. "Kaliah Grace, I don't want to hear another word about going dark. This is all in your head, and you need to move past your fears. I will not let anything happen to you. Not during training or when we go to the Otherworld. You need to believe you're safe; otherwise, this will be a waste of time for all of us."

"You don't understand. I can't control it!" I screamed in his face as my frustration hit a new high.

"Yes, you can. You are more than you believe, and I'm going to prove it. It's time to sink or swim, young one."

With those final words, Stryx snapped his beak and began to flap his wings, but instead of flying away, he hovered above the table while wind slapped me in the face.

Glancing back at the others, they all stared wide-eyed, likely just as surprised as me at Stryx's actions. Though, none of them intervened. Then, the burning sensation within me turned into a scorching one, and panic raced through me more than ever before.

"Stryx, you have to stop. Whatever you're doing isn't working!" I yelled above the roaring of the wind coming from him.

He ignored me, even as I fell to the ground and a glow began to surround my body so bright that I couldn't even tell what color it was. Suddenly, I realized this was exactly how it felt when I'd "died" before being brought to Arvayta.

Stryx was trying to kill me for real this time.

Yelling could be heard through the roaring, but I couldn't tell where it was coming from as I fought to keep consciousness and not die again. I wasn't sure how many times I could do that and actually come back. Once seemed like more than enough.

The magic within me raged until it found a way out through different exits. Some left my hands like I was used to, then some of the power seemed to go straight through my heart like an electrical current that made me start convulsing on the ground.

Lastly, when I tried screaming through the agony, magic poured out of my mouth and went who knew where. My only hope was I hadn't hurt anyone other than Stryx.

Hands grasped at me as I flailed around, unable to control any aspect of my body. A loud snarl sounded near my ear, and I was raised off the ground. When I dared to open my eyes, I still couldn't see anything other than bright lights, as if I was staring directly into the sun, so I had no idea how someone was able to carry me, but whatever they were doing was working.

The power began to calm within me, but my energy was completely gone by the time the pain began to dissipate. So, even though I could probably see again, opening my eyes seemed like an impossible feat.

"It's going to be okay, Kali. Just hang on," Ryland's voice whispered in my ear, and a wave of excitement ran through me.

Why was he, of all people, helping me? Wouldn't life be easier for him if I was dead, considering how angry he'd been at our bond? I would have thought for sure he'd have been sitting back enjoying my torture. But at the same time, I couldn't deny the joy that coursed through me knowing he'd come to my rescue.

Stupid soulmate bond was screwing with my emotions.

Before I could question much more, I heard the splashing of water. As soon as the cool liquid touched my skin, a sizzling sensation traveled along my body, and I was finally able to open my eyes. When I did, I was nose-to-nose with Ryland, whose concerned face didn't once waver from mine.

"Are you okay?" he asked, voice gruff and low as he fully submerged my body into the water except my head.

Nodding, I did an internal check. Nothing was burning any longer, except for the parts of my body that were currently being cradled against Ryland, which I was choosing to ignore.

He smirked. "Can you talk?"

"Yep. I can probably stand, too, if you set me down," I replied, trying to keep any feeling from my voice.

"Stryx almost blew you up. I wasn't sure what to do except get you to the falls before things got worse," he said as he loosened his hold on me.

When he let go of my legs, the moving water shoved me down and my body ended up flush against his. "I'm sorry," I stammered, trying to push away from him, but the water seemed to be fighting against me.

His face creased in confusion. "It seems we're literally being pressed together. Are you doing this?" he snapped, letting anger replace the confusion.

"Of course I'm not. You're the one who brought me here. Maybe I should be asking you the same thing," I retorted.

He huffed. "Listen, Kali. I'm sure you're nice, but someone made a mistake. You're not my soulmate. Don't make this any harder than it already is."

I heard his words and I understood them, but I also felt his fingertips tracing circles around my wrist in the water and wondered if he should be telling *himself* we weren't soulmates instead of me.

"Ryland, all I care about right now is keeping myself alive and making sure other people don't die because I'm alive. And maybe if you're so against the Fates saddling you to me, then you shouldn't touch me like you can't stand the thought of letting go. The water isn't doing *that*."

His eyes widened as he glanced at his fingers around my wrist. "I didn't mean…"

"Yeah, I know. Now get us out of here."

The current in the pool beneath the falls was only around us, and I knew without a doubt that something bigger than me was interfering in whatever was happening, but there had to be some way around it. I couldn't stay stuck to Ryland in the water all day.

The current pushed us closer together until my face pressed into his chest and I could hear the rapid thumping of his heart against my ear. I fit perfectly against him while his palms lay flat against my hips. If he wasn't being so stubborn about the whole thing, I'd probably attempt to make a move on him, but I wasn't pathetic and didn't need him if he didn't want me.

Correction, I didn't need him to *like* me. I did apparently need him to help me get out of the mess I'd found myself in. Then, we could never speak again if that's what made him happy.

The tearing pain in my chest said it wasn't going to be so easy to walk away from my soulmate, even if he was a jerk, but others had said it was possible. So, I'd survive it and do my best not to let myself be completely shattered by a stranger in the process.

With those thoughts, I'd officially decided that magic sucked.

"What are you two doing?" Jordan screeched from above us as she came racing toward the water with Stryx and an older lady right behind her.

Focusing on the newcomer I wasn't familiar with, I watched in fascination as she moved her hands in circular motions and then thrust them at Ryland and me. When the magic came closer, instead of hitting us, it dove into the water and the pressure keeping us locked together finally gave.

Ryland scrambled away first, and I followed immediately after. When I was back on the grass, Stryx landed on my shoulder. "Dry yourself off."

Peeking over at Ryland, I realized he was completely dry; the only evidence we'd taken a swim was the disheveled appearance of his hair.

Not wanting to be shown up, I connected with my inner fae, but ended up on my ass instead as Stryx flew away to avoid being crunched on the ground underneath me.

Jordan snickered, but the newcomer shushed her. "Kaliah, my name is Lorelle. Let me help you." She reached a hand to me, which I gladly took and stood up. "As you've learned, your power is too strong for your body, and you're unable to handle the full amount gifted to you. In time, this will not be the case, but I have something to help you in the interim."

She backed away before reaching into a bag that was draped over her shoulder. When her hand came back out, it was holding a crown. A real freaking crown with purple gems made from something very shiny and silver—white gold, chrome, platinum? I had no idea, but there was no way I was wearing it. Nothing screamed "look at me!" more than a crown, and I had zero desire to have that kind of attention on me.

"Don't look at the crown like that. It's not going to bite you," Lorelle chastised.

"But do I *have* to wear that thing? Or can I just keep it in my pocket or something?" I asked.

She shoved the crown at me. "You should be proud of your heritage, not ashamed of it. This crown will help you control your erratic magic, and possibly save your life. As soon as you accept who you are, the easier this will be for everyone."

Then, the crazy old lady disappeared.

"Who the hell was she?" I asked, fidgeting with the crown that warmed in my hands.

Stryx landed back on my shoulder. "That's Lorelle. She's the second most powerful person currently in Arvayta."

"Who's the first?" I asked.

His beak snapped at me as if I should have known the answer already. "Me. Now, put the crown on and get dry, then let's break for the afternoon before coming back this evening."

Grinding my teeth, I reluctantly put on the crown and heard

Jordan snickering to Ryland, who I assumed was waiting to call me Princess again, but surprisingly, kept all opinions to himself.

When the crown was placed on my tangled mess of hair, it was almost as if it melded to me. I shook my head, but it didn't budge. Then, I tapped into my abilities and was thankful when I stayed upright the second time around.

As my magic spread throughout my body, I thought about what I wanted it to do. Within a few seconds, I was completely dry, including my hair, which was softer and fuller than it had ever been. Euphoria filled me. Sure, I didn't want to look like or be a princess, but having control over the power within me filled me with a completely different kind of joy I'd yet to experience.

Then, I remembered something Lorelle had said. "What did she mean about me accepting who I am? Does this have something to do with the Arelia thing Jordan mentioned before?"

Stryx narrowed his eyes at her, and she shrugged. "Hey, I was just guessing. If you didn't want her to know, then you should have let the rest of us know."

"It is what it is. Not that it makes any difference, but yes, you are the next Arelia. Your grandmother was the last one, and it appears you've inherited more than just her eyes," Stryx answered.

"It sounds like it should be a big deal if there hasn't been one alive in a couple of centuries," I said, hoping he would expand.

Stryx flew to me, and I held out my hand for him. "Listen, Kaliah. You need to focus on one thing at a time right now. If you try to take on too much, it will only hinder your growth. Being an Arelia doesn't change anything about what we're doing, but I promise when the time comes, I will make sure you know more."

My mind wanted to argue with him, but my heart was at peace with the answer. I trusted Stryx with my life, and he was right. There were a lot of other things going on, and I was okay with circling back to the Arelia subject later.

"Now, if that's all, you two port home and I'll find you later.

We'll work on funneling your abilities through the crown now that Lorelle has provided it. Once you get a real handle on your magic, we'll take a trip to the Otherworld."

"Is that wise?" Ryland questioned.

"We have to show Alaryk we're not afraid, and our allies need to know Kali is capable of doing what needs to be done or they won't stand behind us. It's the only option we have," Stryx answered.

Once again, the pressure was on, but just maybe with this crown and access to my magic, there was a chance I wouldn't fail at everything that was asked of me.

I wasn't ready to give up, even if I was beginning to realize I was in over my head.

CHAPTER 14

A week later, the crown had become almost a permanent part of my body and had changed me in more ways than one.

My skin was brighter and firmer, my eyes even more vibrant than before, and my hair was now rocking some interesting blonde highlights that appeared purple whenever I had the crown on. Though, the most obvious change to me was the new points at the tips of my ears. They weren't sharp, but there was a definitive alteration that had left me in freak-out mode for a solid forty-eight hours.

There was no denying what I was any longer. I was fae.

Along with the physical changes came the mental and magical ones. I was no expert, by any means, but my affinity for water had my skin constantly feeling like I had goosebumps no matter where I went. Water was everywhere, and until I had a real handle on everything, Stryx said I would be on constant overload with my senses, but the crown would keep it from being completely overwhelming.

Unfortunately, he was right.

The only time I took the crown off was when I slept and only because Stryx sealed me in my room. As mad as I wanted to be at him for doing so, he only started locking me in when I ended up accidentally calling water to me in my sleep from the fountain on my parents' porch and flooded the guest house.

Later that afternoon, I had my last test before we headed to the Otherworld, which was scheduled for the following day. I was nervous, but also eager. While the books hadn't done crap to help me understand my erratic powers, they were useful in understanding the other races and history.

"You know, I'm going to have to stop calling you Chuck if you begin reading more than you train. It's ruining your cred," Jordan teased as she plopped down next to me on the couch, making me lose my place. "The crown isn't helping much, either."

Glaring at her, I reached a hand up to touch the titanium metal, but in my attempt to look cool, I ended up pricking my finger on one of the sharp points. There were six of them, apparently one for every main race within our two worlds, past and current: Fae, Arvaytans, Shifters, Witches, Vampires, and Demons.

When demons were mentioned, I instantly pictured grotesque beings with leathery skin and horns, but apparently most of them were just descendants from demons and kept a human form like succubus, incubus, djinn, and more I really didn't care to ever meet.

"Yeah, well, shove it. You might know more about your magic than me, but I could still kick your ass," I said as I dabbed my finger against my jeans.

"You think so? Tonight, after your final test, let's see just how true that statement is." She smirked, and something told me I was going to regret agreeing, but I did anyway.

"You're on."

"I need to run to town. Do you need anything?" she asked as she stood back up.

I waved my book at her. "I've got everything I need right here."

Her eyes rolled. "Get a life, nerd."

Ignoring her, I waited until the door shut to begin reading again. It was a section on past fae with water affinities, and I was mentally taking note of several things I wanted to try that evening. Maybe even against Jordan.

The door opened just a few minutes later, and I let out a sigh. "You ready for your ass-whooping now instead?" I said before looking up to see who was walking through.

Ryland raised a brow at me. "Bestie problems?"

His use of "bestie" had me snort-laughing. "Not exactly. What are you doing here?"

His feet shuffled side-to-side before he finally grabbed one of the two chairs at the table and brought it over to sit in front of me. He was visibly sweating, and I didn't think I'd ever seen him so nervous.

"Is everything okay? Did something happen to my parents?" He was still technically their assigned guardian, but they'd been so busy communicating with the higher-ups in the Otherworld, and he was so busy helping me train that Ryland hadn't spent much time with them.

"Sorry. Yes, your parents are fine. So is everyone else for that matter," he answered gruffly.

"Then, I'll ask again. What are you doing here?" I wasn't trying to be rude, but we weren't exactly friends. Even though we had formed a sort of truce we never talked about, any communication we'd had over the last week was strictly related to my training.

Irritation flashed on his face, but he managed to rein it in quickly before answering. "I wanted to speak with you privately if you were willing."

"About what?" I asked. I was definitely willing, because ever since the day he'd carried me to the falls, my body hummed whenever he was close. As much as I hated it, I also loved it, which made me hate it even more. My emotions were putting me through a vicious cycle I hoped would end sooner rather than later.

"Well, as awkward as it is, we need to speak about us and the bond."

Taking a deep breath, I sighed. "It's only awkward for you. I mean, does it bother me that you've shunned me and been a jerk a majority of the time? Of course. But I won't let it stop me from moving forward and doing what needs to be done."

He ignored me and began speaking again. "When we're young, our parents tell us about what it means to find a Meraki, how special it is and how it should be cherished for life. As a boy, I laughed at that stuff. As a teen, I did my best to stay away from new women, afraid my life would be forever changed in the worst ways.

"After a couple decades? Well, you start to look for that special bond, and when I did, I found it. Not with you, but with another. Someone who stole my breath away the moment I saw her and changed my world for the better when I needed it most after losing my parents and everything I ever owned in a house fire. Her name was Sara, and I loved her more than anything in all the worlds."

This was not at all going how I thought it would. I really wanted to interrupt him, but he seemed to be lost in his own story as he stared past me and out the window, so I let him continue.

"She was mine for only a few years, and then she was killed. I found her body, and it ruined me. Arvaytans live long lives, but yet, the one I was supposed to spend mine with was gone when I was only in my forties. If it hadn't been for Jordan and Oliver, I might have willingly gotten myself killed and searched for her in the afterlife.

"But as time went on, I focused on work and taking care of

your parents, because I owed them a great debt for taking me in after my own had died. I'd lost the three most important people in my world within a few short years of each other, and it was another decade before I was even close to the man I'd been before they were all taken from me."

Reaching out to him, I said, "I'm really sorry for your losses." His pain was real, and I felt it in my own soul. My eyes brimmed with tears as he spoke, and I wanted nothing more than to take the agony away from him.

Though, before I could grasp his hand, he pushed away. "I'm not here for your sympathy. I'm here so you understand. I've already loved another, and I can't do it again. I don't know how this happened, and honestly, a part of me wonders if there is a dark magic at work here, but I can't prove it. I lost my life book in the fire that took my parents, but if you're willing, I'd very much like to see yours."

Pain rocketed through me. He still didn't believe that we were meant to be soulmates. Him asking to see my book made me feel as if he thought I was lying to him in some way. As much as I wanted to snap back at him, I decided to just ignore the hurt and get it over with.

I'd actually forgotten about the book my parents had given me on my birthday and never even opened it. Apparently, I wasn't questioning things enough.

Getting up, I didn't say anything to him as I headed toward my room and opened the dresser drawers until I found what he wanted. As my hand closed around the book, a shock ran through my body and buckled my knees.

Catching myself on the dresser, I checked to make sure my crown was still in place, then slowly took a few steps until I was steady again.

When I made it back to the living room, Ryland was pacing, and I threw the book at him without thinking. It hit him in the chest and fell to the floor, and he actually looked appalled I'd done such a thing. So much for ignoring the hurt.

"You want to see it, go for it," I bit out before taking a seat back on the couch.

He reached down for it, but the book zapped him, too, only much harder. "I can't open it. Only you can."

Sighing, I reached toward the ground and grabbed it with ease that time. "What am I looking for?"

He hovered over me. "Find the index and see what page 'Family' is on. It should be there."

Family was only on page five, right after a section called "Before Arvayta". Apparently, my prior life wasn't really worth documenting since it had been spent on Earth. Turning the few pages, I stopped and shoved it toward Ryland. "Look at that. Meraki: Ryland Grey. Guess I'm not a voodoo witch playing tricks on you after all. Or wait, do you want me to prove the book is real, too?"

"Kali, that wasn't what I was implying."

Standing, I pushed him away. "Really? Listen, I get it. The situation sucks. Was I happy about being told who I was supposed to spend the rest of my life with? Absolutely not. Would I have grown to accept it? Most likely. But I won't be made to feel like a burden. If you don't want to be here, or don't want to help stop Alaryk, then don't. Stay away from me and let the bond break or whatever it does when it's not accepted. I don't care anymore."

His hand reached for my arm, and the moment our skin connected, power flared between us and drew us together instead of pushing us apart, just like it had when we'd been in the water.

Ryland froze as my body pressed against his, and I glared at him. This whole situation was screwing with me, and I didn't like it one damn bit.

My soul kept telling me I wanted Ryland, but my mind was screaming at me that I didn't need him. The two parts of me were going to ruin any progress I'd made if Ryland stuck around much longer.

"Please, just go. Leave me alone," I said softly.

He nodded, and the magnetic pull between us finally fizzled out. When he stepped away and closed the door behind him, I allowed myself a few minutes of tears falling freely for a love I was destined to have but never would.

If I ever saw the Fates, I'd be the first to tell them what a bunch of assholes they were.

When my allotted time was up, I headed for the shower, washed away the evidence of my heartbreak, and got ready for my final test.

It was time to shed away the hurt and do what needed to be done. Most importantly, I was going to do it proudly without a man by my side.

CHAPTER 15

RYLAND

Walking away from Kali was harder than I thought it would be. My plan had been to tell the truth, hopefully dissuade her, and it would be a mutual understanding, but the sympathy I'd seen on her face told me the bond was in fact very real. She had truly only wanted to heal the hurt within me.

Only, it had made me angry and I'd insulted her by forcing her to show me her book of life. I wasn't supposed to feel anything for her. My soulmate had already walked our worlds, and I wouldn't disrespect her memory by accepting another, not even when my heart had been telling me it was the right thing to do from the start.

Kali couldn't be mine, or so I kept telling myself. Except there it had been in black and white, proof that none of this was a ruse. I'd really been given two Merakis in one lifetime. None of it made sense. I was furious with the Fates for doing this and not sending a heads up.

I knew they couldn't interfere in most things, but with an

abnormality like this, it would have seemed pertinent for them to do so. Considering Kali was the key to everything we were trying to prevent, I would have assumed they wanted things between her and me to go more smoothly than they had been.

When her eyes met mine, they told me she wanted to give things a shot and accept what had been forced upon her. When I really looked at her and was honest with my feelings, I was overwhelmed with guilt. Guilt for wanting the same things but knowing my first love had been murdered. There was no way I could move on like she had never existed.

I just couldn't do it. I couldn't disrespect her memory by taking another Meraki. Instead, I'd been rude and distant and angry, all things Kali hadn't deserved or put up with. When she'd retaliated, a part of me had been grateful she wasn't taking my crap. She deserved better.

Porting to the only place that brought me peace as of late, I arrived at the falls and settled myself against the rocks at the edge of the grass. I closed my eyes, focused on the roar of the water, and felt the vibrations beneath me while the magic within the core of our world eased my pain.

My body warmed, and I felt a presence before me. Deciding I wasn't in the mood to speak with anyone, I kept my eyes closed and hoped they'd get the point and move along.

When a foot slammed into my shin, my eyes flew open. "What the hell?" was my immediate response, but I quickly realized my mistake and bowed before the man in front of me.

"I'm sorry, Fate. I didn't expect your company," I said reverently.

The Fates very rarely made an actual appearance in our worlds, so I'd either royally screwed up or whatever they had to tell me was so secret they couldn't even send it in writing the normal way.

"Stand, Ryland. You don't need to bow to me. We are all

equals here." His voice was angelic, and there was an ethereal glow around his russet skin and ocher hair.

When I stood, I averted my gaze, because I had no clue what I was supposed to do. Usually, only council members spoke with the Fates. I was way out of my comfort zone.

"Take a walk with me," Fate said.

None of them had names. We simply called the group of them Fates. Since they worked so cohesively, it was as if they were one person anyway.

"Are you sure that's a good idea? People will question your presence," I said.

"Nobody can see us. You're still sitting on the ground." Fate grinned as I whipped my head back.

Sure enough, it appeared as if I was sleeping next to the falls, completely at peace. What I wouldn't give to actually feel the way I was seeing myself.

Trusting Fate was right, I followed him down the dirt path. "Have I done something wrong?" I asked.

"Not at all, child. I'm here because we made a mistake and we need to remedy it."

I knew it. Kali wasn't really my Meraki. Thank the Fates I hadn't actually done anything to lead her on. She didn't deserve that.

"You have it wrong, I'm afraid," Fate said, interrupting my thoughts.

"What do you mean? What other mistake could you have made?"

"We kept something from you when we shouldn't have. We thought you would work through it on your own, but we underestimated your loyalty. For that, I am very sorry for the grief we've caused you."

I was very close to cussing out a Fate who could very well end me where I stood. I didn't understand anything he was saying.

"Sara was never your Meraki. I am deeply regretful we let you believe it for so long, but I need you to know we thought you'd figure it out yourself when you managed to move on with your life without completely losing yourself."

My head shook. No, they had it wrong. Sara had been mine in every way. She knew me soul deep, and our love…it couldn't have been fake.

"You're wrong. Sara was my perfect match in every possible way. Kali is the one who isn't my Meraki," I responded with so much hate, my hands shook at my sides.

Fate reached for me, but I backed away.

"Don't touch me. Don't take away my memories. Don't take Sara from me. I won't let you."

I knew the Fates were capable of pretty much anything, and I wouldn't bend to their will and accept Kali just because they deemed it necessary for whatever was going to happen with the dark fae. They needed to figure out another way.

"Ryland, I'm not trying to take anything away from you. I want to show you something we should have shown you long ago, but at the time, we didn't see it pertinent to interfere."

He snatched me before I could port away, and I was locked within his grasp. His fingers pressed against my temples as the world around me faded and images began to assault me.

Sara with another man. Them laughing and pointing at pictures of me with my friends. Sara kissing this other man and whispering into his ear.

Then, Sara the day I met her.

She was positively stunning in a white summer dress, sitting peacefully on a swing in the Otherworld all by herself. Her presence had called to me like a siren. A need to go to her had been so strong, I still vividly remembered it even all these years later.

The image skipped forward to our first kiss and the hug that followed it. Her face was scowled when my past self couldn't see it, as if she was repulsed.

My body flinched at the image, and I tried to jerk away, but Fate wouldn't let me.

The last thing I saw was so real, I felt like it was playing out right in front of me. Sara was back with the man in the first glimpse.

"He's fallen hard and fast. It was almost too easy. I've even won the admiration of the Queen and King. It's disgusting, really. Why couldn't we have postponed this until she was pregnant? Being nice is so draining," Sara complained.

The man cradled her face. "I know, love, but we need there to be no doubt of your loyalty to them. If you can't get me that child, I won't be able to get the vengeance my ancestors deserve. I was made for this, and you were made for me. Together, we will make them pay."

Sara pouted. "It could be years before that happens. You're going to let another man touch me for years*?"*

He snarled, then captured her mouth with his before Fate cut the image and released me from hell.

"We really are sorry. We spent months trying to avoid you meeting her, but there was only so much we could interfere without repercussion. Our hope was that you'd heal and move on when Kaliah came home, but Alaryk's spell had been stronger than we thought."

My eyes narrowed. "Alaryk? What does he have to do with this?"

"The fae you saw with Sara. That's Alaryk. He has been trying to get Kaliah since before she was even born. He believes they're meant to be together and he can convince her to become a dark fae. He was told from a young age that the only way to true power was to be stronger than anyone else. For some reason, he believes Kaliah will be the partner he needs to fulfill his greatest wants."

Fury like I'd never felt before flooded through me, and I lost all control of my abilities. Wind whipped around us as I let go of all restraints. I'd been played for a fool. As much as I didn't want to believe the Fate before me, I also knew they didn't meddle with things lightly.

My heart was shattering into a million pieces as I recalled my time with Sara, all the moments that I'd held on to for decades and cherished. My mind was still unwilling to believe they were all a lie, but my heart? My heart was conflicted beyond comprehension. Half of me filled with hatred at having been tricked, and the other was filled with grief for a love I had thought was true but wasn't.

How could everything with Sara have been false? I didn't understand it. I didn't want to accept it. Everything within me ached at not only the loss of the woman I once loved, but the memories that were now tarnished after what Fate had shown me.

I'd made so many mistakes, because I'd believed in what I had with her.

Kali. I'd pushed her away. Told her I didn't want her when everything about her drew me in. I'd lied to both of us and probably made her want to hate me, but she'd never be able to. The bond wouldn't allow her to, no matter how much I had denied it. Eventually, if I'd never given in, she would have moved on, but indifference is all she would have been capable of with someone else.

Sucking in a deep breath, I drew the air back within me. "What do I need to do?"

Fate smiled at me. "You need to make things right with Kaliah. The bond needs to be accepted by both of you before she faces Alaryk, or she will be highly susceptible to his attempts at luring her to his side."

If he'd been able to trick me into thinking Sara was my Meraki, I had no doubt he was more powerful than I'd given him credit for before.

"Why does he want her?" I asked between gritted teeth.

"Alaryk believes that a union between the last dark fae and

light fae royalty lines will bring about a reign of power like their ancestors had never been able to achieve. He is deceptive and will do anything to get what he wants. You need to understand just how dark he's gone, Ryland. He killed his own parents when he was only thirteen years old, and he's been on his own ever since. With every kill, he becomes more powerful, and he won't stop until there is nobody left that he considers a threat."

My jaw tensed as fury flooded through me. This was not good, and I needed to get back to Kali. I needed to apologize for being an idiot. Though, my mind and heart had loved another for so many years that even though my mind now believed she was my Meraki, I was still hesitant. To make my heart believe what I'd seen wasn't going to be as easy as it sounded.

"I can't stay any longer, but we need to know you understand now. That you believe what you've been told and seen," Fate said.

"It's not going to be something I can quickly fix, but yes, I believe what you've shown me today. We'll figure out a way to make this right," I replied.

He placed a hand on my shoulder. "Do you want me to make you forget she ever existed? We never want to take your free will away, but if it will help you move forward, I can take those memories away."

Did I want that? Would it really make things easier? No, it wouldn't. I wanted the rage that settled deep within me. I wanted the motivation it gave me to find Alaryk and make him pay for all he had done and all he planned to do.

"No, I'll be okay, so long as Kali forgives me for not accepting what I should have known as truth," I said.

Fate grinned. "You're going to have your hands full, but we have faith it will work out. Though, she has her own free will. We might have deemed the two of you the perfect match, but it's up to both of you to make it work. Meraki doesn't mean utopia. You still have to fight for the love you desire."

I'd already been fighting, but it had been for the wrong reasons. I'd been fighting the feelings Kali stirred within me, but not anymore. I'd show her I could be the man she deserved, and I'd never stop, even if or when she forgave me for pushing her away.

CHAPTER 16

Ryland didn't show for my final test, but I told myself a million times that it didn't bother me. I didn't need his approval of my progress. I didn't need him for anything, no matter what my soul thought. I was a badass, and I'd do what needed to be done with the people who actually gave a crap about me.

Stryx was perched on the edge of the table and hooted at me. "So, your final test isn't so much a test, but more like show and tell. I want you to demonstrate to me what you're comfortable doing and answer a few questions. There is nothing you can do that is wrong. We just need to simulate some scenarios to make sure it's safe for you to leave Arvayta."

Nodding in agreement, I kept telling myself I was ready enough for whatever little test they wanted me to complete. I wouldn't let any obstacles keep me down.

Jordan and Oliver were present and standing beside Stryx. Without notice, Jordan tossed a fire orb at me, but I doused it in water before it could burn my skin.

"Not today, Satan." I grinned and thought about how I had

called her Satan before I knew she had an affinity for fire. It was constant entertainment for me.

"I'm only warming up, and it's two against one, so I wish you luck, Chuck."

Just as she reminded me Oliver was capable of taking me down as well, a vine raced up my leg, but I pulled my training dagger from behind my back and cut it into bits before the creeper wrapped around my waist.

All without cutting myself, which was an improvement on its own. Normally, I was fairly good at drawing blood whenever I was using the blade Stryx said would help me prepare for the ones I needed to wield against Alaryk.

Jordan continued to distract me with flames or fire orbs while Oliver attacked me with vines and the occasional hole in the ground. Those would randomly appear when I was dodging the fire before using my water affinity to keep as many of their hits at bay as I could.

After I'd been singed no less than five times, twisted both ankles, and had bruises from the vines strangling me all over my body, Stryx finally called them off. "I think that's enough defensive work. You did well, Kali, but that's not enough to keep you safe. There are a certain number of people surrounding us right now. Call out the location of each one or you're as good as dead."

This was always harder for me, because while I could call on water easily when I was in danger, I still struggled with properly utilizing it when I couldn't see my attacker coming for me.

Closing my eyes, I took in a deep calming breath and connected to the water in the air around me. Then, I moved that connection further down and into the ground beneath me. Water was everywhere, which should have made wielding it that much easier, but instead, it was almost overwhelming.

Picturing the connection like a bubble, I pushed it slowly away from me while keeping my eyes closed. I sensed the moment Jordan, Oliver, and Stryx were within it, even felt the warmth in Jordan's hand as she likely considered playing dirty and hitting me with fire while I was focused on something else.

The further out I searched, the more strained my body became, and my jaw tensed as I pushed my senses beyond any distance I'd attempted before.

"Behind the boulder to our right, one man," I called out. "Two more in the trees to my left." The process continued until I'd found nineteen people and was barely standing upright from the amount of energy and focus the task was taking from me.

"One more, Kali. Can you find them?" Stryx asked, and I groaned.

I'd searched everywhere, high and low, and there was no one else. He had to have counted wrong.

"Don't give up on me now. You're almost done. You don't want to be a failure, do you?" Stryx taunted, clearly listening to my thoughts. Jerk.

Gritting my teeth, I tried one more time. This time instead of searching further out, I moved my bubble further into the ground as I bent down onto my knees and sank my fingers into the dirt. Water raced toward me and coated my arms, but there was no one hiding beneath me that I needed to worry about.

Next, I tilted my head toward the sky and glanced around, no longer needing my eyes closed to focus since I'd been connected for nearly twenty minutes. There was nothing visibly out of place that I could see when I turned in circles, but if someone with the wind affinity was hiding up there, then I'd never find them unless I pushed harder.

Glancing at Stryx before I used the last of my energy, he nodded for me to continue, which hopefully meant I was on the right track.

Pushing myself beyond anything I'd ever been capable of before, I arched my power high into the sky and felt tiny pin pricks against my skin as the water began to speak with me.

Higher. Left. Further left. Slow down.

Gotcha.

"There's someone about a hundred feet in the air, shielding herself with the wind," I said triumphantly and felt pretty good until I was smacked in the face with that wind and my mom appeared before me.

"Nobody has ever found me before." She glared. Then, just as I worried that I'd done something wrong, she winked and wrapped her arms around me. "Very well, Kaliah. You have no idea how proud I am of you."

Dad blinked into the picture. "We're both really proud of you."

They each gave me a hug before I turned back to Stryx. "Did I do okay?"

"You did very well. There is still plenty to learn, but if we get separated for any reason, I wouldn't worry about you finding a way to survive on your own. At least for a short amount of time."

Geez, that was encouraging.

"We wish we could come with you, but we also have every faith you can do this on your own," Dad said, and I smiled.

Even though I was their only daughter, they'd given me all the room to grow into my own person for my entire life. They always supported my decisions and never tried to make me into someone they thought I should be instead of who I wanted to be.

Granted, becoming a princess of sorts in a magical world hadn't been on my horizons, but they were at least letting me handle things on my own terms and had yet to pressure me to do any of the training if I wasn't ready.

"What do we do now?" I asked.

"Now, we change and head to the Otherworld. Jordan has proper attire for you to wear," Stryx said, but when my face paled, he added, "It's standard clothing. Calm down."

The last time I'd let Jordan dress me when we were on Earth, I had ended up in hooker boots, a tight black mini-skirt, and the brightest pink sequin top I'd ever laid eyes on. My entire body shuddered at the memory and I even saw Stryx's feathers rustle. There was no way he missed that image in my head.

"What about Ryland?" my dad asked.

"He's welcome to come if he shows, but we haven't seen him all day," Stryx replied without looking at me.

That feathered tyrant knew at least one of us had seen him today, but I owed him one for not saying anything. I'd rather not have his rejection be discussed publicly. If they wanted to chat about it when I wasn't around, that was fine by me, but we definitely weren't having that conversation right then.

"See you at the house!" I called out before porting, and Jordan was right behind me.

"Is everything okay?" she asked as soon as she was at my side in front of the house.

"Everything is great. Now, show me my new badass warrior clothing."

She eyed me suspiciously. "That was too enthusiastic, but I'll let it slide. I expect you to tell me what's going on when we get back. If I need to kick someone's ass, don't rob me of that joy by keeping information from me."

I wrapped an arm around her and gave her a squeeze. "While I appreciate your words, the actions aren't necessary. I'm just ready to get this over with and see what the Otherworld is all about."

She raised a brow at me. "So, you're telling me the weirdness I sense from you has nothing to do with why Ryland is missing?"

"Yep. Ryland's a big boy. I'm sure he's fine. He doesn't concern himself with my business, and I won't be concerning myself with his."

She shook her head, but thankfully let it go. "Alright, then. Let's get ready."

While she got the clothes, I took a quick shower to rinse off the dirt and sweat from the test and felt like a new person once I stepped out of the water. Even after almost two weeks, I still was fascinated with the effects water had on me. Hopefully, I wouldn't ever tire of it or take it for granted.

Jordan was nowhere to be seen, but there was an outfit on my bed when I got out of the shower that was actually something that I was okay with. It was a one-piece suit with a hard, two-tone exterior and a soft layer on the inside. The outer layer was black and dark grey, possibly made from Kevlar or something similar. Though, I hoped it wasn't for dodging bullets and only to protect from magical hits.

The last two items were a jacket made from the same material as the outfit and a pair of sturdy boots that went all the way to my knees. Everything fit perfectly, like it was made just for me. Even with the hard exterior, the clothes formed so well to my body, I could move with absolute ease.

Once I was dressed, I headed to the bathroom and forcibly removed my crown in order to manhandle my hair into submission. After it was brushed and braided and the crown was placed back where it belonged, I took a long look in the mirror.

My blonde highlights shone brightly through the plait, and my eyes were crystal-like against my tanned skin from being outdoors training so much. There was almost a flow about me, a sense of accomplishment and power flooding through me.

Just a couple of weeks ago, I was petrified of this place. Sure, I had been curious, but knowing magic was real wasn't as fun as it sounded. It came with complications humans didn't have to worry about, but as I stared in the mirror, I could see the changes I'd already made in such a short time. No matter what came my way, I'd be able to give my best without any doubts.

Jordan came rushing back inside, seeming out of breath. "Oh, good. You're ready. Let's go."

"Uh, where have you been for the last five minutes?" I asked, surprised to see she was already dressed, but still somehow seemed disheveled.

"Just checking on something. Come on. The others are already at the portal, and Stryx said he'd leave us behind if we don't hurry."

He was way bossier than I would have ever expected, but in a way, I loved it. He was always honest when he was able, and he seemed to truly care about what happened to me. So, even though I sometimes wanted to pluck all of his feathers out when he tortured me, I still loved him.

My parents were waiting outside the guest house, and my mom's eyes welled up when she saw me. "You look exactly like your grandmother."

My parents never talked about our family when we were on Earth, for good reason, and we hadn't had much time since arriving in Arvayta, so for the first time, I truly sensed the grief pouring from them. My heart broke, and I made a silent promise to ask more about my ancestors when we got back.

They deserved to be remembered and talked about. The dead weren't something to avoid; they were to be celebrated even if their time was cut too short.

"I love you, Mom," I whispered when I hugged her tightly.

"I love you, too."

Dad hugged me as well, but it didn't last long as Jordan huffed impatiently. "Come on."

With one last wave to them, I followed Jordan's port, and we arrived at a row of smaller waterfalls that led to who knew where.

"Alright, we're here. Let's go." Jordan tugged on my arm.

She was being awfully pushy, even more so than usual, so I knew something was up, but I had no idea what. Stryx didn't seem to mind, and Oliver was already present, dressed in the same outfit as us except a two-piece that was baggier where needed.

"I'll punch in the coordinates for the Otherworld, and then we can walk through," Oliver said and headed over to what I had thought was just a rock, but it revealed a pin pad as soon as it was touched.

"So, we step through the water, and then the Otherworld will be on the opposite side?" I asked Jordan.

"Well, sort of. We walk through, you float through time and space, and then you stumble into the Otherworld, but you'll be fine. We've only lost two people in a few thousand years."

My eyes widened, but before I could say anything, the waterfall lit up in a golden hue and I was being dragged toward it, all the while hoping I wasn't going to end up in some void for the rest of eternity.

"Wait!" a deep voice called, and Jordan cursed.

"We were so close," she grumbled.

Turning around, I saw Ryland leaning against a rock and glaring daggers at Jordan. "You lied."

"Did I? I think I was just confused. How about we catch up later? Bye!"

Jordan pushed me into the portal with no notice, and I screamed louder than ever before while praying to the Fates I wasn't about to die.

CHAPTER 17

About thirty seconds later, I crashed onto squishy ground while still screaming. I'd never been so scared in my entire life, including when I had known I was going to die and turn into a magical being.

"What the hell, Jordan?" I snapped as she appeared right next to me, landing softly on her feet.

"You don't need any distractions right now. Ryland is one of those, so I took care of him. You have other things to focus on today. Like blending into the Otherworld, meeting with some important people, and making them love you like I do. Ryland doesn't need to be a part of any of that with his brooding attitude."

While I was still pissed that she pushed me into the dark abyss, she did make a point. Especially after my earlier conversation with Ryland, I didn't need him around reminding me of his rejection. It was really stupid that I even let it bother me in the first place.

I hardly knew the guy. He barely spoke to me and usually made me feel like crap when he did have something to say. The only good things about him were that he was nice to kids and an alright guardian.

Okay, he was better than alright, but I'd never tell him that. Or tell him how every time he got really frustrated with me, his eyes darkened just a few shades and I lost myself in them. Or how I noticed the tick in his jaw every time Oliver put his hands on me to help my form in training.

The tension with Ryland was more than I could stand some days, but I was drawn to him regardless. I hated it just as much as I adored it, which further pissed me off.

Jordan's fingers snapped in front of me. "Did you hear anything I just said?"

When I turned around, I noticed Oliver and Stryx were also present, and they were all looking at me expectantly. "Uh, no. Being thrown into an abyss messed with my head. You only have yourself to blame for that."

The trip through the portal wasn't all that scary once it was over. The only part that had frightened me was the unknown. As I was sucked into the vortex, everything around me darkened until, about halfway through, there were twinkling lights that reminded me of the stars I used to admire at night when I was at Multnomah Falls.

Then, just seconds before I was spit back out, the light around me grew so bright, I threw my arm over my eyes and spun around until I landed my ass onto ground that I hadn't even really checked out yet. Of course, I'd arrived in a new world and been completely oblivious to the beauty around me.

Jordan huffed and walked away as Stryx landed on my shoulder and Oliver took off after Jordan. "What do you think?" Stryx asked.

"I think I'm in way over my head, but I'm going to keep doing my best, because I'm stubborn like that and refuse to fail." Complete honesty was the only way to go with him since he knew my true heart anyway. Stupid bonds.

"Our bond isn't stupid, Kaliah. I know you don't mean it that way, and I don't take offense to your words, but I need you to understand something as we move forward. A bond, whether it be like the one we have or a Meraki, is meant to provide you with strength in more ways than one. While inconvenient at times, I promise you'll appreciate it one day."

My hand stroked his silky white feathers. "I love our bond, and I never want it to go anywhere. I just don't like feeling vulnerable. Between you in my head and Ryland rejecting me, I'm feeling overwhelmed on top of all this new magical world stuff. Oh, and let's not forget the fae who wants me dead."

My life was a hot mess.

His head nudged against me. "The Fates have not given you anything more than what you can handle. Just keep your head up and have faith. Believe in yourself, and the rest will fall into place at its own time."

Believe in myself.

Those three words pierced right into my heart. Before magic had become a very real thing in my life, I'd always been confident. Yet, somewhere along the way, I'd lost some of that pride. Maybe Stryx was right and I needed to let everything else go.

It sounded simple, but I wasn't so sure it would be an easy task to accomplish.

"Let's catch up to the others. I've blocked the portal, so Ryland won't be interfering with what you're going to do today. Unless you'd rather him come along, we need to move," Stryx said and gave me pause.

Sure, there was a tugging sensation that was calling me back to Arvayta that I'd felt from the moment I'd gone into the portal, but if I was truly going to believe in myself, I needed to do this on my own.

"I'm sure he'll still be there when we get back, and whatever jerk comment he wanted to make to me can wait," I replied as I began jogging to catch up with Jordan and Oliver.

While we moved through the land, I paid more attention to my surroundings. The ground had an odd buoyancy to it that made running easier and my strides longer. The sky was broken up into four sections as I searched further ahead. The first to catch my attention was an aqua one that reminded me of the waters in Hawaii: crystal clear and welcoming.

Next was a fiery-red sky that consumed a flaming sun and made it hard to stare for long. The area around it contained plumes of smoke and appeared ominous, but even still, I yearned to go to it and provide the water that the lands likely desperately needed.

My body twisted, so I could take in the next section. The sky was covered with storm clouds that ripped through the horizon as wind constantly seemed to be jerking them around. That particular area, I'd have been happy to avoid.

Last was a peaceful landscape that Jordan and Oliver were headed toward. The sky above was a pale green color, and there was a bright yellow sun hanging above the clear horizon. This section was closest to us, and I could make out the silhouette of a town and a much larger castle-like structure on the back side.

"Welcome to the Otherworld," Stryx said. "As you noticed, there are four sections to the Otherworld: earth, wind, fire, and water. The four elements that make up the fae race. Even though there are no pure elementals left, a small amount of those elements still live within those descended from the fae, as you've learned."

Hmm, now that I saw it all together, I realized the council and/or the Fates were smarter than I gave them credit for originally. Our little team was made up of each of the elements: Oliver was earth, Jordan was fire, I was water, and Ryland was wind. We'd yet to actually work together on anything, and even though they weren't as heavy on their fae heritage, I wondered how it would work when we combined forces.

"We'll work on that soon enough, and good job for putting it together. I don't think the others have yet. Guardians have always worked as warriors instead of fae, but you'll need to think harder and smarter before going up against Alaryk."

Jordan and Oliver had paused, waiting for us just before a gate. An oversized one made from what appeared to be the same titanium as my crown, except instead of purple jewels encrusted in the overhang, there were burgundy ones.

"Come on, slow pokes. We don't have all day, and I want to send word for Yelah as soon as we can," Jordan said.

"Yelah is the dragon queen, right?" I asked.

"Yep, and I want her to meet you. If we're going up against a dark fae with who knows how many at his side, I want the dragons to stand with us. Yelah will fight with us, because it's the right thing to do and because she owes me." Jordan smirked, and I wondered if she'd be that cocky around the queen of dragons.

I was already intimidated just from hearing about her.

"We're here to meet with several people, but if Yelah won't come to the earth sector, I'm not willing to allow Kali to go to the fire one in order to find her. While I have no doubt that she's capable of handling her own, there are far greater risks, and before we venture out of the neutral territory, your whole team needs to be together," Stryx said and surprisingly, Jordan didn't disagree.

My fluffy little friend seemed to be the only person she didn't argue with.

When we were all standing before the gate, Oliver stepped forward and placed his hand on what I thought was a lock of some sort. He flinched and hissed, causing me to take a step forward, but Jordan grabbed me.

"He's fine. Just wait a minute."

I did as she said and sure enough, when he finally pulled his hand back, a grin graced his face and the gates began to open. "Welcome to the Otherworld peace sector."

I'd heard bits about this place during my training, and as soon as we stepped aside, I realized that none of it had been exaggerated.

All had appeared quiet from the outside, and the only visible building had been the castle, but as soon as we stepped foot inside, chaos of the best kind erupted in front of us. My mind instantly tried to make sense of it all, but there was no use.

The Otherworld is filled with magic unlike that within Arvayta. It pulls from its inhabitants and is a mix of many different races, which means it's capable of so much more. There is a shield around this entire area that keeps it invisible from anyone on the outside, Stryx said within my mind as I continued to take in everything around me.

The gates we went through provide the only entrance into the sector and would not have let us pass if it sensed any threat. This area of the Otherworld is the only known location where creatures from all over can congregate and feel safe. Outside its walls, it is every being for themselves with no laws to say otherwise unless someone is trying to offset the balance.

Like Alaryk? I replied.

Yes, he threatens the balance, and you'll find that even the most unexpected allies may surface in order to help us end him before he gets to you.

Interesting. I eagerly looked forward to meeting the creatures he hinted at, but first, I took a few minutes to truly appreciate where I was.

As my eyes ventured around, the castle was the first to grab my attention again as it seemed to glow under the sun above. The golden hue sparkled all over the pearlescent structure with three turrets and probably over one hundred windows ranging in sizes.

People all around us strolled from one place to another, seeming to take their time and socialize as they went. Nearest to our group was a marketplace and where Jordan seemed to be headed. There were booths lining at least ten rows that seemed to go on for as far as the eye could see.

Some of the booths were named with things I'd never heard

of nor understood, but others were easy enough to get the gist of what they might offer. Messenger was the one Jordan stopped at while my gaze perused a few others like spells, hexes, and bones. My entire body shivered as I wondered where they got the bones from and what they might be used for.

"I need a message to be sent to Queen Yelah as soon as possible. Please let her know Jordan is in the peace sector and needs to speak with her right away," Jordan said to what I thought was nobody until a gnome appeared from behind the counter standing on a ladderlike structure that seemed to move with him like extended legs.

"As soon as possible will cost you. What do you have to offer?" the gnome grumbled.

Jordan reached for the bag on her back and pulled out a handful of emeralds. "Will these do?"

His eyes lit up and he reached for them, but Jordan pulled them back. "Within the hour, little man, or I'll be back, and you won't be happy to see my face."

The gnome snarled at her, showcasing pointy teeth. "I'm never late. Now pay or leave and don't ever come back."

Jordan dropped the gems into the grotesque hand of the gnome. "Nice doing business with you."

Oliver pulled her back before she could get herself into any trouble as she seemed to have more to say. Once we were out of earshot of the gnome, he said, "You couldn't have just said please and thank you?"

"What's the fun in that? They need to know we're not to be messed with. Arvaytans are already perceived as weak. I won't give them any reason to prove that fact," she responded with a sneer.

This was a side of Jordan I'd never seen before. She was always so carefree and lighthearted. If she was taking this situation that seriously, I knew I needed to up my game.

"Now, where do we go?" I asked, because I knew contacting Yelah was not our only goal for the trip.

"Now, we stroll through the marketplace and see who comes to us. It's no secret that Alaryk is out there and hopes to use you to increase his power in order to tip the scales toward the darker part of the Otherworld. Those who wish to stand against him will come forward, but some in their own ways and when we least expect it," Stryx said.

Oliver moved to stand at my side with Stryx, and Jordan slid in close, looping her arm through mine on the opposite side. We continued to walk, and I kept my face neutral for the most part, smiling at those who made eye contact and leaving alone those who didn't. Assuming that they all knew who I was with the crown on my head, I didn't bother to try to hide myself.

There were witches, vampires, more gnomes, pixies, and so many other creatures I didn't recognize, but the most disappointing part was that nobody approached us. Besides the few smiles thrown our way, everyone kept to themselves, which was a huge discouragement once we exited the marketplace about an hour later.

"Yelah or one of her people should be here soon. I'm going to go wait at the gate for her. Do you think you guys will be good without me?" Jordan teased.

Oliver flexed his arms and grunted. "I got this."

I patted his shoulder. "Oh, whatever would we do without you."

"Likely suffer without my handsomely good looks." He flashed a grin at me that featured adorable dimples.

While I considered Oliver extremely handsome with his longer blond hair and pale hazel eyes, there just wasn't any attraction present when I really looked at him. I'd never be able to see him as anything more than my friend.

"Let's head to the castle," Stryx suggested once Jordan took off.

I had no objections to that, because I'd been curious about it ever since we arrived, mostly wondering if the golden glow around it was real or a trick of the eyes from the bright overhead sun.

After a five-minute walk, we were met by a group of guards and one stepped forward. "What is your business at the castle today?"

"We'd like to speak with Queen Navi," Stryx said.

The guard eyed the three of us several times before speaking. "Follow me."

He led the way inside, which surprised me because he'd asked no other questions. He'd simply trusted us, which didn't make any sense until we passed through the entrance.

Brace yourself, Stryx whispered in my head just before an invisible gel-like sensation covered my body and it took every ounce of strength to move through it to get inside the castle.

"What the hell was that?" I heaved once we were through.

"That was our security system. Seems you passed the test. Pity. It's been a rather boring morning and I was hoping for some excitement," the guard said, and I immediately wanted to throat punch him.

"Where do we meet the monarch?" Oliver asked.

The guard pointed to me and Oliver. "You two wait here. Only the owl is allowed any further. If the monarch wishes to see you, she will do so when she's ready."

I really didn't like this guy.

It's okay. I expected this and should have told you ahead of time. You're perfectly safe in here, and I won't be long, Stryx said before he flew after the guard and left us alone.

"Well, this sucks," I complained as I plopped onto the chairs in what I assumed was their version of a waiting room.

"Nah. This is easy. Just wait until you're faced with a horde of hungry vamps or some pissed off dragons. Then you can say 'this sucks'," Oliver replied, not helping at all.

Leaning my head back, I glanced up at the ceiling that was made from some sort of sparkling tile and wondered, not for the first time, just what the hell I'd gotten myself into and if there would ever be a day when I was used to all the craziness.

Before I could ponder much more, I heard Oliver grunt, followed by a thud. Moving to my feet, I prepared for a fight and my body called on my magic. Then I froze when I laid eyes on an extremely pissed-off woman holding a knife to Oliver's throat.

We were so screwed.

CHAPTER 18

Within a second, I'd surveyed our surroundings and realized there was no one coming to our aid. The woman behind Oliver had sharp fangs and red eyes, causing me to assume she was a vampire. She was dressed similarly to me and Jordan, but had several knives tucked into places I didn't realize were pockets.

She flicked her sleek burgundy hair back and glared green eyes at me as she whispered something in Oliver's ear. When his head shook, she yelled, "Don't lie to me!"

"I swear, Brooke. She already has a Meraki. We're just friends," he pleaded with her as a drop of blood trailed down his neck.

Were they talking about me? Was this a woman scorned? I really wasn't in the mood to deal with a volatile woman, but maybe I could pretend I was on her side and reason with her for Oliver's sake.

"Uh, Brooke, is it? I'm Kali. Oliver is a new friend of mine, but we're not close enough that I wouldn't mind assisting in his ass-kicking if he's done something wrong," I said, hoping she'd ease her hold on him if she thought she had back-up.

Oliver's eyes widened at my statement, but hopefully he'd trust me enough not to stop me. I'd do my best to keep Brooke from hurting him.

Her eyes widened. "Did he tell you about me?"

"No, but I've been there." Okay, I hadn't really been, but she didn't need to know that. "So, how about you tell me what he did, and I'll help you get your revenge on him that doesn't include getting you in trouble for murder?" I smirked at the vampire, surprised I was able to remain as calm as I was on the outside, because internally, I was getting nervous. Her fangs were still out, and Oliver was sweating bullets.

After a minute to think about what I'd said, she retracted her fangs and shoved Oliver, and he tumbled to the floor. "I could never kill Ollie, but he does deserve to learn a lesson or two."

Ollie? I was going to have to remember that nickname for the future. Brooke sat down across from where I had been sitting, and Oliver made himself scarce while I took my same place.

Brooke spent the next five minutes giving me too many details about a night with Oliver I had no business knowing about, but when she was done, she informed me of how he promised to meet near the castle the following week and never did. That was a few weeks ago.

"Ah, I feel like maybe I need to apologize a little as well," I said. "That's about the time I arrived in Arvayta, and Oliver is part of my training team. It's been keeping him pretty busy."

"Wait, *you're* Kaliah? The light fae descendant?" she gaped, and I nodded. "Holy hell, this just gets better and better."

"And why is that?" I asked when I sensed heaps of sarcasm within her voice.

"Well, I'm part of your additional guard whenever you're in the Otherworld. Queen Navi has been preparing for your arrival for the last year. She does not want to see Alaryk gain more power. Even though she doesn't have fae magic within her, she's a powerful sorceress with an affinity for all things earthly. When her land hurts, so does she."

This was great news. Well, for me anyway. Sure, I'd been keeping Oliver busy, but he wasn't with me all day, every day. He was just going to have to own his actions and apologize, then deal with the consequences, because something told me Brooke wasn't going to be okay with a simple apology.

Oliver crept back into the room, his neck cleaned up and only a pink mark left behind from where Brooke's blade had nicked him. "Uh, Jordan is back and waiting outside, but Stryx isn't. She said you need to go meet Queen Yelah."

So many queens around, and there I was standing in a castle, wearing a crown, feeling like an imposter.

You're not an imposter, Kaliah. Go see Yelah and tell Oliver to wait for me. Brooke can escort you and Jordan. Then, we'll meet you out there shortly. Queen Navi won't be seeing all of us today, Stryx said, somehow always in tune with my conversations and his own.

It's a gift you'll learn eventually. Now go before the dragon queen gets angry from waiting and decides to eat you for dinner, he added.

You're a horrible mentor and bonded animal, I snapped before ignoring his soft chuckle and relaying the pertinent information to Oliver.

Brooke wasted no time grabbing my arm and dragging me from the room. "Please tell me he won't be with you *every* time you're in the Otherworld."

"Um, I can't say for sure, but I think so."

She mumbled several incoherent thoughts as we moved through the main doors we'd come in earlier, but this time there was no pressure.

Jordan was waiting for us, and she eyed the vampire holding on to my arm. "Who are you?"

"Brooke. Vampire and guard assigned to assist Kaliah with whatever she needs in the Otherworld. And you are?" Brooke sized up my best friend. Both of them seemed to be on edge, and I had no clue if this was going to end badly.

"Jordan, Arvaytan, guard assigned to Kaliah no matter where she is, and her best friend."

Their gazes locked while I held my breath wondering what the hell was happening, but then Jordan cracked a smile and Brooke let go of my arm.

"Nice to meet you. Now let's go see Queen Yelah. Last I heard, things weren't good with the dragons," Brooke said as if nothing awkward had happened just two seconds prior.

Jordan visibly tensed and didn't wait for a reply before turning to run toward wherever Yelah was waiting for us. Brooke tugged me along, and we both ran, though I knew I was slowing her down.

Calling on my magic, I tapped into my general fae abilities to pick up speed. Mostly, my training had been connecting with my strongest power, being the water affinity, but a few hours had been spent explaining some things I may or may not be able to do that past fae could.

Thankfully, speed wasn't an issue, and my legs began to move faster until we caught up to Jordan. She didn't slow until we entered a forested area still within the gates of the peace sector.

"The snarky little gnome said we needed to meet her near the trees. I swear, if he lied and this is a trap, I'm going to chop his knobby little fingers into bits," Jordan growled, but then a deep rumbling laugh came from the shadows and she relaxed.

"You haven't changed a bit during our time apart," the dragon said as she broke through the darkness of the forest.

Jordan gasped, and I did the same. Yelah had a large wound on her chest that was very fresh, almost two feet long. "What happened?" Jordan asked as I took in the rest of the massive beast before us.

Deep teal scales covered her body and seemed to shimmer with hints of darker blue and silver as she moved out of the shadows. From her clawed feet to the horns on her head, Yelah was around ten feet tall and packed with muscle.

"That weasel of a dark fae happened. I was going to travel to Arvayta as soon as I was healed if I didn't see you before then, so I could tell you." Her massive head swiveled toward me as her silver eyes glistened. "Kaliah, I presume?"

"That would be me." Would I ever grow used to people knowing about me before they'd even met me? Probably not.

"Alaryk caught word that the dragons would stand with you, and he took it upon himself to visit my land without permission to leave a message for you, but it was more for us and anyone who would love to see him dead."

"What message would that be?" I asked, doing my best to hide the tremors from my voice that I felt on the inside.

"Anyone who dares to assist you in fighting against him will face his full wrath. He killed eight of my best dragons and left me severely wounded. I have no doubt he's capable of doing as he's threatened. While that should make any reasonable queen back away from the situation, I want you to know, the dragons will still fight by your side, but it won't be until the last moment. I need to keep my people safe for as long as possible."

I turned to Jordan. "Do you think this is why no one talked to us in the market earlier?"

"Most likely. If Alaryk is making threats and following through on them, our allies will be few and far between."

Yelah's massive wings ruffled. "Alaryk is more powerful than any other being I've faced before, but I sense a greatness within you, Kaliah. Do not let fear hold you back from your destiny."

Nodding, I stepped away and let Jordan speak with her dragon friend while I processed more of our craptastic situation, or at least attempted to. More lives were being threatened because of me. Because some psycho fae thought I was the key to world domination. It wasn't exactly what I enjoyed hearing about.

"Are you okay?" Brooke asked from behind me.

Damn, I hadn't heard her come closer and she'd scared the hell out of me. "Yeah, I'll be fine. It's just a lot to take in."

"Something tells me you're going to be just fine." She grinned at me, once again showing her fangs, but they were more subtle than when she'd been ready to kill Oliver.

Before I could thank her, Stryx appeared and landed on my shoulder while Oliver was still running behind. "It's time for us to go."

"Is everything okay?" I asked.

"Yes," he said out loud, and then added mentally, *The visit didn't go quite how I hoped, but we'll talk about it when we're back in Arvayta.*

Without questioning him, I went back to Jordan and Yelah. The dragon queen kneeled when she saw Stryx. "It's good to see you again, Stryx."

"You as well, Queen Yelah. As a thank you for standing with us, would you like some help with the healing of your injury?" Stryx asked in a formal voice I wasn't used to.

"I won't say no to it, old friend."

"Kaliah, please pull a feather from under my left wing, and then place it in Queen Yelah's wound," he said, as if that was supposed to be some normal thing that we did all the time.

"Excuse me?" I asked.

"I'll do it," Jordan said. Then, Stryx lifted his wing and I watched my best friend swiftly pluck a singular full-size feather before turning back toward the dragon.

My feet instantly moved closer so I could see how the magic worked, and I was glad I did. The moment Jordan let go of the feather, it seeped into the damaged scales, and white smoke began to trickle out from the injury.

Yelah hissed, and her dragon legs buckled until she was almost lying down in the dirt. Stryx flew closer to her and flapped his wings in steady succession until the smoke dissipated. Once the smoke was gone, Yelah stood back up and shook out her wings. Her chest was completely healed.

"I forgot how much that hurt, or I might have told you no." She grinned at Stryx, showcasing a mouth full of razor-sharp teeth.

Shudders ran through me, and I was even more thankful she was on our side.

"We all need to go. Please let us know if you hear anything else and stay safe," Stryx said to the dragon before we went our separate ways.

"I'm going to head back to the castle now. Are you sure you can't stay longer?" Brooke asked, avoiding Oliver who seemed to be trying to gain her attention.

"Next time will be longer," Stryx promised, and Brooke nodded before turning and practically disappearing as she ran back to the castle with full vampire speed.

I'm going to need to leave you once we're in Arvayta. It's time to bring the bonded animals back, Stryx said as we quietly headed back toward the gates.

I badly wanted to ask more questions, but I could feel Stryx shut me out, so I let him be until we were in a safer talking area. All the while, I couldn't decide what was worse, having him be gone for who knew how long or knowing that things had gone so badly with Queen Navi that Stryx felt a strong desire to rush bringing the bonded animals.

Either way, things were about to escalate quickly, and our team was not at all prepared.

CHAPTER 19

Going through the portal back to Arvayta wasn't nearly as terrifying as the first time. Staying as far away from Jordan as I could, I watched Oliver walk through first, then followed after. My eyes stayed open, taking in the void and vibrant lights off in the distance that I assumed were other portal entrances.

When the light before me got too bright again, I closed my eyes and stiffened my body to hopefully stay upright and not stumble like before. Thankfully, it worked and I was able to walk right onto the ground. My only confusion was the darkness surrounding me.

"How long were we gone?" I asked, as I glanced around. It had been early afternoon when we'd left, but the sun was nowhere to be seen and we'd only been gone a couple hours.

"For too long," a deep and not-very-happy voice grumbled from the shadows.

Ryland stepped closer, and I'd never seen him more livid, not even when I hit him with the orb full of bee stings.

"What happened?" I asked, looking only at him, afraid something had happened to my parents.

When his eyes met mine, they softened and surprised the hell out of me. "Nothing around here, but you may want to say goodbye to your best friend."

Jordan stepped through the portal right as he said that. "Oh, serves you right to be left out. You've been a Class A jerk lately, so I don't even want to hear it. Don't think I don't know what you were up to, because I do. As did Stryx, and it still needs to wait about another hour."

What in the world was she talking about? I tried asking Stryx, but he was conveniently ignoring me through our bond. Ryland was up to something that had to do with me, and they really should have let me know. Or maybe I should have already known due to our Meraki bond that wasn't really a bond. Stupid soulmate stuff was really frustrating.

Ryland's eyes moved from Jordan to Stryx to me several times before he finally nodded. "I take it things didn't go as planned in the Otherworld?"

"They went just fine, and we have the full support of Queen Navi and Yelah, but we need to move swiftly and without notice in order to keep everyone safe. Alaryk is making moves in the Otherworld, and I don't believe it will be long before he shows up here," Stryx said from his perch on a rock.

"Let's go speak with Brooks and Daliah. They can fill the council in for us," Jordan said with a shudder.

"Is there something wrong with the council?" I asked, wondering if there was something else that I was missing.

"No, I just hate having to keep my mouth shut for meetings with them. It gives me a headache." She shrugged and moved on as I shook my head.

Stryx flew to my shoulder and positioned himself between me and Ryland, who seemed to be sticking pretty close to my side.

Are you seriously going to make me wait? I asked Stryx through our bond.

Wait for what?

Don't play coy with me. What is going on with Ryland and why wasn't he allowed with us? I demanded.

Ryland may have received some news that made him feel guilty for some of his actions. I knew from the Fates, and Jordan figured part of it out on her own. I'm sure that once we're done speaking with your parents, you'll know all about it. Just be patient, he said with a bit of a laugh at the end. We both knew I had zero patience.

However, I was eager to get the full story about what happened with Queen Navi, so I stopped questioning Stryx and we all ported to my parents' house.

Our entire group entered through the already-open back door, and everyone moved around the spacious living room in various places. I then understood why this part of the house was so much bigger than the one we lived in back on Earth.

Oliver stuck close to Jordan, and they kept whispering about stuff that was really starting to irritate me. Stryx took residence on the back of the couch near my parents who continued to stand even after they both hugged me tight.

"You'll have to tell us what you thought about the Otherworld later," Mom said, and I nodded at her before flinching at the shadow near me.

Ryland was still following me like a lost puppy dog, and I was freaking out about his nearness. I really needed to know what was going on with him. At least my heart was happy about whatever was happening, even though my mind was thoroughly confused.

There was a sort of pulsing sensation running through me that increased as he dared to move closer to me, similar to how I'd felt the first time I'd been in the falls, but this was different and felt bone deep. Before I could continue analyzing it, Ryland's hand grabbed my elbow and led me to an empty couch.

His touch was gentle but had my heart rate increasing, and when my eyes inadvertently met Jordan's, she was smirking. If she was finding enjoyment in this, then it couldn't be good.

After I took a seat, I assumed Ryland would sit next to me. Instead, he chose to stand right behind me where I couldn't see him, further frustrating me. Before I could decide to stand myself, my dad began speaking.

"We have the council on standby to go over what you've learned. Is there any imminent danger we need to warn them of?"

"No, but we may need to prepare for it soon. Queen Navi has been sending her people out into the different sectors of the Otherworld, and things are progressing quickly now that Kaliah has come into her power. Alaryk is getting reckless, and nobody has been able to stop him," Stryx answered.

"The dark fae even attacked the dragons without provocation, killing eight of them and severely injuring Yelah. She will still stand with us, but also asks that they only be required to help at the last minute as not to put her clan further in danger," Jordan added.

Mom nodded. "That's completely understandable, and the council will appreciate any help they're still willing to provide. What about Queen Navi, though? What support can we expect from her?"

Stryx took the conversation back over then, and I took in everything that I could. They might not be saying it right then, but I knew if I didn't get my crap together soon, I was going to be the reason Alaryk succeeded. I refused to let that happen.

"When I met with the Queen, she was rather distraught and afraid. She feared that if she met directly with Kaliah that Alaryk would know and strike sooner. She still has her wits about her, and I'm not worried about her taking action, but the damage to her lands has her on edge," Stryx said.

"Rightly so. Is there anything we can do as a show of gratitude to help them?" Dad asked Stryx.

"That is also something we talked about. Our capable fighting guardians aren't big enough to take over scouring the Otherworld in place of the queen's people, but I suggested we begin to work together. Send some of the guardians with earth affinities to the most damaged areas in an attempt to heal the lands while also assisting with patrols. It would not only give us direct access to what's going on over there, but it would also appease Queen Navi."

"I'm happy to lead a group of us over there if needed," Oliver offered.

"No, we need you here. The four of you need to stay together, on the same world at all times," Stryx answered sternly.

"So, what's your suggestion then, Stryx?" Mom asked.

"Tonight, I'll leave for Dásos, and when I return, I will be bringing the bonded animals back with me. Every fighting guardian will be matched, regardless of how much fae blood they have. Each of them has at least a trace of their ancestors, and that's all I need to complete the ritual."

Mom and Dad shared a worried look that had me wondering if maybe the bonded animals weren't such a good thing, but before I could question it, the conversation switched.

"As soon as we're prepared, we need to move on the Otherworld. There are too many vulnerable guardians in Arvayta, and if we can avoid it, we need to keep the fight in the Otherworld," Stryx added.

"But doesn't that give him the advantage? Can't we just ask those who aren't able to fight to at least hide? From what I've learned, Arvaytans are strongest when powered by the magic of the falls. If we leave the falls, won't we be putting ourselves at an even greater risk?" I asked, knowing that even if that wasn't all true for everyone else, it seemed to be for me. The water gave me a boost like nothing else I'd found yet.

Mom raised a brow. "She has a point, and it will be an option we propose to the council. Ultimately, it's up to them, and we should get going so they can decide. Stryx, do you need help bringing the bonded animals back?"

"No, but I will be making several trips over the next twenty-four hours. By the time I get back, the council needs to be decided on how they want to move forward. Alaryk isn't going to give us much time."

Mom and Dad nodded, then began moving around as they prepared to leave. I stood and moved toward Jordan and Oliver. Ryland was still right at my side, and I kept trying to avoid him, but it wasn't working.

"Can we speak privately, Kali?" he finally asked.

"Uh, sure. Just give me a minute," I mumbled.

He nodded, then walked toward the back deck.

Jordan snickered, but Oliver seemed just as confused as I was. At least I wasn't the only one.

"What is happening?" I whisper-yelled at her.

"Why don't you go find out? I promise it's nothing horrible. I don't know all the details, only what I could guess, and before there was time to ask questions, we had to leave. So, I expect a full debriefing when you're done."

Stryx landed on my shoulder, interrupting our conversation. "I need to go. Keep your crown on, and do not bond with anything while I'm gone. I'm not sure how much that crown can handle and you're not ready for your full powers just yet, but you're getting close."

"What? Bond with another animal? Of course I wouldn't do that," I said, even more confused.

He pressed his head against mine just like he used to, and I stroked his feathers as he changed the conversation. "I've left your daggers that you'll need to start training with in your bedroom. Don't touch those before I get back, either. Your power is volatile until certain things fall into place, but we're almost ready. Just wait for me."

"Is everything okay with you?" I asked quietly. He was beginning to freak me out, and I couldn't lose him or I might really fall apart.

"Yes, or at least it will be. Now, I need to go. Don't blow anything up while I'm gone." With those final words, he took off out the back door and disappeared into the night sky.

Jordan nudged me. "Go put that boy out of his misery."

I looked back at Ryland, who was pacing on the porch and casting glances at us every few seconds. "Okay, fine. But go find lots of chocolate. I'm sure I'll need it when I get done." Remembering my last conversation with Ryland, when he officially rejected me and told me about Sara, already had my heart hurting.

Even though I understood his reasonings and couldn't really argue them, a deeper part of me was going to take a long time to heal from knowing I'd never have my soulmate. Though, maybe if Ryland could have two, then so could I, even if I had to wait decades to find another.

As soon as I stepped foot onto the deck, Ryland stopped pacing and met my gaze. His eyes, still identical to mine, shone brightly in the dark sky and called to my soul.

Yeah, there was no finding another soulmate. No matter how much we'd fought or how rude Ryland had been over the last few weeks, there had been one too many moments where I had brief glances of his kindness, like when he'd helped that young boy near the fountain or taken me to the falls when I'd been overwhelmed with power.

Hell, I'd even seen how much it pained him to tell me he could never accept me. Somehow though, we were going to need to work out a solution, even if it was temporary until we defeated Alaryk. Then, maybe I'd walk away. Go back to Earth or find a nice place in the Otherworld, so we could let the bond break without having to be near each other.

"Kali, are you okay?" Ryland asked, wiping a stray tear from my cheek.

Crap, I hadn't even realized I was crying.

"Yeah, I'm fine. Just a lot going on. What did you want to talk about? I kind of assumed we'd sorted everything out earlier."

He flinched at the hurt in my words. "Can we go somewhere to talk? There's a place I'd like to show you."

"Uh, sure." Suddenly, my palms were sweating, and my heart was racing. This bond was going to be the death of me before I even had the chance to reject it.

He grabbed my hand and ported us to a remote area surrounded by trees, and the rushing sounds of water could be heard over the pounding of my heart. The moon sat high in the sky, giving us just enough light to see about ten feet in front of us.

"Where are we?" I asked, very much aware of his hand still holding mine.

"The only hot springs within Arvayta. I stumbled upon it one day when I'd been out hunting, and I come here from time to time when I want to think. I thought it might be somewhere you'd enjoy as well."

I had no idea why he was telling me this or even sharing it with me, and to be honest, I didn't like it. If he was simply trying to torture me so I'd disappear faster, it was working. I wanted nothing more in that moment than to run as far away from him as I could.

My heart couldn't take his rejection followed by his kindness. If he was trying to make up for earlier, he was doing it all wrong.

"Well, thanks for showing me, but I think I should head back now." I tried to pull away from him, but he tightened his hold on me.

"Will you stay a little longer? I'd like to apologize for earlier."

"No apology necessary. Let's just keep the interactions to a minimum and we'll sort out the details later," I said, once again trying to pull my hand away and just barely succeeding.

The hurt on his face when I did that confused the hell out of me. I took a step away, trying to decide where I wanted to go before porting. I had no desire to face Jordan, because what I really needed was some therapeutic crying. The kind that was loud and ugly and included some yelling at the top of my lungs to help me get over whatever Ryland was doing to me and needed to be done alone.

After that, I could have my time with Jordan, filled with wine and music and laughter, because even if nobody had said it yet, I knew in some way I was already bonded to her. She was my best-friend soulmate, and I'd count on her to see me through whatever came next.

"I'm sorry, I don't know how to do this. I wish the Fates had come to me before I spoke with you, but they didn't, and I've made things worse. Please just sit for a minute," Ryland begged with not only his words, but also his eyes as his hand reached for me once again, and my window to disappear was gone.

My heart won, and I accepted his hand. When we touched, I embraced the power that flowed between the two of us and briefly let myself pretend he was mine.

He led us to a rock that overlooked the hot springs. Steam rose from the water and had me itching to dive in, but Ryland once again demanded my attention. As soon as he spoke, everything else around us disappeared.

"I don't know how else to explain it, so I'm just going to say it. Sara was not my Meraki. One of the Fates came to me today after I left your house and explained some of my past. I was deceived by Sara, who had been working with Alaryk.

"The dark fae has been fighting to get you since long before you were even born. I'm sorry I fell for his tricks and hurt you in the process. I hope you can find a way to forgive me, but I understand if you can't. Though, I need you to know that I will do everything I can to erase the hurt I caused you and earn your forgiveness. I won't be able to move forward without you by my side as my true Meraki."

Cheese and rice, what was happening in my life? I could barely process his words. They'd hit me like a freight train and broke every bone in my body, leaving me unable to move or speak. My soul was dancing, but everything else was numb.

"Kali?" Ryland waved his hand in front of my face, then grabbed both of my shoulders. "Kali?" The frantic tone in his voice had me snapping out of my stupor, but not in the best way.

"I have to go." Scrambling from his grasp, I wasted no time before I disappeared.

His words were everything I had hoped for, but also everything I feared. Ryland held too much power over me. The Meraki bond was more than I could handle on top of everything else, and I wasn't sure I could accept his apology.

At least, not in the way he seemed to be expecting.

CHAPTER 20

Porting without thinking of the exact place I wanted to be probably wasn't the smartest thing I'd done since learning how to use my magic, but I'd been in such a panic that I didn't care. Thankfully, I'd landed right at the edge of the falls and not somewhere I'd never been.

Deciding I wanted to remain as unseen as possible, I searched for a spot near the rock wall and took a seat within the shadows. I needed time to think. Time to figure out what I wanted, or more importantly, what was best for me.

The one thing I was sure of was that the Meraki bond was starting to piss me off. Sure, the idea of it was great. Having one perfect match for yourself, finding them, and—*bam*—happily-ever-after like I'd read about in the princess stories.

Even though I was technically a princess, this was no fairytale.

Things hadn't transformed into a utopia as soon as I saw my soulmate. Far from it. Ryland hadn't swooped in and saved the day, making me fall immediately in love with him. No, he'd pushed me away, because he'd been mad at himself. All of the nice things that I knew about him did not make the other stuff go away.

At least, not easily.

Leaning back against the rock, I closed my eyes, which probably wasn't a smart thing to do since it had been an extremely long day and I was ready for bed, but I wasn't prepared to face my best friend. I knew I wouldn't be able to keep any of this hidden from Jordan, and once I said certain things out loud, I wouldn't be able to unsay them.

I needed more time.

But I didn't have more time.

Alaryk wasn't going to wait for us to be ready, and I needed to make a choice, but it wasn't fair that I needed to forgive Ryland merely for the benefit of Arvayta. When or if we decided to trust each other and really get to know each other, I wanted to do it because I knew without a doubt it was the right choice.

Eventually, my thoughts slowed down and I drifted off. When I did, images flashed within my mind of happier and easier times back on Earth. Then, they transitioned into my first meetings with Stryx and all those insane but very real moments that followed.

Just when the weird slideshow of a dream was ending with my human death, the vision of my dying body burst into a vivid yellow light, and my eyes flew open. Except the light wasn't only from my dream; it was standing right before me, too brilliant to look directly at.

"Hello, Kaliah," the angelic voice said softly as the glow around her began dimming to a more manageable level.

"Uh, hi?"

"Do you know who I am?" she asked, and my head shook, though she did look incredibly familiar. "I'm your grandmother Taliah."

Crap, was I dead for a second time? If not, I didn't imagine her being in Arvayta was a good thing, considering she was supposed to be in the In-Between with the Fates. I certainly wasn't ready to be there myself.

"No, you're not dead, but you do need help, and that's what I'm here to give." She smiled softly, and I finally saw the spitting image of Mother in her.

My heart softened, and my throat burned as emotion built within me. This was my family. Family I'd never had the chance to meet. She had the same brunette hair as my mother, but she also had shimmering blonde running through it like I did. Her eyes were a light golden brown that stood out with the radiant light around her.

"Do you mind if I sit with you? I can't walk any further from the falls or I could disappear," she said.

"Of course not." There was no letting her disappear on me, so I scooted over, allowing her to sit nearest to the water. Then, I immediately felt weird about having a past queen sit on the ground with me. She should be on a throne, not the grass.

"Definitely not, my sweet granddaughter. When I was queen, I was never higher up than my people. They were my equals, I merely helped to guide them when needed. Right here, next to you on the earth, is exactly where I want to be."

Damn, she was even better than I'd heard or read about. "Stryx does the same thing where he can read my thoughts. Will I be able to do that one day to others?" I asked, since she seemed to know what I was thinking as I thought it.

"Most likely, but you won't know for sure until all of your bonds are in place. You need as many trustworthy people by your side to help support the strength of your full force. Once you have accepted what is meant to be, there should be nothing you can't do."

Ugh, so we were back to that. Take a man or be weak. Hell, no.

"That's not what I meant, and it saddens me you feel that way, Kaliah. Our kind was created by powerful women. Merakis were not created to make us less powerful or show that we were weak without them, but to do the opposite, in fact. For you, Ryland would be your anchor to the worlds that you need in order to access your full power. He would cherish you and everything you're made of, protecting you from anything that means you harm.

"He would love you so fiercely, your abilities would only grow stronger and more powerful, even though he is helping to carry the weight. Together, the two of you would become an unstoppable force, sharing a love and bond like no other in your lifetime. But only if you are open to the future possibilities, instead of being stuck in the past."

I snorted. "In the past? Him treating me like crap just happened this morning. I get what you're saying, and it all sounds great, but it seems to me that Fate is the only one who wants us together. I had been open to accepting him, faults and all, before he flat-out rejected me this morning."

"I'd like to show you something. Do you mind?" She raised a hand, and I nodded before she cupped my cheek.

As soon as her skin touched mine, images rolled through my vision as if I was watching a movie. Beginning with clips of Ryland pacing in his house, mumbling and being angry. Then it switched to him outside of my house, scared and sad. Followed by him when he was with me, but with the ability to focus on his face when I wasn't looking at him.

There was admiration in his eyes and lots of despair, which was breaking my heart as I saw it. Then, it showed him leaving my house earlier that day, and porting right to the very spot I sat. He'd come to the safety of the falls and hidden exactly where I'd chosen.

And just like me, he wasn't alone for very long. A man appeared before him and they walked away together, or at least a spirit form of Ryland did as his body stayed put. With the final scene, it showed Ryland waking up, joy radiating from him, along with a brightness in his eyes I'd yet to see and a renewed determination.

"Do you see what I see?" Taliah asked when she was done with her mind invasion.

What did I see? I witnessed a broken man, a selfish and angry-at-the-world man. But I also saw someone fighting a battle alone. Though, we weren't in his head. There was no way to know what he was fighting.

"He was fighting against you. I know that doesn't sound appealing, but Ryland knew from the moment he laid eyes on you that you were special. When he realized how much you were to mean to him, he ran from his feelings of love and turned them into anger. Anger at having to betray the one he thought deserved his loyalty even though she no longer walks these worlds.

"While I wouldn't normally let my granddaughter settle for anything less than her worth, and Ryland hasn't proved he's deserving, I do believe he has realized his mistakes. I have full faith that he is capable of being a worthy Meraki to you if you give him a chance. His loyalty was his downfall, but it could also be what keeps you safest."

Damn it. She was completely right, but I was still having a hard time wrapping my mind around the fact I was supposed to just accept him as my soulmate after the last few weeks of rejection.

"In order to bond, you don't have to do anything you're not ready for, but you can accept him as your other half, which you're already fully aware of, and let the connection blossom naturally. You don't have to begin a serious relationship with him just because he's your Meraki. He still needs to win your love, and you're more than entitled to ask that of him while utilizing the benefits of a completed bond."

"Won't the bond push us together whether I want it or not?

I've had some serious feelings toward Ryland already, and I'm not sure how I feel about it."

"The bond will only strengthen feelings already present. There is a reason Ryland was chosen for you. He is your perfect match in every way, and maybe this has all worked out exactly as it needed to. Just forget about the bond and get to know Ryland as a person. You just may find the Fates gave you the greatest gift you've yet to receive."

Sighing, I leaned my head back and admitted to myself that everything she was saying was true. The moments I saw Ryland be his true self—the one who wasn't mad at the world—he was kind and gentle, yet strong all at the same time. That was a man I could love one day, and he at least deserved a chance to redeem himself.

"Thank you," I said, turning toward her, knowing she'd already heard my decision.

"Before I go, please know I won't be back. This was a loophole from the Fates, because they'd already interfered with Ryland earlier. I wish I could be here to teach you all the things I knew, but I know you'll make a fine successor. Just keep learning as much as you can and be open to the impossible. You wear my crown as if it was made for you, and I eagerly await you showing the worlds what you're capable of."

Her hand settled over mine, and a feeling of peace filled me.

"I wish I'd been able to grow up here, with you and my ancestors. I'd be more prepared for what's to come," I said.

She leaned in and kissed my forehead before giving me a firm hug. "Just remember, everything happens for a reason. Even if we don't understand or like those reasons, bigger things are always at play. Accept that, and everything else will fall into place, my sweet granddaughter."

She stood and we hugged before whispering words of love and goodbyes. Once she was gone, I knew what I had to do, even if I wasn't looking forward to apologizing.

Deciding to postpone the moment, I began walking back toward the town instead of porting. I had no idea where Ryland lived, but hopefully I'd pass by someone who could tell me. It wasn't like they wouldn't know who I was.

Just as I rounded the first set of rocks past the falls, I collided with a hard body, and a scream ripped from my chest before I instinctually flung magic from my hands. My probably-not-an-attacker fell to the ground, convulsing as if he'd been shocked by a defibrillator.

When the moonlight landed on the face of Ryland and I knew my mistake, I immediately withdrew my magic and apologized a million times as he recovered from the blow.

"It's okay, Kali. At least we know your reaction time isn't going to be an issue." He smirked at me, and I was surprised. I thought he'd be upset that I'd disappeared on him right after he confessed his mistakes to me.

"Uh, yeah. I was actually coming to find you," I forced out the words before I could chicken out. We needed to get this awkward moment out in the open as quickly as possible. At least it was awkward for me. I wasn't the most comfortable speaking about my feelings, so it was either going to be word vomit or nothing at all.

"Is everything okay?" He glanced around, moving in closer to me without seeming to realize it.

"Yes, everything is fine, or at least it will be. Listen, you surprised me earlier, but I do understand where you're coming from."

He cut me off. "So, you accept the bond?" Excitement poured from him, and I almost felt bad for what I was about to do.

"Yes and no. I accept that you're my Meraki, the other half to my soul, but it doesn't mean I'm ready to marry you or move in together or anything remotely close to that. We can date and get to know each other alongside my trainings where I learn to manage my abilities with you at my side. I can't bring myself to just accept things because some higher being told me it's what's best for me. I need to know it without doubt for myself. If you can agree to that, then I'd like to move forward."

The grin on his face grew wider with every rambling word I spoke. "You want to be courted."

"Um, no. We're not from the early 1500s or whatever. We can date like normal people. I realize I'm not human any longer, but it's how I grew up, so this is what I need."

His hand reached for mine, and he lifted it to his mouth, placing the softest of kisses in my palm. "There is no challenge I will let get in my way of making you mine. I accept your offer, and we can begin tomorrow by accepting our bond to each other in front of the council. Then, I'll take you out to dinner for our first date."

Cheese and rice. It sounded like we were getting married at the courthouse, then heading to the diner to celebrate like crazy people.

What in the world had I done?

CHAPTER 21

Ryland walked me back to the guest house, and we kept the conversation light. He mostly chatted about things around the town that I didn't know enough about yet. Like the bakery who made donuts only on Sundays and the Italian restaurant that had the best chicken tortellini in all the worlds.

I had to give it to him. He seemed to already know the quickest way to my heart was through my stomach.

When we arrived at the driveway, I stopped. Lights were on in the guest house and the main house, so remaining in the shadows was probably a good idea.

"I don't want to push you into something you're not ready for, but if you want to complete the bond, I can arrange everything with the council for tomorrow afternoon," he said nervously while avoiding eye contact.

"Like I said before, I'm willing to accept the bond and all that comes with it, as long as you're willing to take the relationship aspect of things slow. How does completing it work?"

We were already connected—I'd be a fool not to acknowledge

the pull I felt toward him—so we might as well take advantage of the benefits while working out the details.

"It's like a ceremony where they bind our souls together. It can still be broken like the bond we have now, but it would take a powerful being to do so, and the suffering would be unimaginable."

Huh, I never had any special ceremony with Stryx, but our connection seemed to be locked down tight, so I guess it was different for the Meraki bond. What was a little more hurt later if need be in exchange for more balance at the present time while we figured things out? I wasn't scared and Ryland didn't seem to be, either. Though, his confidence seemed to be more from believing nothing would tear us apart than anything else.

"I'm not worried about it. Do we want to train tomorrow beforehand or take the day off?" I asked, then felt like an inconsiderate jerk for suggesting we work on the day we were practically getting married.

"Um, the day off would be better since I have to coordinate things with the council. We can pick up the day after, though. The two of us will have a lot of one-on-one training with the help of Stryx as he releases more of your abilities and I help you from being overtaken by magic."

"Okay, well, I guess I'll see you tomorrow afternoon, then?" I had no idea how we were supposed to say goodbye. If he was my actual boyfriend, I'd be kissing him senseless, but he wasn't. He was more than that in so many ways, most of which were terrifying.

His eyes took on a sparkle that was more mischievous than innocent, causing me to take a step back. It was a look I'd yet to see and didn't know how to read.

"I know this is a lot to take on, but I promise, I'm going to be everything you need me to be, Kali." He closed the gap between us and gently cradled my head between his calloused hands before pressing his lips to my forehead. When he pulled away, he winked, then disappeared from existence, taking my breath with him.

I hadn't expected him to be forward, but that was the perfect amount of persistence for me, and if he kept it up, I wouldn't have a chance in fighting the attraction he was throwing my way.

While walking slowly to the guest house, I thought about all that had happened throughout the day. It had been one of the longest in my life, yet it was turning out to be one of the best.

When I opened the door, Jordan instantly pounced on me, shaking my shoulders with both hands. "Where. Have. You. Been?"

"Uh, out?"

Her head shook as she backed away and headed toward the fridge. "No, that doesn't work for me. You left with Ryland, then he showed up here looking like someone kicked his dog. Once he realized you didn't come home, he took off, and you've been gone a long while. So tell me, where have you been?"

During her little rant, she managed to grab a bottle of something unlabeled from the fridge, along with two glasses, and made it to the couch before drawing her next breath. I still hadn't even moved from the doorway.

"Come on. We don't have all night. I've got fae wine to loosen you up, and I'm not afraid to force it down your throat, either." She grinned wickedly, and I held my hands up in surrender.

"Okay, okay. Calm down before you catch the place on fire with an unintended orb or something," I teased as I took a seat next to her on the couch, then proceeded to catch her up on the last hour or so of events.

"Holy crap. You got to meet Taliah. *The* Taliah? I wish I had been there. And Ryland? I did *not* see that turn of events. I mean, I had a feeling. Hence, why we ditched him when leaving for the Otherworld, but wow, that moved fast. So, how do you feel about it all?"

"I don't know. Nervous, relieved, excited, anxious, scared. All of that in no particular order and so much more," I answered honestly.

"Understandably so. Finding and accepting your Meraki is a big deal. I can only imagine those feelings all at once." There was a hint of longing in her voice, and I instantly felt bad.

There I was, only a resident of Arvayta for a few weeks, and I was lucky enough to find my soulmate but not willing to go all in. While Jordan, who was decades old, had yet to find hers, but was clearly yearning for the connection.

"As soon as this mess with Alaryk is all over, you and I will have a real girls' vacation. We can go wherever you want and maybe we'll find your other half. Too bad it wasn't Oliver." Having her Meraki be mine's best friend would have been quite convenient.

"That's disgusting, and don't ever say anything like that again. Those two boys are like my brothers. I don't want to hear about any sexy times with you and Ryland, nor any hopes of me being with Oliver. It will never happen." Her body shuddered at the thought, and I couldn't help but laugh.

"Easy enough for me. But I really do hope we find your happily-ever-after."

She leaned into me. "At least I've already found my soul sister. That will be enough for now."

"Ahhh, you do love me. What's funny about that, though, is I had very similar thoughts earlier. I have all these bonds in my life, and while things are unbelievably insane around here, I really do feel grateful for you, Stryx, and well, now Ryland."

Her eyes widened. "Oh, speaking of Stryx. I wonder what kind of animal I'm going to get. He better not stick me with a rabbit or something docile. I want one with bite. Like a tiger or panther."

Shaking my head, I finally took a drink of the fae wine she'd offered me, and my tongue was hit with several flavors. Apple, strawberry, and cinnamon were the most prominent, and I eagerly gulped down more.

"Easy, Chuck. That might taste good, but it will knock you on your ass if you're not careful," Jordan said before taking a sip.

A hiccup escaped my lips, then we burst into laughter, falling on top of each other. The rest of the night was spent talking about all the good things in our life, those from the past and even the present. Hours later, when I finally fell into bed and the room was spinning, I decided that no matter what came next, this was the best life I could possibly be living.

THE NEXT MORNING, I SILENTLY THANKED RYLAND FOR CANCELING training. My head was pounding, and my body felt like I'd run a dozen marathons. When I stumbled into the kitchen for some sort of soothing tea, Jordan didn't look like she was faring much better than me.

"I hate you," I mumbled.

"I warned you, and you can't hate me. We're soul sisters. Agreed upon it less than twelve hours ago. Even if you don't remember in your hungover state, you're still stuck with me for life. Plus, you'll love me forever once you taste this concoction." She slid a mug across the counter to me.

Lifting it up, I could see a clear liquid in the cup that was steaming and smelled like mint chocolate. Without hesitating, I took a long pull, then immediately spit it out. "That's the most deceitful drink I've ever had. It smells delicious yet tastes like death."

Jordan smirked. "If you can choke down a few gulps of that, the hangover will be gone. I promise, it's worth it."

Ugh. She better be right, or I was going to pay her back. Trying once more, I plugged my nose and took two small yet quick drinks while attempting to swallow the warm liquid before tasting it.

"Now go get ready. You've got a date with the council, and I don't think your Meraki would appreciate it if you were late."

My eyes widened and pulse quickened. Holy Fates. I was tying myself to a stranger later that day. What had I been thinking?

"Oh, calm your tits. You're going to be fine. It's not like you have to have—"

"Do not finish that sentence. I'm getting ready now." I stormed off, slammed my door shut, then stared at my closest.

What does one wear to their not-wedding?

An hour later, I'd yet to come out of my room, and Jordan was throwing a fit because I wouldn't let her help me. Finally, a softer knock sounded, and I heard my mom's voice.

"Kaliah, can I come in?" she asked sweetly.

Of course, I wasn't going to tell her no, but as I went to open the door, I realized I'd never told my parents what was happening. I was supposed to be officially tying myself to someone this afternoon and I'd never told them. I was the worst daughter ever.

When I opened the door, I instantly wrapped my arms around my mom. "I'm so sorry I didn't come see you guys last night. I don't know what I was thinking."

She laughed and pulled back. "It's okay, sweet girl. Ryland came to see us before finding you, and we knew if you needed anything, you'd come to us. Your dad and I knew you'd need space to grow on your own if we truly wanted to see you succeed in Arvayta. It's why we've been a little distant lately. This is your time to shine on your own while making mistakes and becoming your own person.

"You didn't and still don't need your parents hovering over your every move, making you more nervous than necessary. We have faith we raised you well enough to know that if there is something important, you can make the right decision on your own and know that we will be there to support you no matter what. You don't need any pressure from us."

I snorted. "Yeah, just pressure from my grandmother."

She gasped. "Taliah visited you?"

I nodded and once again explained everything from the night before. I was beginning to think I should just write it down, so I didn't have to repeat myself.

"Wow. I wish I had been there. I was young when she passed, but nobody I've ever known had a bigger heart than hers. I'm glad she was able to help you and you met her. It is my greatest regret not allowing you to know your heritage before it was time, but keeping you safe was more important."

"What does Dad think of me pretty much getting married today?" I asked, hoping he wasn't going to go all papa bear on Ryland and me.

"Your father is very familiar with how the Meraki bond works. He knows there is nothing he can do to stop it, so while he wishes you didn't have to grow up so fast, he's happy it's Ryland. We've known that boy his whole life, and the Fates couldn't have chosen a better equal for you."

My cheeks flushed, and I turned away. Then, I remembered that I still wasn't ready, and we needed to leave soon.

"What do I wear today?" I asked, eyeing her silk green gown and really hoping she didn't recommend something from her closet.

"Now that is something that I will gladly help you with." Mom stood and went to the choices I had out on my bed. I didn't want anything too fancy, but also not too casual.

She glanced at the items on my bed and then shook her head. "Those won't do, but I have an idea and I'll be right back. Jordan's gone ahead of us, so why don't you use the bathroom and begin on your hair. Something simple and keep your curls. Be your natural beautiful self."

Before I could object, she was out my door and headed

outside. Deciding she couldn't be nearly as bad at dressing me than as Jordan was, I did as my mom said and started on my hair. Using a curling iron, I made my curls even bigger. Then, I braided two sections of hair, one on each side of my head, before pulling them back and tucking each plait under my crown, giving the appearance it was half-up and down.

My mom returned just as I was touching up a few of the curls, and she was holding a garment bag. "Oh, honey. You're perfect. Now, let's see what you think of the dress." She shoved me into my room, excitement rolling off of her in waves, which made me more nervous even though I trusted her.

She hung the bag from the back of my door and unzipped it slowly, revealing an icy blue dress that almost exactly matched my eyes. It was fitted with two-inch straps at the shoulders. There was absolutely nothing flashy about it, yet the fabric was luxurious and far from casual.

"Where did you find this?" I asked in awe.

"I had it made just for you." She beamed from ear-to-ear.

"How did you know? Or when did you do this?"

She laughed. "Just now. I saw what you were considering, and I knew what it was missing. Your color choices here were too dark or the fitting wasn't right. You needed a little something of everything you had laid out. I went to Carletta and asked for a rush. She magicked this right up and sent her well wishes."

I didn't know who this Carletta lady was, but I needed to meet her. The dress was absolutely stunning, and I was shedding my pajamas before I even knew what I was doing. My mom helped me step into the dress and zipped me up. When she did, tears pricked at her eyes.

"I hope you know how proud you've made us. Not just today, but everything you've done, the young woman you've become. Your dad and I are so honored to be your parents."

Hugging her close, I whispered, "I love you, Mom. Thank you for everything."

"There isn't anything in this world I wouldn't do for you. Now, let's get to the council chambers. The process is quick and painless. Assuming you already feel a connection to Ryland, it should be relatively the same, just amplified. Though, how much depends on how close the two of you get, but you can work that out on your own. Or remember, I'm here for whatever questions you might have."

She hugged me once more, then took my hand as I followed her outside.

My heart was bursting with love and joy. Getting ready with my mom had been everything I needed, and I was ready to bond with Ryland more so than even the night before.

Dad was already on the porch and stood when he saw us. His eyes lit up with pride, and I went straight into his arms as soon as he stepped off the porch. He didn't say anything to me but held me tight, which spoke more to me than words could.

As the day went on, I began to feel like this was more of a wedding than Ryland had let on, but I didn't care anymore. Everything within me knew what we were doing was the right step forward. Somehow, it would all work out the way it was supposed to.

When I pulled back from my dad, I took his arm. My mom took the same position on his opposite side, then we ported to the front of town hall. Not many people were out, which I was thankful for, but when we entered, I became overwhelmingly nervous out of nowhere.

"Where is Jordan?" I asked.

"She should already be with Ryland and the council," Mom answered.

"What about Stryx? Shouldn't he be here for this since I'm already bonded to him?" My little feathered friend better hurry back from Dásos before I got cold feet.

"He doesn't need to be, but if you'd rather wait for him, we certainly can." Mom didn't sound confident that would be the best choice, but I was beginning to consider it. As the realization that he wasn't present really set in, my stomach began to knot up.

"I'm not sure. Something doesn't feel right now that we're here," I said, glancing around for any signs that something was amiss.

Dad wrapped an arm tighter around me. "You have full say in what happens today, sweet girl. If you'd rather wait, then that's what we'll do. None of us are going anywhere."

"Let's just get to the council room, and I'll see if anyone has heard from Stryx. Maybe he'll be here soon. He did say he'd be back today." I really hoped that was the case, because all of a sudden, there was a heaviness pressing down on me. Any positive thoughts I'd had back at the house were long gone. Something on an instinctual level was telling me nothing was okay anymore, and I was afraid to find out I was right.

My pace picked up as we moved through the town hall, eager to figure out what had me so on edge. Except, when we rounded the corner to the meeting room, my steps faltered, and we stopped. "There's something dark in that room. It's pulling me forward, yet everything within me says to run the other way. Who is in there?"

Concern was etched deeply into both of their faces. "It should just be the council, Jordan, and Ryland. I don't sense anyone else," Mom said warily.

Before we could decide what to do, there was a scream muffled by the walls, though there was no mistaking the terror that induced it. With trembling hands, all three of us ran for the door, and I wondered just where Jordan and Ryland were. If they weren't okay, I wasn't sure how I was going to get through anything else.

When we arrived, my dad flung open the door to a setting that would forever be engraved into my darkest memories.

CHAPTER 22

One of the council members was lying stomach-down on the table, eyes open, yet lifeless. There was blood splattered everywhere, but I couldn't see her wounds, making me assume they were all in the front pressed against the table that was also covered in crimson liquid.

My eyes found Ryland, who was standing next to a furious Jordan and staring at the back of the room. I followed their gazes and met the smirking face of a stranger who didn't belong in Arvayta. With stark-white hair that was shaved short at the sides and a few inches long at the top, his pointed ears and sharply angled cheekbones stood out, along with the nearly black eyes staring at me.

"My love, I'm so glad you finally arrived. And look at you! Positively exquisite," the man who I then assumed to be Alaryk purred.

Everything about him was light except for his eyes, and it was hard to believe he was supposed to be a dark fae, but when he smiled at me, my skin crawled and I didn't question the evil I knew he was capable of. It radiated off of him in rapid pulses.

"What are you doing here, Alaryk?" Dad roared.

Taking a moment, I glanced around the room, trying to see if anyone else was hurt besides Rosella, whose name I finally remembered when I had a moment to breathe. While the rest of the council wasn't hurt, they were pinned to the wall by an invisible force.

Mathias, the head of the council, was red in the face as he fought against whatever magic was being used against them, but it seemed pointless.

"I'm here to claim my mate. I heard there would be a bonding ceremony today and assumed I should be present. She is destined to be mine after all." Alaryk spoke with such confidence, he had me worried.

But what I was most concerned with was how in the hell he knew I was supposed to be bonded to Ryland when we'd only decided the night before. Who had betrayed us and why?

"I'm not yours. I don't care what some prophecy said decades ago. I'm my own person and make my own decisions," I said, taking a step forward.

If Alaryk wanted me for himself, I wasn't worried he would hurt me, so I wanted to keep the attention on myself.

"Tsk, tsk, my darling. You've been poisoned to think the worst of me, but I promise you a lifetime of happiness with the world at your fingertips. All you have to do is take my hand and you can have all you ever dreamed of." His voice was smooth and words hypnotic, but I fought against their power.

"You came here uninvited and killed one of my people. Why should I trust you?" I asked, while moving closer to Ryland and Jordan with my parents at my back. If anything happened to any of them, I wasn't sure what I would do.

He raised a hand toward me. "Let me show you what I'm capable of, and then you'll understand I'm not here to hurt anyone so long as I get what I want." His fingers snapped, and a white light flashed around the room.

When my eyes adjusted from the glow, we were no longer in the council chambers. We were outside, near the fountain I so often admired, but only Alaryk and I had been transported from the room.

"Where is everyone?" I snapped, moving a few paces back from him. The road was empty, I couldn't see a single Arvaytan, and considering it was late afternoon, something was really wrong.

"Your people are with mine. You didn't think I came to collect my bride without a backup plan in case you refused, did you?" His lips lifted into what I assumed was supposed to be a grin but came out as more of a sneer.

"Wishful thinking, I guess." With every step I took away from him, he took two more closer to me.

Stryx, where are you? We could really use some help here before this psycho kidnaps me, I pleaded through our bond, hoping like hell he could hear me in Dásos.

Just stay calm and indulge him. I'll be there as soon as I can, Stryx responded, sounding fearful for the first time ever.

"So, what will it be, my love? Will you come with me willingly, or will you have your people slaughtered all because of your stubborn pride?" Alaryk asked when he was only an arm's length away from me.

"Well, can I ask some questions before I decide? Ever since I arrived here, things have been decided for me, and while I appreciate that you're giving me an option here, I'd like to be well-informed before I choose. You say I've only been told lies about you, so tell me why I should trust you?"

My hope was that I could convince him I wasn't exactly happy in Arvayta, give him a little faith that I'd be easily swayed to his side. If the prophecy said I would be, he should hopefully buy my lies the first time around.

"Because you're destined to be mine. Isn't that enough?" he

snarled, clearly angry I wasn't showing fear and caving to his threats.

"You'd think so, but you see, I've also been told I was destined to be with another. How am I supposed to know who's right? The only family I've ever known, or you? A complete stranger I'm inclined to get to know, but I need a reason. While I'm not happy here, I know I'm safe. Would I be safe with you?"

His hand reached for me, and it took every ounce of strength within me not to flinch at the cold touch of his fingers on my cheek. "I'd never harm you, Kaliah. I'd worship every inch of your body and give you all your greatest desires. There is nothing in all the worlds you'd ever want for with me."

I forced myself to lean into his touch. "What would you expect of me in return for your graciousness?"

His head moved closer until his lips were nearly touching my ear as he whispered, "Everything that you are would be mine, and everything that I am would be yours."

Cheese and rice. If I wasn't a million percent certain he wanted to destroy the worlds with our combined powers, then I'd have a hard time resisting him. The pull he had on me was real and powerful. Whatever magic he was using wasn't child's play.

My eyes met his as he licked his lips before grasping my face. "What do you say, my love? Will you leave this world behind and be mine forever?"

Just as I was about to answer him, a flash of light distracted us both as a portal opened. On the other side was a thick forest and a horde of fierce animals waiting to come through. Stryx led the way, and as they poured into the center of town, the portal kept growing. More creatures than I ever imagined waltzed through the opening, and I began to let hope sink in that we could beat the dark fae.

Alaryk grabbed my arm and jerked me into his chest, forcing

my head up with his other hand. "Were you playing me, darling?"

"Did you honestly believe I could love someone who would kill innocent people in an attempt to hold power over others? Everything about you repulses me. Now let me go!" I pressed both hands to his chest and shocked him hard enough to force him several paces back.

Wasting no time, I ported to the portal that was about fifty feet from us and surrounded by animals I hoped would keep me out of sight. "Stryx, what do we do? He has others here, and he's keeping our people locked inside. Probably tortured." My whole body shook at the thought of what the others were going through while we waited for help to arrive.

"The animals will go search for their other halves and help. Just keep an eye on Alaryk and don't let him get his hands on you. If he takes you…" Stryx didn't finish the sentence and he didn't have to.

Speaking of other halves, I would have thought my parents, Jordan, and Ryland would have followed us out of the council room, but I'd yet to see them.

"I have to go find them," I yelled to Stryx, assuming he heard my thoughts.

He swiveled his head around in the creepy and nearly three-hundred-sixty-degree way I found impossible. "They're on the steps of the town hall, and Oliver is with them, too. They'll be here soon. Just stay by my side. The portal magic will help to mask yours from being found by Alaryk."

Speaking of the devil.

"Kaliah, my love. Where did you run off to? It's time to go home," Alaryk yelled over the stampeding animals racing by him to help my people.

Stryx finally came down from the sky and landed roughly on my shoulder. Thankfully, even though they weren't covered, his claws were magically enhanced not to tear my skin up. Perks of the bond.

"We need to get to the others. We can't wait for them to come to us," Stryx said, and then did something he'd never done before.

Suddenly, my mind went blank, and when my vision returned just a couple of seconds later, my eyesight was doubled as my brain was somehow processing what Stryx was seeing and what I was at the same time. Together, we could see from every angle around us.

Then, Stryx's thoughts began mixing with my own, and I grabbed the sides of my head as I adjusted to the changes. *How is this happening?* I asked without speaking.

I'm allowing you access to everything I am. Preferably, we would have practiced this, but we don't have time for that. You have to get to the others, and they're being targeted. So, let's move before Alaryk finds you. I can only mask you for so long.

A dizziness rolled through me as I fought to focus on the double vision, and within a minute, I had a decent grasp on it. By then, the animals had stopped coming through the portal and we were no longer hidden by the seemingly endless stream of them.

Once Stryx closed the portal, he urged me to move toward the town hall. Screams and roars from the animals sounded from all around us while plumes of smoke rose into the air, and my heart was slowly breaking. This place wasn't ready for a war, but it had been forced on them, nonetheless.

On your left, Stryx said. My hand shot out instinctively, grabbing the throat of my attacker.

He was about six inches taller than me, and carried about twice the weight, but I didn't let it frighten me. "Leave before you get yourself killed," I said with a sneer.

"We're not leaving until our king gets his queen," he replied with a strangled voice.

I really couldn't fathom killing someone yet, but I couldn't just let him go and didn't have time for hand-to-hand combat, so I did the next best thing.

Calling on my power, I let it build higher than ever before on my own and sent a blast straight into the man's chest. I didn't even know if he was part fae or something else entirely; all that mattered was he was unconscious on the dirt within the blink of an eye.

"Keep moving, Kaliah, and remember they won't all be that easy to take down. That shifter perceived you as an easy target, most others will not." Stryx's words sank in, and I kept my power at my fingertips.

I'd be ready for whatever came at us next, because there was no way in hell that I'd let Alaryk get his hands on me. The more I tried to imagine what he wanted from me, the angrier I became. As I let my emotions build, I became a bubble of energy.

Magic radiated from every point of my body and there was a slight purple glow coming from skin everywhere I could see. *Did you lift the blocks on my abilities?* I asked.

No, you're breaking through them, just how I wanted. This is how I hoped you'd do it, though not under these circumstances. On your backside, turn now!

Without missing a beat, I ducked and slammed my fist full of magic into the stomach of the beast before me, but he wasn't the least bit fazed by my powers. Standing back up, I took in his nearly seven-foot frame before noticing the scales that lined his skin and the measly cloth shorts that he was wearing, nothing else.

"Hello, Princess." The man-beast grinned, showcasing a mouth full of teeth that reminded me of Yelah.

Uh, Stryx, what am I supposed to do against this thing? I asked mentally.

You fight him until help arrives. The others can see us now, and they'll be here soon. Do whatever you have to in order to keep him from getting a hold on you.

My jaw clenched as I realized that meant if I was able to, then I needed to kill the creature before he could do the same to me. If it was my life or his, I didn't really have a choice, but I didn't like it.

Crouching down to make myself a smaller target, I felt my dress begin to rip, so I gave it a little help and myself more room to move by making two slits midway up my thighs.

The beast swiped his hand out for me, and Stryx flew into the sky while I rolled out of the way on the dirt, losing my shoes in the process. Thankfully, my crown was practically plastered to my head and stayed in place.

"Oh, come on, Princess. I mean you no harm. Just come with me and everything will be fine," the beast jeered as we faced each other once more.

"That's never going to happen," I snapped back.

He grinned once again, making my insides turn with fear. "That's what I was hoping for."

He's a dragon hybrid. There are only two ways to kill him: free him of his head or remove his heart from his scaled chest, Stryx said as I practically did the two-step with the dragon-man, evading his attempts to grab me.

So, considering I have no weapons, what the hell do you want me to do? My voice was full of rage as the shouts from others could still be heard around us.

Just keep fighting, and I'll be back.

You're leaving me? I yelled in my head as I once again found myself on the ground, but Stryx never responded and I wanted to kill him.

Using all of my frustrations, I charged at the dragon-man, hands out and full of as much harmful magic as I could muster. When we connected, I grabbed onto his scales and began pulling, hoping I could find skin and cause more damage, but I'd stayed too close for too long, and his clawed hands took hold of my arms

Lifting me off the ground, the beast brought me even with his face while blood trickled from where he grabbed me. "Enough, Princess. I'm not supposed to hurt you, but I will if you continue to refuse me."

"I will fight until my last breath," I sneered, then called on everything I had, remembering that magic wasn't just what I had within me. It was also in everything around me.

Water was another part of me, just like magic, so I reached far and called it to me, asking for its help. Within mere moments, an overwhelming amount of power slammed into me, and I did the only thing I could think of.

I released it and froze the dragon-man in place before wiggling free of his grasp and dropping a couple feet to the ground.

Just as I landed, Jordan came leaping out of nowhere and chopped the frozen head clean off, then proceeded to stab it for good measure.

"A little late, but thanks for the assist," I said, looking around for the others. Ryland was still fighting near the town hall against an opponent who kept disappearing and reappearing every time Ryland came too close.

"Come on, we have to help them," Jordan said, grabbing my hand, then immediately dropping it. "Care to turn the cold off, Chuck?"

"Actually, no, I don't. Let's go."

She grinned and nodded, then proceeded to plow through the crowd of fighting animals and creatures.

Heat slammed into my back, but I ignored it because it didn't hurt. Though, when the voice that followed spoke softly in my ear, I froze on the spot. "You were made for me. What you did to that dragon was the sexiest thing I've ever seen in my existence."

Alaryk's voice was alluring, but I fought the pull with everything I had. His hand trailed down my bloodied arm. "I won't let anyone else hurt you. Just come with me."

Then it hit me. He kept asking me to come with him when he

could have easily just grabbed me and disappeared. "You can't take me." I turned around and faced him, no longer afraid. "You need me to come with you willingly, don't you?"

His face went from caring lover to murderous in a split second. "I don't *need* for you to do anything. I'm offering you a life of luxury, but if you continuously refuse, then I will show you the consequences of that decision."

There must have been something in the prophecy he believed in so much that stated I had to become his on my own terms, a loophole I so badly needed. It told me I wasn't doomed, and we had a real chance at stopping this psycho.

"You don't scare me," I snarled before thrusting my arms at him, trying to freeze him like I did the dragon.

He shook his finger at me, completely unaffected. "You're going to regret that." His dark eyes stared above my head and nodded.

Taking the chance, I followed his gaze to where my parents were being held by two of his men at the top of the stairs to the town hall. Neither of the fae holding them appeared to be in great shape. My parents had fought hard against them based on the black eyes, torn clothes, and magic scorches I could see.

Though, none of that mattered when my eyes landed on the glowing knives each of the men held in their hands.

"No!" I shouted and began to run for them, but I was too late. The two monsters keeping them paralyzed plunged blades into my parents' chests at the same time before disappearing, but I'd remember their faces and they would face my wrath one day.

Alaryk yelled after me. "This is what happens when you fight destiny, my love. Remember, this all could have been avoided if you'd just come with me, but don't worry, I'll give you time to grieve before I come back for you."

Alaryk's words cut straight through my heart as a darkness began to come over me with every step I took. The fury raging through me took precedence over everything else as creatures began to disappear and the path to my parents cleared.

Their lifeless bodies lay at the footsteps of town hall with their eyes open, both bleeding from daggers in their chests. Using a hand, I wiped the stray tear from my mother's cheek and closed her eyes, then my dad's.

I collapsed between them, wrapping an arm around their waists as tears streaked down my cheeks. There wasn't an inch of me that wasn't breaking from the anguish of seeing my parents motionless on the ground.

I could hear my voice being called, but I ignored them as I let the hate for Alaryk rise to the surface. I wanted it to consume everything I was, and I wanted to kill him. He'd taken my only family from me, and I wasn't going to let him get away with it. Not even if I had to go dark to accomplish the task.

As I attempted to dry the tears I'd shed for my mother and father, thunder sounded in the distance. It was a noise that didn't belong in the perfect climate of Arvayta but called to me, nonetheless. As I raised myself up, I looked to the sky, calling the powerful energy of the storm brewing to me.

"Kali, you need to stop," Jordan said cautiously, and when my eyes met hers, she took a step back.

"Who's going to make me?"

Just as lightning shot down from the sky, straight for my body, Ryland wrapped his arms around me, absorbing the hit alongside me. His hands moved to my face, and everything around us faded except the glow of power I wanted all to myself in order to remove Alaryk's existence from the worlds.

"Let's do this together, Kali. You and me. We will end him. You're not alone, and I will help you carry this burden." His words were strong, forceful, and demanding.

My head shook as tears still trailed down my face. "He took them. I have to make him pay."

"And you will. I'll make sure of it, even if it's the last thing I do."

His eyes called to the darkness growing within me, forcing it down by the second. When I finally nodded, the storm dissipated, and Ryland pulled me into his arms. I allowed him to take some of the weight from my shoulders, but as I glanced down at my parents' prone bodies, I knew it was just the beginning.

A storm was about to rage, and I was going to destroy everything in my path.

OF BLOOD AND SACRIFICE

BOOK THREE

DEDICATION

To anyone who has ever lost someone so precious and irreplaceable, yet managed to continued on.
May your fortitude keep growing with every passing day.

CHAPTER 1

Lightning struck all around me as my hair flew across my face and tears flowed down my cheeks. The anguish came and went, some moments better than others, but most of them worse. Today was not a better day. After just laying my parents to rest, my grief was in full force.

It wasn't right, nor was it fair, but there would be retribution. Alaryk would get what he had coming to him. I wouldn't stop until he paid for taking the two most important people in all the worlds away from me—he and the two men who had done the dark fae's dirty work.

"Kali!" Jordan's voice sounded like a whisper through the thunder that followed the fit I was throwing, and I pretended not to hear her.

Kaliah, you need to stop before you hurt someone, Stryx sounded in my head.

That was the only thing that could give me pause.

Enough innocent blood had been spilled and I refused to be the cause of any more.

Fine, but I don't want to talk. Make her go away, I replied, not caring if I seemed unreasonable.

Jordan had done her best to be there for me, but no amount of consoling could heal the hurt in my heart. My parents were gone, and they were never coming back. Alaryk had taken them from me when I refused to go with him and be by his side in some asinine quest for control.

Ryland is here, too. Shall I send him away as well? The disappointment in Stryx's voice wasn't missed.

As the thunder quieted and the lightning began to dissipate, my shoulders hunched. *I don't know.*

Ryland hadn't been hurt by my lightning before, but he'd yet to force himself on me since the moments after the fight. I'd asked for space and he'd given it, but not easily.

You can't be afraid to care about people anymore. Your parents' deaths were not your fault, and they would be devastated to know you were doing everything you could to push away those who care for you most.

Stryx was the only person I couldn't make disappear. The feathered annoyance was always there in my head, reminding me of things I'd much rather forget.

"I'm not leaving, Kaliah Grace. Neither is Ryland. You had your time, and now you've forced our hand." Jordan glared from across the training field as the storm around me died down.

I'd at least had the forethought to go outside of town before I let the power rip from my core and through the sky. Power that had been unleashed just moments too late. Useless then, but I'd make sure the next shot I had at Alaryk wasn't wasted.

Ryland was next to Jordan with Stryx on his shoulder. They both stared at me, but with more patience than my best friend.

Deciding I'd let enough of the rage out for the afternoon, I caved and went to them. I didn't have the energy to deal with Jordan if I refused to speak with them once again. Her level of annoyance with me was only increasing as the days passed, and I knew deep down she didn't deserve the treatment I'd been giving her. None of them did.

She opened her mouth, but Ryland covered it with his hand. "You yell at her one more time and I'll deal with you myself."

She bit his hand, and he pulled away. "She's *my* best friend. I'll do whatever I want."

Stryx snapped his beak. "Enough. Both of you. Kali, how are you feeling after utilizing that much power?"

What I appreciated most about that question was that he had specified it to my abilities, not my actual feelings. It was possible Stryx knew me even better than Jordan did, but I'd never tell her that. She'd probably murder the owl.

She could certainly try. It would be fun, Stryx replied to my thoughts.

Jordan caught my grin and crossed her arms. "Hey, no mind speak. It's rude in front of other people."

"I'm doing fine with the power," I said, answering Stryx's question. "The crown helps more than I realized before. Though, if I take it off for even a second, my body begins to shake, and breathing becomes hard. Will that last forever?"

I hoped not, because I didn't want the crown to be a permanent fixture on my head, but I'd deal with it over my magic taking control any day.

"Do you remember us mentioning something about you being an Arelia when you first arrived?" Stryx asked instead of answering me.

I recalled when Jordan had mentioned it during my first meeting with Oliver. Stryx had said that would come later in my training, and I'd been perfectly okay with that, considering all the changes I'd been going through at the time.

"Is that what this is?" I gestured toward the sky where the last few flashes of lightning were fading away.

Right after the fight ended with Alaryk, something in me had snapped and I'd been struck by my own power. So had Ryland, but he'd absorbed the lightning nearly as well as I had, which I still didn't quite understand.

The power I'd somehow summoned had turned my water affinity into something more, something nobody around me had ever seen. While it seemed to make most people afraid of me, I was basking in the charge of the storms I created.

"Yes, your emotions broke the last of my blocks on your abilities, and we need to get them under control. The longer we wait, the harder it will be," Stryx answered.

"What do I need to do?" I asked eagerly. Anything that needed to be done in order to beat Alaryk, I'd do without a second thought. Plus, it was a welcome distraction from the grief.

"You need to formally bond with Ryland like we planned before. He will level out your power and take on whatever you can't handle, like he did when you first created the lightning."

Well, I'd do everything but that. Or, at least, I didn't want to.

Ryland was my Meraki. My soulmate. I'd promised him I would accept our bond officially, but we'd never made it that far and I'd pushed him away ever since.

I was a hot mess and didn't want to take him down with me.

"Alaryk mentioned time for her to grieve. We don't need to do it now," Ryland said when I didn't answer right away. The hurt in his voice broke my heart.

I wanted everything the bond promised. I wanted it more than he knew. More than all of that, though, I wanted to keep everyone else safe. The closer they got to me, the more I had to lose, and I couldn't handle any more hurt.

"If you continue on this path, it will only result in your failure," Stryx said before flying away. I knew exactly what he meant—if I kept pushing people away and chose the darkness—but the others didn't, and they never would if I had anything to do with it.

"What does Mr. Know-It-All mean?" Jordan snapped, clearly past offering me her sympathy.

"Nothing. I'm sorry I've ignored you all, but I appreciate you being there today."

The burial for my parents had been rough, harder than I'd attempted to prepare myself for, but Jordan and Ryland had each held one of my hands as I'd stood above their graves and watched the dirt be filled in.

Instead of a headstone, trees had been planted over their graves as the only marker for where their bodies laid, and I'd vowed to visit often to make sure the trees grew tall and strong.

"We wouldn't have missed it for anything," Ryland responded. "We thought after everything this morning that you might like some company back at the house."

My head shook, but before I could speak, Stryx was back inside my mind.

I mean it, Kaliah. Push those who wish to help you away and you will fail.

Stupid, intrusive owl. *I'm going to figure out how to block you and it will be the best day in the world.*

I hope you do, he replied smugly.

"Sure, you can come back with me," I answered, then ported home without another word.

By the time I took the first step on the porch, they were right behind me. I turned around to find them silently yelling at each other, mouths moving and hands flailing.

"Uh, what's wrong?" I asked.

"Oh, nothing. Ryland just needs to run an errand, so it will just be the two of us for a little while," Jordan replied with a forced smile.

"Actually, I don't have anywhere I'd rather be," he snarled.

I moved toward them, placing a hand on each of their chests. My eyes went to Ryland's as warmth flowed from me to him, our incomplete bond flaring to life, reminding me of the peace he provided to my soul. Which made my next words even harder. "Give us an hour, then I'll kick her out."

She jerked away from me. "Like hell you—"

"It's either that or I continue to ignore you both," I cut her off with a raised brow.

"You wouldn't dare."

Ryland reached for my hand that was still resting on his chest. "I'll be back in an hour."

Emotion I wasn't prepared for rushed through me. It was the first intentional contact I'd had with anyone in five days. Sure, I'd received hugs and handshakes from others, but I'd felt nothing then. I'd refused to allow their sympathies to have any impact on the rage I clung to, but welcoming Ryland's touch showed me Stryx was right.

I'd had my time to be isolated and guarded, but it was time to let others back in.

Ryland kissed the back of my hand and then disappeared from sight.

"Just because he's your Meraki, doesn't mean I'm going to let him monopolize all of your time," Jordan huffed.

"I know, and I love you for that. Now, let's go inside, but if you comment on the chaos, I will kick you out."

I'd been staying in the main house while Jordan and Ryland stayed in the guest house. I hadn't let either of them in, and I'd made quite the mess during my isolation.

As I opened the back door, even *I* cringed at the disaster. Broken glass crunched beneath my shoes, and dying flowers were scattered around the room from when I'd thrown a vase someone had left on the porch. I'd never even glanced at the card to see who they were from.

Boxes and bags of food had been left on the counter. When I'd bothered to eat, I had only chosen food I didn't need dishes for, afraid I'd break more things.

Jordan walked toward the hall closet and pulled out a broom and dustpan. "Why don't we therapy clean?"

Instead of answering, I threw my arms around her and held on tight as new tears leaked from my eyes.

Her hand held the back of my head as I shook against her. "It's going to be okay, Kali. Not today, tomorrow, or even next week, but you're going to get through this. I'll make sure of it."

I nodded but didn't reply. My throat was thick with emotion, and words refused to come.

A few minutes later, I managed to mostly pull myself back together. "Thank you."

Tears of her own fell freely, and I felt like a jerk for not thinking about her pain. Jordan had been close with my parents, like another daughter to them. Yet, I'd only thought of myself after their deaths.

"I'm sorry, Jordan. We both lost them, and I left you by yourself because that's what I needed, but I didn't think about what you needed as well."

She wiped away the tears. "I had Ryland and Oliver. Before you came along, they were my only friends. They let me beat the hell out of them while I wished for nothing more than to be able to offer you the same relief from the heartache."

I let a smile tug at my lips. "I bet you made them regret allowing you to do so."

"That I did, but they never said one word. They're good men, Kali."

I understood the double meaning to her words. "I won't push any of you away anymore. Stryx wouldn't let me if I tried anyway, but I don't know that it's a good idea to bond with Ryland now."

Jordan began sweeping, remaining calmer than I expected. "Why is that?"

"He's already had to experience the loss of one Meraki—even if it was fake. I don't want to put him through that again." I grabbed a garbage bag from the kitchen to pick up the bigger pieces of glass, followed by all of the trash.

"Who says he would lose you? Do you plan on dying?" Jordan countered.

"No. I don't know. It could happen, though. I don't want to have to worry about risks and hurting others when I'm so dead set on making sure Alaryk pays for what he did. I can't be the person Ryland deserves when the hate and darkness are so strong."

The prophecy that I would turn dark and work alongside Alaryk was never far from my thoughts. Every time I contemplated killing him, the darkness became more profound, and I wondered just how true the foretelling might become.

"That's not darkness, Kali. That's grief and rage. You lost your parents just five days ago. You're not supposed to be whole right now, and we all understand that. Ryland more than anyone. He lost his parents, too, you know."

I let her words sink in and wondered if they could be true—if I could overcome the ugliness growing within me. I was a shattered version of a past me that I no longer recognized or understood. I used to think I could put everything back together, but I wasn't so sure anymore.

And taking anyone else down with me besides Alaryk wasn't on my agenda.

CHAPTER 2

After we finished cleaning up and the house didn't smell like a garbage can, I sat with Jordan on the couch, simply enjoying her company. She could be crass at the best of times, which I loved about her, but she also knew when I just needed her presence.

"It's going to be okay," she said, not for the first time, while leaning her head down onto mine.

My finger touched my temple. "I know that here, but it's hard to convince my heart of the same thing."

"Just don't push us away anymore. We only want to help, and you need to remember you can't do this on your own. Don't let vengeance consume you or Alaryk will win, even if you beat him. He wanted to break you and turn you into something you're not. Don't give that to him."

I knew she was right. Deep down, I had already acknowledged why the dark fae had done what he did, but still, the rage that wasn't leaving anytime soon was so much louder than anything else around me.

The lines between right and wrong were being blurred as I

thought of all the things I wanted to do to Alaryk. No, not wanted, I *needed* to do.

Before I could get worked up again, a knock sounded at the back door, and Jordan stood to answer it. Glancing back, I could see Ryland through the glass with Stryx on his shoulder, making me wonder how close those two were getting.

Even though I'd told Ryland we could talk, I still wanted to run away. He wanted more from me than I was able to give, and I wasn't sure how to explain that to him. As much as I didn't want to hurt him, I didn't know what else to do. He didn't deserve half of a person as a Meraki.

Stryx sighed in my head, but I ignored him. I wasn't in the mood for one of his lectures, and apparently, he knew it, because he kept the verbal opinions to himself.

Jordan glanced at the non-existent watch on her wrist. "Punctual as ever, Ry. Couldn't even give me an extra five minutes?"

"I gave you an hour. Now, go," he grumbled, and I cracked a smile.

Ryland and I hadn't really gotten anywhere with whatever relationship we were trying to establish, but when he'd held on to me during the lightning strike, the action had shown me I could count on him, even if I didn't want to. It made my current predicament really frustrating when he reminded me of what I was trying to give up.

Jordan hugged me goodbye, holding on just a minute longer than usual. "Be kind to him. He's not handling this well, either," she whispered in my ear, and I nodded.

"Jordan, wait for me outside? I'd like your help with something," Stryx said, still perched on Ryland's shoulder.

Jordan pointed to herself, shocked. "Me? Really?"

"Yes, you. Really."

Jordan flushed and stared at me wide-eyed, but I merely shrugged. I had no idea what he wanted her for. When she finally went out into the yard, Stryx gave me his attention.

"Before the two of you speak, I need to say some things."

My eyes rolled. Here he went with his *wise* words. Yes, I knew the grief was making me a jerk, but I didn't care. Didn't everyone realize I'd just buried my parents? Didn't they realize I didn't want to talk about anything other than killing Alaryk?

Sure, I had been convinced there was no way I could complete the task when I first found out what I was supposed to do, but Jordan was wrong when she worried the deaths of my parents would push me exactly where Alaryk wanted me.

It had done the opposite. It had given me the push I needed to woman up and have zero qualms about ending the bastard.

"Kaliah, that's enough. Yes, I realize it's only been five days, and I'm not trying to be insensitive to your emotions, but you need to get it through your stubborn head that you can't do this on your own. It's not you versus Alaryk. It's us against him. We need to work together as a team, or he *will* win."

I huffed. "How do you know that?"

"Because Alaryk has a few decades of rage on you. The hate in his soul is far superior than I hope you ever experience. He has had the drive to either kill you or turn you to his side for nearly fifty years. It seems he's settled on making you his mate, which is almost worse. This is not something you can fight on your own, no matter how much you wish to. None of us can."

Ryland's feet shuffled. "Maybe a few more days, or even a week, won't hurt to allow Kali the time she needs."

Stryx clicked his beak. "Time will not heal what ails her."

His beady eyes narrowed on me, and I really wanted to stick my tongue out at him, or better yet, drop kick him across the yard.

Our relationship was turning into a love-hate one, and I didn't like it.

Our stare-down lasted a solid minute before I caved. "Was there something else you wanted to say?"

"Why don't we have a seat?" Stryx suggested.

Great, that was never good.

I took the only chair so I could have some space. I didn't figure anything he wanted to tell us without Jordan was going to be something I really wanted to hear.

"The reason I didn't ask Jordan to stay is because the two of you need to make this decision on your own. I know Ryland's standpoint, but Kaliah, you need to know what it means when you make certain decisions."

"Like what?" I asked.

"First, before Alaryk showed up, you were ready to complete the bond with Ryland, but you've been avoiding it ever since. Your powers are erratic, and that's because your bond isn't complete. Your crown is not enough to contain what lies within you."

A rumble sounded within my chest. "Why not? I know you keep saying this, but I think I'm handling it well enough."

"You were never meant to carry the burden of this magic alone. You were always meant to have a partner. Someone who would stand by your side and lift you when needed. Someone who would protect you with their own life without a second thought. Ryland is your anchor to the goodness you were born from."

My fingers tapped on the arm of the chair as I recalled my conversation with my grandmother. She'd, too, called Ryland my anchor, telling me I didn't need him because I was weak. I'd believed her then, but I'd had a hard time remembering it as of late. My stubbornness was out in full force, and I didn't know how to stop it.

"Yes, Stryx. I know Ryland is my Meraki. I understand all of what you're saying, but it doesn't change anything. I won't be forced into something I'm not ready for."

"Is it really that you're not ready, or because you believe it's what is best for everyone else?" His feathers ruffled, and I wanted to strangle him. I really hated that he was in my head at all hours of the day. Learning how to kick him out was high up on my priority list.

Ryland stood. "Stryx, I know you mean well, but this isn't working. You shouldn't put this on her. Circumstances have changed, and I respect her wishes to wait, as should you. We all know what's at stake, and we will handle it. I won't bond with her just because you believe it's the only way we can win."

Well, he just earned some major bonus points with me.

"If that's what you both wish, then I'll stop trying to help." Stryx flew out the door, more frustrated than I'd ever seen him before.

Leaning forward, I let my hair fall in front of my face and rubbed my hands over my eyes. Hurting Stryx wasn't what I had planned. I was well aware he was only trying to help, but I had my own thoughts I couldn't ignore. I knew what I thought was right, and I just wanted to make the hurt go away.

Why was that so hard to do?

Ryland kneeled before me. "Do you want me to leave?"

My first thought was to say yes. I'd been doing fine on my own the last five days. Well, fine if you considered starting lightning storms and breaking things in the house fine.

Though, I couldn't find the willpower to send him away.

"You can stay if you want, but I'd understand if you chose to leave." At least he still had an out if he wanted one.

I didn't imagine he felt great about being saddled to me. I would bring nothing but trouble into his life if he decided to stay.

"Kali, look at me." His fingers nudged my chin, not forcefully, just enough to give me the push I needed to quit hiding.

His eyes stabbed me right through the chest. They offered nothing but comfort, compassion, and understanding. He wasn't there to judge me or push me or anything else. He was just there.

"I'm sorry," I murmured. Though, it wasn't for anything specific. I knew I hadn't made all the right choices, and he'd probably paid the price for at least some of them.

"You have nothing to apologize for. You are in mourning. We all are. We understand your hurt, even if ours isn't exactly the same."

"You were really close with them?" I knew he had been their assigned guardian, but I didn't know what that actually entailed.

He nodded. "I was. They took me in after my own parents died and treated me like their own. You know, they didn't think they could have kids. There were decades when they'd done everything they could to get pregnant, but it wasn't until they least expected it that you came along."

The hole in my heart tore a little further. I'd never known that. I ached for my mother who had deserved as many children as she wanted, because she was the best mom anyone could ever wish for.

"When they found out about you and the prophecy, I'd asked to go with them, but Arvayta needed me more than them, or so they'd said. That was, until you were twelve and something big happened. I don't know what it was, but it scared them enough to ask for Jordan."

This piqued my curiosity. "I'd almost drowned around that time. I wonder if that had anything to do with it. But why didn't they want you?"

He grinned, a dimple I'd never noticed before appearing in his left cheek. "You were just figuring out what boys were. Do you really think they wanted one trying to get close to you?"

So very true. I'd probably have refused his friendship anyway. Boys hadn't always been kind in middle school.

"So, what now?" I asked, because I really had no clue.

He took my hands in his and squeezed tight as his smile faded away. "I won't force you into something you're not ready for, but I will remind you of a few things. The first, I'm all in with this. Whether we're bonded or not, I will have your back, either as your friend or your Meraki. I won't let you go against Alaryk alone. I will follow you wherever you go, no matter the danger."

A lump lodged in my throat as I tried to swallow. His words struck emotions in me I'd much rather have ignored.

"Second, I know you're afraid, and it's okay to be scared, but you need to remember one thing. You are my life now. No matter what happens, I accept you for who you are. There is nothing I've learned about you that I would change."

I opened my mouth to interrupt him, but he held up his hand. "I'm not done yet."

My eyes widened at the demanding tone, but I quite liked it and wished he showed that side of himself more often.

"You are not perfect, but neither am I. We are both incomplete, but together, I really do believe that we can do whatever we set out to accomplish. I'm not trying to pressure you. I just need you to know that I'm still here and always will be. Nothing has changed for me."

He paused, seeming to wait for me to say something, but I was speechless. I didn't know how to respond.

For a brief moment, I let myself begin to wonder if Stryx had let Ryland in on any of my internal thoughts, but I shook away the notion. The owl might be a righteous pain in my ass, but I trusted him fully. He wouldn't betray me in that way.

"Even though I plan to give you space, I want you to know, I also intend to pursue you when appropriate. I won't have you thinking just because I respect your need for time that I'm no longer interested," he added with a slight grin.

His hands cupped my cheeks, completely taking me by surprise as he slowly moved in closer, clearly giving me time to push him away if I wanted, but I couldn't.

There was nothing in me that didn't want him to do what he was doing. So, instead, I met him in the middle and a soft sigh escaped my lips as his pressed against mine. Once, twice, and then a third while I held him closer.

He only let the chaste kisses last for a moment before he pulled back. "One last thing. That won't always happen. I won't be used. You either want more with me or you don't, but I won't get stuck somewhere in the middle. Just remember, I'm all in, Kali. Whenever you're ready."

He stood and turned for the door while I was left on the chair, completely in shock.

What the hell had just happened? *How* had it happened?

I had no idea, and I wasn't even sure what it meant.

Suddenly, I was back to being alone again, and, for the first time since I saw my parents' prone bodies, I didn't want to be.

CHAPTER 3

The next day, I got up at a reasonable time and took a shower. Getting ready for the day filled me with equal parts relief and anxiety. In order to stop Alaryk from hurting anyone else, I knew I would have to train harder. I wasn't stubborn enough to think I could stop him as I was, but at the same time, taking this step and leaving the house, I was moving forward.

Without my parents.

I wasn't ready to live a life in Arvayta without them. We'd only had mere weeks together in this new-to-me world, and it wasn't fair that they hadn't been able to show me everything they loved about this land.

None of it was fair.

But today wasn't about that. Today was about becoming a better me, so I could do what I'd been daydreaming about for nearly a week.

Jordan came out of the guest house as I opened the back door. "About damn time," she huffed.

"Have you been waiting for me?"

"Duh. But Ryland said if I forced you to go to training that he would burn my favorite shoes. So, I decided to wait by the window until I saw you at the door. I knew you'd eventually come out, even if I wanted it to be a little earlier." She reached for my hand. "Now, let's go kick the asses of Ryland and Oliver."

Before I could respond, the air was pulled from my lungs and everything went black for mere seconds until my feet were on the grassy grounds of the training fields.

"Who said I wanted to be here?" I asked, even though it was exactly where I had intended to head. A part of me had missed bantering with her, and I couldn't pass up the opportunity to prod at her.

"You had no choice. As your best friend, I made a vow to make sure you don't do anything stupid unless we're doing it together. I know there is still a lot of healing left to do, but I won't let you do it alone all the time. You had five days. Now, give me this one."

I smiled at her, probably my first true smile in days. "I love you, Satan."

"I love you, too, Chuck. Now, go show the boys how you earned that nickname." She winked. "They already know I'm the devil."

Shaking my head, I had no doubts. They'd known Jordan a hell of a lot longer than I had, and I actually felt bad for all they'd probably had to endure before she was sent to Earth.

We walked toward the training building and found only Ryland and Oliver in the center, both using swords against each other.

"Are they trying to take the other's head off?" I gaped, then hissed as Oliver got awfully close to making contact with Ryland's shoulder.

"Oh, calm down. Neither of them will actually bleed, at least not intentionally. If they do, that's what we have Lorelle for. She's the healer of all things. She once healed my feet when there was nothing left but bone and burnt skin."

I shuddered. "Do I even want to know how that happened?"

"Dragons. Dirty, nasty beasts when they want to be, but I showed him who was boss in the end. I might have crawled away, but at least I was still breathing."

She had no fear whatsoever, and I drew on that courage, knowing I'd have to channel my inner Jordan to get through whatever was coming our way.

"Hey, losers. Quit fighting like sissies and let us show you how it's done," Jordan yelled from the doorway.

Ryland met my gaze as he lowered his sword. "You sure you're up for this?"

"I am. Maybe not every day, but I'm going to take things one at a time for now."

An owl hooted from outside, and I'd yet to see any others in Arvayta besides Stryx, so I turned back around. As soon as I walked back past the corner of the building, Stryx was perched on a boulder.

"It's time to see what you're capable of with some guidance. Are you ready, Kaliah?"

"I thought you said I had to be bonded first?" I countered, hoping he wasn't up to any tricks.

"If you wish to be successful, I still stand by my words, but it doesn't mean I can't teach you a few things. Now, come."

I eyed a stray rock on the ground, really wanting to throw it at him for commanding me like a dog, but I resisted as the others appeared outside as well.

"We're training with *him* today?" Oliver said with a layer of shock to his voice. I still sometimes forgot Stryx was a bit of a celebrity around Arvayta.

"Don't make his head bigger than it already is. He's just an owl," I replied, then wind promptly knocked me on my ass.

"What was that, Kali?" Stryx asked from above me with his wings still flapping and keeping me pinned to the ground.

There was so much pressure, I couldn't even speak, but I hoped the glare in my eyes told him exactly what I thought.

After my feathered frenemy was done showing off, I stood from the ground, wiping the dirt off as I followed the others. Stryx took us out into the furthest part of the fields, away from anyone else.

He landed on a boulder, moving his gaze between each of us. "The four of you are unique in your own ways. You balance each other out in methods you're unaware of just yet, but I hope for you to learn."

Jordan raised her hand like we were in school, though she didn't wait to be called on. "What about the bonded animals? Where did they go after the fight?"

Ah, that was a great question and something I had completely forgotten about.

"They are near but need time to adjust. This is a different world for them, so they need a bit more time before being overwhelmed with their bonded. I thought they'd find them during the fight, but only a select few did. The rest will need to be done more carefully," Stryx answered.

Maybe I could hang out with them and take my time away as well. I knew exactly how they felt.

"Kali and Jordan work well together because they are polar opposites," Stryx continued while stretching his wings out and making himself a focal point.

As he paused again, Jordan produced a flame from her hand, which I instinctively put out with water without thinking.

"How did I do that?" I asked, shocked my reflexes had taken over so easily.

"It's the Arelia power seeping through. It wants to be used. Your mind knew what needed to be done, so it did it." Stryx turned his head toward Oliver. "Kill that bush."

Oliver grimaced, but did as he was told.

As soon as the leaves began to turn brown, my hands twitched to provide the plant with life, to give it water and let it thrive, but I held back.

"Kali, let it out," Stryx demanded when I didn't let my instincts take over again. The action made me feel like I was losing control, and I wasn't fond of that.

Regardless of how stubborn I could be, I trusted Stryx and opened my hand. Magic flowed out the ten feet toward the bush before turning into water as it covered the branches of the bush. Relief poured into me as the green began to come back.

"Oliver controls the earth. He could have healed it on his own, but if he was ever unable, Kali, you need to know you're capable of assisting him. Though, we need to do something about the mental restraints keeping you from reaching your full potential," Stryx said as soon as I cut off the water to the plant.

"Yeah, easier said than done for someone who didn't know a whole lot about this world until a few weeks ago," I grumbled.

"And you're not going to learn with that attitude," Stryx retorted.

Ryland stepped forward. "What about me? Kali seems to create her own storms just fine. How do we help each other?"

Stryx spread his wings again, but this time, drifted off the rock and circled the two of us. "You and Kali are nearly one in the same. Should you complete your bond, the shared power between the two of you will be nothing like we've seen since the last King and Queen.

"Ryland, the wind you yield will complement the storms Kali cannot control. Where one is weak, the other will be strong. You will need to rely on each other when faced with uncertainty. One cannot succeed without the other."

Stryx was going to pound those words into my head until I gave in, but he was only making me more resistant. I wasn't a fan of being told what to do, even if I was beginning to remember why I wanted to complete the bond in the first place.

The only reason I was standing in the training field was because of Ryland, but even that wasn't going to last long if the owl insisted on taking every opportunity to remind me of what I was *supposed* to do.

"I think that's enough, Stryx. Kali gets the point, so unless you have something new to address about that particular situation, then I suggest we move on," Ryland said sternly. The others gasped, but I merely smiled.

Ryland continued to show me everything that he was, including standing up for what he was passionate about.

I glanced back at Stryx. "So, what next? Besides each of us blending well together with our different elemental abilities, how do you propose we beat Alaryk?"

"You can't merely *beat* him. You have to kill him. From what I've learned, there is only one way to succeed in doing so, and it's going to take a group effort. Hence, the purpose of my display just moments ago."

"I have no problems killing the dark fae. I just need to know how," I said confidently.

Stryx twisted his head. "It's not that simple, and we're going to have to do some leg work before we can make it happen."

I swear, if he mentioned me bonding with Ryland one more time, I was going to...

"Alaryk will have spell after spell in place to keep himself alive. Like I've said before, he's been preparing for this possible fight for decades, so we need to think beyond our own abilities. There is a dagger that is said to kill any being that it strikes the heart of. We need to make that blade and use it against the dark fae before he learns what it is."

"What do you mean 'make'?" Jordan asked.

"The blade is not yet forged. It will take pure metal from the gnomes, blood of a vampire, and a heart stone gifted from a succubus in order to create the weapon you'll need to kill Alaryk," Stryx answered.

I'd already met a gnome, and, while not appealing, he didn't seem completely unreasonable. Though, I wasn't too keen on meeting the other two beings unless all vampires were like Brooke, but something told me that wasn't going to be the case.

"I love the succubi." Oliver waggled his eyebrows, and Ryland punched him in the kidney.

"We won't be there for pleasure, so keep your mind clear," Ryland snarled.

Oliver's hands went up. "I was just kidding. Calm down, man."

"You weren't kidding, and we all know it," Jordan added as I recalled the scorned vampire from the Otherworld. Oliver apparently got around quite a bit, but he had seemed remorseful about Brooke, and I wondered if there were more feelings there than he let on.

"If we're going to be in the Otherworld, will Brooke be escorting us?" I asked Stryx.

Oliver flinched at my question, which gave me the confirmation I'd been looking for.

"Queen Navi will lend us her people, and I believe Brooke is one of them, so it's possible she'll be with us while we're traveling through the different sections."

Oliver mumbled something under his breath, but I didn't catch it. All that mattered was that if Brooke was tagging along, he'd hopefully be on his best behavior since she didn't appear to put up with his crap.

"Kali, I want you to work independently for today, and the others will assist you as needed. You three keep an eye on her. Don't ask, just act. The four of you need to work together seamlessly if you intend to keep yourselves alive."

Well, that wasn't ominous or anything.

Taking a step forward, my hands went to my crown, making sure it was in place and still plastered to my head.

The first day I'd gone out on my own to let loose after losing my parents, I'd almost lost control. Power had been pouring so furiously from my body, even the crown had had enough. When I'd felt it slip down my forehead, everything within me began to ache. I knew then that Lorelle hadn't been kidding about what the crown could do for me, so I'd been extra careful the last few days when I'd needed a release. Even if, at times, I'd been tempted to see what would happen without it.

"What should I do first?" I asked, ready to show them some of the things I'd been working on in private.

I was certain Stryx was already aware of them, but the others had no idea what I'd grown capable of since letting some of my restraints go.

"I want you to create a storm, but only keep it the size of this boulder," Stryx demanded.

"But I can do one much bigger."

"I know that, but bigger is not always better. Control is the ultimate weapon. If you have no control, your power is useless."

The smugness of his voice grated on my nerves, but I'd left the house that morning so I could accomplish something. I needed to get closer to beating Alaryk, and if I had to put up with the know-it-all owl, then so be it.

I tightened my ponytail, then rubbed my hands together. Magic began to gather at my core, and I marveled at how easily it came to me. Almost too easily as I fought to keep it from dumping out of me like I usually allowed when I was on my own.

It was incredible to think that just the month before, I was technically only human. I might have known of Arvayta, but none of Stryx's training prepared me for the well of strength that flowed through me as I focused on creating the mini storm.

A cloud formed above me, and I guided it with my hands next

to the boulder Stryx still sat on. From the cloud, water poured into the ground hard and fast.

Sweat built on my brow as I concentrated on pushing my abilities. The cloud was growing bigger by the second, and I could already feel my control slipping, but I doubled my efforts and contained it once more.

The rain turned to ice, and thunder sounded from the cloud as small flashes of light flickered through the ten-foot-tall storm. A smile grew on my face until one of the lights ricocheted off a piece of sleet and smacked me in the face.

Blinded, I lost my control over the storm and felt power rip from my chest. Pain tore through me like the storm I'd created, and I cried out.

Wind began to whip around us, and I was certain I'd ended up in the center of the storm, but when I opened my eyes, Ryland stood next to me, his hands glowing and his face full of concentration.

I followed his gaze and saw he was containing my storm. *He* was controlling my power. Power I simply let flow freely when I needed the release and had yet to take true command of on my own.

Jordan nudged my shoulder, bringing me out of my shock. "He can't keep it locked down for long. Bring your magic back to you, Chuck."

Shaking my head, I cleared my distracting thoughts and focused. I closed my eyes and called the storm back to me, starting backward from how I'd created it. When Ryland let out a sigh of relief, I finally opened my eyes.

He reached for me, his fingers wrapping around my elbow. "Are you okay?"

"Yeah, thank you."

I wasn't exactly sure what I was thanking him for. For stopping the storm from getting out of hand like it usually did? For caring about me? For simply being kind? Maybe all of the above, and hopefully he knew it.

Ryland nodded and released me, giving me the space that I needed to catch my breath and focus on what had gone wrong.

"Did any of you learn anything just now?" Stryx asked.

"Kali is dangerous, and we shouldn't piss her off?" Jordan offered.

Stryx snapped his beak at her. "Anything useful?"

"I acted on instinct and helped her. I listened to my gut when it said Kali needed my help," Ryland said, proving Stryx's earlier point.

"Yes, that's what I was hoping would happen." The owl's feathers ruffled.

My arms crossed. "So, you were counting on my failure?"

"As I've said before, you're not capable of—"

My hand went up. "Nope. I don't want to hear it. I got it."

I didn't need to listen for the hundredth time about how I wouldn't be any good until I accepted my bond.

I might have been broken, but I was also a strong woman. I didn't need a man to accomplish what I set out to do, and I'd be damned if I didn't prove it just to spite the owl, even if it meant denying myself happiness in the process.

CHAPTER 4

While porting back to my house, I'd decided there had been enough training for one morning. Maybe I'd feel up to going back out later in the afternoon, but Stryx had pushed my buttons one too many times. I needed a break before I did or said something I couldn't take back.

Slamming the door closed, I stormed into the living room and really wanted to destroy something. Though, seeing the house clean after Jordan had done most of the work gave me pause. I was never a violent person before, but the rage swirling within me had changed everything I thought I knew about myself.

Tapping sounded on the glass, and I turned around to find Stryx hovering at the door. My head shook, hoping he would go away when I didn't let him in.

The stubborn owl glared at me. *I'm not going anywhere, Kaliah. We can have this conversation mentally or out loud, but either way, it's happening. Right now.*

What's left to say? I already know what you want from me. My arms crossed in defiance. Yes, I was aware I was acting like a child, but he seemed to trigger the response out of me as of late, and I couldn't stop the attitude from spilling out.

I promise, what I have to say is not what you think. Please, let me in.

Stryx's eyes stared me down, and the walls I'd erected around myself over the last five days wavered as memories traveled through my mind of how close we were before everything had gone to hell.

Stryx had been a true friend. My bonded animal. Yet, I didn't understand why he had pushed me so hard. He'd pushed me until I was furious, even though he was already aware of my thoughts.

After ignoring him for a solid minute and realizing he was as stubborn as I was, I finally let him in. He flew to the couch, and I followed, choosing to sit across from him.

"I'm sorry," he began, and I felt the sincerity of his apology through our bond. "I thought you needed pushing, but I realize now that you need a friend more, and I've done a horrible job of that."

Feathered owl says what? I couldn't believe Stryx was apologizing, but I appreciated it more than he knew.

"I understand why you were pushing, and I'm pretty sure you were chosen for me because we're a lot alike. I'm not going to say I told you so, but you should have known better." I smirked at him, unable to stay mad for very long, especially when, just by those couple of sentences, it really did seem as though he learned his lesson.

He clicked his beak like he loved to do when I irritated him. "We are much too alike. In that you are right, young one."

"So, will you drop the bonding thing? Let me do this how I want to?" I asked.

He sighed. "I wish I could. You don't know how much I wish you weren't going to be forced into this choice, but you *need* an anchor to your goodness, Kali. You need someone to keep you from succumbing to the darkness I can already feel growing within you, and Ryland is that person."

"Why can't it be you? We're bonded, aren't we?"

He flew to me, and I held my hand out, bringing him close as he brushed his feathers against my cheek. "Yes, we are, but not in the same ways. Before you were created, your soul came to me. I knew you before you even existed in the physical sense. Even still, our bond is not the same as a Meraki one. While I will always be a part of your life, I cannot do for you what Ryland can."

This magic stuff was beyond what my mind could sometimes handle. I didn't understand how it was possible for Stryx to know my soul before I was born, but it was also fascinating.

"Taliah also mentioned Ryland would be my anchor. That I didn't need to bond with Ryland because I was weak, but because my abilities were too great," I said, once again remembering why I had been so ready before.

"Your grandmother is one of the wisest fae I have ever had the pleasure of knowing." His beak parted as if he was trying to smile. "I thought I would never have another bond like the one with her, but if you can forgive my persistence, then I'm certain I will be proven wrong."

I lowered my forehead, pressing it against the side of his head. "Of course I forgive you, but only if you teach me how to keep you away from my every thought. We need to set some boundaries if all is to be forgiven."

"I won't say no to that. Your thoughts can be rather distracting at times. It might be better for the both of us." His feathers ruffled, and I almost shoved him away, but I knew he was joking. Well, at least partially.

"So, how do I block you?" I asked.

His wings came around both sides of my face. "Close your eyes and build a wall within your mind. Make it out of whatever you want. Wood, brick, cement, metal, anything that is sturdy. Do it slowly and precisely."

Concentrating, I did as he said, choosing brick and mortar, laying each row piece by piece until I was satisfied. When it was done, I added a bit of magic to it in my mind, sealing it with power I still didn't quite understand, but felt right anyway.

"Very well. That was the final step and I didn't even have to tell you," Stryx praised.

"What was?"

"Sealing the wall. With that magic, you should be able to take the wall down as you please, and it will remain in effect for as long as you will it to. I can no longer hear your thoughts, but I can sense your feelings still."

My eyes narrowed. "How do I know you're not just saying that?"

"Kaliah, would I lie to you?"

No, he wouldn't. He would drive me insane, but Stryx had never lied to me.

"Thank you for teaching me." I hugged him close.

"I'm sorry it took so long, but I needed to know you were safe. I had preferred to wait until you were bonded, but since you insist on delaying that, I hope you can accept this as part of my apology."

Pulling back, I brought him up to eye level. "You really feel that strongly about my bonding with Ryland?"

"I do. It is what will keep you safest, and your safety is of the utmost importance to me. It would crush me to lose you in any sense."

What hurt most about agreeing to the bond again was knowing that my parents wouldn't be there to see it happen. It was part of the reason I'd been so hesitant. The last time had been so perfect with my mom helping me get ready and my dad waiting outside to escort us to the town hall. Everything had felt right that day until it wasn't.

No longer would the bonding ceremony be something I could look back on fondly. The memories would always be tainted with the images of the bloodied room and my parents' death. Even if nothing went wrong on the second try, I couldn't ever forget the first.

Pressure pushed against the wall I'd built around my thoughts, and I recognized Stryx's essence. Lowering the block was hard, not only because it took a significant amount of magical effort, but also because, in doing so, I made myself vulnerable again. Once I worked past the obstacles, the love Stryx had for me flowed through my mind, and I was instantly relieved of the sadness that had been creeping in.

"I know you still hurt, Kaliah. I wish I could make that go away, but it is also my duty to guide you onto the right path. Please don't mistake that for me being insensitive to your feelings. If I didn't believe you care for Ryland, I would not push so hard."

I hugged him once more as overwhelming emotion overcame me, and I let fresh tears fall down my cheeks. "I know that. I've known it all along. It's just hard to think about moving forward without them. My heart doesn't know how to move on. Bonding with Ryland is like getting married. How am I supposed to do that without my parents?"

Agony tore through me as grief stronger than ever before took over my every thought. I was only nineteen. I might be strong, but a girl still needed her parents. Watching them get murdered... It was too much. The hurt was too much. I didn't know how to move past it.

"You are not moving on without them. Even though you can't see them, they are here, and I can guarantee with every tear you shed, they shed twice as many. But you need to know how proud of you they were. You were their everything, and all they wanted for you was your happiness. If you choose to bond with Ryland, it won't be something you're doing without them. I can promise you that."

I had no more words to say, because I wanted so badly to believe he was right. To believe that my parents were there even if I couldn't see or feel them. So, I just squeezed him tighter.

Warmth filled me from the inside, spreading through my chest and out toward my arms and legs. Love and pride swelled within me, and I went from crying to sobbing in a matter of moments.

They really were there. I had no tangible confirmation that the feeling had come from my parents, but I let myself further believe Stryx was right and they were proving his truth.

Moments later, when the tears dried up, I finally released Stryx from my clutches. "Okay. If Ryland will still have me, then I will bond with him, but I still stand by my previous decision to take things slow."

His feathered head pressed against my arm. "I understand, and I know he will, too."

"So, what now?" I asked.

"Now, you tell your Meraki what you want, and we make it happen, on your terms. After that, we resume training and then head to the Otherworld within two weeks' time. The guardians who already bonded with other animals are scouting Alaryk's known spots. So far, they've seen no sign of him, and I consider this a good thing."

My face pinched. "How so? Wouldn't it be better to know where he is at all times?"

His head shook. "If he isn't surfacing, he's hiding. You scared him, and that's good. Though, if we wait too long, we risk him doing something drastic. So, we will train until our time is up, then go in search of the items we need to forge the dagger."

I shuddered at the thought of purposely seeking out vampires. It didn't seem wise to me, but all I knew about them came from fictional movies and books back on Earth.

"Brooke wasn't so bad, was she?" Stryx asked, reading my thoughts and reminding me I hadn't put my wall back up.

Before answering him, I fixed that problem and realized he was right. But where there was good, there was usually bad. Nothing was perfect, and I wasn't naïve enough to believe we wouldn't find trouble with the creatures we needed to help us.

However, I wouldn't let that stop me from completing the challenge given. We would gather all of the pieces and forge the dagger.

Then, I would hunt Alaryk to the ends of all the worlds if I had to. One way or another, he would die by my hand, and, for the first time in days, the thoughts of his death brought me peace instead of the growing darkness I'd been clinging to.

CHAPTER 5

Randomly just telling someone you were ready to be bonded for all eternity wasn't as easy as I first thought. Of course, we had already discussed it, but this was awkward territory, and Ryland had been much too nice.

My heart still hadn't completely let him off the hook for pushing me away in the beginning, but my more sensible side was trying to be reasonable. He came from a completely different world than I did. He had old school values and principals. His commitment was overwhelmingly intact.

When I really broke it down, I didn't blame him for being angry at the thought of being forced to disgrace his first love. Fabricated or not, it had been real for him, and he'd made a life-long promise to her that he'd intended to keep, even after death. Well, until he learned she'd deceived him.

Knowing he was willing to give me that same vow once he knew the truth was equally overwhelming. The conversation and emotional outpour with Stryx had definitely pushed back the growing darkness and rage I had within me, but it didn't make what came next any easier.

After finding Jordan, she let me know Ryland and Oliver were back at the training center and helping some of the newer guardians. It was a task they used to take on often before dealing with the drama I'd brought into their lives.

I showed up at the facility and watched from the door. My Meraki was kind, caring, and strong. He truly enjoyed helping others, but even seeing and telling myself all of that, didn't help me with what I had to do next.

Accepting the bond was daunting but necessary according to Stryx, who I trusted with my life. The connection between Ryland and me wasn't going anywhere, and making it official didn't change anything. Well, except it would put Stryx at ease and help me control the abilities within me well enough to kill Alaryk. When I really broke it down, I'd be a fool to deny it any longer, but I wouldn't stop myself from wanting some distance until we truly knew each other.

Ryland noticed me as he turned to adjust the form on one of the guardians. He grinned as he took a step forward, then paused, likely trying to decide if he'd be welcome. Instead of making him suffer, I waved him over.

"What's wrong?" he asked when he got closer.

"Uh, nothing. Why?"

His body was suddenly tense as he stared intently at me. "Your eyes. They're brighter than normal and red around the edges as if you've been crying. Did someone say something to you?"

I grinned, pretty sure if I told him someone had hurt my feelings that he was prepared to hunt them down and torture them slowly. That was the commitment I was drawn to, even if it was a lot to take in. I knew it was his way of showing he cared.

"I was talking with Stryx—" I started, but he cut me off.

"I told him to leave you alone. I'm going to rip his feathers out one by one," Ryland snarled, and I reached to grab his arms before he could port away.

"It was good and exactly what I needed. Stryx didn't do anything wrong. He actually helped me a lot."

Ryland softened and stepped closer. "How so?"

"Well, the growing darkness from the grief is more manageable than it was an hour ago," I answered, avoiding the reason I'd come to find him.

He placed a hand over mine that was still holding on to him. "That's good. He probably could have killed me, but I still would have tried to make him stop forcing things on you that you're not ready for."

Warmth filled me, and there was a pull within me that yearned to step closer to Ryland, but I ignored it as I said my next words. "He also helped me to understand why I was so afraid of bonding with you now when I had been so ready before. I still want to take things slowly, but I'd like to try again if you would."

The gap between us became smaller as he cradled my face in his hands, forcing me to look at him. "No. We won't do this because you feel there is no other option." The words felt harsh, but there was also a different kind of care within them I'd never experienced before.

"I'm not being pushed into this. The bond is there regardless of whether or not we let the council do their official…sealing… whatever it is. There are too many benefits to ignore, and I just want to get it done."

He flinched at my words, and I realized how cruel they sounded. Cheese and rice, I was a jerk. Now, it sounded as if I was using him. I was no better than Alaryk at this point.

"I'm sorry. That came out wrong," I mumbled.

"No, it didn't, but I understand. You didn't grow up here. You don't understand how special and uncommon this type of bond is. This isn't the way it's supposed to go, and I'm sorry you don't get to experience the process as it was created to be, but I will do this for you if it's what you really want."

Sigh. I was screwing this all up, and I wanted nothing more

than to port home and find my mom in the kitchen cooking something amazing and ready to tell me everything would work itself out.

Ryland's thumbs brushed away the stray tears I'd let fall. "It's going to be okay, Kali."

My chest tightened as he said the words I so badly wanted to hear. Even though it wasn't the same as hearing them from my mother, I did believe that Ryland thought they were true. He had an absolute faith in me that continued to surprise me with every interaction.

When I didn't respond, he pulled me closer and wrapped his arms around me. I fought to keep my emotions in check, especially since we were still in public. I'd cried enough that day, and it hadn't been my intention to continue doing so when I found Ryland.

Still holding me close, he spoke softly near my ear. "How about I set up the bonding ceremony, but not for a couple of days? You wanted to get to know me, and I'd like to learn about the you that didn't grow up in Arvayta. We can have a date or two and ease into the transition."

I nodded. "That sounds perfect to me." It really did. It would give me some more time to wrap my mind around everything. I should have been getting used to all the changes in my life. Something life-altering seemed to pop up around every corner for me lately, and I hoped that would soon end.

"I'll go set everything up and pick you up in two hours for our first date if you're good with that." I nodded, and he kissed my forehead. "Good. I'll see you then."

Stryx flew in and landed on my shoulder just as Ryland was getting ready to disappear. "Not so fast. I already took care of the council. The ceremony will take place at an outside location instead of town hall and will be at dawn in two days' time. That gives you this evening and all day tomorrow to do whatever you'd like."

"What about this afternoon?" Ryland asked.

"The bonded animals are recovered, and I'd like for you to meet them before you take off."

A sense of excitement rushed through me. I'd seen a lot of the animals coming through the portal during the fight, but stress levels had been so high, I hadn't taken a moment to appreciate them in a proper way.

"Thank you for coming to get us," I said with a sweep of my hand over his wing.

"Yeah, don't get used to it. With that wall of yours up, it's not as easy to find you," he grumbled, and I grinned. Served him right after all the intrusions he made on my inner conversations.

We ported to a field I'd never seen before and found Jordan and Oliver already there. Jordan was bouncing on the balls of her feet and I'd never seen her giddier.

"This is the best day ever," she squealed, and I laughed.

"Calm down. What if there isn't an animal for everyone?" I asked and glanced at Stryx with a wink.

Jordan shoved me. "Hey, Debby-Downer. Piss off."

"Oh, don't be so sensitive. Stryx already said everyone was getting one. I was just joking." When I glanced back at the owl, he shook his head.

"Actually, not everyone, but Jordan shouldn't have anything to worry about."

Well, that was cryptic.

"Follow me." Stryx flew toward a forested area I'd yet to venture to. We moved through the dense, shadowed area, and it opened up again after several yards to a much smaller clearing packed with exotic animals from all over the earth.

Tigers, panthers, cheetahs, lions, monkeys, snakes, foxes, bears, birds, and so many more I was probably missing. Each species came in different colors and sizes, and it was the most unreal experience to see them staring at us with so much humanity in their eyes.

"What now?" Jordan whispered.

"You wait. The animals will come to you when they're ready. Some will just want to meet you; others may approach because they're your bonded pair. Don't assume until you're certain, and I promise, you'll know. Also, don't touch until you've been given permission. These creatures haven't interacted with anyone outside our world in many years. Be patient."

Patience and Jordan didn't often go well together, so I was surprised at her restraint as she stayed put. Oliver, on the other hand, shocked all of us by inching further from our group and toward the animals.

"Should we stop him?" I asked.

"Not yet," Stryx replied.

"So, we wait until after he's lost a limb to one of the big cats?" Jordan joked, and as she did, a panther stepped out from the crowd and stalked toward Oliver.

The beast of a cat–if you could even call it that–had to weigh a few hundred pounds, and muscles rippled through its legs as it crouched with its tail flicking behind.

Oliver paused when he was about halfway between us and the panther. Stryx hadn't budged from his perch on the tree, but I still began to get nervous. We might live long lives, but none of us was invincible.

Just as I was about to call Oliver back, the sleek shadowy animal launched itself at our friend and tackled him to the ground. Each of us took a step forward, but an invisible wall stopped us in our tracks.

"What the hell, Stryx?" Ryland roared, but I tugged on his hand.

"Look."

Oliver was laughing and rolling around in the grass with the panther as they played like children together. There were no claws extended from the oversized cat, and they both seemed to be enjoying themselves.

The wall before us shimmered out of existence, and Jordan marched forward, intent clear in her stride.

She mumbled under her breath about how she should have been the first and charged right into the crowd of animals perfectly capable of killing her. My best friend was certifiable.

"Are you going to do anything about this?" I asked Stryx.

"Nope."

"What happened to the 'the animals will come to you' spiel?" Ryland added.

Stryx ruffled his feathers. "Now that I'm seeing it, this seems like more entertainment. The animals won't hurt her. Much."

Charging forward, I went after my best friend with Ryland right behind me. There was no way I was going to let her get mauled by wild beasts. That was until I found her groping each one before she shook her head and moved on.

As she was playing with a monkey, I spotted a lion creeping toward her backside. I launched forward at the same time he did and tackled his hind legs.

He roared in my face, catching the attention of everyone around us. "Get off of me, Guardian," he spat.

"Like hell I will. You were going to eat my best friend," I snarled back.

His back leg kicked me in the gut, and I let go as Ryland grabbed my arms to pull me back.

"I was only going to take a little nibble." The lion purred as soon as Jordan grabbed on to his mane.

"Did you attack her? Bad kitty." Their heads pressed together, and I narrowed my eyes.

Freaking wild animals. Jordan included.

"Well, I guess everything is fine after all. Stryx warned us for no reason." As I said the words, Jordan's fist sailed past my head and collided with a snake.

"Not exactly."

My body shivered. "Ry, if you could find your bonded animal, that would be great." I was more than ready to leave the clearing before something else tried to kill me.

Stryx flew closer and landed on the back of the lion. "About that. Ryland doesn't have one as of now. I thought it would be best for the two of you to focus on your bonds and not have the distraction of another."

My eyes immediately went to Ryland. His face didn't show any emotion, but I knew he had to be disappointed. Seeing the excitement from Jordan and Oliver was contagious, and I knew the joy firsthand with Stryx. My heart broke a little for him, because even though he agreed with Stryx, I knew he was lying through his teeth.

CHAPTER 6

We left Jordan and Oliver with their new animal friends, allowing them the time they needed to get acquainted. Which seemed fitting, because Ryland and I were off to do the same thing.

"So, I was going to plan everything after I went to the council, but since Stryx already took care of that for us, is there anything you'd like to do?" Ryland asked as we walked back toward town.

Even though we could port wherever we wanted within Arvayta, I still enjoyed strolling through the lands. There was always something new to see, and I was easily entertained with anything unusual like what I saw next.

"What is that?" I pointed to a small creature staring at us from a bush.

"That? You don't want to know." He shuddered, causing me to laugh.

I took a step forward. "It looks perfectly innocent." The furry thing had massive ears that stood straight up, big round saucer eyes, and grey fur I wanted to sink my fingers into.

Ryland grabbed my arm. "Seriously. It will kill you before you can even blink."

"I thought this place was like utopia. Or is it more like Australia? It just looks stunning, but you're likely to die no matter where you go, even in your own home."

He laughed. "I don't know much about Australia, but there are only a handful of animals here vicious like that thing. Thankfully, the rest of the bad ones don't look near as innocent."

We kept strolling, finally arriving at the training center where the beginning of town came into view.

"So, our date. Are you still up for it?" he asked.

"I am if you are. I know the news earlier might have made your afternoon not so great," I said, hoping to get him to open up about how he really felt not having his own animal.

"Honestly, the moment Stryx said not everyone would get one, I had a feeling he was speaking to me. Everything happens for a reason, and I'm not worried about this one. He was right. I have more important things to focus on right now."

Well, maybe he really was okay with it. He was a bigger person than me. I knew I wouldn't have been very accepting of being the only one without a bonded animal.

"Well, then. How about you surprise me for our outing? I don't know much about Arvayta, and I haven't eaten out much, so you pick."

He stared off at town as we kept moving along and finally smiled. "Okay, I think I have an idea. How about you go home and change into something comfortable. Jeans and a t-shirt are just fine. I'll meet you at your place in less than thirty minutes."

"Sure, I can do that."

He leaned in and kissed my cheek, reminding me that he had promised to take every opportunity to show me his interest. The small kisses and touches he kept providing were definitely hitting home. I'd never been much for affection like that, but Ryland was quickly showing me how much of a difference it made in me opening up to him. When he did things like that, it felt natural. Easy, even.

Without saying anything else, he ported away, and I continued to walk the rest of the way to town. I hadn't been there since the fight with Alaryk. I hadn't been able to force myself to confirm the aftermath had been properly cleaned up, but maybe it was time.

I was trying to heal, and if I was constantly afraid, then there would be no moving forward.

Just as I stepped off the path and onto the main road, a hand reached out and grabbed me.

"I don't think that's a good idea," Lorelle said from the shadows of the nearest building.

"And why not?" My fingers itched to defend myself, but thankfully my instincts had shown some restraint before punching the old lady in the face.

"Aren't you supposed to be getting ready for a date?" she asked, and I nodded. "Well, causing yourself to spiral into an emotional battle of the past might just put a damper on the mood, don't you think?"

"Wait a minute. How did you know I had a date?"

She waved away my words. "That doesn't matter. Just know there is a time and place for grief. Today is not the day for you to walk through town."

This old lady was crazy. I barely knew her, but she was speaking to me as if she was family.

"Why do you care?" I asked.

"Because if Arvayta falls, then I have to move back to the Otherworld, or worse, Earth. I'd rather not do either. So, when I see a chance to keep things on the right path, I take it. Now, listen to this old lady and go home."

It wasn’t that I wanted to obey her, but I also didn't have any desire to argue any longer, so I let her win.

"Fine, but I'll be back tomorrow."

"No, you won't. Tomorrow is too soon as well. You must wait until after the bonding ceremony, Kaliah. If you don't—" She shook her head and grabbed both of my hands, still remaining in the shadows. "I know you have no reason to trust me, but please heed my warning. I can't say any more."

Remembering back to my first day in Arvayta. Lorelle had been there when I'd woken. My parents had called on her to make sure I was okay. If they didn't have absolute faith in this crazy lady, then they wouldn't have done that. Deciding to use their judgement as my own, I consented.

"Alright, I won't be back until then, but only if you promise to tell me why at some point."

She grinned. "You're very much like your mother, you know. That's something she would have said as well."

My chest tightened with sorrow. *Mom*. I missed her so much.

"We have a deal, but only after you've killed Alaryk, and things follow a certain path, will I tell you."

Hmm, that last bit intrigued me. "I will do that. Thank you, Lorelle."

Then she was gone.

Maybe she wasn't so crazy after all. Nah, she was definitely far from normal.

I ported home and headed to the guest house where most of my clothes still were. Jordan wasn't there yet, and I didn't expect her to be anytime soon, either.

Once I was changed, I headed back to the main house and brushed out my hair before putting it in a braid. It had been in my face most of the day and was driving me crazy. The crown did nothing to help either.

Glancing at the clock, it was already dinner time and I hoped Ryland was taking me out to a restaurant. Then, I remembered Lorelle's warning and wondered if there were any places to eat that weren't on the main road.

Another ten minutes later, Ryland showed up, red faced and

carrying three bags. "That old bitty and her rambling. She's lucky Francisco was there."

"What are you mumbling about?" I laughed, because he seemed beyond irritated, and I had a feeling I knew why.

He set the bags on the kitchen counter and began taking boxes out. "Lorelle. I was making reservations for us, trying to have our first date be something to remember, but she stopped the whole thing before I could finalize it."

For an older lady, she sure moved quick.

"She got to me, too, and I already figured we wouldn't be able to go anywhere. Don't worry about it. What if we take the food somewhere and watch the sunset? I've yet to do that since arriving, and it used to be one of my favorite things to do at my parents' house on Earth."

A smile grew on his face until the one dimple I rarely saw appeared. "I have the perfect place." Boxes were already going back into the bags, and he was walking out the door before I could say another word.

After following him outside, I took his outreached hand and he ported us to the hot springs he'd shown me before. The last time we'd been there, I'd been enthralled with the area, but I'd also been a hot mess and hadn't had the chance to appreciate it as much as I would have liked.

I pulled my hand from Ryland's and found a spot we could sit where I'd be able to put my feet in the water. When I started taking off my shoes and rolling up my pants, he just stared at me with a silly smile on his face. "What?" I asked.

"You. Your enthusiasm for the things that make Arvayta special that most of us take for granted after living here for so many decades. It's refreshing." He took a seat next to me but opted to keep his feet out of the water as he put the food out. "I got a little of everything since I wasn't sure what you liked."

"There isn't much about food I don't like, so this is perfect."

We began eating while asking questions about each other,

keeping to the basics and random stuff. Favorite color, childhood memory, books, movies, and anything light. I learned he loved fishing, but rarely was able to do it. He also had a knack for woodworking and promised to show me some of his pieces one day.

"Thank you for this. It feels normal, and there hasn't been much of that lately," I said as I dried off my pruny toes.

His hand settled on my leg. "You're welcome. We can do it again tomorrow if you'd like. Not this exact thing, but I can take you to other places. Arvayta isn't huge, but there is plenty to explore."

Dropping the towel, I placed my hand over his. "I'd like that. A lot." And I really did mean it. We'd spent the last hour with no distractions and no worries, and I'd almost been able to forget how crappy my life had been the last week. If I could have more moments like this, I would take them at every opportunity.

Surprising me, he gave my hand a gentle tug, and I toppled into his lap. "That wasn't how that was supposed to go." He grinned as I tried to right myself, but he grabbed me first.

As he pulled me over, I found myself practically straddling his lap and my heart was racing. We'd kept a physical distance between the two of us for the most part, and I wasn't sure what he was thinking, but I wasn't going to move until I figured it out.

His fingers moved up my arms until both hands held my neck. "I'm going to kiss you." There was no question in his words, but he gave me the opportunity to object, which I appreciated but didn't do.

Instead, I leaned in and welcomed the contact. His lips were soft, and I yielded to him with no apprehension as I moved closer. It was our first real kiss that was more than a quick whisper, and he'd made it one I'd never forget with the sound of water around us and the stars glimmering above.

When we finally pulled apart, both of us were holding on to

each other, and I was a little embarrassed I'd practically mauled him, but he made it seem natural.

"How about I get you home so you can rest before tomorrow? I already have some ideas, and you'll need your energy," he said. My mind instantly went to places it probably shouldn't have, but I couldn't help myself after the kiss we'd shared.

Feeling my face get red, I agreed and moved to get my shoes and socks back on while he packed up everything that we'd brought with us.

After arriving back at the house, we shared one last kiss at the door, then I watched him disappear from the deck. My heart and head were finally in the right place, but as I stepped inside the house, I just hoped that the memories of our perfect date were enough to keep the nightmares away for the night.

CHAPTER 7

The following day was the first good day I'd had in a while, and I was able to keep my emotions in check for a majority of the day. It had begun with Ryland showing up at dawn, stating our second date couldn't be done at any other time. He'd taken us to caves filled with vay bugs—the Arvaytan equivalent of Earth's glowworms, but these ones glowed like the Northern Lights when gathered together.

Between the colorful glow of the bugs and the small stream rolling through, I'd been in heaven for the few hours we'd ventured around the caves. When lunch time came around, the bugs began to disappear, taking our light with them. I had then understood why he'd gotten me up so early. An extra couple hours of sleep wouldn't have been worth missing that experience.

Ryland dropped me back off at the house, so he could tend to some of his guardian responsibilities, and I finally caught a glimpse of Jordan through the guest house window. Before I could twist the handle, Jordan came barreling outside.

"Where the hell have you been, Chuck?" Her arms wrapped around me and held on tightly as we stumbled to the ground.

"Uh, out? What about you? It's not just me who's been busy."

She brushed her blonde hair away. "Why didn't you tell me how awesome it was having a bonded animal? Dominic is obnoxious, stubborn, and handsy. He's my spirit animal, and I love him!"

Jordan rolled onto her back, the most excited I'd ever seen her, and I reached for her hand. "I'm really happy for you, Jord."

Her head twisted toward me, and she smirked. "You seem pretty happy yourself, and I've seen Ryland come and go a few times. Care to share anything with your best friend?"

"Not a chance, Satan."

"Oh, come on. I'll behave. I promise." There was a twinkle in her eye that told me she was full of it, but she wouldn't stop bugging me until I caved, so I gave her the cliff-notes version of the last day.

"Holy crap, girl. He's not wasting any time, is he?"

"He is being equally patient and persistent. Both of which are appreciated. Being around him keeps me grounded and the worst of the grief at bay," I answered before sitting up.

She raised a brow and sat up as well. "Hmm, sounds familiar. Isn't that how several people have described having a Meraki to you, but you still refused? Someone you didn't need to make you stronger, but a partner who would keep you grounded and balanced."

I waved my hand. "Yeah, yeah. That's why I agreed to the bonding ceremony, but it's not like I want to move in with him tomorrow or anything. I still want some space and time to get to know each other."

"As much as I would kill for a Meraki, I get it, and I'm proud of you for making that choice. For letting this be your decision just as much as it is fate's."

"Thanks, friend. How about we go inside? Unless you have somewhere to be with Dominic."

She shook her head. "He's off with the other animals. They're preparing for our group training tomorrow."

I shuddered. Training with a bunch of wild animals did not sound like much fun, especially when that snake had tried to kill me the day before.

Stryx had better be able to keep his people in line, or I was going to start frying some reptiles.

MORNING CAME MUCH TOO SOON AFTER STAYING UP UNTIL THE WEE hours of the night. Ryland had surprised me with another dinner, but instead of taking the food out, I'd convinced him to stay in and we watched some of my favorite book-to-movie flicks. I had to hand it to him. Even though some of them were extremely cheesy, he didn't complain once.

After an amazing night, though, reality had returned and the time had come to do something I'd been avoiding for the last couple of days while I focused on the good in my life instead of the bad.

Before the bonding ceremony, I wanted to visit my parents.

It might not have been the smartest thing to do, but it felt right. So, I crept out onto the porch before the sun rose and ported before Jordan could spot me. She wasn't known for being a morning person, but today wasn't a typical day.

I was pretty much getting married later that morning, and I wouldn't put it past my Satan of a best friend—who was very upset I hadn't let her give me a bachelorette party the night before—to show up and do something over the top in the morning.

When I appeared at the hill where the trees marking their burial sites were growing quicker than I thought possible, my chest tightened, but I managed to hold in the tears. That was progress I hadn't expected this early in my grieving.

Sitting down, I fidgeted with the grass and thought about how to begin. "Hey, Mom and Dad. I know it's been a couple of days since I've been by, but I was doing things that I hope are making you proud up there. You were right, and Ryland isn't that bad, but don't worry, Dad. I'm still not rushing anything. Though, we're going to try the bonding ceremony again this morning."

I paused as tears fought for release. I didn't want to cry. I wanted to get through this knowing I'd at least moved through a tiny bit of the grief.

"Stryx said you'll be there in spirit, and I really hope that's true. I don't want to do this without you. Well, whatever this is. I never got to ask what would happen at the ceremony, but I'm assuming it can't be that bad if the two of you were in support of it. Then again, you had also been okay with me dying in order to get into Arvayta." I snorted at my own twisted humor.

Then, my mind circled back to the bonding ceremony. If it felt too much like a wedding ceremony, there was a decent chance I'd bolt. The whole "cold feet" saying was really starting to claw at me, so I changed the subject.

"Can you guys see these trees? They're starting to grow together as they move inward, and it's one of the most striking things I've ever seen. Whatever magic they were planted with is definitely doing its job." My hands pressed into the bark of each tree. "I miss you both so much."

My throat burned, and I let a few tears fall but kept the worst of my anguish at bay. Just as I wiped the last of the tears away, wind blew at my back. I sighed, thinking it was a sign from my parents. Instead, my bond to Stryx flared to life as he landed next to me.

"Kaliah," he said softly, then waited.

I squeezed the trees once more and blew kisses to each of them before I stood and held my hand out for Stryx. "Am I late?"

"Not at all. I just wanted to check on you. That wall of yours is a little too effective. You can't even seem to sense when I'm trying to politely reach out."

"Politely, huh?"

His feathers ruffled. "I could break through it if I wanted, but it would hurt you and I'm not that cruel."

"Only part of that statement surprises me." I winked at him and pulled his body closer for a hug. I'd missed him during my time with Ryland. "How do I make the wall strong enough to keep you out, but transparent enough to hear you if I need to?"

His wing swept up and brushed my cheek. "We'll worry about that later today. Let's head to the bonding site."

I glanced down at myself. "I'm wearing yoga pants and one of my dad's old shirts. Shouldn't I change first?"

"You're perfect as you are. Now, let's try something new while we're at it. I want you to close your eyes, ready yourself to port, but don't think about where you want to go. Focus on my energy and follow it instead. Trust in me."

That sounded like something that would be helpful in the future. I did as he asked, but I couldn't sense him. So, I lowered my wall that kept him out and found the energy I knew to be uniquely Stryx.

"Very good, Kali. I'm going to port in just a few seconds. Keep that link and be ready to follow."

Assuming he was looking at me, I nodded and kept my concentration. His energy began to change, and I braced myself. For what, I wasn't sure, but it was new, so I couldn't help being cautious.

Stryx disappeared from my senses, and I followed him, or so I thought. Instead, I ended up back at home with him nowhere to be seen.

"Cheese and rice. Now what am I supposed to do?" I said to myself.

Port to the forest entrance where we entered to meet the other animals. I'll meet you there, Stryx replied since I still had my wall down.

Without saying anything, I did as he asked. Just as my feet landed on the soft ground, Stryx came gliding through the trees. "Don't be disappointed, Kali. It's a perk that takes great concentration and a lot of practice. With all you have going on, I didn't expect you to get it the first time but wanted to see how you'd do without giving you any doubts."

He thought he was so smart. No, he was just a pain in my ass.

I heard that.

Immediately, I threw my wall back up and glared at him. "Where are we going, and is everyone else already there?"

"Ryland and Lorelle are there, but no one else. Lorelle didn't think it was a good idea."

"How did Jordan take that?" I asked, disappointed my best friend wouldn't be there, but also okay with it. The less people there, the less it would feel like a really big deal.

"I'm not sure. Dom told her instead of me."

"Chicken," I muttered.

His beak snapped at me. "No, I'm smart."

He took off into the forest, and we headed the opposite way we'd gone before until I heard a stream. Another minute later, the trees thinned out, and I saw Ryland standing in the water while Lorelle circled around him with what looked to be some sort of smudge stick. I tried to use one once in Portland and ended up doing it wrong and smoking us out of the house. Jordan had promptly thrown it away.

Ryland was wearing all white, and his hair and clothes were wet, as if he'd been swimming. Thankfully, nothing was see-through, so I didn't have to worry about inappropriate thoughts.

The two of them ignored us until Lorelle stepped out of the water. "Perfect timing." She snapped her fingers and flicked some sort of magic at me. "Now you're ready. Please step into the water, but don't touch Ryland."

Glancing down, I noticed I was wearing the same clothes as Ryland, only several sizes smaller. Stryx nudged me forward when I didn't move on my own, and I smiled back at him. "Where is the council? I thought they had to do this ceremony."

He landed on the ground since there was nothing nearby to keep him at eye level. "Normally, yes, but there is nothing normal about this situation, so Lorelle made different arrangements with their permission."

"She seems to be doing that a lot lately," I said with a pointed stare at her as I remembered her demanding I stay away from the main part of town, then ruining Ryland's dinner plans.

My feet went into the water, and it was surprisingly warm. When I was knee deep and about four feet from Ryland, Lorelle began to circle me with her smudge stick that smelled heavily of sage and something else that I couldn't identify.

Her greying hair was pulled back into a braid, and she wore clothes similar to those of Ryland and me except hers were dark grey, almost black where the water had touched. After she'd done a few more circles, she stopped in front of me. "Sorry." Then, she pushed me into the water.

I spat and sputtered as I tried to catch myself, but it was useless. Instead of fighting it, I dunked myself completely. When I emerged, I pushed my hair away from my face only to find I was missing something vital. "Where is my crown?"

Whatever calm Lorelle had been building within me with her juju was long gone as panic began to fill me. I turned to search the water, but she grabbed my arms and caught me off guard with her strength. "I have it in a safe place. You are okay here. I promise."

My heart slowed, but the anxiety didn't subside completely. I didn't like not knowing the whole plan, and she should have warned me.

"Why isn't Ryland moving?" I asked when I realized he hadn't reacted to my freak-out.

"He is in stasis as you will be soon. Now, stand still and let me clear your aura again," she demanded, then added, "And remove any blocks you have. You need to be completely open to what's about to happen."

Stryx nodded, so I put down my wall. It wasn't like my internal thoughts were anything new to him, so I hoped I had nothing to worry about.

Once my shoulders relaxed, Lorelle started murmuring words I couldn't understand, and I grew calmer by the second. My body swayed, and I was convinced I'd fall back into the water, but I couldn't find it in me to care. Then, everything else faded away. I found myself floating in the air, but it was dark around me.

I tried to move, but I was immobile, and dread filled me. *Stryx?* No response.

My brain was screaming words, but no sound would come out. A heaviness settled over me as a familiar energy filtered into the emptiness around me.

"Hello, Kaliah."

CHAPTER 8

My head swiveled around, but I couldn't see anything through the surrounding darkness. There wasn't even a flicker of light visible around me. My stress levels reached new heights as Alaryk continued to call my name. It rolled off his tongue in a sensual way that made my skin crawl, but at the same time, intrigued me, which then turned into fury.

I would not find him attractive. I *couldn't* find him appealing in any way possible.

I refused to be the reason people died.

"Kaliah, why do you fight me?" he whispered in my ear, and my arms flung out but didn't touch anything.

"Get away from me." I tried to access my magic, but it was as if it had been stripped away from my core.

"Stop struggling. It's pointless. We're in a realm of nothingness that I created, and neither of us have power. We are equal and can be ourselves without any obstacles. Now, do you care to tell me what you're up to today?"

Damn it. How did he keep finding out about the bonding ceremony?

"None of your business. Now, send me back," I demanded, while trying to figure out how to do so myself.

"You see, it doesn't work that way. I didn't bring you here all on my own. A part of you wants to be with me. I called for you, and you answered."

"Lies!" I screamed.

I shuddered as his breath brushed over my neck. "Keep telling yourself that, my sweet."

He'd yet to actually touch me, but he seemed so close that I should have been able to reach him.

"What do you want?" I asked, trying to reason with him.

"You know the answer to that, so why do you ask the question?" he replied.

My head shook. "I thought you wanted to kill me."

"That's plan B. Given that you're here with me, I still have hope for plan A, but don't take that for weakness, my sweet. I won't hesitate to kill you, given the opportunity, if you continue to refuse me and offer yourself to that worthless guardian."

My mind raced, trying to figure out where we were and how I'd gotten there—most importantly, why I couldn't feel anything physical. My emotions were heightened, but every physical sense seemed to have vanished.

"They're not teaching you enough in Arvayta. If you'd have come with me, you'd know exactly what was happening to you," he grumbled.

"I will never go anywhere with you unless it's to kill you. You murdered my parents. I can't let that go unpunished," I snapped.

"Am I the one who needs punishing? Because, let's be honest, who's fault was it really?"

Anguish soared through me like never before. I couldn't stomp the emotions down as they took over every facet of my being. Rage, sorrow, and vengeance were all so prominent within me, yet I couldn't do anything about them as they bubbled within, demanding to be released.

"That's it, Kaliah. Feel so deeply that you have to see the truth. See that you're no good for anyone else but me. We were cut from the same cloth. *We* belong together."

Power burst from me as I exploded—literally, or so I was certain. Everything around me shredded in my mind as light began to filter through, and Alaryk's screams faded into the distance.

My name was being called, but I couldn't respond. I didn't know what would happen if I did anything other than hold on to what was left of me, which didn't seem like much.

Ryland's hands yanked me from the water. "Kali, wake up!"

His fear finally penetrated whatever had been holding me hostage, and I opened my eyes, fury filling my every thought. "He took me."

"What are you talking about? Who and when?" Ryland asked as Stryx hovered right behind him.

"Alaryk. I was gone. Didn't you see?" Panic filtered through as I tried to remember everything that happened, but it was fading away by the second.

"Your physical form never left, Kaliah. You went to a shared realm with him," Lorelle said disappointingly.

"I don't understand. How did that happen?"

"He called for you and you answered."

Ryland's grip on me tightened. "Did you?"

My head shook. "It's not possible."

Lorelle sighed. "It's not your fault. I thought this might happen. I did my best to give you the greatest chance at avoiding him, but he's stronger than I had hoped, and your connection to him is there, whether you want to admit it or not."

I snarled at her. "The only connection I have to that man is the one that drives my need to kill him."

Stryx landed on my knees that protruded from the water I still lay in. "I'm sorry, Kaliah. I didn't know until just yesterday."

My glare turned on him. "What are you talking about?"

Ryland was fully invested in the answer to that question as well. He had just as much of a stake in this as I did, it seemed.

"The prophecy is there for a reason. Even if it doesn't come true, even if we can stop it from happening, it doesn't change the facts. The two paths before you are each very possible. If you choose it, you could bond with Alaryk the same as Ryland, even though he is your Meraki. I was going to tell you the moment I found out, but Lorelle didn't want those thoughts interfering with the process."

What in the actual…

Ryland's face turned several shades of red and purple before he finally spoke. I was still trying to process what the owl was saying.

"So, are we unable to bond now that Alaryk interrupted the ceremony? What does this mean for us?"

Lorelle moved closer. "You can bond, but Alaryk will fight it every chance he gets."

"Ha. He's probably not feeling too great right now. I exploded whatever hellhole he'd lured me into."

Lorelle raised a brow. "Tell me what happened. Every detail, no matter how small."

I gladly did as she asked, and poor Ryland was losing it as I continued.

"If the two of you are still open to completing the ceremony, I think now is our only shot. Kali would have weakened him with that move. Not his physical form, but the one that will keep getting in the way of any connection you share."

"Let's do it," I said immediately, then realized maybe Ryland didn't want to. Maybe knowing his Meraki was tied in some sick way to another was too much for him to handle. "Well, as long as Ryland agrees."

He didn't answer right away, and my heart began to break, but Ryland had yet to move away from me, so I was taking that as a good sign he wasn't going to bail. Though, if he did, I wouldn't blame him.

"Will Alaryk be able to get in my head through our bond if Kali and I can complete the ceremony?" he asked Lorelle.

"No, I don't believe so."

Ryland grimaced. "Well, that's unfortunate. Regardless, let's try again. We'll deal with Alaryk soon enough," he said, and I breathed a little easier.

Lorelle didn't hesitate before she placed one hand on each of our chests. "This is going to hurt."

I was still sitting in the water with Stryx on my knee and Ryland next to me. Lorelle bent beside us and lowered herself as magic seeped into my body that didn't belong. Smoke rose from my chest and, when I glanced at Ryland, I could see the same was happening to him.

Stryx had flown out of the way, and I couldn't see him any longer as Lorelle pushed us both further into the water until our bodies were completely submersed.

Fear of drowning clawed at my mind, but it was quickly forgotten as the voice of Ryland sounded.

Kali?

Yeah? I was weirded out, even though I did the whole mind-speak thing frequently with Stryx. Having another in my head wasn't exactly appealing.

Are you okay? he asked.

I think so. You?

It's painful, but manageable.

We stayed in silence after that as I focused on fighting my body's desire to pass out. I wanted to be awake and alert for as long as I could, just in case Alaryk came back.

A roar tore through my mind, and the agony reached a new peak. My body rose from the water, steam rolling off of me as everything within me burned, and it reminded me of when my human side had died. My eyes finally closed, and I tried to reach out to Ryland, but my connection to him was gone, though I swore I could sense his panic.

What felt like forever later, I dropped back into the water without an ounce of grace and choked as the stream rushed over me. Once I was back in control of my body, I sat up in the shallow pool, wiping water and hair away from my face. When my vision cleared, I searched for Ryland, but I couldn't see him.

Then, hands grabbed on to me, and I didn't hesitate to flip the person onto their back and position myself on top of them. "Woah, Kali. It's just me." Ryland was beneath me, head barely above water as my fist hovered just inches from his nose.

"Sorry." I blushed and cringed as a throat cleared.

"Are the two of you done?" Lorelle chastised.

Moving off of Ryland, I let my weak body fall back into the water. I wasn't sure how long we'd been out there, but I felt like hell. Everything within me was zapped of energy.

"Did it work?" Ryland asked as he reached down to help me up.

"I believe so, considering both of you are still breathing," Lorelle replied coolly.

A response was at the tip of my tongue, but a reaction was likely what she hoped for, so I didn't give her one. Instead, I found my footing and let Ryland guide me out of the water.

Stryx flew to me with my crown in his talons. "You may or may not need this anymore, but I'd recommend keeping it on until we know for sure. How are you feeling?"

"Exhausted and like I could sleep for a week," I answered honestly.

"The two of you should go back to the house and rest," Stryx suggested, and dread once again flooded through me.

Just because I'd bonded with Ryland didn't mean I wanted to be with him all the time. I still wanted to be my own person and get to know him slowly.

Calm, young one. You do not need to do anything you're not ready for, but it will speed up your recovery to remain within close proximity to Ryland for a while. You don't need to rest in the same room, but the same house would be preferable.

The wall was still down, and I remembered Ryland had been in my head during the bonding.

Can he *hear me, too?* I asked.

No, this perk is only between animal and human.

I heard him while Lorelle was doing whatever she did, though.

The two of you were at your weakest yet strongest as the bonds merged. It shouldn't happen again.

Stryx seemed so sure, but suddenly I couldn't wait to get my wall back up and reinforce it. I was tired of people being in my head, and the physical and mental exhaustion was making me cranky.

Slamming the block back into place, I at least took the owl's suggestion of remaining close to Ryland seriously. "Yes, the house would be good. You ready?" I asked Ryland, and he seemed surprised at my agreeance.

"Sure, but I don't have to stay if you don't want me to."

I ignored his last words and grabbed on to his hand. After waving goodbye to Lorelle and Stryx, I headed back home with Ryland in tow. The sun was high in the sky, and at least a couple of hours had passed while we'd been out there.

The guest house was quiet, so I assumed Jordan was with Oliver or Dom and was thankful. I didn't have the energy for fifty questions with her. She'd have to wait until we woke up again. Or, at least, until I did.

"I'm exhausted," I mumbled as I eyed the couch and considered the effort it would take to walk up the stairs to the room I'd been staying in.

"Do you want me to help you to your room? I won't stay if you're worried about that."

"Quit being so nice. I kind of miss the asshole version of you." As soon as the words left my mouth, I couldn't believe I'd said them and covered my face. Exhaustion also made me lose some of my filter, apparently.

He laughed, deep and throaty. "I'll remember that. Now, let me take you to your bed." The words were more of a demand, and my body warmed. That was better.

Ryland picked me up and carried me toward the stairs. By the time we hit the top, my eyes were already heavy, especially as he murmured comforting words to me. Holding on to me with one arm, he pulled the covers back, then lay my lax body into the bed and covered me up.

He kissed the top of my head, and I reached for him. "Don't leave me." There was an ache in my chest that I feared would only get worse if he left.

"I'll sit right here." He pulled the chair from the corner of the room to the side of the bed and held my hand once he sat down.

When I was certain he wasn't going anywhere, I let the weight of sleep pull me under as our bond flared to life and a sense of security settled over me for the first time since losing my parents.

CHAPTER 9

Apparently, bonding wasn't all that easy to recover from. Waking up with a raging Jordan in my face wasn't exactly what I had been expecting, either, but it happened, nonetheless. Along with Ryland still next to my bed. Our hands were intertwined, and he was sleeping near my shoulder, only partly still in the chair. Well, that was until Jordan woke us both up.

"It's been three days! I'm going to lose my mind," she huffed.

"Calm down. They need time," a deep voice rumbled and had me instantly on alert. That definitely wasn't Oliver.

When I peeked, there was a freaking lion in the room. "Uh, Jordan?"

She rushed over to me, both hands shaking my shoulders. "You're awake." Her relief was palpable.

Glancing over, Ryland was just beginning to stir and, when his eyes opened, there wasn't a bit of happiness coming from him. "What do you want, Jordan?" he snarled.

"Oh, calm down and get the stick out of your ass." Jordan winked at me. "In case you didn't know, your Meraki isn't a morning person."

"Good to know, so why don't you go wait downstairs and we'll be there shortly?" I asked as nicely as I could in hopes she'd comply.

When it appeared as if she was going to argue, the lion whipped his tail around and the fluffy end went straight into Jordan's mouth, effectively shutting her up.

My mouth fell open in surprise, as did hers, but only had her gagging on hair.

"We'll be downstairs," said Dominic, then the lion nudged her out of the door with his massive head.

I glanced down at Ryland. "Can you believe that?"

He grinned. "I've been waiting decades for someone to do that to her and get away with it."

Those two were like brother and sister.

Ryland was still holding my hand and stared at it before he spoke. "How are you feeling?"

Taking a minute, I internally checked myself out. Nothing seemed different—maybe a little calmer—but my magic still swirled just the same in my core. Then I remembered my crown and found it still on top of my head.

The bonding ceremony seemed a little hazy in my memory until I remembered Alaryk trying to crash it. If he did that again, I wasn't sure what I would do, but I needed to figure out a way to prevent any part of my mental state from allowing it to happen.

"I'm good, I think. I don't really feel any different. Is that bad?" I hoped my words didn't offend him.

"No, that's why I asked. I don't either, but they said it worked, so I guess we'll see." Ryland stood from the bed and walked toward the door. "I'll give you some privacy and meet you downstairs?"

"Thanks. I'll be right there."

As soon as the door was closed, something flared within me—a tightness within my chest. Then, a thud sounded at the door and Ryland poked his head back in. "Well, that was different."

"You felt it, too?" I asked, and he nodded. "I remember on occasion feeling a tugging sensation toward you before. I guess this is the same thing on steroids?"

"Probably. Bonded guardians don't do well apart. I'll probably need to sleep in the house until we get the hang of things."

Or forever, I thought, then shook my head. No, I wasn't rushing anything. He was right. We would figure it out and then go back to taking things slow.

"Alright, I'm going now. Just be prepared to miss me like crazy." He winked and disappeared.

A grin plastered to my face, and I couldn't make it go away. I felt like I was experiencing puppy love and couldn't help but be happy, which made me feel out of control of my own life. Then, I began a downward spiral of thoughts as I made my way to the bathroom.

As I took the longest pee of my life, I wondered if I'd made a mistake bonding to Ryland, but then our connection began to grow with the distance, and I knew it was only crazy thoughts I needed to make go away.

Ryland was a good man, one who was faithful, kind, and passionate. There would be no regrets, even if it happened a little too fast for my liking.

I took a quick shower and dressed in workout clothes. My body was charged, and as soon as I satisfied Jordan's need to grill me, I'd be heading to the training fields. I needed a release before I did something without thinking.

As more time passed, I realized the subtle differences in myself. My skin was more sensitive, my awareness was on hyperdrive, and I felt like I was on caffeine overload. Taking the steps two at a time, I raced downstairs as soon as I was ready.

Ryland was pacing the living room. He, too, was already changed and seemed out of sorts, but the moment our eyes met, my nerves calmed, and I could breathe normally again. I was going to kill Stryx if this continued to happen forever. Neither of us could live like this.

Then again, my parents had been Merakis and were apart on occasion and survived without showing signs of distress. Maybe it was just temporary for me and Ryland since everything was so new.

Before I could process much more, he was standing before me and pulling me into a tight hug. "This is going to take some getting used to."

"You forgot to prepare yourself for how much you'd miss me," I teased, using his earlier words against him.

"Apparently."

Jordan shoved us apart. "I haven't spoken to my best friend in days. Go. Away."

Remembering back to when I was convinced that I had a bond with Jordan as well, I sympathized with her. "Do you think you and Dominic can go outside for a bit? You don't have to go far," I said to Ryland.

He moved in and kissed my cheek while squeezing my upper arm. "Sure. Come on, Dom."

I watched the two of them go out the back door, still having a hard time wrapping my brain around the fact that there was a lion roaming my house as if he was a person.

"What. The. Hell?" Jordan jerked my attention back to her. "You ditch me, get married, and then sleep for three days straight. I should divorce you for that, Chuck."

My chest already ached at having Ryland be further away, but my heart broke even more for my best friend. "Come here, Satan." My arms opened for her, but she didn't budge, so I threw myself at her. "I'm sorry. Please, forgive me."

I didn't even try to pass the blame on Stryx or Lorelle. I wished she had been there, and I should have fought to make that happen. Then again, things didn't go exactly as planned, so I'm glad she didn't have to stress about it during the process.

"You owe me. Big time," she grumbled.

"I know. How about the next shopping trip is on me? I will buy you all the shiny things."

She smirked. "Even better, you can let me pick out all the shiny things for both of us and you'll still pay."

I cringed but agreed anyway, because I really did owe her.

"So, officially bonded, huh? How's that feel?" she asked.

"Well, I passed out pretty much right after it was completed. Did Stryx tell you what happened during the process?"

She pulled me to the couch, and we both sat down. "He did. I can't believe that psycho has that kind of reach. What did it feel like?"

Remembering the void was harder than I realized, but not impossible. "Every emotion in my mind was heightened. I was confused and hurt and angry, and so pissed off that I ended up blowing the realm he created to bits by the end of it."

"That's my girl. Show that asshat who he's messing with."

"What about you and Dom?" I asked, knowing she'd gone through some pretty significant changes as well.

"It's been amazing. Not like having a Meraki, I'm sure, but still something I'm honored to be able to experience. It's like what I feel with you, but deeper, you know?"

I nodded, because I really did understand.

"We postponed training with them until the two of you were ready. Do you think you'll be up for it tomorrow?" Jordan asked, seeming excited about getting started.

"What kind of training?"

"There were over fifty guardians matched with animals. They'll all be going to the Otherworld with us. Stryx wants everyone to practice communicating and fighting alongside their bonded ones, with you and him setting the example."

Well, at least we were going to have a lot of help when we went searching for Alaryk. Hopefully it would be enough.

"I'm actually feeling pretty good as long as I'm near Ryland.

The bond feels like a rubber band, though. We're stretching it and testing it. The farther he tries to move away, even right now, the more constricted my chest gets. Might be good for us to work with Stryx on ways to sort that issue out."

She waggled her brows at me. "Don't lie and tell me you don't want to spend every waking moment with him. It's okay and perfectly normal."

I sighed. I was still struggling with the independent human side of myself. I might have died and come back fae, but some habits were harder to break than others.

"Come on, Chuck. Let's go get our boys and have some fun." Jordan grabbed my hand, and we headed out the door.

A tension I didn't know I was holding on to released from me as soon as Ryland was in my sights. His icy-blue eyes softened as they met mine, and I instantly wanted to run to him, but the more stubborn part of me refrained. Instead, I watched Jordan run for Dom and jump onto his back, then they both disappeared.

"Everything okay?" Ryland asked as he reached for me.

Slowly, I took his hand and nodded. "Yep. She's better now, but I wouldn't put it past her to retaliate later, so watch your back."

"Oh, I have no doubts. Some of the things she used to do to Oliver and me would make lesser men cry."

"I wish I had grown up here with you guys to experience it firsthand, but Earth wasn't so bad, either." I had a lot of good memories there. Pretty much the only ones I had with my parents, so I'd never truly regret my time there now that I wasn't able to make new ones with them in Arvayta.

"Come on. Let's go see what Stryx has planned." Ryland tugged on me and then ported us onto the training fields.

Jordan and Oliver were fighting each other with their animals, but before I could watch for too long, Stryx approached us, landing on my shoulder. "Good to see the two of you out of the house."

I nudged him with my head. "Yeah, you could have warned us that we'd be out of commission for a few days."

"And take all of the fun out of it for me? No, thank you." It wasn't often that Stryx joked around. He was more often an obnoxious know-it-all who was well aware of how special he was. So, it was nice to see him in a good mood and so light-hearted.

"Do you need help with getting ready for tomorrow?" Ryland asked.

"No, I've got it handled, but just know the two of you will be students with the others."

I nodded. "Jordan mentioned you and I would be setting the example, but what about Ryland? Will he be working with us?"

"The bond between guardian and animal works very much the same as a Meraki one. So, we will incorporate both our bond and your Meraki one into the training whenever possible. The most important piece will be the two of you maintaining a presence in front of the others. Training with them will put a sense of faith in you that they need to be certain what they're about to do is worth risking their lives."

So, we had to show everyone else that I knew what I was doing and our bond was strong and we weren't leading them all to their deaths. Great. No pressure or anything.

CHAPTER 10

Stryx had freaked me out for no reason. Oddly enough, working with the animals hadn't been any different than our previous training sessions. Most everyone worked in pairs for the first few days, then we were sectioned off into groups.

I'd learned how to "listen" for Stryx, so that I didn't completely block him out when my wall was up, and he'd even allowed me inside his on a few occasions. I was disappointed to learn his thoughts were just as organized as he was on the outside. A hot mess had been what I was hoping for to make myself feel better.

Stryx had also taught Ryland and I how to sense each other. Our bond allowed us to feel emotions and know when the other was near or too far away to connect with. It was an interesting concept I still hadn't quite wrapped my head around but hoped it would come in handy at a later time. The connection seemed like it would only be pertinent if we were in danger.

Everyone trained together for just over a week, but then our time was up. Queen Navi was getting anxious and had sent word to us that we either came immediately or she was going to look at other options for keeping her people safe, options that wouldn't bode well for any of us.

Ryland watched me with abandon as I finished braiding my hair and put my crown back in place. Disappointment filled me that it didn't make my hair glow purple anymore now that my power was stable.

Ever since I had officially bonded with Ryland, the crown hadn't been necessary to wear all of the time like Lorelle had thought, but I'd grown surprisingly attached to the security it gave me. Knowing I had a failsafe if my power got out of hand, and Ryland wasn't around, helped to ease my worries.

"How are you feeling?" he asked.

"Ready. Though, everything feels like it's moving so fast, yet not fast enough. How much damage has Alaryk caused since we bonded? Not hearing from him makes me nervous," I replied.

Ryland and I had taken time for a few more dates that included many more kisses, a lot of conversations getting to know more little details about each other, and a lot of moments that helped confirm I hadn't been a fool to bond with him.

He knew my every want before I did. He anticipated things as if he'd known me my whole life. Where I moved, he moved as well. It was overwhelming at times, but similar to how I had finally found my crown reassuring, I was beginning to cherish everything about Ryland.

There was still a part of me that refused to allow him to sleep in my bed or think of us as bonded for life, but that cautiousness was getting smaller by the day.

When I was done getting ready, I glanced at the picture of my parents on my dresser. I kissed my fingertips and placed it on the glass. "I'm counting on you to have my back," I whispered.

Grief still came in waves, and I expected it to for many years to come, but I'd kept busy enough to keep the worst of it at bay. When I couldn't, Ryland was right there with me, supporting me as I processed things how I saw fit. Sometimes it was tears, other times I broke more glass, and in only one other instance had I called the lightning to me.

Creating a storm was the most freeing feeling I'd ever experienced. There was something so raw about it that called to me, and I wanted badly to figure out a way to do it without putting anyone else at risk, but that was a problem we'd solve once Alaryk was dead.

In the meantime, we had a dagger to build and needed to be on our way.

When turning away from my dresser, I collided with Ryland's chest, and his hands reached out to steady me. "Is there anything I can do?"

"You're already doing it just by being here," I answered honestly and pushed up to kiss him.

It was something I had been doing often over the past couple of days and without hesitation, and the closer we got, the easier things came to me. The path before me was clear. I knew what needed to be done, and I wouldn't waste time fighting feelings in case not everything went according to plan.

"Come on." I grabbed his hand, and we headed downstairs.

I'd never gone back to sleeping in the guest house. I let Jordan and Dom have that space while sticking closer to the things that kept my parents' memory near and allowed more room for Ryland to be around, but also have his own space.

I took one more look at the house I'd only known for the last month or so and hoped like hell it wasn't the last time I'd see it. Ryland seemed to sense my nostalgia and tugged me along to the porch before I could get my head too far out of sorts.

"About damn time," Jordan whined from the grass with Dom at her side.

"Oh, shut it. I've waited hours for you on many occasions. You've maybe been out here two minutes?" I replied teasingly.

Dom grunted. "More like one minute, but it felt like an hour with her droning."

She glared at him, and I grinned. It made my heart happy to see Jordan have that special bond with someone. Even if it wasn't the one that she most craved, it was still something to be valued.

Oliver and Cynder arrived next. The black panther wasn't nearly as vocal as Dom, but she seemed to care fiercely for Oliver based on their interactions in our trainings, and that was what mattered most. She hadn't been sent here to be our friend, but hopefully she'd open up more as time went on.

"Alright. Let's go." Ryland ported and I followed, knowing the others would be right behind us.

Stryx told us to meet him late that morning at the portal to the Otherworld. Our group was arriving last since he insisted on getting the other guardians sorted and assigned to their locations without us. I'd checked in with him several times through our bond already, and he promised everything had been going according to plan.

So, when we arrived and he wasn't there, *I* wasn't happy.

Where are you?

"I'm right here, and you're early, so I don't want to hear it," Stryx said, appearing on the boulder next to the entrance.

He was lucky. I wouldn't have hesitated to go through the portal without him if I thought something was wrong.

Once everyone was accounted for, I focused on the area around us. The last time I'd been there, I remember there was a tranquility about it, but the ethereal glow I had recalled was no longer there.

"What's wrong with this place?" I asked.

"Ever since Alaryk was here, it's been changing. It was part of the reason Lorelle didn't want you to be in town. He left behind a darkness that has been affecting the falls," Stryx answered.

"I think telling us about this sooner would have been appreciated," Jordan snapped, and I was relieved I hadn't been the only one in the dark about the changes.

"It's only gotten bad the last day or so, and there wasn't anything you could do, but now there is."

We all seemed to agree he was right. Knowing would have only caused more stress on the rest of us, more need to rush and possibly make rash decisions.

"Everyone ready?" Stryx asked when nobody objected to his reasonings, then he wasted no time flying back toward the waterfall opening. "Let's go then."

Taking a deep breath, I shook out my arms and peeked back at Arvayta one last time. There was no coming back until either the dark fae was dead or I was. Either way, I wouldn't be the same me when the fight was over.

Jordan looped an arm through mine and pulled me toward the entrance. "We'll jump together."

"Better than you pushing me." I shrugged.

We stepped through at the same time, and the feeling of air being pulled from my lungs hit me hard. Harder than any time before. Realization came too late that I shouldn't have left without Ryland, considering our bond was so new, but as the pain peaked, I sensed Ryland getting closer.

When we landed, my feet hit hard ground, and I was instantly on alert and forgetting about the hurt in my chest. The land hadn't been solid before. It was supposed to be buoyant and full of life.

Moving out of the way for the others to come through, I took in our surroundings. Gone was the peaceful place I'd first visited, and in its place was a barren land with everything around it dying.

I dropped to my knees, calling for water, trying to feed nourishment into the dirt, but there was nothing left.

Oliver gasped in pain when he arrived with Ryland, and my

heart hurt for the earth guardian. Oliver's connection to the lands was much stronger than mine, and I couldn't imagine how this was affecting him, but Cynder seemed to as she wrapped herself around his legs.

"How?" he asked.

"Alaryk," was all Stryx needed to say.

"We need to hurry." Oliver and Cynder began moving, and the rest of us trailed after with Ryland and me in the middle, Stryx flying above, and Jordan and Dom watching the back.

As we moved along, I searched the skies and noticed even the four sections above us were dulling. No longer could I see the aqua of the water lands, the crimson sky, or the stormy one. The only one remaining strong was the pale green above the lands Queen Navi ruled over and where we were headed.

The titanium gates still stood, blocking the market from outside view, and I watched as Oliver once again took charge of letting us in. Each of us moved through with a sense of urgency, knowing there was no more time to waste.

The booths were open, but there were very few around buying anything. I assumed most of the smart people were at home, hunkering down and trying to stay out of the fight they had nothing to do with.

When we arrived at the pearlescent castle, it didn't have the same golden hue I had noticed before, and I suddenly wondered if we were too late.

"The queen is expecting all of us," Stryx said, not at all seeming worried, so I dismissed my negative thoughts.

Jordan leaned in closer. "I've only met her once that I can remember. She's either very intense or seems to have no idea what she's doing. I'm not sure which is better, so just be careful."

Super. A sorceress who couldn't control her emotions. Just what we needed.

"Or maybe she just likes to keep people on their toes," Stryx added, his advanced hearing coming in handy.

Jordan rolled her eyes as she stepped onto the palace stairs. Once again, we went through the shield that felt like it was trying to peel my skin off and entered into the main atrium of the castle. This time, there was no escort for us as we followed Stryx up the stairs.

He moved too fast for me to really look around, but it seemed the same as any castle I'd seen in the movies. Old pictures, armor, doors—lots of them—and confusing hallways for intruders to get lost in.

We finally arrived at a set of wooden doors carved with filigree and flowers beneath two large bronze knockers. Ryland did the honors, using one of them at Stryx's request, and then we waited.

"Where are the door handles?" I asked.

"There are none. It only opens with the queen's magic," Oliver replied beside me.

Interesting and hopefully, for her sake, more effective.

Finally, both doors opened without noise and we entered into the queen's chambers, which were more like a whole house.

There was a formal living room to the right that was inset into the ground. To the left was a small kitchen, which was still fancier than any other I'd ever used, and cleaner, as if it'd never been touched. On the far wall was a door and a hallway that veered to the left, and I couldn't see beyond the first few feet.

What caught my attention the most were the windows overlooking the lands the queen so obviously cherished. Without being invited, I moved further into her space and stared out the glass.

Stryx tried to get through my wall, but I had a feeling he was going to reprimand me for being rude and I didn't want to hear it. My heart was hurting at the signs of carnage. Charred lands, barren fields, toppled trees. All of it was devastating, and all of it was my fault.

"He works quickly, doesn't he?" Queen Navi said from my side.

"Unfortunately so. I'm sorry."

Her head cocked to the side. "What for?"

"He's doing this because I won't do as he wants."

"And if you did? If you joined him in the darkness, what do you think would happen to these lands or the people who live here?" Her hand gestured toward the window.

I didn't have an answer to her question.

She continued, "This is nothing compared to the destruction he could cause with you by his side. *You* are the reason it's not worse, so don't apologize for his actions." Her voice was stern, pushing through the blame and making me almost believe her.

The others had moved further into the room, and I felt bad at seeing Ryland tense. He worried for me too often, and I needed to be more aware of his feelings, like he was of mine.

Nobody sat. There was no time for that based on what we'd seen so far, and the queen addressed Stryx while I took a moment to take in her regal gown that hung loosely from her hips and trailed behind as she walked. Her golden hair was combed perfectly into a bun so tight that I wondered if she lived with a constant headache.

Her crown was twice the size of mine, gold in color and without gems, while her eyes were a deep forest color, bordering on hazel with the flashes of brown in them.

"Are your people in place?" she asked Stryx.

"Yes. They met with your guardians, and the groups have already set out. Were you able to acquire any of the pieces we need ahead of time?"

She shook her head slightly. "The gnomes don't keep the metal you need here, and the vampires have gone underground, it seems."

"And the succubi?"

Queen Navi grimaced. "A lot of them have perished. Seems

one of them tried to woo Alaryk and he punished the lot. Brooke has been searching for information on those who are left and hiding. The last known locations were in the wind sector and possibly some in the water lands, but I haven't had the extra help to confirm that."

"That's a lot of pissed off women," Jordan said what I was already thinking.

If they'd already suffered so many losses, it wasn't likely they were going to help us unless we could find a way it proved to benefit them as well. Hopefully promising to destroy Alaryk would be enough. I wasn't sure we had any other options.

"Brooke will be your liaison to the other warrior groups. All of my people are fitted with communication devices and can give you updates on your guardians if needed, as long as they stay together," the queen added.

We hadn't been around Brooke for very long the last time we were in the Otherworld, but she was a vampire, and I was hoping she would make one of our tasks easy. We needed vampire blood and hopefully she had some to spare.

"Anything else before we go?" Stryx asked.

"As you collect the items needed to forge the dagger, you'll need a safe place to store them as you make your way back to me." She snapped her fingers and a box appeared. "This should be more than sufficient."

Ryland reached for it since Stryx obviously couldn't take the heavy object. The wood was carved just like the doors with bronze hinges and a lock, but I didn't see a key.

Queen Navi turned to me when Ryland was putting it away. "You have two days' time before my wards will weaken and my land will die out completely. Use your time wisely, and may the Fates bless your journey."

I wasn't sure how I was supposed to respond to her statement, so I simply nodded and began moving toward the exit since it seemed like we were done. The others followed, and the doors opened once again. The queen watched us go, and I worried we were putting too much faith in her.

All the sorceress had done was give us a box and put my nerves on edge. Neither seemed helpful, but I trusted Stryx and hoped like hell his plan was staying on course, because we couldn't afford any mistakes.

CHAPTER 11

After overcoming the uncomfortableness I felt leaving the queen's chambers, I realized we had no real plan. At least, not one I was aware of. We knew what we were supposed to do, but I had no idea *how* we were going to do it. I had assumed we were meeting with Queen Navi so she would give us guidance, but that didn't happen.

Frustratingly so, I was feeling completely lost and we'd only just begun.

"So, what now?" Jordan asked, running her hands through Dom's mane as we stood on the castle steps.

Everyone looked to Stryx, but it wasn't him that answered.

"Now, your circus show follows me into the lair of your worst enemies." Brooke appeared from nowhere, her stealth unprecedented by anyone else I'd met so far. It was no wonder she worked so closely for the queen.

"Circus show? Okay, bloodsucker." Jordan rolled her eyes, clearly not as impressed with the vampire as I was.

"Is she always this surly?" Brooke asked me.

"No, but snarky, yes. She likes to keep things interesting, but something tells me you do as well."

Brooke and Jordan had been on guard around each other before, which I contributed to Jordan being wary of the newcomer, but hopefully that wouldn't last long. We didn't need any added tension as we searched for the vampires, gnomes, and succubi.

Jordan and Dom were in conversation, and I went to Ryland, the bond between us reminding me it had been a while since we'd been near enough. Casually, I brushed my arm against his and turned back to the others.

"So, is that what we're doing? Going to find the vampires first?" I asked.

Stryx flew to me and I held my hand to him, then put him on my shoulder. "Given we have Brooke's help now and can't guarantee it later, I think that's the best course of action."

"Why don't we just use the blood from Brooke? She is a vampire," Oliver suggested.

"Because she is not the vampire we need," Stryx answered.

Sigh. Of course, there was going to be a specific one.

"I know some people who can help us. Queen Navi told me what you need, and I already have some connections doing the leg work for us. We'll be done in the wind sector in record time. Then, I'd recommend searching for the succubi. Small pockets of them still exist, and you'll either find them hidden amongst the vampires or in the water lands."

"What about the gnomes?" I asked.

"They're in this section, but further out where there aren't as many people. We have to come back here for the queen to cast the final spell for the dagger. So, we won't be wasting time by bypassing them now," Stryx answered.

I turned to ask Brooke a question about the vampires, but she was in a heated discussion with Oliver, so I left her alone. Whatever was going on between them, I hoped they worked it out or I got the chance to figure out what the problem really was, and maybe help.

"Well, let's get moving then. Brooke?" Ryland said her name loud enough to interrupt whatever argument she was focused on.

She shook her head, snarling at Oliver and pushing him away as he reached for her. "Let's head to the southernmost point of the sections. That's where the easiest entry to each land is."

Jordan shuddered. "I remember going through the fire lands when Yelah needed our help. As long as we avoid that place, I don't care how we get where we need to be."

"The fire sector is the worst," Brooke droned and then launched into her story about a time she'd had to hunt down a newborn vampire.

Jordan listened intently, and I had hoped they'd get along just fine. Then again, maybe that wouldn't bode well for me. Jordan was already a lot to handle. I didn't really need two of her.

Ryland grabbed my hand, and I squeezed tightly. "Sorry if I worried you back there."

"I won't ever stop you from doing what you want to do. I just need to remind my heart that you're capable of doing things on your own even if it isn't always safe." He grinned.

"Were you really worried the queen would hurt me?" I asked.

He shook his head. "Not really, but we're in unique times. Never a bad idea to be overly cautious while we're here."

"I'll remember that, and thank you for giving me space to be me." I gave him a quick kiss and then went back to paying attention to where we were going. The lands only got more devastating the further we moved along, including not only dead plant life, but animals as well, further breaking my heart.

It didn't take long to get to the border. Apparently, the market was the most central location in all of the Otherworld, and everything else wouldn't be as easy to find. Since we didn't know exactly where we were going, there would be no porting, either.

The lands were separated by titanium fences, identifying each sector, with designated paths leading into different terrains. A part of me longed to enter the water lands. I could see a glistening lake with water so still, I imagined I'd be able to see the bottom of even the deepest parts.

Though, as soon as we entered into the gloomy lands of the wind section, my skin pricked as magic swirled within me and a storm ahead called to me.

"Easy, Chuck. We're not here for play," Jordan teased.

"Fine, but we'll be back here at some point, right?" I asked, because it seemed like the only truly safe place in any world that I could fully let myself go without fear.

Brooke grinned. "Hell yeah, as long as you let me tag along."

"Deal," I replied as I watched Cynder catch her attention.

Oliver didn't seem too thrilled with the panther's action, so it further encouraged Brooke to move closer to the animal. She really was just like Jordan.

Turning toward my best friend, I went to tell her that, but she was on Dom's back and running ahead of us.

"Is that smart of her to do?" I asked Ryland.

"Normally, I'd say no, but Dom seems to have enough sense to keep her out of trouble."

That was so very true.

Stryx's feathers ruffled, and I tensed. "What's wrong?"

"Someone is coming."

I searched for Jordan, but she and Dom were too far ahead to call back. Brooke was suddenly at my side and Oliver right behind us with Cynder.

"It's them," Brooke hissed.

"Who is *them*?" I whispered, but nobody answered me.

Instead, a group of three men appeared before us, one standing just a step ahead of the others. Each of them stared at us with crimson eyes and a hunger that had me stepping closer to Ryland.

"Brooke, I heard you were looking for something," the one in front said.

"I am, but we don't need your help, and we're not here to cause trouble, Cole," she replied stiffly.

He sniffed the air. "But there's so much magic in the blood of your company. You shouldn't be so selfish to your kind, or have you forgotten where you come from now that you're the queen's pet?"

Brooke sneered, and I latched on to her arm before she could retaliate, something I would have known Jordan to do, so I assumed she was thinking it.

The vampire flinched at my touch, but she stayed at my side. "Unless you're on Alaryk's side, I'd recommend letting us pass," she said.

Cole stepped even closer. "That fae has been through here, but he's yet to follow through on his word. Lucky for you, it gives you the opportunity to one-up him."

"What do you want?" I asked when Brooke didn't say anything.

His gaze traveled up and down my body. "Well, I could think of a few things."

"Not a chance in hell, bloodsucker," Ryland snarled, holding me tighter.

What kind of vampire blood do we need? I asked Stryx since he'd yet to say anything.

Blood from an original line vampire. His will work, but it'll cost us. Brooke was supposed to have connections with other pure vampires, but given they haven't found us by now, we may want to consider this option and avoid being here any longer than necessary.

So, you won't be mad if I…

Without finishing, I put the wall back up.

"What about Arelia blood?" I said, and Stryx's talon's dug into my shoulder through my jacket.

Cole leaned forward, taking another whiff of air. "Ahh, I haven't tasted one of you in much too long." The vampire grinned, showcasing fangs I could have lived the rest of my life without seeing.

"Not like that," Stryx's voice boomed.

"And who's going to stop me?" Cole smirked.

"We don't want a fight. What if you can have the blood and something else you won't ever have the chance of getting again?" Stryx flapped his wings, power rippling from him that had even *my* skin crawling.

Cole backed up a pace. "Okay, Owl. I'll bite. What do you have?"

"One of my feathers."

A roar sounded from the shadows and my worry for Jordan and Dom far exceeded any fear of the vampires before us. As I inched forward, Stryx pushed against my wall and I let it back down.

She's fine. You can't make any sudden movements right now, he said, and it was hard as hell to trust his word, but I managed to stay put.

Brooke pulled two needles from her bag, handing one to me and holding the other out in front of her. "Do we have a deal, Cole?"

He snatched the needle. "Feather first."

Stryx nodded to me and lifted his wing. Without wasting any time, mostly because I was still worried about Jordan, I yanked the feather out, and Ryland took it from me without asking. Apparently, he wasn't going to let me get any closer to the vamps than necessary.

Cole took it and then stuck the needle in his arm himself. "Same time, Arelia."

"Fine." I moved to do the same, but Ryland was already back at my side and gently took over, which was good, because my hands were already shaking from so many warring emotions. Blood would only make it worse.

Each needle had a vial attached to it, and I stared off into the shadows hoping to spot Jordan while Ryland and Cole drew blood. Still, there was no sign of Jordan, and there hadn't been any more shouts, so I was counting on that being a good thing.

I wouldn't lie to you, young one. They are both fine.

If you're wrong, there will be no stopping the storm I unleash.

His wing spread out around my shoulder, but it did nothing to quell the fear.

Brooke stepped between Cole and Ryland, holding both of her arms out, palm up. Ryland dropped my blood into her hand, but Cole hadn't.

"If that fae shows up here and threatens us for helping you, we won't hesitate to join him," the vampire stated.

Brooke snarled. "I'd expect nothing else. Now, hand it over and disappear."

"And if I don't?"

"Then you'll find out just how nice this group is being. You have no idea what they're capable of."

I stiffened. Brooke was going to get us into a fight I wasn't sure we could win. I knew nothing about vampires, and I was sure she didn't know anything about my powers.

Cole handed the blood over. "Alright, *Brookie*. Have it your way today, but if we catch you out here again, we won't be so lenient."

He snatched my blood, then blurred out of existence along with his cronies.

"Thank you, Brooke," Stryx said, and I was confused as to what the hell for.

She shrugged. "He wasn't going to just hand it over. He needed to know we were willing to fight him. Cole has always been known for going back on his word, and most vampires don't associate with him anymore because of it."

"Kali!" Jordan's voice screamed in the distance.

Pushing Stryx off of me, I began to run for her with Ryland right at my heels.

If there was a single scratch on her, heads were going to roll.

CHAPTER 12

My legs moved faster than ever before, and when I entered the dark depths of the forest where I'd heard Jordan's screams, all I could think about was who I would kill if anything had happened to her. I focused on the rage as I powered through the dense area, staying as quiet as I could to listen for her again.

No longer did I find any comfort in the wind section. There was no sun, which made it much harder to find my best friend. Branches bit at my arms as I ran through the trees, and a rage began to build within me as darkness slithered its way to my core.

Just as I was about to let a scream of frustration rip from my lungs, I heard Jordan's voice. "Kali? Where are you?"

"She's back to the left," Ryland said, but I was already circling around.

When I thought we should be close, a massive form slammed into the side of me and we crashed into a tree, snapping it in half.

"Kali, wait." Ryland's voice was full of panic, but I didn't care as power slithered along my skin, changing my every emotion and want within seconds.

Suddenly, I didn't even care about finding Jordan. My speed picked up, and my only goal was to get away from them. The people who reminded me of all that was wrong with my life. The people who made me feel and do things I'd rather not.

A sense of numbness crept into me, pushing me to accept the darkness that simmered within my depths as I raced along the forest and ignored those around me, including Ryland who screamed my name over and over again.

"Dom, don't touch her," I heard Jordan call out, but it was too late.

My instincts took over, and I slammed enough volts of magic into the chest of my attacker that I was certain he was dead.

What surprised me the most was that there was hardly any remorse filtering through me. It was as if my humanity had been turned off and I was finally free.

Jordan raced past me without a second look, her eyes wide with fear. "Dominic? Dominic, wake up!"

Her cries sounded behind me, and the realization of what I'd done finally registered, but I still didn't move to do anything about it. It was time for me to leave them for good, though as I took my first step, Stryx and the others arrived, giving me pause. Deep down, something in me still cared for them.

"What happened?" the owl asked me.

"He attacked me, and I think I killed him," I answered with very little emotion.

Stryx hooted and soared past me to Jordan who was hysterical on the ground, trying to wake up her bonded animal.

Ryland grabbed a hold of me, forcing me to look at him. "Kaliah Grace, snap out of it. You can't do this."

Confusion filtered through me. I wasn't doing anything. There was nothing wrong. For once, I didn't feel anything, and it was amazing.

"She must have gone through some dark magic or someone hit her with something while you were running," Brooke said, and I laughed.

"I *am* dark magic." I spoke the words, but I didn't recognize the voice.

"No, you're not. You're better than this. Fight it, Kali." Ryland's fingers grasped my chin and pulled me close as I tried to get away from him.

I didn't want to be bonded to him anymore. I was done being what everyone else wanted me to be. I was done caring.

"No. I won't let you do this." Ryland slammed his lips down onto mine and kissed me with every ounce of goodness he held within him.

I tried harder to push him away, even bit his lip and drew blood, but he wouldn't stop until I yielded beneath him.

Feelings began to rise within me. Love, guilt, sorrow, friendship, companionship. Things that had and could hurt me. I didn't want or need them in my life. I just wanted everything to go away.

Power rippled through me, and I was finally able to push Ryland away. "Leave me alone!" I screamed in his face.

Cynder circled me while Oliver and Brooke watched my every move. I wasn't afraid of them. I could kill them all with a single snap of my fingers.

That gave me an idea, and I called a storm to me. First with the rain and wind, followed by thunder, and I saved the lightning for last.

Clapping hands sounded in the shadows as two men appeared. "Alaryk will be so pleased, Kaliah. Come with us, and we'll take you to him."

My head twisted as new emotions tried to enter my mind. I knew these men. They were full of darkness like me, but they were monsters. They'd taken something from me that I'd never get back. They'd taken the only good left in my life.

These men had to die.

"Where is Alaryk?" I asked before making my move.

"Your king awaits you, and we will bring you to him," the blonde one said proudly.

"Tell me where he is." I demanded.

He tsked. "I don't think so. Our spell might have worked, but nobody gets that location without proving their loyalty."

"Fine. I'll find him myself," I snarled.

Hands tried to wrap around me once more, but there was no stopping what came next. I called the lightning to me. I let the storm within me rage like never before. These lands were made for me, and I would soon rule them. This would be my home, and anyone who didn't like it could either leave or die.

The first bolt of magic struck the blonde one, and he burned to a crisp within seconds. *Worthless magic user.*

The second one was smarter. He'd hung back, but he wasn't fast enough. I threw a paralyzing orb at him and stalked closer while lightning struck the ground around us, inching closer by the second.

"Are you going to be smarter than your friend?" A purple orb swirled within my palm, ready for use.

"Go to hell, you psycho—"

I didn't let him finish before I threw a punch. I had no time for insults. I knew what I was, and I didn't care.

Shouts sounded from all around me, but nothing could stop me from killing my parents' murderers. The darkness within me recognized my need for vengeance and fueled me along, urging me forward. I called the inky blackness of my core to my palm, watching the purple orb lose its light until it was merely a murky blob.

Slowly, so that he suffered, I pushed the magic into his chest and let my power do the rest of the work.

The storm continued to rage around me, and I stood, smiling

at a job well done. The euphoria of victory was a high like no other.

That was until talons clawed into my shoulder blades, making my knees buckle, and I fell to the ground as the world around me faded away.

I'm sorry, Kaliah. It's for your own good.

A NIGHTMARE PLAYED OVER AND OVER IN MY HEAD UNTIL I WAS finally able to force myself awake. My chest ached from the anxiety of the visions that kept being forced into my mind. Reaching over, I tried to find my comforter, but all I felt was grass.

Where the hell am I?

I opened my eyes to find Stryx standing on my chest and Ryland kneeling next to me. Both of them were eerily silent. "Where are we?"

"You don't remember anything?" Ryland asked, his voice rough and filled with a sadness that had me reaching out to him.

He flinched at my touch, and a piece of my heart crumbled.

Oh, God. What had I done?

"Kaliah, we're in the Otherworld. Do you remember coming here?" Stryx asked next.

Closing my eyes, I tried to remember, but all I could see in my head was the nightmare. I'd gone dark like everyone had feared. I'd lost control. I'd killed people.

My body shuddered. "No, just a nightmare."

"That's not a nightmare, young one. I can see what you're seeing, and it really happened."

My head started to shake slowly, then I remembered more. Jordan and Dominic. How could I have hurt my best friend like that and not even care?

I was the monster.

Anguish consumed me until I was quivering uncontrollably.

Stryx flew away, and Ryland moved in. His arms lifted me up and tightened around me, but I didn't want his comfort. I didn't deserve it.

"Kali, it's okay," he murmured.

"No, nothing is okay. I...I..." I couldn't even say the words. I was a coward.

Footsteps approached, and I opened my eyes, staring over Ryland's shoulder. Jordan had burn marks on her arms and tear tracks down her face, but she didn't appear as furious as I expected. I was going to welcome her punishment, and a small part of me even hoped she killed me to end my suffering.

I would never be able to live with myself after what I'd done.

Ryland moved aside at Jordan's request as she kneeled next to me. "Kali? Is that you?" I nodded and she smacked me across the face. When I didn't retaliate, she began to cry. Then, surprising the hell out of me, she hugged me.

"I thought we lost you," she mumbled into my shoulder. "I'm sorry I wasn't there. I should have never left your side."

What? She was apologizing to *me*? I didn't understand. She should hate me right now. I killed her bonded animal.

Stryx came back, and wind smacked me in the face. "Kali, listen to me and trust my words. You did not do any of this. You were struck by dark magic and had no control over yourself."

I gently pushed Jordan aside and stood since Stryx was on a branch. "How can you say that? I knew exactly what I was doing. I murdered the people who actually killed my parents. I not only ended their lives, but I enjoyed it. I. Am. A. Monster."

His beak snapped in frustration. "No, you're not. Yes, you made a mistake. You acted out of darkness instead of light, but there is nothing you did last night that is unforgivable."

Turning toward Jordan, I didn't understand. "What about Dominic?"

"You hurt him, but Stryx healed him. It's why it took him so long to get to you. Ryland and Brooke tried, but your lightning burned them both when they got too close. It even got me after you were passed out."

A miniscule amount of relief seeped through at knowing I hadn't taken Dom from Jordan, but it still didn't excuse my other actions.

"Kali, Alaryk did this. He sent his people to look for you, and they spelled you. Do not take blame for this," Stryx said, but I had a hard time believing him. Even Jordan being okay with it all seemed unreal.

Jordan stood. "I need to go back into the cave. Dom needs me, but everything is fine, Kali. Nobody is angry with you. We all understand."

My shoulders shook. They shouldn't have needed to "understand."

Stryx left with her, and I was once again alone with Ryland. I wasn't sure where he stood. Yes, he'd hugged me and offered me comfort, but he'd also flinched at my touch when I'd first awoken. This was exactly why I hadn't wanted to bond with him. I was bringing him down with me.

Who knew how many more times this would happen before I was able to kill Alaryk? Hell, *if* I was even able to do it.

The last day, or night—or whatever it had been—completely took any confidence I'd been building right out of me.

"You don't have to stay with me," I said without looking at him. I didn't want to see whatever emotions might flicker across his face.

"Kali, I'm sorry I—"

I waved him off. "You have nothing to be sorry for. This was all my fault."

"No, it was those two pieces of shit who did this. They began all of this the moment they sided with Alaryk and touched your parents."

His voice was stern and truthful, but I still couldn't believe him, because for me, all of this started the moment I was born and prophesied to be anything other than good.

He reached for me, but I was the one who flinched this time. "Kali, don't push away from me."

"It's for your benefit, not mine," I snapped. "You should go back to Arvayta and get as far away from me as possible."

This time when he grabbed me, one hand wrapped tightly around my waist while the other gently tilted my chin up. "Kali, we are forever. Don't you ever say otherwise." His lips pressed to mine in a demanding kiss that took my breath away. My hands gripped his shirt as I clung to him and the light he provided.

The harder he kissed me, the more I began to see reason. He was bringing me back with every sweep of his tongue and press of his body against mine.

"You are mine, Kaliah Grace. Nothing and nobody can ever change that," he whispered in my ear as I finally gave in.

"Don't let me go."

"I have you, I promise." He kissed me once more, and I let myself believe his words were true, even if it meant the hurt would be all-consuming later when things ultimately got worse. Because, if there was one thing I was certain of, it was that our situation wasn't going to get any easier.

CHAPTER 13

Ryland led me into a dingy cave. The only light came from a small fire lit in the back that our friends currently sat around. Jordan was off to the side with Dominic, and I really wanted to go to them and apologize but chickened out.

"Come eat something." Ryland squeezed my hand and I agreed.

I had no idea how long I'd been unconscious, so food was probably a good idea. He handed me a bottle of water and a meal bar from his bag.

"How long was I out?" I asked and opened my snack.

"Most of the night. It's nearly dawn now, but the sky doesn't really give anything away for the time of day," he answered me while taking a seat next to me.

"Have you opened the box yet?" I asked, referencing the one Queen Navi had given us.

"No, how come?" he replied between bites of his food.

"She said we should keep the items we need inside it. We should probably get the vampire blood in there," I said, trying to be useful.

Brooke came closer, and I cringed at the sight of the burns covering her body. "I tried to open it while he was with you, but it wouldn't budge, and I didn't see a key."

"Brooke, I'm so sorry." I didn't understand why she wasn't trying to pummel me into the ground. "Stryx, can you heal her?"

She shook her head before he could answer. "The owl has given enough already. I've already healed considerably. The rest of the marks will be gone by end of day."

So, accelerated healing was a vampire thing. Good to know.

Trying to shake off the guilt, I reached for the box, giving myself something to focus on since nobody was saying anything. The fact that they were neither mad nor surprised that I had gone dark hurt worse than anything else.

My fingers traced over the mahogany wood until they landed on the lock. I'd remembered thinking we needed a key but assumed the queen wouldn't forget something like that. Bringing the box closer, I peeked at the latch and noticed a button. I swiped my thumb over the metal, and it popped, drawing blood.

"Ouch." I set the box down and pressed the pad of my thumb against my pants. "That thing bites. Literally."

Ryland was already moving closer, inspecting the container. "Your blood unlocked it. Interesting that she wouldn't have told us that."

Brooke took a deep breath. "Man, you're lucky I don't hold grudges. You really do smell good."

My eyes widened, and she winked before walking away.

"Was she kidding?" I whispered to Ryland.

He shrugged like it was no big deal.

Before I could press further, Brooke returned and snuck up on me again, her head right next to mine. "You should probably lock this up."

I made an inhuman sound and almost peed my pants. The

vampire was definitely pissed I'd hurt her, and she was getting back at me without even touching me.

Once I recovered from the scare, I took the vial of vamp blood. Placing it in the box, I closed the latch and watched as the lock reengaged on its own.

"Looks like you'll need to be the one to open it every time we need to put something in there," Ryland said as he began cleaning up our food.

I took a long pull from my water bottle and didn't respond. Instead, I wondered if I was going to be around long enough to even help them. The dark magic spell I'd been hit with had shaken me. It showed me the truth about who I was, and the worst part? I'd enjoyed who I'd turned into.

The girl who was in control while killing those monsters didn't have any distractions. She had a singular goal and made it happen at whatever cost. At one point during my initial grieving, I had felt the same way without needing dark magic, but I'd let my friends and Ryland back in, and it had changed things.

Though, I'd yet to really decide if it was for the better, especially after the night before.

Oliver approached us with Cynder at his side. The panther narrowed her cat eyes at me, then turned her head up as if she didn't have time for the likes of me.

"Glad to have you back, Kali," Oliver said with a smile.

"Yeah, thanks."

He turned away awkwardly, only making me feel worse instead of better.

"Things will go back to normal soon," Ryland said.

I turned to him. "Which normal? The one where I'm still me and Alaryk is threatening us, or the one where I'm no longer your problem and the rest of you can go back to the way things were before I ruined everything?"

"Kali, that's not what I meant. Don't dwell on what happened.

You need to focus on the good things, or the next time…" He cut himself off, but he didn't have to finish. I knew what he meant.

The next time I went psycho on them, I might not come back.

Wind brushed against me, and I glanced around until I saw Stryx. He was still with Jordan and Dom but looking right at me. *I can't change the way you feel, Kaliah. Only you have control of that. As much as I would like to make this better for you, you have to do this on your own. I know you're hurting, and you feel guilty, but you have to find a way to work through it.*

Instead of replying, I slowly put my wall back up. Stryx didn't need to be saddled with the dark thoughts rolling through my head. He already had enough to deal with.

"There are a few succubus hangouts I'd like to check out if everyone is ready to move," Brooke announced.

Jordan stood first, then wrapped her arms around Dom's hips to help him up. When he was finally on all fours, Stryx landed on the lion's back and spread his wings, covering as much fur as he could reach.

Ryland moved in next to me, wrapping his arm around my waist. "Keep watching."

It felt like a private moment we shouldn't be intruding on, but since nobody else was leaving, I stayed put. A minute later, Stryx's wings began to glow, and sparks of magic flew off of him. Dom shook, barely keeping himself upright as Stryx continued whatever it was he was doing.

Jordan's shoulders hunched over as she covered her mouth. Without thinking, I went to her and hugged my best friend. She was hurting, and I wanted nothing more than to make it better.

"Stryx healed most of him throughout the night, but there were some lingering side effects." Jordan's words were muffled, but I heard enough to have the guilt slam into me again.

"I'm so sorry, Jord. I never meant to hurt anyone." Tears pricked at my eyes as I continued to watch the lion quake under the weight of Stryx's power.

"Just because I'm sad doesn't make it your fault, Kali. Bad shit happens all the time. Don't make this about you. Understand that you were a victim like the rest of us and move on. None of us are dwelling on it, so why should you?"

I flinched at her words. They were harshly spoken, telling me she was still upset, but maybe it wasn't for the reasons I assumed. Maybe she was telling the truth.

Backing away slowly, I went to Ryland, who held his arms open for me. When I stepped into them, he whispered, "She's right. She could have said it more gently, but that's not how Jordan does things."

A flicker of light expanded in my core. I tried to grasp on to it, but just as hope glimmered, the spark vanished.

The lion roared, and within the confines of the cave, I had to cover my ears.

Stryx flew to my shoulder. "Dom is going to be fine. Let's head out."

Brooke, Oliver, and Cynder led the way, followed by Jordan and Dom, who held his head high as if he hadn't just been in massive pain.

Stryx stayed with us, and we left last. "What did you do just now?" I asked.

"When he was first hurt, I gave him one of my feathers. It healed the worst of his wounds, but he needed more time and magic to be back to normal. Unfortunately, my feathers aren't never-ending. I have to use them sparingly, or there could be lasting repercussions. So, I did what I could initially, and when enough time had passed, I infused him with my magic to dull the remainder of the pain until he heals on his own."

"I'm sorry you had to give one up to the vampire in order to get his blood. I didn't realize it could hurt you," I said.

He snapped his beak. "You gave your blood; I gave a feather. Then, we got what we needed. There's nothing to be sorry about."

His irritation at me seeped through like Jordan's had. Maybe I really was making a big deal out of nothing. Obviously, what I'd done hadn't been nothing, but I was surrounded by people who truly cared about me. They weren't going to walk away because I messed up. They knew I wasn't perfect and accepted me anyway.

The spark within my core reignited again and I held on to it with everything I had. Closing my eyes, I let Ryland guide me as I focused on bringing back the light within me. Stryx's wing came around the back of my head, further motivating me to find a glimmer of joy and let go of what I'd done.

Yes, I'd hurt my friends, but they were going to be okay. I'd even killed two people, but as much as I didn't want to be a murderer, I couldn't have let them live, even if I wasn't under the influence of dark magic.

If I hadn't stopped them, then how many more innocent lives would they have taken? Too many.

"That's it, young one. Hold on to your light and let it lead you. It will never take you astray," Stryx whispered in my ear.

Ryland's grip tightened on me, and, when I finally opened up my eyes, he was staring at me with admiration. "You are incredible. I hope you realize that."

Instead of replying, I merely smiled at him and accepted the compliment. I wasn't entirely sure I believed him, but I was trying to, and that was progress.

"Brooke found something," Stryx said, bringing our attention back to the task at hand.

"The succubi?" I asked.

"I don't know." He flew from my shoulder, and I began to run with Ryland at my side.

We caught up with the others, and they were standing around a female body. "I can smell the blood. They were recently attacked," Brooke snarled, fangs protruding, and I was having a hard time deciding if that was because she was hungry or angry. Maybe both.

"Maybe there are some survivors," Jordan suggested, looking around.

Cynder wrapped her body around Brooke, instantly having a calming effect on the vampire as she took a deep breath and focused. "There's at least one heartbeat within the trees." She blurred and disappeared into the surrounding forest.

The rest of us followed after her with Cynder leading the way. I found it interesting that Oliver's bonded animal had taken such a liking to the vampire.

Brooke was walking slowly between a grouping of trees when we caught up. She was intent on her task, so we stopped and waited for her next move. Suddenly, she slammed her fist into a tree, and it splintered, sending the top half toppling into the forest.

A scream cut through the air as Brooke pulled a kicking and screaming child from inside the stump. "Let me go!" Little arms flailed as her head shook and blonde hair blocked her face. "My mother will kill you all."

Brooke held the girl closer, whispering something in her ear. The child stopped fighting, but still wasn't trusting. "Where is my mother?"

"Can succubi even have kids?" Jordan asked.

"I didn't think so. Their mothers are always human, and no human has ever been in the Otherworld or Arvayta before," Stryx replied.

"So, then, where did this kid come from?" Oliver asked.

"Hopefully, Brooke can find out."

Two shimmers appeared in the air, and Ryland tucked me behind him, crouching and ready for a fight. Without a thought, my magic was already building inside me, but I couldn't see any danger.

Brooke still held the child, Oliver and Cynder with her as well, none of who seemed on edge like Ryland, but Dom was growling, and Jordan stood ready at his side with sword in hand.

Stryx still hadn't flinched from his spot on a branch, but he was observing carefully. "Show yourselves," he demanded.

When nothing happened, he spread his wings and flapped them three times until the shimmers I'd seen turned into something else entirely.

CHAPTER 14

Two tiny pixies appeared out of the shimmer, identical in facial structure and body, but where one was light, the other was dark. Blonde hair and ebony hair. Silver eyes and nearly black ones. Pale skin and umber. It was a startling, yet fascinating contrast between the two of them.

"What do we have here, sister?" the blonde one asked.

"Hmm, seems to me we've found ourselves some new toys. Shall we take them home or have our fun with them here?" the other snickered.

Dom wasn't having it and flicked his tail, forcing one to bounce into the other. The ebony-haired one hissed. "Watch it, furball. We didn't arrive here looking for a fight, but don't tempt me to change my mind."

A darkness that was all too familiar to me rolled off the tiny pixie in waves and called to me. Ryland held on tight as I took an involuntary step forward.

"Myrina, take it easy. We don't need anything from you, so you and your sister can be on your way," Stryx said, landing on my shoulder.

The darker one Stryx had called Myrina flew toward us but spoke to her sister. "Did you hear that, Sephira? They don't *need* anything from us."

"That I did, and I find it interesting unless what we've heard are lies."

Ryland leaned in closer. "Pixies are the most manipulative of the creatures in the Otherworld. Don't fall for anything they say."

Unfortunately for him, that only made me want to know them more, and I fully recognized how that should have been a warning sign for me, but I blamed the fact that I didn't care on the lingering effects of the night before.

"Word around the sectors is that you're looking for a few things along with a dark fae," Sephira said as she circled closer to me. "Seems things around here might have gotten a little out of hand during your search."

"We were looking for the succubi and found this child. The others were already gone when we arrived," Stryx replied.

The tiny pixie winked at him. "Sure, they were. That child is a witchling. She doesn't belong with the succubi. Regardless, we don't care and that's not why we're here. You have something we want, and in exchange, we'll give you what you want."

A witchling? That was a term I hadn't heard yet, but assumed it meant a child witch.

Myrina joined her sister, and they flew toward me and Ryland, sharing a look before addressing us.

"Your secret lover isn't happy with you. He's throwing fits all around our lands, and we don't like it. So, you need to go to him or deal with us as well," Sephira said sweetly, but there was nothing sweet about it.

"Sounds to me like it would be better for you if we killed Alaryk. You can't be stupid enough to think he'll stop his destruction if he has me," I replied calmly.

Myrina lunged for me, but Sephira stopped her. "Dear sister, we don't resort to violence. We're negotiators. Now, tell me, Guardian. Why shouldn't I let Myrina have her way with you?"

"Because I'm not a guardian, and I'd probably kill her, and then I'd have to kill you and who wins then? Nobody, because then you can't give me what I want. You'll just have wasted our time. So, how about you tell us what you want, and we'll see if we're interested in making a deal?"

Myrina was turning red in the face, but Sephira kept her composure. "Give me your hand."

"No," Ryland interrupted.

The pixie's wings fluttered. "Oh, really? Well, here's how I see it. The girl is right. Things are either about to get real messy or real friendly. So, if you want us to make a deal, let me prove what she is."

"Ryland, let Kaliah go," Stryx demanded, but my Meraki didn't comply.

I turned around to face him. "I'm okay. I won't do anything like before." As much as I wanted to add "I promise" to the end of that statement, I knew I couldn't. All I could do was hope my words were true.

Except there was a little part of me that wished they wouldn't be.

"What do you need with her hand?" Jordan asked while Ryland battled with his need to protect me.

"I want to poke her finger. One test of her blood will tell me all I need to know. You see, I know who she *thinks* she is, but not everything is as it seems any longer," Sephira answered cryptically.

Jordan's sword was still in her hands. "You hurt her, I don't care how messy it gets, I will feed you to the lion."

The pixies looked at each other and grinned. "We look forward to any attempts."

They really were sinister little things.

"Ryland, the sooner I do this, the sooner we can be on our

way. We need to find the heart stone," I said.

His chest rumbled as he held me tighter. "I don't trust them."

"Neither do I, but my gut is telling me this is our best chance."

Sephira appeared right between us, her four-inch frame glowing near my cheek. "Heart stone, you say? Well, you'll definitely be interested in our deal now."

Before anyone could stop her, Myrina was at my other side and bit my fingertip.

My hand jerked away. "What the hell?"

Jordan joined Ryland at my side in an instant. "You're going to pay for that, bug."

Myrina ignored her as she licked my blood from her lips. "Oh, she's unique. One of a kind even."

"What do you taste, sister?"

Myrina licked her lips. "Fae, both light and dark. Guardian magic and ancestral power, strong and commanding, but untapped. Disappointing, really."

Well, these pixies were idiots. We already knew all of that, and I was pretty sure half of the Otherworld did as well.

"Why do you wear a crown on your head, but yet you hold no title?" Sephira asked me.

"It's a family heirloom. I've grown fond of it."

I didn't want to tell her its use in case she had any bright ideas, but not having all the details didn't matter to the pixie.

"Well, I want it, along with some of your magic." Sephira turned around. "And some of that." She pointed to Brooke.

"Some of the vampire?" Stryx asked.

"Yes, her venom. I have a spell I've been working on, and the air around her tastes divine."

These pixies were extremely odd creatures. They seemed more like miniature vampires to me with their biting and smelling than anything else.

"You can't have my crown," I finally said. Even if I didn't

technically need it anymore, I would never give it up knowing it was the only thing of my grandmother's that I had.

Myrina pulled a small dagger from her side that grew larger as she got closer to my face. "She can have *whatever* she wants."

"Easy, sister." Sephira grabbed her shoulder, then spoke to me. "I just want it as collateral along with the deal since our end of it can't be guaranteed right away."

Ryland stepped forward. "What deal would that be? All I've heard you speak of are the things you want. Yet, you haven't proven why I shouldn't suggest that Kali unleash her power now and make the two of you disappear."

Surprise filtered through me, but I was pretty sure Ryland was bluffing. And if he wasn't, maybe things weren't so bad, and he really did accept the darkness within me after witnessing what I had done the night before.

"Oh, don't get your magic in a twist. Let's start from the beginning, so those of us not keeping up can understand. We know where Alaryk is. We've made a deal with him, but you don't get to know that deal. Just know if you prove yourself, it won't happen." Sephira smirked at me.

My fingers twitched as I fought to lash out at her. Knowing my friends were so close was the only thing holding me back.

"You can have the crown back as soon as Alaryk is killed, and I want to be there when *she* unleashes what's inside her." Sephira pointed at me but continued to speak as if it wasn't present. "I will take what I want from the darkness lingering within her blood and do with it as I please."

"Not a chance in hell," Jordan snapped, interrupting the pixie.

Sephira shook her finger. "Not your magic, not your deal. Stay out of it before I play with your cat a little too roughly."

Dom wrapped his tail around Jordan's waist, keeping her in place, but I was disappointed. The more these pixies talked, the more I wanted to fight with them.

"Pixie, you're pushing your luck. You might be powerful, but you're outnumbered by just as much magic. Remember that before you speak again," Stryx said.

The pixies hovered in the air next to each other and seemed to take Stryx seriously, which thankfully released some of the tension from Ryland and Jordan.

The little girl Brooke was holding began crying and screaming for her mother again, giving the pixies the push that we needed to move things along.

Sephira sighed. "Fine. I still want the crown as collateral. Alaryk is causing trouble for us, trying to put others higher up on the food chain. We don't like it, nor are we fond of the deal we made with him, but we're not opposed to it, either. So, for the time being, as long as you can prove yourself, the enemy of our enemy is our… consort. Remove our annoyance and you can have your precious crown back."

"That's not a deal. You better keep speaking and stay away from my crown," I snapped as Myrina inched even closer.

"Ah, yes. If I wouldn't keep getting interrupted, then we might have gotten to that point already. So, the succubi," Sephira paused, glancing at her sister once more.

"What about the succubi? Do you know how we find them?" I asked.

"No, we don't bother ourselves with the likes of demons, but we have something better, and it will cost you," Myrina answered.

"What would that be?" Oliver asked, having moved between Brooke and the pixies after they mentioned their interest in her.

"We have a heart stone," they said in unison.

Stryx pressed on my wall and I let him in. *Pixies don't lie. They must really have one, but you cannot give them any part of your dark magic. We will find another way.*

"And you'll take my crown and some of the vampire venom in exchange?" I asked.

Myrina cackled. "You better dig a little deeper than that, princess."

"One of my feathers," Stryx offered up, but I backed away with him still on my shoulder.

"No, you said that using too many of them had consequences. You've already used two since we've been here," I hissed.

Just let me give them my magic. Your life isn't worth whatever they could do with it, I added mentally.

But it is. His head turned toward Jordan. "Please take one from the right side."

Jordan's apologetic eyes met mine. "I wish there was another way, but we need their help."

"And here I thought you were a stupid girl," Myrina snickered.

Jordan's sword arched in the air, stopping only a centimeter from the pixie. "Don't. Push. Me."

Myrina was smart enough to keep any other words from coming out as they stared each other down. Finally, Jordan sheathed her sword and came closer to Stryx, who was still perched on my shoulder.

She apologized once more as Stryx outstretched his wing and she yanked one of his silky white feathers from its rightful place.

Sephira zoomed between them and took the feather. "Hmm, this is quite the bargain. I've never encountered such magic. I'm not sure what I'll do with it."

"My suggestion would be to save it. It could save your life one day," Stryx said calmly, likely hoping that's exactly what they would do instead of using it for not-so-great purposes.

"Fill two of these full of the venom and then you can have the heart stone." Sephira snapped her fingers and two vials floated in the air.

Oliver grabbed them and walked back to Brooke, who was rocking the now-sleeping child on a rock.

"The crown?" Myrina asked with glee.

Seal the crown with your magic before you give it to them. Tell the crown to protect itself, or you'll never get it back, Stryx said through our bond.

How am I supposed to do that? I replied.

You just do it. Focus on the task, and the rest will follow.

Taking the crown from my head, I jerked it back as the greedy pixie's hands reached for it. "Do you want to die? Nobody can touch it until I remove the protective spell over it."

Complete lie, but I didn't care. It worked, and they both backed up a little. Trusting Stryx knew what he was talking about, I spoke to the crown while calling my magic forward. As the light around it began to glow silver then purple, I hoped like hell the words I used were good enough.

As soon as the light died off, Sephira moved in. "Place it in the shimmer." Next to her, the air changed and darkened.

Slowly, I lifted the crown and regretfully handed it over as Oliver came back with the two vials of venom.

"The heart stone?" he demanded while holding the murky liquid out for them to see.

Myrina clapped her hands, the stone appeared out of nowhere. "I'd recommend not touching it."

Ryland took the box out, and I opened it so he could get the stone.

"It was a pleasure doing business with you. Hopefully, we'll be seeing each other again. Really soon, if we're all lucky," Sephira said. Then, they both disappeared.

CHAPTER 15

Irritation built deep inside me after the pixies disappeared. I wasn't sure why we had made a deal with them. The longer my crown was gone, the more I realized our mistake.

I might have had a handle on my magic and didn't need the crown to filter it any longer, but the darkness within me was still volatile and I found myself reaching for the forbidden magic as I paced the forest floor.

"What about the child? Since the pixies called her a witchling, I'm assuming we don't want to leave her here for them to come back and take?" I asked.

"I'll take her back to the castle. The queen will make sure she's cared for by a coven until we can locate where she came from," Brooke said.

"We'll go with her," Cynder added.

I'd noticed that the panther hadn't left the vampire's side much. Interesting, considering there were no actual bonds between them, but at least Cynder was being friendly with someone other than Oliver.

"Tell Queen Navi we'll be there soon. The gnomes shouldn't take long," Stryx said.

Oliver stepped forward and tossed a bag from his backpack to me. "You're going to need what's inside of there. Lorelle gave it to me but told me not to say anything until the time was right. In case we don't make it back before you're with the gnomes, I figured now was as good of a time as any."

Opening the tote, I found a note at the top that merely said, "Don't trust the gnomes." Well, that was useful.

Digging past that, I found a crystal with blue string around it and a brick of gold weighing as much as a newborn baby.

Stryx peeked in as well. "The crystal will tell us if they're lying, and the gold will be sufficient leverage. Only silver is mined in the Otherworld, and gnomes despise Earth, so the brick will be something we can offer them in exchange for the raw material."

"Raw?" I asked.

"In order for the dagger to be pure and filled with original magic, the metal has to come directly from the gnome mines and not be contaminated. It's why we didn't melt anything else down and use it to forge the dagger," Stryx answered.

"So, Oliver, Cynder, and Brooke will port back to the queen, drop the child off, and meet the rest of us at the gnome mines?" Ryland asked, and Stryx confirmed.

It didn't feel right splitting up, but we didn't have time to go back and forth. I didn't trust those pixies with my crown, and Alaryk needed to cease breathing sooner rather than later. Even at the mere thought of his impending death, glee bubbled within me.

Be careful, Kaliah. You're toeing the line with power that isn't meant to be taken lightly.

Damn it. I'd forgotten to put my wall back up.

I know. Everything will be fine as soon as he is dead.

Slowly, I blocked him out again, trying not to be rude, but also giving myself some privacy. I didn't need to be judged for how much I wanted the man dead. He was responsible for making my life a hot mess.

Jordan nudged me. "First chance I get, I'm going to use my sword as a bat, and the ball will be one of those pixies."

I'd been nervous there was irreparable damage to our friendship since I'd almost killed her bonded animal, so I couldn't stop the smile from rising on my face when she gave me a glimpse of the best friend I was used to.

"I'll be the pitcher," I replied with a laugh, but not at all joking.

Stryx flew over to Oliver and spoke to him about a message for the queen, and the rest of us grabbed drinks while we waited.

Jordan began sparring with Dom, which ended up being hilarious as he put her on her back more than once, but she never gave up. Even with sticks and leaves in her hair, she was having a blast.

"I don't think I've ever seen her so happy," Ryland said from my side as he took the bag from Lorelle and put it in his since I hadn't brought an actual backpack with me.

"And to think I almost took that away from her." I grimaced.

He turned me toward him. "You need to let that go, or it will only leave you more susceptible to the darkness. You are a good person, Kali. I know that, and so do those who you call friends. All that's left for you to do is figure out how to believe it yourself."

He kissed my forehead and tried to pull away, but I didn't let him. Instead, I clung to him and pressed my lips to his. Grounding myself to him helped to take away the guilt, helped me to remember who I was and the strength I held buried inside.

When I thought I was on the right side of my mental state, I pulled back only far enough to press my forehead against his chest as he left his arms around me. "Thank you."

"I am always happy to do that if it's what you need to

remember who you are," he said, and I glanced up to find him smirking.

"Don't let it go to your head," I replied teasingly.

"I wouldn't dream of it." He kissed me again while I was looking up, and we only parted when leaves rained down on us.

"Hey, love birds. We have gnomes to irritate. Let's move," Jordan called out with Stryx on her shoulder.

Oliver, Brooke, the girl, and Cynder were nowhere to be seen. It was time to port to wherever the gnomes lived.

Glancing back at the sky, I sighed longingly. As wrong as it was, I still couldn't forget how good it had felt to let loose. If only I could do that and not tap into dark magic, I would be unstoppable. But maybe that's why I couldn't.

No one person should have that much power. The addiction it caused was real, and even after only a taste, I was having withdrawals. I could almost understand why Alaryk was doing what he was. The dark fae probably had little control over his actions, which was sad and pathetic.

Though, even if I was right, it still didn't excuse his actions, and he would pay for them with his life.

"Ready?" Ryland asked with his hand out.

I happily slid mine in his. "Of course."

As soon as we were all huddled together, Stryx led the port and we arrived back in the Earth section, one after another. The sky was still a pale green where we were, but it was missing the peaceful vibe I normally got from the queen's part of the land.

"Are gnomes normally good?" I asked since Lorelle had said we couldn't trust them, but they lived so close to the castle.

"They're neutral. They have a leader who wishes for peace and keeps his people in line enough to appease Queen Navi, but things still slip by," Ryland answered.

"They're a pain—" Jordan began, but once again Dom's tail came into use and gave me ideas to replicate it somehow so I could shut her up when he wasn't around.

"Watch what you say. We're not alone," the lion said in a low voice.

Stryx flew back to me and landed on his usual spot. "Please let me handle this. Gnomes are finicky creatures, and we don't want to upset them. If you're asked a direct question, answer it respectfully, but other than that, try to stay out of it."

"Hey, I'm not like Satan over there. I know how to be reasonable," I said defensively.

"It has nothing to do with you, young one. Just trust me."

That was one thing I could do. I trusted the owl with my life, even if I didn't always agree with him.

The gnomes lived in a mountain covered mostly in rock with very few trees, which surprised me, considering how green everything was just a hundred feet beyond the peak. The closer we came to the opening, the more on edge I felt.

Eyes could be seen in the hills of the mountain as the light around us dimmed. There were hundreds of them, and I was suddenly glad we'd saved this place for last. It gave me the creeps.

"As soon as we arrive at the opening, we have to wait until they come to us. Do not step foot into the mountain until you're invited, or you may not live to regret it. They take their security very seriously," Stryx said to everyone.

Dom tightened his tail around Jordan's waist. "Test that theory and I will kill you myself."

"I love you, too, Simba," she cooed, and I couldn't help but laugh.

Even though it was the middle of the day, when we arrived at the base of the mountain, darkness fell around us, making it so we could only see shadows and eyes. We stayed close enough to touch each other, but not so close that we appeared scared.

Minutes passed and still no one came. My nerves were getting the best of me as I began bouncing my left leg. Something was clawing at me. I couldn't pinpoint what it was, but the magic deep within my core was stirring.

My eyes moved rapidly around the area, but still, I couldn't see a damn thing. "We need to leave. Something isn't right."

Stryx stretched his wings out. "I don't sense anything out of the ordinary. What do you feel?"

"It's my magic. It's reacting to something, but I don't know what."

Nobody replied to my statement, and I wasn't sure if it was because they didn't think it was as big of a deal as I did, or if it meant something more and it was already too late.

Stryx pressed against my wall and I gladly let him in. *Can you sense anything?*

His presence swirled within my mind but didn't calm any of the anxiety I was experiencing. *No, everything seems normal, but we should leave if you think that's the right move. We can come back with more people and try again tomorrow.*

We didn't have that time. Queen Navi made that very clear. Plus, Arvayta hadn't been faring well when we left, and even more time had passed there since we'd been gone.

Unless anyone else senses anything, let's wait it out, I finally replied.

He nodded, and we continued to stand there silently. Maybe another five minutes later, footsteps could be heard, and a dozen torches appeared in the opening.

"What brings you to our home today?" a gnome in the center said with a booming voice. I couldn't make out his facial features under the flickering flames, but they were all of similar height—under four feet tall—and wore very little clothing.

Knobby fingers wrapped around the torches, and bare chests puffed out as they waited for our answer.

"Good day, Leader Spiro. We come by request of Queen Navi. She requires pure metal if you'd be so willing to provide it from your well," Stryx announced.

"Are we not good enough to forge what she requires?" Spiro asked, voice full of indignation.

"I'm sure she would be grateful to have your expert hands craft the item she requires, but as the matter is extremely sensitive, your presence would be needed to complete the task. She did not want to ask you or your people to inconvenience yourselves with her problem."

Damn, Stryx was good at this. Even *I* was sold on his reasoning.

Spiro didn't seem as convinced, though. He stepped closer to the opening. "What do you bring for payment?"

Stryx turned toward Ryland, who was already removing the gold brick from his backpack. As Ryland held the mound in his hand, Stryx continued to speak for us.

"The purest gold from Earth in exchange for your silver, and we only need half of what we offer in return."

The gnome's eyes glowed in the shadows, showing a scarred face and bald head. "This is a payment we can accept, but I will not allow strangers to roam my home. I will only invite you and the holder of the gold inside. That is my only offer."

My mouth opened to object. I wasn't okay with this option whatsoever, but Stryx already knew it.

You, Jordan, and Dominic need to go back to Queen Navi. Ready the other items, and we will be right behind you. We need this to happen and cannot negotiate with them.

Biting my tongue, I listened to him and let things continue to play out.

"That is a fair request, and we accept your offer," Stryx announced.

Ryland's eyes met mine, and they blazed with a fury I didn't often see from him. Neither of us spoke for fear of upsetting the gnome leader, but the shared intensity was enough to tell me he would be hurrying back.

The entrance to the mountain shimmered, and Stryx hopped

from my shoulder to Ryland's. *I mean it, Kaliah. Straight to the castle, and do not leave until we are back. It is the only safe place for you. Keep our connection open, and I will let you know if anything doesn't go as planned.*

I understand, and we'll be waiting. Just make sure to hurry up, I replied just as they stepped through and the darkness swallowed them.

The torchlight began to fade, and I prayed like crazy to the Fates who were supposed to keep the balance that we hadn't just made the biggest mistake. Lorelle had said not to trust the gnomes, but Ryland would have had eyes on the crystal. So, if he didn't say anything, all we could do now was have faith.

As soon as silence descended around us, Jordan took my hand. "Let's get the hell out of here."

She began to port, but just as she did, the uneasiness that I'd been feeling exploded within me and I crumpled to the ground, watching her and Dom disappear without me.

CHAPTER 16

Alaryk stared down at me with a gleam in his soulless eyes. "We meet again, my sweet." His words were a sharp contrast to his next actions, which included punching me in the face, making my nose bleed immediately, and grasping on to my neck.

My mouth moved to speak, but with his grip, the words I so badly wanted to say were stuck as I tried to breathe. I didn't know if he was trying to kill me, but I wasn't going down without a fight if so.

"Let's take a trip." Alaryk grabbed on to my hair and we disappeared just in time for Jordan and Dom to see the dark fae take me as they reappeared.

At least they would know what happened to me, not that there was anything they could do about it since we'd never found out where Alaryk was hiding out.

We landed in a cavernous bunker of sorts. I couldn't tell if we were underground, in a mountain, or somewhere else entirely. The walls were made from dirt—rough, but seemed solid and were several stories high.

The temperature was cool but tolerable, and there was no natural light filtering in. Instead, orbs hung from various spots, providing a soft glow that somehow made the oversized area seem more welcoming.

There were several tunnels leading out of the room, but the only one I had an interest in was the exit. Unfortunately, Alaryk wasn't kind enough to label them.

"I've waited decades to have you in my home. No, in *our* home. I know it's not a conventional house, but once I can trust you, I'll claim whatever place you want as ours," Alaryk said as if I was actually going to stay with him.

I wasn't sure how to take him. I'd been told from the beginning that he wanted to kill me, that I was the last heir to the throne he despised, even though it no longer existed. Yet, every time I'd met him, all he wanted was for me to be his partner.

Sure, it was for sinister purposes, but still, if he hadn't hurt so many people in the process…

"Now, we have to do something about your soul. The moment I heard what you did in that forest…" He paused, closed his eyes, and let out a moan. "Oh, you have no idea what that did to me. Sure, you took out two of my best men, but it was a sacrifice I was happy to make to show you the possibilities."

"You mean, to show me I was capable of being a monster? I almost killed people I care about," I sneered, but even as I said the words, excitement bubbled within me that I couldn't stop.

His fingers caressed my chin. "Oh, Kaliah. Don't fight me. We were made for each other. The Fates had it all wrong when they scared you away from me. We will make these lands prosper and bring back the old ways, with me and you as their king and queen."

My skin tingled everywhere he touched, and I hated that a part of me loved it. Closing my eyes, I pictured Ryland and the care he'd shown me, the light he provided and how he grounded me to the goodness I believed in.

I didn't want to succumb to the dark magic. I didn't want to soak it up and drown my sorrows in it.

But the longer Alaryk spoke to me and touched me, the more I could see how right he was. My humanity was slipping away, along with any guilt about what needed to happen next.

Deep down, I knew this wasn't the way I was supposed to stop Alaryk. There was a line I shouldn't cross, but every time I dipped my toes across, the darkness fought harder to keep me there.

"I'm not a monster and neither are you, my sweet. I've done things I shouldn't have, but they've all brought me to you, and I won't regret them. Now, let me fix you so you can truly be free." The dark fae's hand pressed over my chest, and a shock ran through me.

My head tilted back and chest rose as the air was pulled from my lungs and grief overcame me, a complete contrast to how I was feeling just moments before. My parents were there in my mind, calling to me to come home, but where was home? There was nothing left of them to go back to. They'd brought me to this world and left me.

Slowly, their image faded, and Stryx came next. His wise eyes stared at me in disappointment until his wings spread and pushed himself out of my mind, our connection gone.

Then it was Jordan. My best friend. My soul sister. My partner-in-crime. She would come for me, and she would understand. She had always understood me, and I would make her see reason again.

Last was Ryland. He was standing in front of me, peering down upon my broken body with disgust. Just like the others before him, he said no words, but his eyes? They told me everything I needed to know.

I'd only ever known him with icy-blue ones that matched mine perfectly, but as he continued to glare at me, they changed into something darker and no longer mine.

"I was never yours," he spat, then disappeared.

My eyes opened to find Alaryk kneeling before me. "I see you for who you truly are, and I will never abandon you."

Power surged inside me as rage built. Darkness called to me from everywhere around us, and I clung to it like the air I needed to breathe.

My fingers sparked with power, and I wrapped them around Alaryk's throat. "You ruined my life." Squeezing tighter until he turned red, I pushed him five feet backward.

Standing up, I pushed my hair back and raised my arms into the air, calling my magic to me as I unleashed the hold that I'd been keeping on myself. Without my crown to keep me in check, the surge came hard and fast.

"You're the most stunning creature I've ever laid eyes on," Alaryk whispered as he stood from where I'd pushed him. "I really don't want to hurt you, but I will if I have to in order to keep you in check."

His hands circled and he waited for me to react first, which was mistake number two. The first had been giving me the push I needed to kick his ass.

Without hesitation, I shoved my hand out and shot lightning across the room as I called a storm to me. We obviously weren't underground, because the air changed and cackled with my magic as I changed the atmosphere within the blink of an eye.

"Fun show trick, but it's not enough to stop me. Though, I do enjoy the foreplay, so let's keep going," Alaryk yelled over the thunder, then blasted me with a stream of magic that was midnight in color and tickled my skin.

"Was that supposed to hurt, *dear*? Or were you really hoping for some foreplay?" I called out as I soaked in the spell, further fueling myself.

He snarled at me and tried again, but I dodged his next attempt.

"You did this to yourself. You could have left me alone, but you were greedy and now you get to deal with consequences of your selfishness," I added right before flinging a paralyzing stream of power at him.

Only this time, he didn't budge. He seemed to soak it up, just like I had.

"On the contrary, my sweet. My greed brought me you, and no matter how this ends, I will have won because you *are* darkness. There is nothing good about you, and you need to realize that without me, nobody will ever love you. You are tainted goods to everyone but me."

His words brought forth feelings I'd been trying to smother. I remembered the way Ryland had looked at me after I'd killed those two men. He hadn't treated me the same. I no longer held an innocence about me, and I was certain he had regretted bonding himself to a psychopath.

"You're wrong. I don't need you. I just need to kill you." Even if his words held a truth I already believed, and I admitted that there was something about him that attracted me, I would never be with him. Even the darkness couldn't convince me that was a great idea.

Alaryk might have set me free, and for that he wouldn't die mercilessly, but he still pushed me into becoming the monster before him.

I threw magic at him rapidly until I grew bored and decided we needed to change things up. Surprising the dark fae, I punched him in the jaw, followed by a knee to the gut, and a secondary hit on the side of his head.

"Good thing for you, I'm not afraid to hit a girl." Alaryk smirked, and I got exactly what I wanted.

We barreled into each other, trading magical blows for physical ones. The more times he hit me, the more irate I became and the louder the storm grew around me.

The rock walls shook around us as we bounced against them throughout the fight. I had no idea how long we continued to beat on each other, but with every punch, I grew more powerful, and there was no end in sight for me.

Even with blood dripping from my nose and cuts through my jacket from the exposed walls, I was on a high like never before.

"Will you give up and die with some dignity?" I asked when I grew tired of the games. My magic didn't seem to be stopping him, but neither was his hurting me. There had to be a way to end this.

He ripped his torn shirt the rest of the way off and used it to wipe the grime from his face. His once-white hair was tinted brown from the dirt, and he added blood to the mix when he used his hands to brush the strands back.

"Oh, sweet Kaliah. I know you're new to this game, but you can't be that stupid. I wouldn't have come for you if there was any risk of me losing. This only ends one of two ways: with you by my side or your death. Either way, I will reign supreme."

His confidence was grating on my nerves. He couldn't kill me. He knew it, and I was sure of it now as well. We were too evenly matched. If only I'd stuck around long enough to get the dagger…

"I think I'm going for a walk," I said casually. Even though I didn't know which door led to the outside, I realized I didn't need it. Alaryk had ported us into the cave, and I would port myself out of it.

Except it wasn't so simple.

"You're only leaving here if I say so. I'm the only person in and out of these walls. Perks of being the creator of the structure," he replied smugly.

"Is that so? Well, what if there were no more walls?" Rage at being held captive grew within my core as I gathered all the power I could summon.

The dark fae would not keep me as his prisoner. I was fiercer than that. I was my own person, and I had control over my life. If

I couldn't kill him right then, I'd leave until I could get what I needed to do so.

Hope welled within me, which was an odd feeling. There was a spark of something associated with it that I'd pushed away, an emotion I no longer deemed relevant. While I didn't consider myself evil like Alaryk, I had no qualms about losing the things that made me soft, like love and hope.

Alaryk watched me with fascination as I drew on my power and flung it toward the wall with little effort. A hole blasted through it, and the sounds of battle poured through. My gaze turned back toward the dark fae.

"You didn't think we were the only ones fighting for something today, did you, my sweet?"

CHAPTER 17

RYLAND

Entering into the mountain without Kali by my side was tearing my heart apart. Something wasn't right, but we needed the dagger to be done with this nightmare, so I was left with no choice. I had to trust Jordan and Dominic would keep her safe.

"We will head straight down to the mine, and you will get your silver, then leave. Don't touch anything or speak to my people," Spiro said as we continued down the hallway that descended lower into the earth with every step we took.

Things wouldn't be so bad if I could speak with Stryx like Kali could, but this wasn't my first time dealing with arrogant creatures. I could remain diplomatic so long as we got the hell out of there quickly.

The walkway began to open up, and we entered into a room with an elevator that didn't hold more than a few people.

"You will go with two of my people to the mine pit. If what you seek is the purest of silver, then this is your only option," Spiro said.

"How long will it take to acquire the silver and come back up?

We don't want to be a bother for you any longer than necessary," Stryx replied.

"No more than half of the hour."

I stepped toward the elevator, wanting to get moving quickly, but Spiro grabbed my arm. "If you cause any trouble within my home, I will bring havoc down on yours. We might be small people, but we are mighty. Don't you forget that."

My head nodded stiffly. "Of course, Leader Spiro. You will have my utmost respect, as will your people and home, while we are here. We greatly appreciate your help."

His eyes narrowed. "There's darkness within the air. Make sure to move swiftly."

He released me and left the room without letting me reply, but I didn't worry about it. He hadn't said anything I didn't already know, so I stepped onto the platform and waited for the gnomes to join us.

The elevator moved faster than I was ready for, and I lost my footing. Even though I quickly recovered, the gnomes hadn't missed my misstep and grinned. If they thought for one second that made me a weak target, they were going to be poorly mistaken should they try anything.

I had a Meraki to save, and nothing was going to stop me.

Fear for her seared into my chest. Knowing I couldn't do a damn thing to stop what was happening to her was going to be the death of me.

My ability to keep her grounded only worked if she stayed away from dark magic, but we were about to head straight to the darkness and ask her to kill him. I knew she was capable of it, but would Alaryk be able to get to her first?

I was so angry with myself that his two men had been able to get to her and I hadn't protected her. She'd done things that hurt her and those she loved, and I should have tried harder to bring her back to us. It was my job to provide her with an anchor to the goodness she was made from, and I'd failed.

Stryx pressed against the side of my head with his wing when we arrived at the mine floor. Torches lit up the area, and it was nearly freezing this far below ground. That was until we moved closer to a well that they'd built to melt the silver.

"Your portion should be ready within five minutes," the gnome grumbled, then walked away with the other one as if they couldn't stand to be so close to us.

Since the well was warm, I stayed close. "This is going better than planned," I whispered to Stryx.

"It's going too well. The blocks they have on their home are cutting me off from everyone else, even Kali. I don't like it. I'm going to keep my eyes on the hallway, and you watch the silver. As soon as it's melted, we need to leave," Stryx replied, his talons tightening from the nerves against my shoulder.

Damn it. Not having a connection to the others made everything in me want to forgo dealing with the gnomes and make sure Kali was okay, but they should have been safe within the barriers of Queen Navi's castle already, so I tried not to worry. Plus, the crystal Lorelle had given us hadn't changed colors when Spiro was speaking to us—I'd kept it in my peripherals as much as I could—so *he* at least wasn't up to something.

My eyes watched the well. It was made from centuries-old brick and contained two levels. The top was small with only one shallow iron bowl that held chunks of our silver. A few feet beneath it was a fire that seemed to be magically controlled as I couldn't see any gnomes beyond the darkness.

I briefly wondered what the purpose of the well was for, but then something struck my chest, and I stumbled, losing all thought.

"What's wrong?" Stryx hissed.

"I don't know. Something… isn't… right."

Spiro appeared. "I've just been told Alaryk was here. He didn't try to breach our walls, but he arrived just as your people were trying to leave."

Kali.

I was going to murder that bastard myself.

"Did he take Kaliah?" Stryx asked.

"Only the blonde guardian and lion remain, and they are causing trouble at our entrance. You will take what is ready and leave my home immediately. You have disrespected my people, and it won't be forgotten." Spiro held his head high like he was above us and I wanted to drop kick the pompous gnome.

"Yet, it was your people who turned against us. Alaryk wouldn't have found us without help. That is something we will remember as well, Leader Spiro. Though, we still have a deal. Please at least honor that before we take our leave."

Was Stryx saying he believed one of these gnomes was on Alaryk's side?

All I could see was crimson as I itched to reach for the daggers tucked against my hips, but I knew starting a fight here wouldn't bring Kali back. We needed to be on the move and come back later to serve justice if necessary.

The other gnomes returned and poured the silver into a canister, which I took and put next to the box in my backpack. Without Kali, we weren't able to open the box, and if the queen couldn't do it herself, I had no qualms about throwing it against a wall until it shattered.

Spiro moved out of our way, and we took the elevator up by ourselves. We could find our own way back, and if we stayed around the gnomes any longer, I wasn't going to be responsible for my actions.

As the door closed and we began going up, I punched the wall and yelled. "How did this happen?"

"I'm not sure, but Kali is prepared for this. She is going to be fine," Stryx replied.

"But at what cost? Alaryk holds the magic that calls to her. What if she decides she no longer wants to kill him? Even if she does find a way to kill the dark fae, she may not be able to recover this time."

Too many "what ifs" were running through my mind, and I wished for some of the darkness that Kali thrived on. I wanted to remove all inhibitions and do whatever it took to get her back without guilt.

"Calm, Ryland. We will get her back. This is nothing we haven't planned for. You just need to have faith that we've done everything we could to help her."

Faith. I'd always had plenty of it. Even when my parents were killed, then again when I lost Sara, who I thought to be my Meraki. I'd always held on to the peace of mind that the Fates had a plan, that there was a bigger purpose for me.

But if anything happened to Kali, if she was taken from me, I would lose that faith. I would gladly hand over any good within me in exchange for the darkness where I wouldn't have to feel, because if I had to *feel* the loss of another, everything in my path would be destroyed.

Once the elevator reached the top section of the mountain, Stryx flew ahead of me, and I ran close behind him. Guards were positioned at the entrance, but we didn't pause. Stryx sailed right over them and I barreled right into them. I had no cares left to give about pissing them off.

"He just took her. We don't know what happened. She was with us and then she wasn't. I'm so sorry, Ryland," Jordan said with absolute remorse.

"It's not your fault. Let's just focus on getting the dagger made," Stryx announced as he flew over the area Kali was last seen.

"What? No. We need to get her back first," I demanded. The thought of her being subjected to the dark fae for too long made me sick.

"The block on my connections is lifted. Kali will not listen to reason right now. The rage within her is too great, which is not necessarily a bad thing. She is not choosing Alaryk, but she still won't stop until he's dead. We need to see the queen first in order to bring your Meraki back, Ryland."

My hands shook at my side. I hated this. I knew she was gone. I knew who had her. Yet, I couldn't do a damn thing about it until we completed the task at hand.

"Jordan, go back to the castle. Tell Queen Navi we are right behind you. She needs to be ready for the spell immediately and send her people to the northernmost region of her lands. Alaryk has been right under her nose this whole time," Stryx said, and my head snapped up.

"He's here?"

The owl nodded. "I can sense Kali. We will find her, but the dagger first."

Jordan and Dom were already gone when I asked why we were still there.

"I sensed her essence was left behind. Her blood is on the ground over there. I need you to dig around it and bring it with us. We need it to tie her to the dagger," Stryx answered.

He flew back to the spot, and I followed without question. As long as whatever he wanted kept us getting closer to Kali, then I'd do it.

The earth was rough, but I paid no attention to the rocks that scraped at my hands as I pushed through the ground. The longer I saw her blood on the ground—though it wasn't much—the more I had trouble controlling my emotions. Wind whipped around us until I was done.

As soon as Stryx confirmed it was enough, we ported to the gates of the castle and market. Jordan was already there waiting for us.

"The other guardians, bonded animals, and queen's guards are already on their way to Alaryk's hideaway. I also sent word to Yelah. Queen Navi was able to pinpoint it when she did another search in only the northern region. He has an army there waiting for us." Jordan held her sword in her hands, not at all afraid of the coming fight.

"Very well, Jordan. Let's go to Queen Navi, so we can join them." Stryx flew ahead and we ran after.

Jordan kept glancing at me but didn't ask whatever she was thinking, which I appreciated. I didn't want to talk about it. I didn't want to say my thoughts out loud. I just needed action. I needed Kali back in my arms.

We stormed into the castle and rushed past the guards still left behind to protect their queen. Thankfully, they were smart enough to let us pass without hassle.

The chamber doors were already opened when we arrived, and the queen was dressed in full battle armor. "Will you be joining us?" Stryx asked as I set the mound of dirt on the table and began getting the items out of my bag.

"No, I cannot abandon the palace, but should the fight come to us, we will be prepared, and I will join my people," she answered confidently.

"You can open the box, right?" I asked.

She dipped her finger in Kali's blood like it was completely normal and opened the lock. "It appears so, but it still remains to be seen if I can properly forge the dagger without her here."

"Won't her blood be enough?" Stryx asked as he perched on one of the chair backs.

"I'm not sure. I've never conjured a weapon like this. This is very old magic I was lucky enough to stumble upon."

"What about Ryland?" Jordan asked.

Queen Navi's head tilted to the side. "What do you mean, guardian?"

"Well, he's bonded to Kali. Can't you use Kali's blood magic, but Ryland's physical presence and tie both of them to it?"

"What type of bond have you made with Kaliah?" she asked me.

"A Meraki one. Lorelle sealed it within the waters of our falls."

"And you accept the responsibility of this blade? If it should kill anyone other than Alaryk, it will have repercussions to your magic. To take a life not destined for the blade could damn your soul."

I nodded. "The blade will be destroyed once Alaryk is dead."

"Very well. We can do it this way, but I make no assurances that it will work," Queen Navi said as she got to work.

There was another box on the table that she opened, which contained a mold of the dagger to be made. Once the heart stone was placed in the hilt area, she started the spell and continued to work swiftly.

The silver went in next and settled into the area, forming one solid piece of metal. As the liquid form began to harden, Queen Navi added the vampire blood, then Kali's last.

Her hands hovered over the forming blade, and magic poured from her and into the box until it started to rattle and crack, then she closed the box, continuing to mutter her spell over and over again.

The minutes ticked by agonizingly slow as I wondered what was happening to Kali. Was she consumed by darkness? Was Alaryk hurting her? Would she even recognize right from wrong by the time we arrived?

Too many questions and not enough answers until we arrived to see for ourselves.

A loud crack sounded through the room and my eyes went back to the mold that was now in pieces. Queen Navi dusted the mess away and revealed the forged dagger.

The succubi heart stone gleamed in the sunlight, and I took in the detail I hadn't expected to be there, like the intricate carvings in the pommel and the beveled edges of the guard.

"Give me your hand," Queen Navi said to me.

I placed my hand in hers, and she promptly drew a pool of

blood in my palm with the dagger, dragging the blade across my hand until both sides were covered in my blood. Then, she shoved the hilt into my hand and wrapped both of our hands around it as she started another spell.

My eyes closed and power flooded through me, followed by a new connection to Kali opening up between us. She was hurting, and my entire being ached to be with her.

"You are now connected to the dagger, and you will sense your Meraki in a different way while the blade is activated. Use it to your advantage, and may the Fates bless you during this battle."

Jordan and Dom were already waiting by the door, and we wasted no time with pleasantries. It was time to get my Meraki back.

CHAPTER 18

After blasting the wall to bits, I climbed the rumble with ease and charged onto the battlefield, curious as to what exactly was happening around us. The bonded animals and guardians were already there, fighting those who stood with Alaryk.

There were over two hundred people gathered, but the fight wasn't even. The guardians and queen's people were outnumbered and losing.

"They're all fighting for you. How does that make you feel?" Alaryk called out to me, keeping a safe distance from my still-glowing hands.

Turning toward him, I smirked. "Thanks to you, I feel nothing but the drive to kill you. You wanted a partner, but your greed will be your downfall. You created that which will end you."

He shrugged. "What then, Kaliah? You said it yourself. You're a monster. Who will love you if you kill me? I'm offering you everything you could ever hope for. You never have to feel again, and I will provide you with all that you desire so long as you share your power with me."

I considered his words; they struck something within me that I'd buried deep, but when I didn't answer, he kept going.

"Don't you see what's missing out there? Your so-called friends have already abandoned you. None of them fight for you like I do. We were created for each other, and I'm not sure what else it will take for you to see that."

Glancing back at the crowd below us, he was right. There was no sight of Ryland, Stryx, or Jordan. If the others had time to arrive at the fight, then my friends should have as well.

"You know I'm right. Just take my hand and we can end this right now." Alaryk reached out for me, taking one step closer.

I eyed the power that rolled off of him. Neither of us had pulled back, meaning neither of us was willing to trust the other. Even if I went to him, I'd never believe it would work. He was darkness. I was darkness. We were two parts of evil that didn't belong together.

But he did make some very valid points.

The people who supposedly cared about me most weren't present. They weren't fighting for me. Ryland wasn't keeping me anchored to the goodness. Stryx wasn't trying to get through my wall. Jordan wasn't slaying everyone in her path to get to me.

None of them were doing what they'd promised.

"That's right, my sweet. Let that rage out. I'll never hold you back. I only want the real you. Set yourself free!" Alaryk was several steps closer but paused as lightning struck within inches of his position.

I did as he suggested. My power seeped through as I called to the storm I'd already begun when inside of the mountain. The dirt beneath me shook with a ferocity and ripped holes in the earth, causing fissures to separate the fight below.

"You're positively stunning, Kaliah. Just come with me." His hand was still outstretched as his dark eyes pleaded with me.

My heart had been overridden by the darkness the moment

Alaryk touched me. I stopped caring about anything other than his death, but I couldn't deny the pull to him I felt.

My legs moved toward him without overthinking it. Maybe I didn't have to kill him. I didn't have the dagger to do so anyway, and if my magic hadn't killed him when I'd struck him in the mountain, I wasn't sure it was possible anyway.

Maybe there was a common ground we could meet at.

Excitement bubbled off of Alaryk, and I stopped.

Something was happening within me. My chest ached, and feelings of hope filtered through. Hope for what, though? Then, there was love and rage. Confusion punched through my core as I tried to sort out what was happening to me.

I backed up once more, and Alaryk roared. "You will be mine, Kaliah." His magic slammed into my center, and I tumbled down the mountain side.

My body landed in a heap at the feet of a dragon. "It's nice to see you again, Kaliah," Queen Yelah said from above me. "You've changed, but we will still fight for you. Remember to fight for yourself."

Her words on top of the growing emotions within me rocked my core.

What was happening to me?

"Kali!" a familiar voice yelled but was quickly quieted by the booming of Alaryk.

"Make your choice now, Kaliah. Our time for foreplay is up, and it's time for the main event. Which will you choose? A life of never being good enough in *their* eyes, or a life where you can thrive while being your true self?"

Again, the dark fae's words hit home with me, but the desire to kill him still simmered somewhere within me.

Rage filtered into me from someone else. The feelings weren't mine, but a part of my mind pushed me to pay attention to the connection that continued to grow with every passing second.

I can't lose her. I have to make it in time.

Ryland's voice sounded inside my mind, further confusing me, especially as our bond flared to life and I couldn't ignore the feelings it ignited within me.

"Your hesitation leaves me no choice, my sweet. If I can't have you, then nobody will." Alaryk's power slammed into me from a close distance, and I flew backward.

After landing on the ground, I moved quickly, refusing to let him catch me off guard again. The emotions from Ryland were weakening me, but I wouldn't make the same mistake twice.

Go away! I yelled inside my head, then charged forward.

We were fighting next to everyone else now. Jordan was there, and our eyes met. She had her sword mid-swing and didn't miss a beat as she struck her opponent. "Sorry we're late, Chuck. Let's finish this together."

I didn't know how to respond to her. I had more control over my actions than the first time I took to the dark magic, but my care was still missing. Her words meant nothing to my mind, but my heart… I couldn't seem to turn that all the way off.

There was no time to continue to wonder, though. Alaryk was coming for me, and I wouldn't let him knock me down again.

He lunged for me, and I met him in the middle, once more trading hits that were more physical than magical.

"You can't stop me. There is no magic in this world that can contain me, and now I'm going to take what's yours," Alaryk hissed at me as he wrapped his hands around my throat.

Gone was the wooing version of him he often presented to me. In his place was the real dark fae, the one I'd assumed him to be this whole time, but I'd also almost fallen for him and his smooth words.

Wrath and madness consumed me, and I fought against his hold as he pinned me against a tumbled rock from the mountain.

Ryland appeared behind Alaryk, holding a blade out to me. His eyes were tinged with fury, and something cracked within me. He was hurting and, suddenly, I wanted to do whatever it took to make the pain stop.

"No!" Alaryk's voice thundered in my ear as his hand slammed onto my chest, searing my skin within his magic.

My body fell slack. Whatever the dark fae was doing instantly sucked the life out of me. My eyes rolled into the back of my head, and I couldn't see a damn thing as shouts sounded.

The pounding in my head didn't help, either. I tried to ignore it, but in my weakened state, I couldn't any longer.

Kali, can you hear me? Stryx's voice came through my mind.

Yes, what's happening?

Have you chosen your path, young one? he asked.

I want to kill Alaryk if that's what you mean.

What will you do if you succeed? Will you keep the darkness within you to control, or will you freely let it go?

I don't want to feel anymore, I said truthfully.

So, you'll choose to live in darkness?

Emotions slammed into my mind: memories of my time with Jordan, the dates I'd had with Ryland before leaving for the Otherworld, the places I'd explored and wanted to know more about.

Stop screwing with my head, I yelled.

I'm not doing anything to you, Kaliah. Your mind and heart are also at war. You have many battles at play today. I'm just here to see which of them wins and stand by your side if you'll let me. So, which will it be? Your time is running out.

Alaryk was still sucking me dry. The press of his hand against my body was also urging me to choose, but I was scared. I'd left behind so much hurt and uncertainty when the darkness entered me. It offered me an escape I wasn't sure I'd find without it.

Kali, don't do this. I know what he's offering seems easier, but I promise if we survive this, the reward will be worth it. Don't let him kill us, Ryland's voice sounded in my mind and my heart stopped.

Ryland couldn't die because of me. He didn't deserve that. I wanted him to walk away, and while normally his loyalty was something that was to be admired, it was really beginning to piss me off.

I don't want others to die because of me, I said, hopefully to Stryx, but since Ryland was suddenly there, I wasn't sure if he could hear me as well.

So, will you relinquish the darkness inside? Stryx asked.

If it will save the lives of others, then yes. I don't want it.

Very well, young one. Just try to remain conscious.

His words were followed by blinding pain as light exploded within me and something stabbed into my chest over and over.

When my body had absorbed the worst of it, my eyes finally opened to see Alaryk still standing over me. "You can't beat me."

"Yes, I can."

Lifting my hand, I did the same to him by shoving my palm against his chest, but instead of taking his power from him, my instincts told me to give him more of mine.

Lead with light, Kaliah, Stryx whispered in my mind, and that's exactly what I did.

CHAPTER 19

Everything slowed as I pushed past the darkness swirling inside of me and had a clear mind again. Emotions filled me, and I thrived on them instead of letting them bury me in sadness.

Alaryk still had one hand on me and the other pointed toward Ryland, holding my Meraki frozen in place as he tortured him. "You turned my prize against me, and now you will watch as I rip her away from you and take away your bond."

There had been a pulling sensation within me the moment I let emotions back in and pushed the darkness away, but I hadn't thought twice about it. Alaryk's words made me frantic that he was actually stripping away the Meraki bond I had with Ryland.

Without another thought, I acted on instinct and called a storm to me once more. This time, instead of it lashing out uncontrollably, it came with ease and perfection, going exactly where I wanted.

The wind picked up Jordan, Oliver, and their animals and brought them to me. I needed them by my side to do what came next. Jordan's eyes gleamed with an unusual happiness, but there was no time to ask what had happened.

Each of them circled around us, and Stryx was at my back, supporting my every move. The agony in my chest grew with every passing second, but I didn't rush.

Ryland has the dagger, Kali. You have to get it from him, Stryx said. I wondered how they'd completed the task so quickly but would have to ask later.

"Let go of him," I snarled at Alaryk, trying to pull his attention to me.

"Not a chance in—what are you doing to me?" He finally noticed I was touching him and had been pushing some of my own power into him. Light magic didn't hurt when it wasn't meant to.

"Showing you how much stronger I am than you without your influence." I turned toward Jordan. "Now!"

She was my best friend, my soul sister. She knew my fight styles, and I trusted her in that moment to do what needed to happen next.

Dom joined in, distracting Alaryk with a bite at his calf while Jordan sliced his hand clean off with her sword that flamed with her fire power. Blood poured from the wound onto Ryland, but he recovered and pulled the dagger from his side pocket.

Alaryk bellowed above the sound of my storm. "You bitch!" Then, he removed his other hand from me and shot something dark and ugly at my best friend. She tumbled down the small hill, and I moved to go to her, but another man I didn't recognize was with her in a moment and ported away.

Fear spiked through me, but Dom wasn't losing it, so I trusted she was as okay as she could be at the moment.

The dark fae then turned toward Oliver and tried to do the same thing to him, but Oliver dodged the first attempt, slamming his fist into the ground and knocking Alaryk off balance. Ryland was recovering and sent his wind out into my storm. All three of us were working together.

As Alaryk began to right himself, Dom and Cynder jumped into the action and attacked each of his arms, effectively pinning the dark fae to the ground with the help of Ryland and Oliver.

"Now, Kaliah!" Stryx yelled at me as he joined the animals, using his wings to assist in keeping Alaryk pinned to the ground, and relieve Ryland who was barely staying upright.

Alaryk was already injured and had depleted heaps of his power in his effort to strip away the bond I'd formed with Ryland, but after fighting with him earlier, I knew he was stronger than the three animals combined, so I didn't bother to move in.

Instead, I waited and used the time to recover and choose my next move carefully, which was to go to Ryland.

"You need to leave before he hurts you again. I can finish this," I said as I gently pulled the dagger from his grasp.

"I'm your anchor, and I will never leave your side. Now, go finish him." His faith in me brought back the last of my sanity that I needed in order to decide what came next.

Turning around, I watched as Alaryk yanked his bloodied arms away and flung magic at Stryx but thankfully missed.

"Not so good with your aim when using your left hand, are you?" I asked, once more trying to get his attention on me.

"One-handed or not, you still can't stop me." He tried to port away, but I was quicker and latched on to him, trying to keep us both on the field.

Even injured, he was still incredibly powerful and ended up pulling me with him in his port after he tried to break my hold, but I refused to let up. We had one shot at this, and I wasn't walking away until he was finished.

We'd only made it to the top of the mountain, and I could still see the others fighting at the bottom. Even though their leader abandoned them, the idiots still kept at it and were beginning to lose.

"I knew you wouldn't let me leave." Alaryk grinned. "I've been waiting for this moment."

I had no idea what he was talking about, but I was done listening. My grip tightened on the dagger in my hand and started to rise, but before I could hit my mark, pain sliced through my back.

"Ahh, that's a good boy." Alaryk cradled his arm with the missing hand and grinned behind me. "Now, take her to the caves and I'll follow behind after I throw the others off course. This time, we won't let anyone see us leave."

Heat pulsed at my back, and I forced my head to turn. A dragon stood behind me with bits of my jacket in his claws.

The bastard had cut through muscle, and I was barely standing, let alone able to move my arm to stab the dark fae.

Alaryk patted my cheek. "I'll deal with you soon, my sweet."

"Wait," I croaked, frantically trying to come up with another plan.

"What is it? If you want to change your mind, it's a little late for that. You've lost, and there will only be pain for the rest of your miserable life. Such a pity, really."

Stryx was in my head, telling me that he was coming to help, but he would be too late.

I had to find the strength within me and finish this once and for all.

Closing my eyes, I dropped my head, appearing weak, but instead I did something I'd never done before. I called to the Fates. I begged them for help. For just enough to help me lift my arm and sink the dagger into Alaryk's heart. As he stepped closer, I wondered if he was either completely oblivious to my weapon or thought I couldn't truly hurt him.

Light filled my chest, and I remembered Stryx's earlier words to lead with light, so I focused on it, moving the brightness through my core and to my arms. Then, I opened my eyes to look Alaryk in the face.

"I'm sorry for the life you've lived and for the path you chose, but I'm not sorry for the path it led me down. Your choices have made me strong enough to do whatever it takes," I said with a confidence I shouldn't have held, considering my back was bleeding profusely and the dragon still lingered close by.

Alaryk laughed in my face and grabbed my chin with his fingers. "Whatever it takes for what?"

"To kill you." My elbow bent just enough so that the dagger could reach Alaryk's chest, given he was so close to me.

With one last surge of power, I poured everything I had into the dagger and plunged it into his heart.

He laughed once more, shoving me to the dragon's feet. "I can't be killed. I've planned this moment for decades. You only had one choice and that was to join me, but you were too weak —" His words cut off as smoke began to rise from his chest and the dagger that was still protruding.

He crumbled next to me, and I stared into his eyes even as the others finally arrived, including Yelah who was commanding the dragon like the queen she was.

Stryx landed next to me along with Ryland as the light left Alaryk. He was dead, and I had killed him, but there was no sadness. Instead, I had relief for the man who had caused so much mayhem amongst innocents.

Alaryk had been in pain and took that anguish out on anyone who threatened his existence. A part of me pitied him and hoped he found relief wherever he ended up next. Now, he was the Fates' problem and hopefully I wouldn't soon be following after him.

"Don't move her," Stryx said, then called for Jordan, who was limping, but back from wherever she'd disappeared to.

I couldn't see what they were doing, but I watched as Dom dragged Alaryk's body out of my line of sight.

"It's going to be okay, Kali," Ryland whispered in my ear, but they weren't words I needed to hear anymore.

Everything was right in my world. There was no more darkness within me. My friends were safe. Nobody else would die because of me.

If it was my time, I'd go happily, knowing I'd done exactly what I was meant to do in this world.

You're not going anywhere other than home when I'm done with you, Stryx demanded in my head.

My lips lifted into a smile as Ryland held my hand, Jordan helped Stryx, and Oliver stood watch over us with Dom and Cynder.

Everything was exactly as it was meant to be.

CHAPTER 20

Stryx ended up using two of his feathers to heal my back, and besides being sore from the fighting, I was back to my normal self. There was no more lurking darkness waiting to take me away from reality. There was only peace and contentment.

Jordan had disappeared with Dom after I was healed, along with Yelah who had taken off with a glint in her eyes and a prisoner confined with her dragon magic. I'd nearly felt bad for the monster that had tried to rip my spine out, but those thoughts were fleeting, and I knew he was about to get what he deserved for siding with the dark fae.

"What about the fight below?" I asked as the rest of us stayed on the mountaintop.

"Most of those people were under the influence of Alaryk's magic. Once you killed him, a lot of them stopped fighting. Those who didn't are being dealt with," Oliver answered, still looking over the edge with Cynder.

"Where's Brooke?" I assumed she was supposed to be wherever he was searching but wanted to be sure nothing had happened to her.

"She's helping round up prisoners. Her speed comes in handy," Oliver answered with a little awe in his voice, and it made me sad they weren't bonded mates.

"You're not going to forget to call her this time, are you?" I asked.

He turned to me with a sideways grin. "We might not be bonded, but she's worth the heartache that might come later if she leaves me for another. I just have to hope I'm worth the same to her."

Ryland slapped a hand on Oliver's shoulder. "I'm happy for you. Now, get out of here and go to her. We're good up here."

Oliver nodded and disappeared without needing to be told twice. Then, Ryland came to sit with me, wrapping an arm around me as I sat in the dirt, still trying to comprehend what had happened.

"When Alaryk got me, the dark magic took over again, but I didn't want him like he hoped. I still wanted to kill him more than anything else," I said to both Ryland and Stryx since we were alone.

"That's usually how it works, and Alaryk should have known that before trying to sway you. With dark magic, the wielder of it needs to be the most powerful person in the room. If you'd have sided with him, you would have eventually killed him anyway. You were always meant to be stronger than he was," Stryx answered.

"Thank you for coming back for me. He almost had me convinced that everyone had abandoned me when I saw the others here fighting, but no sign of any of you."

Ryland's grip tightened on my hip. "It was the hardest decision not to chase after you the moment I found out you were gone, but Stryx convinced me we needed the dagger. It was the only way to truly save you."

My heart warmed. I might not have any blood family left walking our worlds, but I'd been given a family anyway, and I wanted to kick my own ass for thinking they'd have given up so easily on me.

"How were you in my head?" I asked Ryland, because I couldn't sense him any longer or the emotions that had been pouring into me.

"The dagger. Queen Navi had to use your blood and mine to power the spell, further connecting us and enhancing our bond, but I think now that you've used the dagger for its intended purpose, it's just a normal blade and the magic is gone."

"Actually, Jordan burned it while I was healing you and took the pieces left back to Queen Navi," Stryx noted.

"When is she supposed to be back?" I asked, wanting to make sure she was actually okay herself after the hit she'd taken.

In Jordan fashion, she appeared just as I asked the question, beaming with a smile bigger than I'd ever seen before, and I remembered how giddy she had seemed during the fight. Then, the same man who'd gone to her in the field showed up. "Kali, I'd like you to meet Luka. My Meraki."

I was on my feet in an instant and flung myself at her. "I'm so happy for you."

"It's really all in thanks to you for almost ending our world and going cray-cray. This one over here left Arvayta before I was born over stubborn pride, but I'm forcing him to come back with us."

My head shook, and I glanced at Luka. "I'm sorry now. Just know it doesn't get any better."

Jordan punched me, then winced. "Damn, those rocks didn't feel good."

Luka pulled her closer. "You need to rest. Say goodbye to your friends."

"Excuse me?" She raised a brow. "Did you just tell me what to do?"

That was my cue to walk away. Oh, their honeymoon stage was going to be the most entertainment I'd ever had. Or it was going to be the death of me. Both were very possible.

Yelah and Dom returned as well, and the mountaintop was getting smaller by the arrival. "Everyone has been accounted for, and Queen Navi's people are taking the captives."

"What about the casualties?" Stryx asked.

"We lost nearly twenty fighters, but proper transport and arrangements are already in the works. Brooke is taking the lead on that. She and Oliver have just left with Cynder, actually."

Ryland moved to stand next to me. "We should be going as well. The council will want to speak with us."

My hand raised to Yelah's chest. "Thank you for your words earlier. It was the beginning push I needed to come back to myself."

She lowered her head to me. "It was an honor to fight with you, and I hope we meet again under considerably better circumstances."

When we parted, she disappeared first, and it was only Ryland and Stryx left with me. The crowd had thinned below, too. "Next stop, home?" I asked.

"Not so fast," a voice said from behind me.

I swear to the Fates, if they'd come for trouble…

"Alaryk is dead for good?" Sephira asked.

"He is. Where is my crown?" We'd had a deal, and I'd forgotten about it until that moment.

"It's safe," Myrina smirked.

Ryland took a half-step forward, but Sephira flew between them. "Dear sister, they've solved a problem for us and followed through on our deal. Plus, it's not like it was useful to us anyway. Just a hunk of metal and rather disappointing. Let's not cause trouble today."

"Or ever would be my suggestion," I retorted, and grinned

that they hadn't been able to break through the protection spell I'd placed on the crown when Stryx had told me to.

Sephira merely smirked back at me while Myrina still fumed.

"The crown?" I demanded once again.

Sephira snapped her fingers three times and a shimmer appeared, followed by my crown. I went to snatch it from the air, but she shoved it out of my reach. "Not so fast."

"What now?" I asked with a huff.

"What are your intentions?"

"To go home. What does it matter to you?" I asked.

They hold dark magic, Kali. Your strength puts them on edge. Remember, they will always strive to be the most powerful, Stryx reminded me.

"Will you be coming back here for any reason?" Sephira asked.

"Only if you give me a reason to," I replied confidently, keeping her stare and making sure she knew how serious I was.

"Very well." She lowered my crown, and I grabbed hold of it. "Here's to hoping we never meet again," she added, then both pixies disappeared.

"Oh, how I hope she's right," I groaned.

"Come on. They're not a problem right now, but I'm going to be soon if we don't get you home and safe so I can breathe a little easier," Ryland said, making me laugh.

"You got it." I turned to Stryx. "Are you coming?"

"No, I need to check on the other animals, but I'll check in with you when I'm done," Stryx replied, and I went to him.

I bent down and scooped him up from the rock he sat on. "Thank you. For everything." I squeezed him tightly until he shifted uncomfortably in my arms.

"I would do it again if need be," he replied, pressing his head to mine.

"I love you, Stryx."

"I love you, too, young one."

Letting him go, I went back to Ryland with tears in my eyes. Stryx had never once wavered in his faith of me, and my heart was filled with so much love and light from it.

Stryx disappeared first, then Ryland led us in a port to the entrance for home. When we landed in front of the portal, I glanced across the open field and toward the castle. "Life is already coming back to this place."

"They'll physically recover within a few days, but it will be months before things are really back to normal around here. Maybe by then, I'll let you out of the house to come explore the good this place holds," Ryland answered.

"Oh, you'll let me, huh? We'll see about that."

He grabbed my hand, then winked as we walked through the portal together.

Our feet had barely touched the ground in Arvayta before Lorelle was in our faces. Her hands were on the sides of my head, and magic slammed into me.

"What the hell, woman?" I screeched.

Ryland tried to pull me from her grasp, but the old lady wasn't letting up. Again, showing she was much stronger physically than she portrayed.

"Calm down and let me finish," she hissed, then moved one of her hands to my chest.

I stood there frozen, wondering if maybe our fight wasn't truly over. Lorelle knew something we didn't and if she didn't spit it all out, I was going to end up hitting an old lady. It had been a long enough day, and I wanted nothing more than to end it on a good note.

Minutes later, Ryland had worn a path in the ground from his pacing and Lorelle finally let go. "You're free to go now." Then she tried walking away.

My hand shot out and grabbed her arm. "Not so fast. What was all of that about?"

She grinned. "That's for me to know and you to ponder."

"Not a chance in hell. Spill it. Now." My grip became tighter on her arm in case she tried to port away. If she did, at least I would go with her.

"Just know there are certain things I'm privy to that not even the council is aware of. I have certain abilities that allow me extra freedoms the Fates count on in times of despair. There were many possibilities of how this fight would turn out. You'd eliminated all but two of them when you killed Alaryk, and I just took away the second. All is well in the worlds again."

She tried to pull away, but I wasn't done with her. "Did you think I was going to come here and destroy Arvayta when I was done?"

She shrugged. "It might have happened, but it's not going to. Now, unless you want to lose that hand, I suggest you let me go and be on your way. Oh, and let's keep this secret between us. We don't need everyone afraid of you, do we?"

Oh, I really wanted to retaliate, but instead, I let Ryland pull me back. "No, we don't. We'll see you around, Lorelle," he said, but I wasn't done with her.

"Who are you really? You're not just a healer." Lorelle knew way too much, and I wanted to know why.

She took a step back and grinned, pausing just long enough to make me believe she wouldn't answer me, but then she did. "You're correct. I'm not a guardian, but I've been alive for several centuries." Her hand gestured to her greying hair. "I've earned every one of these. I was born in the Otherworld. My mother was a seer, and my father was a powerful warlock. My magic is similar to that of a guardian but is drawn from different sources."

Ryland seemed just as shocked by her answer as I was, which was nice, because it meant I wasn't the only one who didn't know.

"Now, this isn't common knowledge, and I wouldn't tell you normally, but you saved our home and I promised you some answers. Only the council and Stryx know who I really am, and I expect you two to keep it that way. Not even Jordan needs to know the truth."

I nodded. "Of course. Will you tell me more about my parents and their time here?" She'd previously mentioned how I was much like my mother, and I'd love nothing more than to know the Arvaytan side of her better.

"Come see me in a few days and we'll talk some more." She grinned, then disappeared.

"I wanted to kick her when I thought she wasn't going to answer, but I guess things make more sense now," I said as soon as we were alone again.

"Agreed, but if you'd have kicked her, she probably would have turned you into some sort of animal as punishment and then I couldn't do this."

He dipped me backward, his hand gently moving down my cheek before coming around to my neck and pulling me close to him. The dimple I so adored appeared just before he brought his lips to mine, and all other worries were forgotten.

All that mattered in the following moments was that we were safe, and we were together. There was nothing else in all the worlds that would ever tear us apart.

EPILOGUE

TWO YEARS LATER

Never before had I been so nervous. I didn't like surprises; yet, for the last few days, everyone around me was completely tight-lipped. So, I'd been left with no choice but to try and coerce the information out of the only person who didn't know what secret or surprise really meant.

"Come on, Cami. Tell Aunty Kali what all the big people have been whispering about."

Cami was only one, but she was the spitting image of her mother and just as mischievous as my best friend. Jordan and Luka had taken the fast train with their bonding, and I couldn't have been happier for them, especially when they gave me my goddaughter.

The precious princess sitting on my lap under the tree in our back yard had her mother's sparkling green eyes and blonde hair that also had curls. I was convinced those came from me even though we had no blood relation.

"No," Cami replied with her favorite word. Had I mentioned she was exactly like her mother? Stubborn and all.

"I have chocolate. I just need a few words, kid. Can you

remember what Mommy and Uncle Ry have been talking about when I'm not around?"

Her eyes widened at the mention of chocolate, and I knew I had her, except I was busted before she could get the words out.

"Kaliah Grace, are you bribing my daughter?" Jordan laughed from behind me. "Pregnancy hormones have made you stoop to a new low."

I was weeks away from popping, and yes, that was also a cause of my nerves. Giving birth to a child scared the crap out of me. I'd been there for Jordan's delivery, and the ring of fire that Lorelle had spoken of had me losing my damn mind.

"Oh, you know one day you'll do the same to your nephew," I replied, not at all feeling guilty, especially when Cami spoke next.

"Party!" She clapped her little hands, then started digging in my pockets.

"Camilla Mae, we don't take bribes." Jordan lifted the sweet baby girl from my lap, but not fast enough to avoid me giving her a piece of candy anyway.

"Are you going to at least help me up?" I groaned from the ground while glancing at my protruding stomach.

"Yeah, yeah, but bribe my daughter again and I will cut you once my nephew is out."

"Bring it, Satan."

She laughed while switching Cami to her hip and giving me her other hand. Moving was getting harder by the day, and if Lorelle hadn't promised profusely that I wasn't having twins, I would have been certain I was. Instead, I was convinced we were having a linebacker.

"Do you think you can waddle your way to your parents' tree?" she asked once I was finally up.

"I think I can manage." Porting in the last trimester was a hard no, and I'd had to get used to walking a lot, but it also kept me in shape, considering my only workouts consisted of punching Ryland for telling me I couldn't do anything to overexert myself.

Still, he didn't learn his lessons. Overprotective brute.

Ten minutes later and we'd arrived, but Jordan stopped us to clean up Cami before we went around the corner. Only about a quarter of the chocolate bar had made it in her mouth; the rest was all over her face, hands, and Jordan's shoulder.

"The payback is going to be so joyous," Jordan murmured once she was done and we continued.

Going up the hill to visit my parents was physically getting harder as the days passed, but I still made the trek once a week to give them updates, because emotionally it made me feel better to keep them involved. Stryx told me they knew regardless if I visited, but even after all this time, I couldn't quite let them go.

When we got to the top and could see the massive oak that was their grave marker, my feet stopped moving. My eyes burned with instant tears as I tried to open my mouth to say something.

"Party!" Cami called out again, and Jordan let her down as she ran ahead to her father.

"Ryland wanted to give you something special, and he called in a few favors owed," Jordan said when I couldn't speak.

Standing before me was everyone I cared about most in all the worlds. Everyone *including* my parents.

"How?" was all I could squeak out.

"Don't question it. Just go enjoy your time and thank your Meraki."

I knew she was being modest. Jordan had been just as involved based upon all of their secret meet-ups, so before I moved on, I awkwardly hugged her with my growing belly in the way. "You're the best friend and soul sister a girl could ever ask for."

"You're not so bad yourself, Chuck. Now, stop with the

mushy stuff. I still have a reputation to uphold, and I can't be seen crying in public."

Motherhood hadn't changed her one bit.

Without needing any more prodding, I waddled as fast as my body would let me toward my parents, who hadn't moved an inch, but held their arms open for me.

"They'd come to you, but they can't be more than twenty feet from the tree," Jordan answered my unspoken question.

Blinding tears flowed freely down my face as it all really set in. My parents were there. I was going to get a proper goodbye.

By the time I tumbled into their arms, I was a blubbering mess and Ryland had moved in behind me while Jordan gave us some space.

"Sweet girl, it's okay," Dad whispered in my ear as I hiccupped against his chest, then switched to my mom.

"You have made us so proud, Kaliah," Mom said as she lifted my chin and wiped away my tears.

"I've missed you both so much," I mumbled through the emotions.

"We know, and we've heard every conversation while wishing we could talk back," she replied with a smile.

"How are you here now?" I asked, glancing back at Ryland.

"Your Meraki is rather persuasive. He's been working on this for over a year," Dad answered while nudging me toward Ryland.

I threw my arms around him. "Thank you."

He brushed my hair back from my face. "I just wish it could have happened sooner."

"Oh!" My hands went to my stomach as pain coursed through it, then I almost died of embarrassment as liquid trailed down my legs. "Um, I think…"

"Kaliah, your water just broke," my mom exclaimed.

"It's fine. I'll be fine. Jordan was in labor for nearly a full day.

We still have time." Panic gripped at me. As much as I wanted to meet our son, I needed this time with my parents.

Another contraction barreled through me, and I doubled over. The Fates couldn't be this cruel.

Lorelle walked closer with a grin on her face. "Brooks, Daliah. Mind if I borrow your daughter for a few hours?"

"You knew, didn't you? You told me I had another week," I growled through another contraction.

"This old lady has to get her kicks from somewhere."

"We'll be right here, sweet girl. Just breathe," Mom said as they both hugged me once more.

Once I was done saying goodbye much too soon, Ryland held both my arms and led me away from everyone who had shown up for the surprise. I'd never even gotten to say hi to Oliver and Brooke who were visiting from the Otherworld. He'd moved there shortly after the big battle and the chance they were still taking was working out. Merakis weren't the most common thing, and even if they weren't officially bonded, they were happy and that was most important.

"We love you," Dad called out, and I turned around to blow him a kiss.

Come on, baby boy. Momma needs you to come quickly so you can meet Grandpa and Grandma.

WITHIN TWO HOURS, I WAS HOLDING OUR SWEET BOY IN MY ARMS with Jordan, Ryland, and Stryx around me as Lorelle came and went from the room I'd been moved to after giving birth in the pool beneath the falls. The delivery went smoothly and all that was left to do was give him a name.

"Are you going to tell us yet?" Jordan asked as she stroked the tuft of russet hair on his tiny head.

"I think we should wait to tell everyone at once," Ryland answered, and I agreed.

Normally, I hated surprises, but since my parents were waiting for us, this was one I could get behind. I wanted them to hear it first as well.

Stryx was at my feet and carefully walked forward until his wing could spread over the baby. "Whatever his name is, he will be destined for greatness."

My spare hand reached for the owl and held on to his other wing. "Thank you."

Stryx had come and gone over the last two years, but our bond remained intact, stronger than ever. We would forever be a part of each other's lives, and I couldn't wait for him to teach my son all the things he'd once taught me.

"How about we get you back to your parents if you're up for walking," Ryland suggested.

I wasn't nearly as sore as I would have expected after watching Jordan's delivery, but I soon figured out why.

"Consider your health my baby present." Lorelle popped back in to check on the baby once more.

Jordan scoffed, but I shushed her. "My parents," I reminded her.

"Okay, fine, but you get no special treatment on the next delivery. If I hurt, then so do you."

My head shook as Ryland took our son from my arms and Stryx flew toward the door. Jordan came around and helped me from the bed. Even though I wasn't hurting, I'd still pushed a baby out. Taking those first few steps without my belly were wobbly.

Once we were outside, Ryland had said we could port with the baby, but I wasn't liking the idea of watching my son disappear so soon after giving birth, even if I'd done it myself thousands of times before I'd been pregnant. So, we walked from Lorelle's back to the hill, this time with a little more speed.

Oliver, Brooke, Cynder, Dom, and my parents were still there and grinning from ear to ear. Oliver and Brooke met us first to get a peek before I got to my parents.

Gone was the gruff man my dad normally presented himself as, and in his place was a sniffling grandfather. Mom nodded to me, and I passed their grandchild to my father first. "Dad, we'd like you to meet Harrison Brooks Clarke, named after his two grandfathers that we'd thought he'd never meet."

Mom began to tear up as well. "It's a beautiful name for a beautiful little boy."

Ryland wrapped his arms around me, and our eyes met. "Thank you for giving me our son."

"You can take some of the credit, I guess," I teased.

His hands cupped my cheeks, and he lightly pressed his lips against mine. "I love you with all my heart and soul."

"And I love you just as much."

Even though we'd had to fight for our happily-ever-after, there was no one I wanted by my side more than Ryland. Now and forever, he would always be my anchor, and I would always be his.

STAY IN TOUCH

Find Heather on Facebook:
Reader Group:
Heather Renee's Book Warriors

Author Page:
Heather Renee Author

Or by signing up for her newsletter:
http://smarturl.it/HeatherReneeNL

ALSO BY HEATHER RENEE

Broken Court

An Urban Fantasy series featuring an unconventional leading lady, a broody love interest, and a fae kingdom with a vile king.

Royal Fae Guardians

A complete Urban Fantasy series featuring fae, magic users, a sweet romance, along with snark and humor.

Shadow Veil Academy

A complete Urban Fantasy Academy series featuring shifters, elves, witches, and more.

Elite Supernatural Trackers

A complete Urban Fantasy series featuring witches, demons, a smart-mouthed female lead, alpha males, and a snarky fairy sidekick.

Raven Point Pack Series

A complete Paranormal Romance series featuring wolves, witches, vengeance, and fated mates.

Blood of the Sea Series

A complete Paranormal Romance series featuring vampires, open seas adventures, and the occasional pirate.

Standalone

Marked Paradox - A complete Fantasy fae story about a realm divided and one fae to bring them back together.

ABOUT THE AUTHOR

Heather Renee is a *USA Today* bestselling author who lives in Oregon. She writes urban fantasy and paranormal romance novels with a mixture of adventure, humor, and sass. Her love of reading eventually led to her passion for writing and giving the gift of escapism.

When Heather's not writing, she is spending time with her loving husband and beautiful daughter, going on their own adventures.

For more ways to connect with her, visit www.HeatherReneeAuthor.com.

www.ingramcontent.com/pod-product-compliance
Lightning Source LLC
Chambersburg PA
CBHW030350310726
48979CB00001B/246

* 9 7 8 1 7 3 5 4 7 4 6 0 1 *